IN THE NAME OF THE REICH

IAN M. WILLIAMSON

Copyright © 2025 Ian M. Williamson

The moral right of the author has been asserted.

Apart from any fair dealing for the purposes of research or private study, or criticism or review, as permitted under the Copyright, Designs and Patents Act 1988, this publication may only be reproduced, stored or transmitted, in any form or by any means, with the prior permission in writing of the publishers, or in the case of reprographic reproduction in accordance with the terms of licences issued by the Copyright Licensing Agency. Enquiries concerning reproduction outside those terms should be sent to the publishers.

The manufacturer's authorised representative in the EU for product safety is Authorised Rep Compliance Ltd, 71 Lower Baggot Street, Dublin D02 P593 Ireland
(www.arccompliance.com)

This is a work of fiction. Names, characters, businesses, places, events and incidents are either the products of the author's imagination or used in a fictitious manner. Any resemblance to actual persons, living or dead, or actual events is purely coincidental.

Troubador Publishing Ltd
Unit E2 Airfield Business Park,
Harrison Road, Market Harborough,
Leicestershire LE16 7UL
Tel: 0116 279 2299
Email: books@troubador.co.uk
Web: www.troubador.co.uk

ISBN 978 1 83628 035 4

British Library Cataloguing in Publication Data.
A catalogue record for this book is available from the British Library.

Printed and bound by CPI Group (UK) Ltd, Croydon, CR0 4YY
Typeset in 10.5pt Garamond Pro by Troubador Publishing Ltd, Leicester, UK

CHAPTER ONE

Detective Sergeant John Highsmith

The final casing clattered to the floor, and the crack of the gunshot, which was no more than a dim echo beyond the ear defenders, faded into the concrete room.

Detective Sergeant John Highsmith sighed as he placed the still-smoking handgun down on the counter and pressed the button to recall the target. Even from here, he could see he had missed his mark – again. This new pistol was lighter and easier to conceal under his suit jacket; however, compensating for the recoil was proving harder than they had made out. He would ask for his old Walther PPK back, but this consignment of PPK-Ls – the new, lighter models – had been sent over especially for the detectives, and John was not one to cause a fuss over something so trivial.

Trivial, until he had cause to use it one day and bloody missed.

The torso-shaped target clanged to a halt in front of him, and John realised with relief that this round was not quite so bad as he had first thought. He had fired seven shots from the Walther, with four hits and three misses: one in the chest, one in the left shoulder, one just nicking the neck (he still counted it), and one in the side of the head where the left ear would have been. It was better than last week anyway, when he had tried the PPK-L for the first time and his third shot left a noticeable mark in the concrete ceiling. At least John would have killed his target this time, had said target been standing still and not returning fire – and bright orange. It was still pulling to the right, though; he ought to be back on the firing range again sooner rather than later.

John reloaded the PPK-L before he left, with seven rounds in the magazine and one in the chamber, just as he had been taught. Not that he had ever fired the weapon outside of this room – nor his old Walther PPK, for that matter – as pointing them with conviction had always been enough to defuse any confrontation during his three years at a detective rank. As far as he was concerned, if he could one day retire without ever having shot at a real-life target, he would leave the Metropolitan Police a happy man.

John returned the PPK-L to the shoulder holster under his arm and straightened his waistcoat and necktie, the former a simple pale-grey and the latter a dark-navy-blue, verging on black. After slipping the matching grey jacket over his shoulders, John checked his inside pocket for the spare pistol magazine he always carried with him (those particular rounds would likely lay dormant for the rest of time), then he exited the cold subterranean chamber with the feigned composure of an accomplished marksman.

*

Presently, John returned to the Drug Enforcement Squad office on the fifth floor of Scotland Yard and sat down at his little desk, which was positioned by the back wall of the room.

Whilst drug enforcement had not been a foremost concern for the government at the end of the war, as it had more important matters to attend to, the foundation and expansion of Drug Enforcement Squads – or DESs, as every police officer called them – across Great Britain since the beginning of the decade was an indication of its newfound determination to rout out this menace altogether. The London DES was no different, with the department growing into this office over the past nine years; today, a series of dull and faded wooden desks filled the room to capacity. This office was home to John and the other men in the London DES, even if the narrow windows and deep-maroon, threadbare carpet made it appear forever dim and miserable. The perpetual haze of smoke from their shared cigarette habit did not help, of course. That, and the weak output of the humming fluorescent lights in the ceiling, which just about illuminated the type on a page.

On John's desk, alongside his telephone and Imperial Model 50 typewriter – a temperamental relic from before the war – was the file containing the work he had finished before his break at the firing range: the monthly *Index of Drug Offences and Arrests* for London. This document outlined DES operations in the city, pieced together in a manner that alluded to the best possible use of its budget. Compiling it was a job the detective sergeants of the DES shared on a monthly rotation, and the task had been left to John this month, not that it was his turn. He had completed this arduous chore only last month, but when Detective Chief Inspector Werner, the head of the London DES, placed the empty file on John's desk the previous afternoon and ordered him to fill it, he had not pointed out his superior's mistake. When none of his fellow officers stepped forwards to take responsibility, John reluctantly resigned himself to the task.

After removing his jacket and lighting a Reemtsma cigarette, John settled in for a final read-through of the *Index* before he submitted it to DCI Werner for his approval.

Heading the report were the more common arrests for cannabis possession, which were large enough in number that the responsible detectives could be pleased with themselves, but it was not a great cause for unease in the grander scheme of things. Then came several pages on opium and heroin, the tools of the more experienced addicts who continued a centuries-old tradition of self-annihilation. Illicitly manufactured morphine was recorded as well (this was an often poorly made and dangerous substitute for the real thing, which some people – mostly former soldiers – had taken to using since the war), as were counterfeit cigarettes and illegally distilled alcohols – products that were laced with anything from sawdust to rat poison. As always, there was a section reserved for cocaine; however, this was an expensive drug used only by those with more disposable income, and its mention was therefore knowingly slight in the monthly *Index*.

From there, John arrived at the heart of the report – the part his superiors cared about above all else nowadays. In fact, he doubted whether DCI Werner would trouble himself to read the other pages, but he would instead skip straight to those dedicated to "Yonder".

Since its appearance only four months prior, the psychedelic drug known as Yonder had become the top priority for Drug Enforcement Squads nationwide. As the name implied, Yonder was being touted as a drug that allowed its user to step *beyond* this world by pulling down the boundaries between this reality and another dreamlike existence. It was supposedly a clean, non-addictive high, whilst still boasting a far stronger potency than anything else of its kind; according to reports, just one of those little blue pills provided whomever consumed it with several hours of uninterrupted, blissful euphoria. But Yonder was not like opium or heroin, which were substances abused by vagrants and vagabonds – those who refused to recognise what was available to them if only they climbed out from the gutter. Nor was it like cocaine, an extravagance limited to the social betters of society for when their lesser urges overcame them. No, Yonder was a different beast entirely because it had become *the* drug of the working class, the single largest populace in Great Britain.

This fact alone would have been more than enough to alarm government officials, given that the British working class had never been of particular concern with regard to drug use in the past. That, and any negative impact on the workers themselves would mean dire consequences for industrial manufacturing levels – the absolute backbone of the whole nation. There was something even more sinister about this drug, though, something dangerous that had caught the attention of some very powerful individuals: since its arrival, Yonder had set itself apart as the figurehead for a fashionable "silent protest" amongst these working-class labourers.

It was no secret that there were many in Great Britain who had not adapted well to life after the Second Great War. And it was also no secret that this sentiment was most prevalent amongst the working class; it was an attitude that had been passed down to their children by the previous generation – those who lived before the fighting. Worse, they were the ones who had benefitted more measurably in the interim. There was employment in the factories for all those who sought it – that was a State promise – and whilst economic growth soared, crime rates had plummeted. Even the once ever-present threat of terrorism had been dashed after the King's Loyalists (not affiliated with the current rightfully ruling monarch) were wiped out during The Purges in the mid-1950s. They were indisputably better off here when compared with others around the world: the latest newspaper reports stated that the Japanese were once again fighting widespread terrorism in south-eastern China, whilst in the United States, police officers continued to clash in the streets with "civil rights" protesters who were demanding equality with their "fellow man".

Still, Yonder had tried to tap into this concept of civil discontent, and it had succeeded with disturbing ease. When questioned on the matter by respective DESs, people across Great Britain had described Yonder as a "medication" rather than a drug and as a so-called "cure" for the oppressive reality in which they found themselves. They claimed that it "freed" their minds, and that it provided them with a means to exist outside of the confines of their dreadful lives. It was a ridiculous notion to which only the truly gullible would adhere, and it irritated John no end that some thought this way.

Even so, the presence of Yonder and what it stood for could not be ignored. The drug had swept the nation in the last four months, and the largest industrial hubs – such as Manchester and Sheffield – now considered it the paramount threat to social order. One particular rumour that had been circulating recently claimed that every single worker in these factory cities had at one time or another succumbed to the temptation of this psychedelic, which – if true – would suggest there were already *millions* of users. It was, without a doubt, a phenomenon the likes of which Great Britain had never before experienced.

It was regrettable, then, that the prevailing impression from John's typed notes was that the investigation in London remained stagnant. Only a handful of arrests had been made in connection with Yonder the previous month, almost all of which were low-level dealers. The *Index* therefore documented in excessive detail these arrests, alongside various other dubious avenues of investigation. The Yonder Task Force – the group of detectives in the London DES who were assigned the job of stopping Yonder – hoped this would placate their superiors until something of a breakthrough could be made; at present, John counted himself amongst this ill-fated few.

This was not to say that the Task Force had been sitting idle. On the contrary, they had worked tirelessly against the "Yonder Organisation" – the official label chosen to designate all those involved with the drug. Over a dozen low-level dealers had already been arrested, and another half-dozen were in their sights who would be brought in and questioned before long. Although it had transpired that most of those arrested were fruitless sources of information, from the dealers who did prove themselves worthwhile, they subsequently hunted down three of their suppliers. Unfortunately, these three individuals – two men and one woman – were unable to offer the Task Force anything other than vague physical descriptions of the people they worked for, and had therefore ultimately been of little value. To make matters worse, in recent weeks it had come to light that London was the central hub for this drug, as details from interrogations around the nation pointed to the distribution originating from somewhere within the city's boundaries. Naturally, this made the Task Force's lack of progress all the more embarrassing when other Drug Enforcement Squads began to declare eagerly that Yonder's continued presence in Great Britain was due entirely to the ineptitude of the London DES. Whether or not it was being manufactured in London was another question altogether, however.

As of right now, the Task Force had no credible leads to pursue.

Their most successful arrest thus far had been one such supplier, a young man in his early twenties named Ben Chambers. Two weeks ago, they had used a detained dealer to set up a meeting, and the Task Force had arrested Chambers with over 3,000 Yonder pills in his possession, a major haul as far as their investigation went. But even after prolonged interrogation, Chambers only gave up a handful of his dealers, so to call him their most successful arrest alluded to the dire situation in which John and his fellow detectives found themselves.

Beyond Chambers and the other detained suppliers, it was pure speculation: the manufacturers of Yonder, the go-betweens who passed it to the suppliers, and those who transported it out of London – the entire Yonder Organisation was unidentified. There were but two other names known to the Task Force, which had been used in relation to Yonder by several of those they had arrested, but they were only nicknames: one was "Uncle Billy", and the other was simply "The Spaniard". Unsurprisingly, anything further about them remained an outright mystery.

John recalled the day DCI Werner had formed the Task Force, a month and a half ago now, once it became evident just how significant Yonder was going to be. He had stood before them and proclaimed the matter as one of utmost urgency to both the London DES and the government, and since then he had only grown increasingly impatient with their perceived incompetence. No doubt their inability to conclude this investigation in a timely manner was causing him to appear ineffective amongst his peers and superiors, and especially so now that Yonder had evolved into an unmistakable sign of protest amongst the working class.

As John finished this thought, a group of DES officers entered the office. Amongst them was Detective Inspector Peter Baer, another of the detectives assigned to the Yonder Task Force. The men arrived in a boisterous manner, discussing a football game from the previous evening; John had never understood the fascination with the sport, and many of the names they used to describe the event passed him by completely. Glad for the intrusion of the noise regardless, if only for the fact that it was louder than his disparaging inner monologue, John stubbed out his cigarette in the already brimming ashtray on his desk and closed the *Index of Drug Offences and Arrests* for November 1969.

After breaking away from this group of detectives, Peter approached John's desk and leant over it. John looked up without speaking. Peter's clear, blue eyes stared down at him, intense and alert beneath the florescent lights. His blond hair – he was of Aryan stock – was styled in the common undercut fashion, that being shaved short at the back and sides but long and parted to one side on the top. From where John sat, he could smell the cologne on Peter's clean-shaven face, even amongst the stale cigarette smoke; it was a heavy, sweet scent that was at odds with Peter's demeanour.

'A constable has just called in a couple of deceased,' Peter announced without any attempt at a greeting. His faultless English accent revealed no indication of his German lineage. 'He claims it was Yonder.'

Fuck, John thought with an internal sigh. Whilst numerous cities had reported deaths related to Yonder, these cases were far fewer and further between than might have been expected since overdosing on the drug was apparently nigh on impossible – again, unlike opium or heroin. London had remained off this list until today, but it was a number that was set to rise the longer it took them to shut down the Yonder Organisation.

Someone else could add these deaths to the *Index* next month, John decided. Considering Yonder's boundless nature, he was beginning to fear for his future in the DES should the Task Force continue to make such little progress, and he did not want to sign his name alongside so precise an indicator of their failure.

Peter gave no hint as to whether this worried him. His future was safe in any eventuality, given who his father was. He instead lit a cigarette with a steady hand and asked, 'Are you ready to go?'

John picked up the *Index* and stood to meet Peter's gaze. 'Just let me put this on DCI Werner's desk,' he said, waving the file, 'then I'll meet you downstairs.'

John and Peter stood equally tall, although Peter's better posture made him appear the taller. He was no more than two years John's senior, with that same German ancestry affording him the opportunity to ascend the ranks of the Metropolitan Police quicker than most. John had found he had worked relatively well with the man since their grouping on the Yonder Task Force, and they would converse in a cordial manner whenever circumstance dictated they do so. However, Peter was far too sure of himself for John's liking, and it was difficult for him to trust the DI as a result. He imagined this was not uncommon amongst those who grew up suspiciously handsome and with a certain prerogative; still, on occasion, this self-conviction was prone to manifest itself in a particular – *fashion*.

True to form, Peter did not acknowledge John's reply before he turned away, and he exited the DES office with a loud farewell to his sports-fan colleagues.

John crossed the room and opened the door to DCI Werner's office, which was the only actual office within the DES, although to describe it as such was generous. The small, windowless space was furnished with a too-large wooden desk that had to be pushed up against one wall before it would fit, whilst a practically brand-new typewriter – he did very little typing, the DCI – sat gathering dust to one side. Beyond this, there was nothing of personal value to remark on: no photographs of family members or of DCI Werner shaking hands with a well-known personality from within the Metropolitan Police, nor a medal of service displayed prominently in a frame as there might have been in another such office. It was instead left bare, as though the DCI did not expect he would be residing here for long. John hoped this assumption was correct, not that he would ever dare share such a notion with Peter and the others; that was much too impertinent an opinion, he had always thought.

Detective Chief Inspector – not that he had ever "detected" anything in his life – Werner was not in this morning, so John placed the file in the centre of his desk. His superior had a tendency to lose track of documents and then blame someone else for them having disappeared; it would now be impossible for him to miss the *Index*.

Extending a polite farewell to the other detectives, who continued to discuss the previous night's sports with a passionate vigour, John left the DES office and made for the fifth-floor men's WC. It was as grubby as usual and beset by that traditional sour air of urine and disinfectant, so John spent no longer in there than necessary. Whilst washing his hands after having used the facilities therein, he looked into the mirror over the washbasin: a clean-shaven, twenty-nine-year-old face stared back, with dark circles under the dull, grey eyes, an unkind consequence of both the stresses of the job and of having stayed up of a night with Alice this past week whilst she suffered an odd twist on "morning" sickness. John ran a hand through his thinning, curly black hair and splashed cold water on his face. The man in the mirror was gaunt, pale, and worn out, yet he wilfully assigned a certain degree of blame to the WC's poor lighting and the fact that this mirror had not been suitably cleaned in some time. Nevertheless, it was not the fresh face of the man John once was before he joined the DES as a detective constable.

With that unfavourable assessment of his bleak physiognomy completed, John exited the WC and headed in the direction of the lifts.

When he reached the foyer, Peter was waiting for him, with *The Times* open in his hands and half a cigarette dangling from his mouth. On noticing John approaching, Peter discarded the newspaper, and without a word they fell in together to navigate the crowd that often gathered down here, comprising other police officers and members of the public who went about their own business on this Wednesday morning.

The foyer was the most modern part of the building. Its façade of polished surfaces and fashionable black leather chairs afforded outsiders the impression that the upper levels must have been maintained to a similar standard. This building on the corner of Broadway and Victoria Street was built as the headquarters for the Occupation Forces, and after the military personnel departed in the late 1940s it was dubbed "Scotland Yard" as a sentimental reference to the pre-war years when the Metropolitan Police moved into the vacant offices.

The buzz of chatter bounced off the stone floor and into the high ceiling, consuming the two detectives' footsteps as they crossed the foyer to the exit on the other side.

On stepping out into the dim December sunshine, they were stopped on the forecourt in front of Scotland Yard by another detective whom John knew only in passing: a drinking partner of Peter's who was assigned to the Murder Squad. He and Peter began to discuss the same football match, and John, uninterested, turned his attention towards the flag that hung from a pole six or seven metres above them. There was a gentle breeze today, and as a result, it danced merrily before the grey building, a symphony of colour against the brick and glass. Blue, red, and white, the Union Jack rippled on the wind. The black swastika in the white circle at the centre stood out bold against the primary colours, whilst the golden rim of the circle contributed a confident elegance.

John smiled. He sometimes took for granted what National Socialism did for them in Great Britain. How people could be so disillusioned as to turn to Yonder was beyond him.

Peter finished his conversation, and together they walked around the corner to the parking bays behind Scotland Yard. When Peter produced the key to his BMW, a red 507 Series III, John did not argue against the assumption that they would take his car. He relished riding in the sports model, with the growl of the German engine beneath the elongated bonnet and the grip of the tyres on the tarmac when Peter entered a corner at careless speed. Being a bachelor, he could afford such a luxury, and although John did suppose it might be due time to upgrade his twelve-year-old Morris Minor 1000 for something more modern, he would trade neither his tired face nor his tired car for Peter's solitary lifestyle.

John climbed in and the BMW purred to life, and Peter set off onto Broadway towards the mid-morning traffic on Victoria Street.

CHAPTER TWO

Porcelain

Peter brought the car to a halt alongside a row of small, two-storey terraced houses on Harper Avenue in a residential area of East Ham. Ahead of them, outside number forty-seven, was a common pale-blue-and-white police car, with a flashing blue light attached to the roof and the word 'POLICE' written in tall letters on the sides. In front of it was a white ambulance with similar markings.

On the pavement beside the police car, a young constable in his green uniform was talking into the dashboard radio. As the two detectives exited the BMW, John heard him say, 'They've just arrived. Out.' He then approached John and Peter, and raising his arm into a high salute, he declared, 'Heil Hitler,' to his superiors.

Although John and Peter both returned this gesture, John did so with a likewise fully extended arm whilst Peter offered only a half-salute, his open palm stopping parallel to his head. That was more his style: Peter demonstrating his authority over the constable. John was yet to become so comfortable with his own position in the Metropolitan Police's chain of command. Neither of his fellow officers of the Reich acknowledged the difference, though, and John hastily lowered his arm to his side after the appropriate second.

'This way. They're upstairs,' the constable said before he turned back towards number forty-seven. Up close, he looked very young – not a day over twenty, John thought – with a boyish face peeking out beneath the wreathed eagle on his cap. This recruit had encountered death early and would be unlikely to forget this outing any time soon.

John entered number forty-seven behind Peter and the constable. He was met with a narrow hallway carpeted in a light brown and decorated with a white woodchip wallpaper. Hanging on one wall was a series of framed photographs, which were a mixture of grainy colour and black and white. John picked out the family who must have been living here, with the same three faces of a man, a woman, and a girl appearing over and over again. A black-and-white snapshot of them at the seaside sat high on the wall; the girl was a young child, and the image was old and faded. The next one along was much more recent: that same girl was a teenager now and wearing a fashionable, bright-red dress. She stood beside the woman, who also showed signs of her age, and both of them smiled into the camera, happy people living comfortable lives.

To the right, a single door let out on to the ground floor. John and Peter ignored it and followed the constable up a steep staircase towards a landing with three further doors, which presumably led to a bathroom and two bedrooms. A second constable on the scene watched them ascend. Although he was noticeably older than their guide, it was still apparent that he was out of his depth. He remained to one side, facing away from the only open door on the landing, and he and the younger constable shared an uneasy glance as he admitted the detectives with a silent salute.

The faintest smell of iron was unmistakable up here, and John felt a surge of anxiety swell in the pit of his stomach.

John and Peter stepped through the open doorway into a bedroom. The same woodchip-effect walls were painted pink, and a white, faux-antique dressing table stood beside a single bed. Trinkets and pieces of jewellery were scattered about the dressing table, folded clothes had been piled on a stool in the corner, and little porcelain statues of dogs sat on the windowsill. The door of a tall wardrobe was ajar, and clothes of various designs and colours were hanging inside. A record sat on a player, the needle moved to the side, with a collection of vinyl discs stacked next to it. It was once the epitome of average for a room belonging to a teenage girl.

Not any more, however. One body lay on the bed, another was slumped in a chair by the dressing table, and a third was curled up in a heap on the floor: two females and a male. The one in the chair was the girl from the photographs, John noted. Her head had fallen onto her shoulder, and her lifeless eyes gazed at the carpet. Her skin had already turned an off-white colour, the same shade as the faded porcelain on the windowsill.

Peter spoke first, which was fortunate considering John's mouth had gone bone dry. 'Murder-suicide,' he stated.

It was a simple deduction to make. The girl in the chair had a devastating blunt force wound at her temple, and from where he stood, John could see dark-purple bruising around the throat of the girl on the bed. On the other hand, the boy – for he must have been no older than fifteen – had fatal lacerations on both his wrists, and his blood was soaked into the brown carpet around his body.

It was the same as the other deaths attributed to Yonder, for which the causes were always violence, accident, or suicide under its influence. The drug was a psychedelic, after all, and it therefore had the capacity to exacerbate certain unideal tendencies in its users.

Without looking away from the bodies, Peter called towards the landing, 'You said this was Yonder.'

'Yes, sir,' came a hesitant response. It was the older of the two constables who was watching them from the doorway.

'How do you know?' Peter asked in a level monotone. His whole composure was that of indifferent professionalism, but then Peter had been assigned to the Murder Squad before the DES, so he had no doubt borne witness to far more gruesome scenes than this.

In contrast, John's hands were trembling in his trouser pockets. He had attended numerous dead bodies during his time as a detective for the DES, but they were all overdose victims who had lost their lives due to their own ignorance. In truth, he had expected to find much the same today, but such brutal killings, and all that blood…

And they were hardly any older than children.

John had not prepared himself for this eventuality.

The constable answered Peter's question: 'There is a girl downstairs, sir. A friend of…' He motioned at the bodies, and did not finish his sentence.

Peter faced him. 'Have you questioned her yet?'

The constable refused to meet his gaze. 'Not properly, sir. She is' – he hesitated again – 'not in the best of ways.'

'We need to talk to her,' Peter stated, and he made for the door.

The constable was still standing on the threshold. 'Sir, she—'

John was about to weigh in on the constable's behalf and suggest they allow the girl at least a moment to mourn her friends before questioning her, when Peter spoke with finality. Getting close to the constable, he uttered, 'I was not asking for your permission. Take us to the girl.'

The constable's eyes fell to his shoes, and he mumbled an acknowledgement of the order before he turned on his heel and went back onto the landing. Peter followed, and John exited the bedroom behind him. The younger constable already had his arm raised in salute, and he dared not even breathe when the detectives passed him to reach the stairs.

The constable led them down into the hallway. At the bottom, he stopped in front of the door to the ground-floor rooms, and it was with visible dread that he placed a hand on it.

As the door opened, the sound of heavy sobbing drifted into the hallway, and John's stomach turned all over again.

On the other side of the door was a living room. It was cosy, with the same light-brown carpet as the hallway, a fireplace set into the wall, and an old three-piece suite that faced an even older television set – the usual orientation for the living room in a family home. To the right, folding shutter doors divided this room from what was the dining room, in which a low window with net curtains faced the street. A large painting was hanging on the back wall, upon which a farmer and his dog herded sheep on a field of green – very "old British".

On the couch, an older woman cradled a young girl in her arms. Both of them together were the source of this incessant sobbing.

The constable explained the situation to the detectives with a muted disquiet: 'The woman is a neighbour. The mother of the girl upstairs is away until this evening, and her father is deceased. She is Mrs Patricia Jones, and the girl is Jennifer Campbell.'

John nodded his understanding, whilst Peter studied the couch.

Peter stepped forwards, obviously intent on speaking to them himself. 'Mrs Jones,' he began in the gentle, unnatural tone he employed when addressing victims, 'I am Detective Inspector Baer, and this is Detective Sergeant Highsmith.' He gestured towards John.

Mrs Jones had only become aware of their presence when Peter spoke, and she greeted them now with two red eyes.

'We need to speak to Jennifer,' Peter said with that same irregular tenderness.

'Leave her be,' Mrs Jones pleaded, and she pulled Jennifer closer. She was elderly, and John at once detected the aversion her generation often expressed towards officers of the Reich, and especially one with a name such as "Baer".

Peter leant nearer to Mrs Jones and his voice became sterner: 'Mrs Jones, we need to talk to her.'

The woman recoiled from him, but she still held on to Jennifer.

'*Now.*' The word was almost a whisper by the time it passed Peter's lips in an unambiguous order.

Mrs Jones's face slipped from sadness into distress. She knew when to concede to an officer of the Reich – and especially one with a name such as "Baer". She released Jennifer from her embrace. 'I'll only be outside, Jenny,' she reassured her.

Jennifer whimpered a reply. When Mrs Jones stood up, the girl lifted her knees to her face and continued to cry.

Mrs Jones shot a vicious look at the detectives as she left the living room, and John felt an urge to apologise for the intrusion and for Peter's abrasive conduct. He knew it was not proper practice to do so, of course. Anyway, it was inevitable that they would talk to Jennifer eventually, and sooner was always preferable to later, so he straightened his shoulders and reminded himself that they had a job to do, irrespective of her current emotional state.

Peter crouched down so he was at eye level with Jennifer. 'Jennifer, I'm so sorry this happened to you. It must be hard.' His intonation had altered again, back to that artificial concern. 'But listen, the only way we can stop the people who did this to your friends is if you tell us what happened.'

Jennifer lifted her head to reveal two eyes redder even than Mrs Jones's. She rested her chin on her knees and tucked herself into a tighter protective ball. A pretty girl with small features and long, blonde hair, Jennifer had a face of pure innocence.

After a moment, her crying subsided enough for her to speak: 'We were sleeping over here for the night. Tommy turned up uninvited and brought the drugs with him. He said it would be fun to take it. He said all his friends were buying it off him but he'd give it to us for free to try.'

The boy upstairs was a Yonder dealer, then? If so, he was the youngest the Task Force had come across. He was likely chosen for this exact reason, given that it would have been easier for him to sell the drug to his teenage friends than for someone even as young as Ben Chambers to do so. Whatever the case, it was nevertheless a terrifying prospect: if Yonder's influence was beginning to spread amongst the younger members of society – be it as an act of "silent protest" against the State or for 'fun' – the whole situation was only going to deteriorate much faster.

Jennifer continued, 'I said no, and they started to call me names. They said if I wasn't going to try it, I should just leave.

I came down here to sleep, and when I woke up this morning, they were… they were…' Jennifer hid her head back behind her knees and began to weep uncontrollably. She could not bring herself to say that final word.

'Thank you, Jennifer. I know that was difficult.' Peter spoke the words with what sounded like true empathy.

With that, John presumed this conversation was over. The girl had given them everything she could, and the incident would be logged as yet another example of their inability to impede the Yonder Organisation. As he watched Jennifer, he too felt hot tears stinging his eyes.

But Peter was not finished. 'Jennifer, I need you to think for me. Think hard. Do you know where Tommy got the drugs from?'

The girl was still sobbing.

'Jennifer?'

She continued to sob, her whole body shaking from the intensity of her crying.

Peter was not deterred. '*Jennifer!*' He raised his voice and seized her arm.

John's foot shifted on the carpet. He immediately checked himself and stepped back, though, to stop himself from throwing Peter off the girl. It was one thing to dress down a lower-ranking officer, and another to speak with such little ambiguity to Mrs Jones, but manhandling an innocent teenage girl was precariously close to the line. It was this exact sort of behaviour that made John uncomfortable around Peter: his propensity to act with hostility at the slightest of obstacles – he was unpredictable.

The forceful contact roused Jennifer from her grief. She bolted upright, startled, and cowered deeper into the couch.

'Jennifer' – Peter's voice was level again, but he did not remove his hand from around the girl's arm – 'where did Tommy get the drugs?'

Jennifer wiped her eyes with the back of her hand. 'Tommy said he got them from a friend of his last week, someone he met in a pub.'

This 'friend' was Tommy's supplier, no doubt.

'Did he mention the name of the pub?' Peter asked.

Jennifer considered it for a second, then said with uncertainty, 'The Rag-and-*something*, I think.'

'The Rag-and-*Bone*?' Peter completed the name of the pub for her. It was clearly familiar to him.

Jennifer nodded and made a soft affirmative sound before she returned her head to her knees and resumed crying.

Peter did not thank Jennifer this time; there was no reason to maintain the façade of compassion now he had what he wanted. He released her arm (leaving white marks behind on the pink skin), stood up, and moved towards the door without so much as a nod to John or the constable.

As soon as Peter crossed the threshold, Mrs Jones came scuttling past him into the living room. She sat down on the couch, grabbed Jennifer with both arms, and held the girl in a firm embrace. John did not look back at them as he took his own leave, but he could still feel the woman's hateful scowl burning a hole in the back of his skull from across the room. He would have tried to explain to her how everything they did was for the safety of Jennifer and her other friends; however, he had the distinct impression it would fall upon deaf ears.

He caught up with Peter by the BMW. 'You know the pub, then? The Rag-and-Bone?' he asked.

'I do,' Peter replied, and that was all he had to say on the matter.

Back in the car, Peter turned the key in the ignition and pulled away from the kerb. As he did so, John glimpsed two men in white step from behind the ambulance. Between them, they carried a trolley towards the front door of number forty-seven.

He shivered in his leather seat.

John lit a cigarette and watched the terraced houses go by as they drove along Harper Avenue. And he wondered, *How many other mornings have begun today with death because of Yonder?*

It was already one too many.

CHAPTER THREE

The Rag-and-Bone

A significant divide existed in London, with the River Thames acting as the partition, and it had done so since the end of the Second Great War. The fighting had been especially brutal as the Reich's forces fought to liberate the capital, and nowhere was it more devastating than along the southern bank of the Thames, where the British forces refused to surrender the vital defensive position. When the Reich's inevitable victory came about in London, this side of the river was already reduced to little more than rubble. Swift housing regeneration followed the war, so as to accommodate both the native Londoners left homeless and the workers who arrived in the city seeking employment in the factories or on the docklands, but such haste predestined the area to its now tired and rundown state. Even the atmosphere was different here, being somehow heavier and restless, and the people appeared out of time with their unfashionable, scruffy haircuts and bestubbled chins – they were an unkempt and unshaven mass. It was as if they had missed out on the evolution of society over the past three decades, hidden away from the bright lights of Central London. In reality, this was a different world to the one John inhabited, and it might easily have been mistaken for a district in one of the factory cities. It remained unspoken, but many from the north side of the river believed themselves to be of a different standing to those in South London. John would not go so far as to call these people "unclean", though, as would *some* detectives.

John and Peter sat looking out of the BMW's front windscreen on to a narrow stretch of road named Burgess Street. They were just north of Blackheath, which was an area in the heart of Southeast London. From there, they could see The Rag-and-Bone on the corner. At odds with its neighbours, this particular corner had survived the war intact – this was apparent when comparing the ornate and impractical masonry of The Rag-and-Bone to the functional brickwork of the post-war buildings at the other end of the road. Beyond this observation, it was an otherwise unremarkable public house. The name was painted in deliberate but faded white lettering against the black of an antique wooden plaque, which stretched along one flank of the building above the windows. The low, frosted glass windows revealed nothing of its interior. The sign hanging over the door did intrigue John, though: on it, a dishevelled man led a pony-drawn cart stacked high with scrap metal down a street. John did not understand the reference, and he decided against asking Peter to clarify.

John and Peter observed the pub in silence, not that there was much to report: a series of men came and went, unaware of the two detectives watching them from a distance, but the rest of Burgess Street was deserted at this time on a weekday.

Inside the car, the scent of Peter's sharp cologne had mixed with that of the leather wrapped around the seats. It had caused a heavy, sweet musk to hang in the air that was not unpleasant to endure, yet they had been here for some minutes now, and John was beginning to suffer a headache from the concoction.

It had taken John the length of his cigarette to feel comfortable addressing Peter after his performance with Jennifer Campbell. When they did speak, Peter enlightened him as to the individual they were heading to see: an older man named Joe Harding, who was the proprietor of The Rag-and-Bone. Peter had chanced upon him once before when he had trailed a suspect to the pub during his time with the Murder Squad, and he had found Harding quite unwilling to cooperate. His daughter would likely be inside as well, along with her husband, and John could only assume that they had both been subjected beyond salvation to the old man's crooked tales of life before the war.

John felt for the comforting weight of the Walther beneath his suit jacket. It was nerve-wracking, waiting for their moment to act. He stole a glance at Peter more than once, but the DI did not appear daunted one bit by the prospect of what was to come. It was unheard of for a police officer to be attacked in the street nowadays, as this decade was much calmer than the previous one, but caution was still advised, and especially so when looking for trouble south of the river.

'Fuck it. Let's go,' Peter finally decided, and he climbed out of the car.

Chasing the abrupt order, John scrambled out onto the pavement and fell in step with him. Together, they crossed the road towards The Rag-and-Bone.

John straightened his waistcoat as they approached the door, attempting to shrug off any trace of unease and project the authority he held as an officer of the Reich – all the while, his heart thumped erratically in his chest.

On the other side of the door, the pub was exactly as John might have described it from his seat in the BMW. Furnished with mismatched tables and chairs and a bare wooden floor, the decor was drab and unappealing, and the aroma of stale ale was overwhelming. Not dissimilar to the DES office, the combination of narrow windows and cigarette smoke had caused a fog-like blanket to settle across the poorly lit room. Parallel with the far wall was the bar, which was lined with a half-dozen tall stools and a man perched atop each one of them. A flight of stairs to the left led up to the first floor. The patrons, who were undoubtedly working men on their lunch break, were dressed in shabby, dull clothes from a decade John did not recognise, and they ranged from the suspiciously young to the much older.

In complete contrast to all of this, the mood in the pub was nothing short of jovial: chatter and laughter rang out around the room, and the sound of somebody tickling away at the piano in the corner suggested that a musical number was not out of the question this afternoon. Such an atmosphere surprised John, to say the least.

The detectives were yet to be noticed, with the pub dwellers going about their day as usual. There were far more of them than John had anticipated, though, with few chairs left unoccupied, and he was suddenly concerned. It was not difficult to agitate these types, and he was unconvinced he and Peter would be able to manage a group this size whilst they spoke to Joe Harding.

Peter had a solution to this predicament, as he so often did. He gave John no indication of his intentions in advance, as was his wont, but in a casual, even blasé manner, he drew his Walther and fired a single round into the ceiling.

The sound of the gunshot rattled off the walls, and when it faded, the only noise remaining in the room was the high-pitched ringing in John's ears.

Everyone was now aware of their presence.

'Everybody out,' Peter ordered, the pistol still in his hand.

Not needing to be told twice, the patrons all stood and made for the door.

As the last of them left, Peter turned to John, who had recoiled and sworn in a low breath at the unexpected gunshot. Seeing what must have been an expression of stunned disbelief on John's face, a slight, sly grin played across Peter's when he walked away. That same arrogant smirk was a regular feature of his, and John was barely able to conceal his frustration with the DI's continued lack of restraint.

Peter stepped up to the door and slid a bolt lock into place, ensuring that they would not be disturbed any further.

A tall man in a shirt and braces was waiting to the side. His hair was shaved short in a ruffian manner, common amongst the workers, and a large head on wide-set, muscular shoulders afforded him a considerable presence. Despite his appearance, when Peter stopped in the centre of the room and addressed the man with: 'Ollie, go get Joe,' Ollie – Joe Harding's son-in-law – also understood that it was best to obey, and he took off up the stairs by the bar without delay.

The barmaid remained at her station.

Peter strode towards her and, tucking his Walther back inside his suit jacket, said, 'Whisky, Abbie.' He then sat himself upon a stool.

Abbie, Harding's daughter, was in maybe her mid-thirties, so not much older than John or Peter. John also noticed she was attractive, with a slim body wrapped in a floral-patterned dress, a small nose, short auburn hair, and bright, hazel eyes. It was a shame she was stuck selling liquor to workmen in such a place as this.

She stared back at Peter when he spoke, and for an instant, John thought Abbie might tell him to fetch the whisky himself, which would have been a bold move. But, eventually, she too submitted, and she plucked a bottle of unlabelled, brown liquor from the collection of spirits positioned along the wall behind her.

Unfazed, Peter retrieved a cigarette and lit it. John copied him and focused on his hand not trembling as he held the lighter to the tip of the Reemtsma.

Abbie dropped a tumbler on the bar and filled it with three fingers of whisky, and Peter tossed it immediately into his mouth. His expression suggested it was not good whisky. Still, he set the glass back down and motioned for Abbie to pour another. She did so, with an unambiguous disdain for the man sat before her.

'Drink, John?' Peter asked through the cigarette between his lips.

The thought of a stiff drink was enticing after his laborious morning of paperwork, death, and gunfire. But John never did partake when on duty, so he replied, 'No, thank you,' with as much dignity as he could achieve whilst refusing a drink.

Peter shrugged and emptied the glass for a second time.

'Detective!' A man had appeared at the top of the stairs. 'What a lovely surprise.' He spoke with a broad and vulgar "cockney" accent, which was an inflection reserved nowadays for the working-class labourers who were natives of South London.

'Afternoon, Joe.' Peter stayed seated at the bar whilst Joe Harding, with Ollie in tow, limped down the stairs with the aid of a walking cane.

The man was older, as Peter had said he would be; John guessed him to be at least in his early sixties by his sagging features. Silver hair poked out from beneath a flat cap, the headwear accentuating his unrefined lifestyle, and his haggard face centred around a bulbous nose. The same as his clientele's, Harding's clothes had suffered long use and were at least several decades out of style by now – if ever they had been in style, that was. He wore a bottle-green trench coat with brown patches stitched over the elbows, underneath which was a burgundy-coloured pinstripe waistcoat, and a thin scarf was draped around his neck to protect it from today's chill. When he came to a halt at the bottom of the stairs, he stood there with better posture even than Peter, with his walking cane placed rigidly between his legs, and he scrutinised the two detectives with curious, sunken eyes.

'And what can I do for yourself and…' Harding offered John a lingering stare when he realised they were not previously acquainted.

'Detective Sergeant Highsmith,' John announced rather too quickly when he saw Peter was about to answer on his behalf.

Harding did not repeat his question. Peter was right: there was something different about this man. He had an air of confidence that left John ill at ease. Even confronted by two officers of the Reich as he was right now, Harding appeared entirely unperturbed. He said nothing with regard to the bullet hole in his ceiling – in fact, he did not acknowledge there had been any gunfire.

Peter came straight to the point. 'We're here about Yonder.'

'Yonder, Detective?' Harding returned a confused frown, feigning ignorance. Whilst Yonder had never been reported on in the newspapers or mentioned on the radio, the drug and what it stood for were common knowledge across Great Britain at this point.

Peter breathed a long sigh. 'The drug, Joe. We're here about Yonder the drug,' he clarified in a weary fashion.

Silence. Harding said nothing in response.

Peter sucked at his teeth. 'Detective Sergeant,' he instructed without looking away from Harding.

At the prompt, John put his hand inside his jacket and watched as Abbie and Ollie both went stiff, the pair perhaps expecting further gunshots to follow. Tediously, Harding remained composed and turned his head to inspect John from beneath the peak of his flat cap.

Instead of a weapon, John produced a leather notebook and flicked to the page he had updated during the drive to The Rag-and-Bone. 'Last week, a teenage boy was supplied with Yonder on your premises, with the intention being that he sell it on to his friends. We know this for a fact, Mr Harding' – he could not call the older man Joe as Peter did – 'and this morning, that boy and two young girls were found dead after taking it. We're here to find out who gave him the Yonder.' John left the notebook open in his hand, ready to scribble down anything important Harding might say, although this did seem to be an ambitious notion.

Harding ruminated briefly on what John had said before he spoke again in that abrasive cockney accent: 'Detectives, many people come in this pub. Some of 'em I know, some I don't. They sit, they talk, they drink – and then they leave. Most'll be back the next day. Others, I'll never see again in my life. Now, I can't be held accountable for every little thing that might happen under one of those tables.' Harding gestured to the room and to the ale-stained tables around them.

'You were shot during the war, were you not, Joe?' Peter asked, rhetorically. He had mentioned in the BMW that Harding had fought in the war – on the wrong side, as had most British men his age.

'I was,' answered Harding in a matter-of-fact tone. 'It happened jus' down the road, now that you mention it.'

Peter did not acknowledge this admission, but said, 'Listen, Joe, we both know you don't have receipts for half of this liquor.' It was well-understood that many pubs on this side of the river bought stolen or homemade alcohol as a means to make an easy profit. They could seize his entire stock right now and put Harding out of business whilst he proved ownership of each individual bottle. If he could not, it would be destroyed, and he would be fined – or worse. The question about his war wound was an obvious ploy to remind the man of his place in society; he would appreciate as well as anybody that the law did not favour those who had once fought against National Socialism.

'Okay, Detective.' Harding made a signal with his hand to indicate his understanding. The promise of menace in Peter's statement had achieved its desired effect. 'A man came in last week, jus' like the detective sergeant says he did. Saturday, I think. I hadn't seen him before, and I ain't seen him since. Called himself Frank, if I recall correctly.'

'You'd better,' Peter warned.

'Yes, yes. Frank Boyd. A Scot.' Harding was much more certain this time.

John took out a pen and began writing in his notebook.

'He stayed a good while, a couple of hours at least, and there must've been a dozen people stopped by his table. I thought it a little odd at the time' – Harding affected contemplation – 'I suppose.'

'And you didn't think to report this irregular activity to the police?' Peter asked.

Harding chuckled.

Abbie snickered from behind the bar.

Ollie smiled and bowed his head.

Bastards.

'I spoke with him for a spell,' Harding continued, ignoring the question, which elicited in Peter a visible irritation. 'He didn't offer me anything, before you ask. Seemed a nice enough bloke.' He was stringing them along, John knew, giving them nothing of significance whilst still maintaining a pretence of cooperation. 'I—'

'Have you ever wondered, Joe, how it would feel to be hanged?' Peter interjected.

Harding did not respond, and none of them laughed this time.

'Illegal liquor won't get you a noose, but I'm sure if I bring some officers back here, they will be able to find something. For an old war dog like you, I can't imagine there would be much fuss if you wound up swinging.' Peter raised an eyebrow. 'I'd put in a good word for Abbie and Ollie, of course.' He aimed a cruel smile at Harding, which was not dissimilar to the smile he had directed at John only minutes before.

The old man broke his gaze and scratched at his bestubbled chin. Abbie and Ollie shared a fleeting glance at the mention of their names, worry having fallen across their faces in place of smug defiance.

Harding grumbled something unintelligible, then conceded: 'He said he lives in Hatcham, jus' round the corner from New Cross Gate station. He's tall, and shaven headed, with tattoos up his arms and a couple of little scars on his face. Can't miss him. He said he walks his dog over on Telegraph Hill of a mornin'.' There was a flicker of regret in Harding's eyes, but it lasted no longer than an instant. 'Happy, detectives?' He looked from Peter to John, then back to Peter.

Peter nodded.

John was taken aback. Some information was never out of the ordinary in these circumstances, usually enough for them to leave the subject of their questioning in peace for the time being, but such specific details were unprecedented. Peter's threats must have made a profound impression upon the man.

With this line of questioning at its end now as far as he was concerned, Harding turned back towards the stairs. But John was irate. That Harding would even consider protecting the man responsible for the deaths of Jennifer Campbell's friends was reprehensible, so he called after him, 'Three teenagers are dead because of what was passed beneath one of these tables, Mr Harding. Surely you recognise the gravity of the situation?'

'I've answered your questions, Detective Sergeant,' Harding replied without pausing in his limped ascent of the stairs. Then, so that it was just audible above the thump of his walking cane as he disappeared, he muttered, 'So take your damned Nazi business elsewhere.'

John's blood boiled. Even before the war, the term "Nazi" had been laden with extraordinarily pejorative connotations by all those who opposed the politics of the Third Reich; nowadays, its use was considered a clear indication of subversive tendencies, or at least of abhorrent disrespect. To have the word spoken in front of two officers of the Reich was, therefore, quite unbelievable.

John had to act – people like this were dangerous if left unchecked. He took a step forwards, determined that Harding would answer for his slander.

'Let's go,' Peter declared.

John stopped still, and Peter stood up to leave.

John was baffled. Why would Peter let Harding walk away after such a remark? Peter, a man who was relentless in his defence of the Reich.

Peter offered no answer to this unspoken question. Instead, he stubbed out his cigarette on the wood of the bar and crossed the room to the door. John followed behind him as daylight flooded the pub, none the wiser as to what had just happened.

*

Back in the BMW, Peter drove them around several corners before he pulled up against the kerb again and turned off the ignition.

It was then that he finally spoke – this short journey having been one of total silence – but the words were not directed at John. 'Base, this is Detective Inspector Baer. Over,' he said, taking the handset from the radio on the dashboard. It was linked to the Radio Room at Scotland Yard and was a minor modification all personal cars had been fitted with – John had one in his Morris Minor – so they were never out of contact with the station in the event something needed to be logged or they found themselves in trouble. From where John was sitting, they needed the radio for neither right now: the information they had on Frank Boyd would be discussed when they returned to the DES office, and beyond that, there was nothing to report.

'What may I do for you, Detective Inspector? Over,' came a female voice through the crackle of static.

'I need ten or twelve officers for an immediate DES raid north of Blackheath. And have Detective Sergeant List ride with them. Over.' Peter released the button on the handset and addressed John: 'That should be plenty of bodies.'

John was about to ask Peter what he had planned when the radio burst back into life. 'Okay, Detective Inspector. I'll check with our officers to make sure we have those numbers available. Please stand by. Over.'

Peter placed the handset back on the dashboard. Then, after a long moment of silent reflection – long enough that

John began to wonder whether he had any intention at all of elaborating on what the plan was – Peter explained: 'We raid The Rag-and-Bone and say we're looking for Yonder, that we think Joe's pushing it. He gave us that name too easily; he doubtless sold this Boyd out to get us to leave. People like Joe don't give up information like that unless they have something to hide. Especially telling us where he'll be walking his bloody dog – it was too specific.'

It was just as John had first suspected when Harding gave them Frank Boyd: it was all a bit too easy. He had credited their success to Peter's hard line of questioning and Harding's desire to be left alone. It did not occur to him that Harding might be overcompensating as a means to hide some greater involvement with Yonder, because to allow for its further distribution to then take place in his own bar would have been utter stupidity.

'You never know' – Peter waved a dismissive hand – 'there might be nothing for us back there. But if so, we'll still find *something* worthwhile to pin on them. And we can take Joe in for insurrection if nothing else and remind these bastards who's in charge.' He had it all worked out, down to the justification he would use should it come to pass that this raid by the Yonder Task Force was misjudged.

In any case, John voiced his support for the plan; not that Peter was waiting for any such commitment from him. The truth be told, he would much rather have returned to Scotland Yard and allowed Peter to wreak havoc upon The Rag-and-Bone with whomever answered his call. Peter's aggressive method of investigation had set John on edge – he was like a wild dog, impulsive and volatile – and John dreaded to think what he might do next.

*

Fortunately, that afternoon presented no further need for the DI's particular capabilities.

Several hours later, with the low-hanging sun now obscured by a dense and overcast December sky, John stood in a ransacked bedroom on the upper floor of The Rag-and-Bone with Peter and Detective Sergeant Arnold List, another of their colleagues assigned to the Yonder Task Force. The constables had been thorough, tearing through the building in order to uncover any secrets it might be withholding. The contents of a chest of drawers and a tall wardrobe were heaped in the corner of the bedroom after having been flung onto the floor, and the pillows and the mattress on the bed were shredded to ribbons. The bedroom across the landing was in a similar state, whilst downstairs more than one liquor bottle had been smashed by careless hands.

Laid out on the ruined mattress were the spoils of their labour, and it did not disappoint.

There had been several thousand unlicensed cigarettes stashed away in the cellar, which was no surprise considering many alehouses – even in North London – sold such contraband over the bar. In the bedroom across the landing, they found some opium (enough for personal use) and two small bottles of morphine with neither a patient's nametag nor a doctor's signature attached – a clear indication that it was either stolen or manufactured illegally. These would no doubt be used together as a numbing cocktail to help Harding sleep of a night, not that the man deserved any peace given how he was injured fighting against the Third Reich.

This was all ultimately of little interest, though, when it emerged that Peter was right about Yonder. Harding was not an innocent bystander in the distribution of the drug: he was a supplier, but on a grander scale than anyone they had previously encountered.

They might have missed it had a clumsy young constable not tripped over the rug in the bedroom. On landing hard against the wooden floor, he felt a crack, and after realising it was not his kneecap, the officer rolled up the rug to reveal several loose floorboards – one of which was now broken. After removing them, he discovered a large metal box with a padlock on it, alongside three war-era rifles, two revolvers, and a cache of ammunition.

They took stock of the weapons first. John listened attentively to the metallic clunk as he pulled back the bolt handle on a rifle to check it was not loaded, and he peered with fascination through the rusted sight at the tip of the barrel. A strip of metal over the trigger bore its markings, which – underneath a crown-shaped stamp – read 'G.R, 1918, S^{HT} L.E III*'. John was not familiar with the lettering, but he assumed from the crown that the rifle was British; this was a weapon with a dark, misguided past.

That task completed, it took Peter and Arnold no more than five minutes to break the padlock on the metal box. And there they were: what must have been tens of thousands of those little blue Yonder pills. They had already been separated into nondescript brown-paper parcels, ready to be allocated to somebody like Frank Boyd, and the fact that a dozen such packages were in the box suggested that Harding was far more integral to this operation than they could ever have imagined. Peter was confident when he claimed it would be one of the largest single finds in Great Britain, never mind the largest for the London DES, and a collective ease settled amongst the three detectives for having at last struck a considerable blow against the Yonder Organisation.

Not only that, but they had just prevented potentially thousands of deaths, John reasoned with delight. If only they had somehow learnt of Joe Harding's involvement a week earlier, this internal evaluation continued, then Jennifer Campbell's friends would still be alive…

With that thought, his brief sensation of joy dissipated into the bedroom without a trace, and it was replaced by a grim, heavy remorse.

CHAPTER FOUR

Paperclip

The following morning, John awoke to the sound of rain lashing against the bedroom window. The change from November into December had been just so, with dim sunshine one day and rain the next, followed by a howling gale or even the odd thunderstorm. John would not complain about such dull weather as he preferred the rain to the sticky heat of summer. Furthermore, like a small boy, he found thunder and lightning exhilarating.

He lay in bed, drifting in and out of a light, comfortable sleep before the weight of the day arrived. That was until the clock hands landed on half past six, and he was disturbed by the sharp peal of his alarm. John swung a hand towards the button, which he hit on his third attempt, and then he struggled to his feet. As he stood, Alice let out a tired sigh and rolled over, her head sinking into the pillow. John smiled and left her to her sleep. She had been up again last night until past midnight with nausea, and she deserved all the rest she could get.

Showered and shaved, John dressed himself in his navy three-piece suit (he wore the same necktie as yesterday, for the dark colour matched the navy as well as it did the grey). All of his suits were of a single, solid colour – anything even as simple as a subtle check would have been too eccentric for him. Downstairs, John sat at the kitchen table, relishing his morning coffee and cigarette and biting intermittently at a piece of toast. The rain hammered against the window down here too; the world outside was buried under an oppressive winter mist.

John had *The Times* open in front of him. He was still barely awake, though – he had stayed up with Alice and not fallen asleep until at least one o'clock himself – and only half-read the words as he browsed the headlines with idle curiosity. A new study proclaimed the great health benefits of eggs, which was in comparison to six months ago when they had been all but deadly. Over the page, a double spread discussed the genius of a new type of oven called a "microwave", something John would never be able to afford. He continued to skim through the pages, skipping over the regular section dedicated to the fashion of Queen Wallis without even a glance at it, and took a gulp of now-lukewarm coffee.

On the radio, the two presenters were discussing the current outbreak of flu that had been sweeping the nation since mid-October. 'Symptoms can include vomiting and diarrhoea, along with drowsiness and stomach cramps. In an effort to stem the spread of this flu, people are asked to stay at home if they are suffering from any of these complaints. Sounds quite terrible, does it not, Judy?' Dieter, the male presenter, expressed his alarm.

'It does, Dieter,' agreed Judy, the female presenter. 'However, our health service is one of the finest in the world, and I am certain that it will have no trouble containing this illness.'

John was lucky he had not fallen victim to this flu himself. It had ravaged London in the latter days of November, and there were already numerous people at Scotland Yard who had been taken ill with the symptoms described. He was less concerned for his own well-being, of course, than he was about bringing such an ailment home to Alice.

The presenters had moved on promptly from this upsetting topic, and they were discussing the official plans for London's annual VE Day celebrations in January, when Alice stepped into the kitchen.

She met John with, 'Good morning,' and kissed him firmly on the mouth.

'Tea?' John asked whilst Alice sat down awkwardly at the kitchen table.

Alice replied that tea would be perfect, then she exhaled a long, exaggerated groan. 'Get out of me,' she said in jest to their unborn child, and she rubbed her stomach with gentle care.

John chuckled as he ignited the stove and placed the kettle over the flame, and Alice laughed happily. She was only two years younger than John, though she never did let him forget it. But then that was one of the many things he had always loved about Alice: the fact she was not afraid to tease him or make a joke at his expense, and was frequently willing to push far beyond the boundaries of good taste. Some disliked women being humorous or – for shame! – sarcastic, they thought it not quite right; John found it overwhelmingly attractive. He kissed Alice on the head when he placed a cup of tea and a plate of fresh toast in front of her. She responded with an adoring smile and a thank you before she curled her golden hair behind her ears and took a cautious first sip.

They sat together, making pleasant conversation. Plans were made to visit Alice's older brother, Mark, on Saturday, granted that nothing happened to keep John at work. Saturday was his scheduled day off, so unless something major broke before then, there was no reason he would not be able to take the day and continue where he had left off on Sunday.

Alice then asked what John had planned for today. First, he explained, he would have to check whether the *Index of Drug Offences and Arrests* was yet to be signed by DCI Werner. Alice offered a frustrated tut at the name: John had lamented to her on many occasions about the ineptitude of his ranking superior.

After that, he thought to himself, *it will be time to find out how Joe Harding has been occupying his days these past couple of months.*

John had to walk a fine line when discussing DES matters with Alice. It was not that he did not trust her with such information – as a matter of fact, they often talked about his work, including the ins and outs of the Yonder investigation. It was more about knowing where to stop in terms of shielding her from this business. There was a reason the newspapers were not allowed to report on particular aspects of crime: it was unhealthy to be constantly bombarded with drugs and rape and murder, and John refused to subject Alice to the world he had chosen as a career. Having been a nurse (a vocation Alice gave up to pursue the noblest of professions – motherhood), she did understand better than most the violent and sadistic temperaments of some human beings, yet John still had a duty to keep certain specifics from her. She had learnt when not to press him on a matter, though, and when John was vague about what he would be doing after speaking to DCI Werner, she asked no further questions.

The conversation proceeded instead to Alice's plans, which turned out to be shopping and lunch with her mother. John tutted himself then, though it was inaudible to Alice. Alice's mother had never liked him, not because of anything he had ever said or done but because he was an officer of the Reich. She was an older woman who grew up before the war and therefore had suffered the Imperialists' propaganda about the "evils" of National Socialism, all of which were revealed afterwards to be unfounded. But Alice's mother – similar to people such as Joe Harding and Mrs Jones – had never been able to accustom herself to the world after the fighting, especially given that her first husband died in it. Even now, she mumbled her grievances behind her teacup whenever she thought John could not hear her. She was also the only person John knew who wore a crucifix, which was hidden away under her clothes where she thought nobody could see it, although he supposed that many older members of the population would still do so, unable as they were to unshackle themselves from decades of religious indoctrination. She did no harm, and moreover, John never actually blamed her for having been exposed to this conditioning as a child. Yet, he admitted only to himself that it had become a chore to spend time with the woman after six years of continued sideways looks and whispered slander. Thankfully, she was never able to corrupt Alice or her brother with her backward thinking.

The clock in the kitchen wound its way to quarter past seven, and John, as always with little time to spare, stood up to leave for work.

With his umbrella already open in anticipation of the short walk to the car, Alice met him by the front door. She stared up at him with those big, twinkling, green eyes of hers. 'Go catch bad guys,' she said, a line they had both heard in the film *The Midnight Detective* during one of their first dates.

John smiled and replied, 'I always do,' as had Albert Finney, the titular detective, though John's impersonation lacked the actor's gravitas.

He and Alice shared a kiss goodbye, then John walked through the heavy rain to the grey Morris Minor, a miserable sight beneath the dark sky, and climbed inside.

In the morning traffic, it usually took forty minutes from where John and Alice lived on Pullman Road in Acton to drive to Scotland Yard, and barring some incident en route, he always arrived at the DES office for eight o'clock. Today was an average day, so on the hour, John dropped his damp umbrella into the stand by the door, gave polite greetings to his present squad-mates (which included neither Peter nor Arnold, he noticed), and settled at his desk.

The drumming of the rain drowned out the hum of the building, and John closed his eyes and allowed himself to forget where he was for a second before the day began. His thoughts returned, as they so often did, to Alice and their child – their daughter. Although it was not possible for them to be sure of the child's gender, Alice had determined for herself that she was carrying a girl, and so this had become the accepted narrative for all those involved with the pregnancy. John maintained that he would be ecstatic either way, but the image of his daughter was now perfectly formed in his mind, alongside the decades of possibilities ahead of them: day trips to the seaside, cold winter evenings in front of the fireplace, family holidays to the furthest corners of the Third Reich, and even future grandchildren. These daydreams of an idyllic future had become much more vivid lately, since Yonder had transformed into a looming spectre over the here and now, and John regularly found himself lost in moments of complete, fanciful serenity.

Reality soon forced itself upon him at the sound of the office door being slammed shut. With a huff, John decided it was time to see DCI Werner. The discernible light through the frosted glass of his office door indicated that the DCI was in this morning, and having crossed the room, John tapped upon it.

'Enter,' called a strongly accented voice.

John opened the door and, when DCI Werner looked up, he declared, 'Heil Hitler, Detective Chief Inspector,' with an outstretched arm.

'Heil Hitler, Detective Sergeant,' DCI Werner replied in his high-pitched, grating tone of voice, with no more than a slight raise of his right hand. He only ever addressed the men by their ranks, a trait that left John wondering whether the DCI knew any of their names at all.

The short, thin man sat behind his desk in his uniform, which was black like the attire of the more prodigious Schutzstaffel – the SS. There were subtle differences, though, that were just enough to separate the police force from the SS, the lack of a Totenkopf – the distinctive skull emblem – on the peaked cap being the obvious absence. The uniform did not become DCI Werner, mostly because it was too big for the small-dimensioned man – he looked like a child who was wearing his father's suit jacket. DCI Werner was only thirty-eight, which was young to be in such a high-ranking position in the Metropolitan Police. He looked younger still, however, with his straight, black hair and clean skin; the job had taken no toll on him physically.

Although he probably does regret the promotion now, John speculated, *what with the embarrassment Yonder is causing the London DES.*

'What do you need?' DCI Werner had already dropped his rodent-like face back towards his desk, whereon he was writing something on a piece of paper in illegible (as far as John was concerned) German. The *Index* was nowhere to be seen, and a recently formed stack of files to his right suggested that the DCI had managed to misplace it – again.

'The *Index*, sir. I was wondering if you—'

'Hmm?' DCI Werner appeared to have paid no attention to what John had said. He looked up again, as if seeing John for the first time. His bulging, brown eyes, which dominated his face from above the sharp point of his nose and his hollow cheeks, betrayed an absolute disinterest for whatever John might have to say.

'The *Index*, sir,' John repeated, hiding his frustration. 'I left it for you yesterday.'

DCI Werner grunted and mumbled something to himself, also in incomprehensible German. John's German was very good – almost faultless, actually, not that he would ever be so bold as to admit it – but with the way the DCI often muttered, he was not sure if they were even fully formed words.

DCI Werner began to search through the files on his desk, removing today's edition of *Das Reich*, the only newspaper to be printed day and date in both the Fatherland and Great Britain, from atop it. John noted the front-page headline: 'Soviet Resistance "all but eradicated" on the Eastern Front, says Generalfeldmarschall Friedrich Dollmann.' He could never understand why the Soviets continued this struggle, especially given that it was now so apparent what National Socialism had afforded for Europe since the end of the Second Great War. How there were any of them left after three decades of unrelenting warfare was an even more daunting mystery. Yes, the conflict on the Eastern Front was referred to unofficially as the "Great Stalemate", but surely the fighting was never all that "stale" and the Reich's superior military capabilities had been punching holes in the Soviets' defences all this time?

John had once considered joining the Wehrmacht. In reality, his future career prospects after leaving school were only ever a choice between that and the police force. Whenever he thought about being sat in a frozen trench somewhere along the Eastern Front, John would concede that he had made the easier decision.

Was he a coward for making the easier decision?

He was never able to answer that question himself.

DCI Werner found the *Index* amongst the other files. Evidently having made no effort to read it yesterday, he proceeded to open the document and skim down the text, with a variety of sounds escaping every so often as he did so. He left John standing in front of his desk, not offering him the seat there whilst he read.

'Hmm.

'Ahh.

'Tsk.'

John could not tell whether the man was impressed or agitated, although he assumed it was the latter: DCI Werner was forever agitated about something.

After several minutes of perusing the document, the DCI came to the section on the Yonder investigation, and John immediately regretted not waiting to write up his report until after yesterday's visit to The Rag-and-Bone. DCI Werner read the pages, then his eyes flicked up at John from over the brim of the file.

John felt his flesh creep.

'You are a part of the Yonder investigation, are you not, Detective Sergeant?' His English was very formal and well-enunciated as if he had been taught it straight from a dictionary, whilst the German accent – even when uttered in his unpleasant falsetto – allowed the words a certain magnitude that was lost by a native speaker.

'Well, yes, sir, I—' John's fumbled reply was a muddle of noises, which fell from his mouth and scattered across the carpet. He had been doubtful as to whether the DCI would read the document at all; therefore, he had expected even less to be quizzed on its contents.

'Can you account for this lack of progress?' DCI Werner cut in. His stare was intense and unforgiving.

'Sir, we—' John would have given him the good news, but he was permitted to speak only the two words before being interrupted again.

'Many people are unimpressed, Detective Sergeant, and there is a lot of pressure to resolve this matter. Commissioner Krüger received a telephone call from Prime Minister Bormann himself last night. He is displeased, as am I.' Word of their pitiful progress in routing the Yonder Organisation had reached the Prime Minister's office, then. It was not surprising. Still, the knowledge that John's own failings were now being deliberated by the most powerful man in Great Britain was humiliating.

'Sir—' John tried again to report what had been accomplished the previous afternoon, but DCI Werner held up a hand and he was rendered silent.

The DCI was also quiet for a moment. Then, from a box on his desk, he removed four paperclips and lined them up side by side on the hardwood. 'It is unacceptable, Detective Sergeant. Murderers are being arrested' – he flicked one of the paperclips at John, and it hit him in the stomach and fell without a sound onto the carpeted floor – 'fraudsters captured' – he flicked a second paperclip – 'and undesirable elements rounded up and removed' – a third paperclip hit John. 'Yet, drug dealers' – DCI Werner placed his forefinger on the final paperclip – '*they* are allowed to roam freely in this city, to do as they please and operate unmolested. Why is that, Detective Sergeant?'

'Sir, yesterday we—'

The DCI picked up the paperclip and began unfolding it. 'It is because you are failing, Detective Sergeant.' The paperclip became crookedly straight, and DCI Werner fiddled with it in his narrow hands. His tone had an unsettling composure to it. 'Failing to capture the criminals who plague the Third Reich.' He held the paperclip at each end and bent it in half.

John swallowed, but his throat was dry. His breathing became irregular, and his pulse became quicker. His chest tightened.

'And when you fail, Detective Sergeant' – the DCI clenched the folded paperclip in a tight fist – '*you make me look a fool!*' As he yelled the words in a shrill screech, DCI Werner slammed his fist down on the desk, startling John and causing him to stiffen to attention.

He looked past the DCI and fixed his gaze on the wall, not daring to meet the man's eye. He had been reduced to the emotional level of a schoolboy who was being scolded for forgetting his homework.

'I do not like to be made to look a fool, Detective Sergeant.' DCI Werner's voice was even again, his immediately concealed anger now only visible in his hand, which trembled ever so slightly on the desk.

John continued to look ahead.

At the bottom of his vision, he watched DCI Werner uncurl his fist into a flat palm to reveal the red-stained piece of bent metal inside. 'Do your job, or I will find somebody else who is more capable.' He tipped the paperclip onto the desk, where it clattered down with a definitive clink.

'Yes, sir,' was all John was able to muster through the thud of his heart pounding in his ears.

DCI Werner scrawled his signature below John's on the front page of the *Index*, and then he hit it with a dark-red-inked stamp that read 'APPROVED, London Drug Enforcement Squad'. The party eagle with its extended wings to the right of the text provided official approval on the matter. Without another word and without waiting for the ink to dry, the DCI closed the file and dumped it atop the stack of documents on his desk.

John lingered in that little room a moment longer, expecting DCI Werner to say something further, but the DCI instead went back to scribbling on his piece of paper as if this conversation had never happened.

Recognising this as his invitation to leave, John extended his arm, said, 'Heil Hitler,' and waited for his superior to respond.

After several seconds, DCI Werner did finally repeat the words. However, this time it was without a salute, and seemingly more out of habit than anything else.

John exited the office and did not pause when the door closed shut behind him. Ignoring the inquisitive stares of the other DES detectives, who had no doubt overheard DCI Werner's outburst, he made a beeline for the corridor and headed towards the familiar surroundings of the fifth-floor WC – the one place he knew he could rely on for privacy in the busy building. There, he found an empty cubicle and entered it, placed the palms of his hands against the flimsy wooden door to stop them from shaking, and took several deep breaths. That was not the brightest idea, given the unpleasant air, so John lit a cigarette and concentrated on the wisps of smoke as they emanated from the tip. The distraction soon stayed his erratic pulse.

Rubbing at his tired eyes with a thumb and forefinger, John cursed DCI Werner for making him, a twenty-nine-year-old detective sergeant, feel so emasculated. And he had a nerve to accuse John of being incapable of his job. The man had never been a detective – nor a uniformed constable, for that matter – before his promotion to DCI. He had attended university in Munich, where he would have studied psychology and criminology and the like, and he believed himself better than the actual detectives as a result. He knew nothing of real police work. He had been dropped into the London DES to dictate work and allocate blame, and he was disliked by all those beneath him. This post was nothing more than another rung on the ladder for DCI Werner to climb, though – a step on the way to some position of greater authority – so he would not be troubled by his lack of popularity.

That pantomime with the paperclip is probably the first time the bastard has bled for the Reich, John grumbled to himself with a dry anger.

With his cigarette at an end and the tightness in his chest now relaxed to a dull throb, John tossed the butt into the toilet and flushed it. He left the sanctuary of the cubicle behind him, and at the washbasin, he splashed cold water on his face and took another deep, sour breath, feeling much calmer after this short respite.

*

Having walked a dawdling, reluctant path back across the fifth floor, John was only several metres away from the DES office when the door was flung open and none other than DCI Werner scurried out in the direction of the lifts. John watched his stunted figure as he went, and whilst he did wonder where the DCI might be headed with such haste, he realised he did not care so long as it meant he would not have to see the man again today.

John was hesitant about how the remainder of that morning would unfold when he stepped back into the DES office. It had started badly, but he felt a fresh twinge of anxiety flitter around his stomach when he found Peter and Arnold waiting for him by his desk.

'*We got the bloody Scot, John!*' Peter shouted at him as he approached them. The desk – or rather, the surrounding area – was already enveloped by Peter's heavy cologne. However, it was stronger than usual, as though Peter had only just applied it, and the sickeningly sweet scent clawed at John's senses when he drew closer.

DS Arnold List – a stout man several years senior to both John and Peter, who was too eager to please his superior and friend – repeated Peter's words in a merry fashion: 'We got the bloody Scot!' He grinned broadly and clapped his heavy paws together in victory. Arnold would never rise to the rank of detective inspector, having neither the aptitude nor the ambition to do so. He had only achieved his detective sergeant rank due to this tendency to side vivaciously with his commanding officers, and his ability to crack skulls on command.

The previous evening, the three detectives had formulated their plan for apprehending Frank Boyd. In the end, this had boiled down to them waiting for him at Telegraph Hill, where he apparently walked his dog every morning, under the tentative assumption that no one had got word to him yet of Joe Harding's arrest. They had also decided that only two of them would go, so as to better maintain their cover in the park. Peter had determined that he, as the ranking officer, should be there, and when Arnold offered to be his second without a breath of pause, John had not argued the point. Well, he had put up a "fight" by claiming with forced enthusiasm that he would be more than happy to go in Arnold's stead, all the while hoping the round-faced lout did not change his mind. He did not, Arnold snatching at the opportunity to prove himself useful to Peter, and consequently, John had been able to spend a peaceful evening with Alice and enjoy breakfast with her that morning.

'Good work,' John said, feeling somewhat uncomfortable anyway that he was not there to help them bring this Boyd in. 'He was at the park then, with his dog?' It was an obvious question, but he wanted to keep the conversation moving.

'He was, just as Joe said he would be,' replied Peter, smiling. 'The bastard sold out his own man just to try to throw us. These types like Joe have no honour.'

'They're animals,' claimed Arnold, backing Peter's sentiment with ferocious insistence.

Peter nodded his head in agreement, and John made a sound to acknowledge that he too felt the same, not wanting to appear peculiar.

'We went to Boyd's house as well. We found one of those brown-paper parcels with what must have been 1,000 Yonder pills left in it, plus at least three kilos of cannabis,' Peter explained.

So they are not using their "own" people, John thought. This had been a debate amongst the members of the Yonder Task Force when the other suppliers and dealers they had arrested only ever confessed to distributing Yonder, prompting the question as to whether they were recruited specifically to move Yonder and nothing else. Three kilos of cannabis was not a small amount by any degree, so Boyd was indeed a more run-of-the-mill drug peddler.

Or perhaps the Yonder Organisation was running out of safer options?

Perhaps the Task Force was actually getting to them?

'We just gave Detective Chief Inspector Werner the good news,' Arnold cheerfully continued. 'He said he would report our progress right away.'

A pit of self-loathing welled inside of John. If he had waited but an hour to go into that office, he could have avoided a humiliating berating about his incompetence. So that was where DCI Werner had just run off to, then: up to Commissioner Krüger's office on the eleventh floor to spin tales of his department's success to their collective superior – the arse-kissing wanker.

'Boyd's downstairs, then?' John enquired, trying not to dwell on his poor luck.

'In the room next to Joe,' replied Peter. 'Are you ready to head down? Because I have a job for you.' At this statement, another of those sly smirks played across Peter's face.

And when it did so, alongside the ominous ambiguity his words implied, an unexpected shiver ran down John's spine and he struggled against it showing physically. 'Of course,' John answered, questioning both what his role in Peter's plan would be and how well he would be able to play it.

CHAPTER FIVE

Interrogation Techniques

John considered himself adept at interrogation. He could play the part of the trusted friend or the dangerous foe well enough, and when required to, he was perfectly capable of getting somewhat rough with a suspect – not that he ever preferred this approach.

Whilst these techniques did work on most, there were those who did not bend and break so easily, and Joe Harding seemed just such a man to John. There was something different about him. And with the way he gave up Frank Boyd, he had planned the whole conversation with Peter at The Rag-and-Bone so that he would "break" only when pushed to the point of a less-than-vague death threat. In doing so, he readily surrendered one of his own in order to protect himself and his family. As for Boyd, if Peter's description was anything to go on, then he would not submit willingly either; it was only because the two detectives were armed that the man had been brought in without trouble.

After a short briefing on the interrogation plan, during which John and Arnold were assigned their roles by Peter, the three detectives made their way down to the subterranean level of Scotland Yard known as "The Basement", a series of detention cells and interrogation rooms that had been left behind by the Occupation Forces when they departed the building in 1948.

Via three flights of concrete stairs, the three men descended deep below street level. At the bottom, a stone-faced man in a black military uniform sat in a booth set back into the wall and protected by thick iron bars, next to which was a heavy metal gate. The detectives produced their identifications on demand. After a moment of scrutiny, a loud buzzing echoed around them, followed by a metallic clank. The gate opened, held from the other side by another uniformed guard, this one armed with an automatic sub-machine gun. The Metropolitan Police had never been left to manage The Basement; instead, they were allowed to concentrate on their work whilst specially trained SS personnel oversaw the needs of the detainees.

Being in The Basement always made John uneasy. Bare lightbulbs hung with menace above them, and their stark glare cast long shadows across the cracked concrete floor and white-tiled walls. Exposed pipework ran across the low ceiling, and it clanged and hummed with the strain of age. Even the air was oppressive, being uncomfortably humid in the summer months yet so frigid by early December that each breath formed a noticeable mist. Its entire atmosphere was a throwback to the dark days of 1944. This was all by design, of course; The Basement had been devised to intimidate the enemies of the Third Reich and overwhelm them with a sense of dread and foreboding. John could say with certainty that it achieved the desired effect.

The people in the foyer upstairs knew nothing of this place beneath their feet, and they were better off for it.

The Basement's main gate led into a narrow hallway. To the left were the SS guards' quarters, in which they passed their long hours of duty in relative comfort. To the right were the detention cells, in which prisoners of the State spent their own long hours of confinement in dismal surroundings, with little more than a chamber pot and a hard bed. Straight ahead was the door to the interrogation rooms, in which Harding and Boyd were already waiting for them. Peter led the way as another armed guard allowed them passage into the long corridor on the other side of the door.

The DES detectives were the only officers using these facilities this morning, but that was not to suggest they were always so empty. John himself had visited The Basement many times since his promotion to detective rank, and there was often a suspicious stain on the floor or a red crust underneath the table, left behind by the previous occupant. Some of the rooms even had small, discoloured patches of concrete dotted about them, as if someone had filled in a hole in more recent years; they were far enough below the station that no one would ever hear a gunshot.

The detectives stopped outside Interrogation Room 6, and a little further along was Interrogation Room 7, with Joe Harding in the former and Frank Boyd in the latter. The two men were visible through circular windows in their respective doors, each sitting at a metal table in an otherwise empty and dimly lit room. A discernible panic was writ large in the body language of each of them, which was not an inauspicious sign by any means. They had likely heard first-hand accounts of what transpired in The Basement, so they would have an inkling about what awaited them.

It had been decided that they would start with Boyd. When the detectives entered Interrogation Room 7, he leant back in his chair, trying to affect an apathy for his current circumstances now there was an audience. The Scotsman matched Peter's description perfectly, John realised: he was unmistakably a criminal, with his hair shaved short, cruel and sharp features, and a series of tattoos running up and down his arms. He was like a cartoon character – perhaps the villain in some Hans Fischerkoesen sketch. Boyd also had a black eye, bruising along the side of his face, and a fresh cut on his lip, which was all no doubt a consequence of that morning's arrest.

Peter and Arnold sat down in the chairs across the table from the handcuffed man, and John propped himself against a wall, ensuring he remained in the shadows. It was his job for now to stand there and say nothing, to be the strong and silent type, so he lit a cigarette and took up his position.

'So, Mr Boyd,' Peter began, 'you remember me and Detective Sergeant List from this morning, I imagine. Detective Sergeant List is the one with the noteworthy right hook.'

Arnold did not move, and it was only now that John noticed the knuckles on his right hand were dark red.

'You've been keeping bad company, Mr Boyd, with all this business distributing Yonder. But luckily for you, that's the only thing keeping you from a noose.' Peter regarded the man with a penetrating intensity.

Boyd shuffled in his chair. It was the same tactic Peter had employed with Joe Harding.

'You do know that, don't you, Mr Boyd? That the punishment for peddling Yonder nowadays is a short drop followed by a long swing? Treason, they're calling it. Anarchy against the State. Anyway' – Peter produced a notepad and a pen, placed them on the table, and pushed them towards Boyd – 'we need names, Mr Boyd. Enough, and I'll make sure you see prison. And the more you give us, the better life becomes for you in there. *And* I might even stop by the vet on my way home and tell them not to destroy your dog.' Peter raised his eyebrows and smiled. 'If I'm not too late.'

'Go fuck yourself,' was Boyd's curt response to this in his thick Scottish brogue. Evidently he did not care much for the dog.

Peter sighed. 'Detective Sergeant, if you would.'

At the instruction, Arnold stood, lumbered around the table to Boyd, and hit him once, square in the side of the head. Boyd slumped sideways in his chair, groaning, and as he tried to right himself, Arnold hit him again – this time in the back of the head. He toppled forwards hard, and his body bounced against the metal table.

Boyd struggled to move after that, the blows having taken him by surprise. He sat back up gingerly, with one hand to his face and the other raised in defence when Arnold gestured towards him once more with a closed fist. Arnold did not hit him a third time, though.

John stayed unmoved in the shadows, concentrating on his cigarette. As a police officer, he had learnt quickly that pain can be a great motivator for the truth, especially in his early years as a young and headstrong constable. He was never comfortable with such actions; in actuality, he often regretted them afterwards. But he was an officer of the Reich who was charged with protecting it, and this was simply another aspect of the job.

'Thank you, Detective Sergeant,' Peter said, and Arnold reseated himself. 'We can do this all day, Mr Boyd, and then we can come back tomorrow and do it again. Unless we find one of your friends who is a little more cooperative. Then you can head to the gallows. Or' – Peter threw his arms up – 'maybe you can go to someplace in the sun where much larger men do this for a living, and you can run out your pointless existence breaking rocks. Don't worry' – he stopped midway through his sentence to light a cigarette for dramatic effect – 'I'll be sure to put in a good word for you with the larger men.' Peter blew smoke into the room in a nonchalant manner, acting as though he did not care whether Boyd ever talked or not.

Boyd said nothing.

In the stillness of Interrogation Room 7, Arnold lit a cigarette too, and he and Peter sat smoking. Boyd cradled his battered head across from them, not looking up from the table.

'Do you know how we found you, Frank? You and your little dog in the park?' Peter ended the silence, his earlier efforts having failed to break this man's resolve. 'Of course you don't.' Peter sat forwards and stubbed his cigarette out on the table, the embers sizzling against the cold metal. 'Well, Detective Sergeant Highsmith – he's the gentleman looming in the corner – and I…'

Boyd looked over at him, and John stared back, glad to be in the shadows.

'…went to Blackheath yesterday, and we paid a visit to a pub called The Rag-and-Bone.'

There was a flicker of recognition in Boyd's eyes at the name.

'We had a long chat with the landlord, Mr Harding. Do you know Mr Harding? Joe to his friends. Well, Mr Harding didn't have much to say at first either, but as it turns out, he feels his own life is more important than yours.' Peter leant across the table. 'He gave you up, Frank: your name, whereabouts you live, and even the park you would be in this morning.'

Boyd looked down at the crumpled cigarette, still saying nothing.

'Did you think you mattered to them? That they liked you? Maybe that they needed you?' Peter laughed. 'You're expendable. You can swing now or die in the dirt for all they care. They'll find someone to replace you, and by next week, they won't even remember your name.'

That flicker of recognition in Boyd's eyes had turned to anger. He would be thinking, *No, Joe wouldn't have done that. The old man with the war wound and a hatred of the State wouldn't have given me up. But if not him, then how else…?*

'You're full of shit,' Boyd whispered with venom in his voice.

John knew Peter was pushing the right buttons.

Peter shrugged his shoulders. 'We can show you, if you'd like? I mean, Mr Harding is just next door.' For theatrical purposes, he looked at both Arnold and John, as if for agreement, knowing full well that this was the exact scenario he had envisioned back up on the fifth floor.

Peter and Arnold stood up, and John stepped out of the shadows. He then hoisted Boyd to his feet by the scruff of his shirt and marched him out of Interrogation Room 7. Ahead of them, Peter unlocked Interrogation Room 6 and entered it with Arnold. The interrogation rooms had thick walls, so they left the door open a crack to make sure John and Boyd would be able to hear what was being said inside.

John pushed Boyd hard against the wall by the door and unholstered his Walther. He jammed the weapon into the base of the man's spine and pulled back the hammer, and in his gruffest detective voice, he warned, 'Make a sound, and I'll tell them you tried to run.'

Boyd struggled against John's grasp, but he obeyed the command nonetheless.

'Morning, Joe.' Peter's voice came from inside Interrogation Room 6 as he began the next phase of their plan. 'This is Detective Sergeant List. You met him yesterday, didn't you, when we were tearing apart your little pit of a pub? Anyway, we need names, Joe: those who work for you and those for whom you work. It's the only thing that will keep you from a noose and your daughter and her husband from doing hard labour in some hole in Africa. Ollie breaking rocks in the sun, and Abbie some... *other* kind of hard labour, I imagine.' They all knew to what Peter had implied by the word 'other'. This was one of his favourite interrogation techniques: describing to a suspect what their life would be like in prison or on the African continent, and then reminding them it was only the interrogator who could help them now. Using Harding's family was the icing on this particular cake.

It was all a lie in any case, as Peter had no influence over what would happen to any of them. Once this was done, they would be handed over to the SS, who would decide whether they were to be imprisoned, executed, or put on a ship and dropped off somewhere out of the way of civilised society. Peter thought Harding would hang, and John agreed; not only was he unfit for work with that limp of his, but he had also fought against the Reich in the war and the SS liked to see old British soldiers swing.

Harding finally spoke up, afraid now not only for his own life but for the lives of Abbie and Ollie as well: '*Stop.*' Peter's tactic was working, as it so often did. 'I only know the ones I pass Yonder on to.'

John heard the notepad and the pen slide across the table again.

'Write,' Peter ordered, and the distinct sound of scribbling followed.

'Do you hear that?' whispered John, performing his role. 'That's the sound of him giving up more names. He won't give us any of the important ones, mind you, just a couple of low-level suppliers or dealers. Maybe even some of your friends. Just like he gave you up.'

Boyd's body went tense under his weight, and a growl bubbled in the man's throat.

There was silence in Interrogation Room 6 as Harding wrote. Then, the pen hit the metal table.

'Four names. Much better than you did yesterday, Joe,' Peter declared, with not a hint of sarcasm. 'Let's see…'

He began to read aloud what Harding had written. With each passing syllable, John felt Boyd writhe more and more beneath him, becoming increasingly enraged. 'Do you know any of these reprobates, Frank?' John goaded the Scotsman as Peter read. Any second now, it would be time to let this dog off his leash.

'Is it easy for you, Joe, to give these people up? It seems easy,' Peter asked when he came to the end of the list. He was looking for a final admission from him, a last affront that would push Boyd over the edge.

'They're only dealers,' Harding replied in his cockney accent. 'There're always more when we need 'em.'

Perfect.

At that statement, John – who was barely able to keep him pinned against the wall any longer anyway – let Boyd loose. Boyd proceeded to burst into Interrogation Room 6, flip the metal table away towards the far wall, and lunge forwards at Harding, whose face now resembled that of someone looking into the eyes of death itself. John followed behind Boyd and joined the already-standing Peter and Arnold. The three detectives watched in silence.

Harding was not fast enough to raise his arms in any type of defence, and Boyd hit him in the mouth as soon as he came within striking distance. Harding tumbled out of his chair and onto the concrete floor with a thud. Without hesitation, Boyd straddled the man, flipped him onto his back, and proceeded to punch him repeatedly in the face.

This assault was hardly a pleasant thing to witness, but John found it equally difficult to feel sympathy for someone such as Harding.

After the fifth or sixth blow, Peter signalled that this was enough, and John and Arnold intervened. Grabbing Boyd by an arm each, they dragged him kicking and fighting back into Interrogation Room 7 and locked him inside. They then returned to Interrogation Room 6, placed the table in its upright position again, and hoisted Harding back into his chair. The old man had been reduced to a slumping, wheezing, bloody mess.

Peter wasted no time in making certain Harding understood the point of this exercise. 'Well, Joe, it looks like you've offended Mr Boyd, and I cannot say I blame him. Now' – Peter was still standing, and as he bent towards Harding, he grabbed the man by his red-stained shirt collar – 'I assume you talked to Boyd when you handed the Yonder over. Sat him at your bar and gave him a drink on the house. Perhaps you even introduced him to Abbie and Ollie. They're safe, whilst they're locked up. But just imagine, Joe' – Peter was whispering into his ear now – 'just imagine we let them go, tell them they're free. Then one night, we take Mr Boyd for a drive and drop him off around the corner from The Rag-and-Bone. Do you think he would remember the way? Would he remember what Abbie and Ollie look like? I'm sure that, with a little bit of encouragement, he would have no problem with it at all.'

Harding caught his breath, and he spluttered through the blood, 'God in heaven, you wouldn't…'

'God can't help you or anybody else any more, Joe. You know that,' Peter snarled, almost maniacally. 'I'm the only one who can help you now, but only if you give me something better than these worthless fucking dealers!'

'I can't!' Harding was weeping.

Peter pushed him aside and stood erect. 'Detective Sergeant Highsmith, go and ask Mr Boyd what he thinks. In fact, bring him back in here. Maybe he can ask Joe for me.'

'*No!*' Harding screamed. '*God, no!*' He had crumbled. The man who, only yesterday, had been brave enough to slander the Third Reich openly now sat in pieces in the chair.

'I told you, Joe, there is no God any more – only me.' Peter loomed over him, victorious. As he did so, that heavy, sickly cologne seemed to billow around him, consuming the detectives and this defeated man. '*Now give me some better names,*' Peter demanded.

*

An hour later, John was sitting at his desk in the DES office once more, enjoying a well-earned cigarette. This had transpired to be the Yonder Task Force's most productive morning since the investigation's inception.

Thanks to Harding, their list of suppliers was now plentiful, and the Task Force would soon begin the process of removing them from the streets. This would look good in the *Index* and stem the distribution of Yonder momentarily. And yet, inevitably, it would only wound the monster, as the sooner they arrested these suppliers, the sooner they would be replaced.

But that was not all Harding eventually gave up.

The individual they knew as Uncle Billy was known only by the same alias to Harding; however, he had overheard that the man was the grand architect behind the entire Yonder Organisation. Harding also thought he was an older man, but his only evidence to support this theory was the supposed origin of his pseudonym: Billy had been the oldest member of his unit in the Second Great War, so the younger British soldiers took to calling him Uncle Billy as a display of affection, and the nickname stuck with him afterwards. Whilst this gave the Yonder Task Force little to work with in terms of tracking the man down, it offered further credibility to the notion that Uncle Billy did exist. Furthermore, the possibility of him being the mastermind behind Yonder meant he was now a person of upmost interest.

The Spaniard was also known to Harding only by reputation. He could give them no real name nor any description, just another story: The Spaniard fought on the side of the Communists in the Spanish Civil War and, after killing scores of Nationalist soldiers, was branded an enemy of the state. He had then fled to Great Britain sometime before the Second Great War began, seeking refuge from his crimes with the Imperialists. As for his connection to Yonder, he was in charge of smuggling the drug into London from abroad, and was therefore a cornerstone in the Yonder Organisation.

Although vague once again, this information was still a huge revelation for the Task Force: it was the first modicum of proof they had found that suggested Yonder was not being manufactured in Great Britain itself, but was instead being imported from overseas. Before today, they had considered both these options to be viable, yet a drug being mass-produced to the scale of Yonder in Great Britain without somebody noticing had sounded so unfeasible. That it was somehow being smuggled in always made much more sense.

If it was The *Spaniard* who was importing it, though, did this mean that Yonder was coming from Spain? That would make sense as well, given the rather sub-standard control the Spanish government maintained in its own country. It was not a part of the Third Reich, with *Generalissimo* Franco having elected to be a close ally instead, and it had therefore not benefitted fully from everything National Socialism had accomplished. That included the expansion of the SS into a European security force and the harmony this had bestowed upon the continent east of the Iberian Peninsula.

As for finding The Spaniard himself, due to the close relationship that had been fostered between Great Britain and Spain since the war, there was now a large immigrant Spanish population scattered all around the nation, so this task had proven impossible. Knowing that he had fought in the Spanish Civil War would narrow their search considerably to men of a certain age, however.

There was but one other name Harding could give them. This time, it was an actual name, and one that was more important than both Uncle Billy and The Spaniard for the time being. James Summers was an average man by Harding's description: average height, slim build, dark hair, glasses, and probably in his early forties. There was nothing out of the ordinary about him, and he was not someone the DES would think to look twice at. Yet he was the man from whom Harding collected his parcels of Yonder, at a warehouse in the East End Docklands. Summers owned an import/export business there with links to mainland Europe, all fully licensed and insured by the city. Harding also claimed Summers was involved in the further distribution of Yonder around Great Britain, but when he was pushed for something more specific, he admitted that he knew nothing beyond rumours and hearsay. Regardless, this was still a promising lead.

It had been a sensational morning for the Yonder Task Force. A niggle of guilt loitered somewhere in John's stomach nevertheless, as it so often did when an interrogation turned violent, but this was one of those occasions when the ends easily justified the means, he reminded himself, and he knew he should feel no pity for Harding. This awareness did nothing to assuage that niggle right now, but John knew from experience that it would be little more than a twinge by tomorrow morning, and no more than a memory by the following day.

An irregularity had been playing on John's mind since they had found those parcels of Yonder at The Rag-and-Bone. Eventually, he put the question to Peter: 'Do you not think it was careless of Harding to let Boyd hand out Yonder in his pub?' He could not understand the reasoning: Why bring it home? Why not meet in the middle of nowhere to give Boyd the Yonder, then leave him to distribute it as he saw fit?

'He's old, John,' Peter explained. 'His generation believe they have nothing left to lose because they already lost everything in the war. You heard him yesterday, and we would have been perfectly within the law to have shot the bastard on the spot. Running Yonder out of his pub will have been just another way to prove to himself that he's not scared of us. They get like that, the older ones, until you give them something to lose, something to fear. I gave Harding that in the form of his family – particularly, his daughter. *Then* they break, just like they did during the war.'

John supposed he was correct.

*

As it had turned out, Harding was little more than a glorified supplier. He had spouted the same nonsense about Yonder being a "medication", though, and even as the detectives had closed the door to Interrogation Room 6, he had continued to shout after them something to do with freeing the British people from the constraints of "tyranny". Given the briefest opportunity, he had waxed lyrical on the utopian marvel that was Great Britain before the war.

John paid little attention to his Imperialist ramblings. It was the same pre-war propaganda he had heard before and had been warned to be wary of when he was young. 'Your grandparents were tricked by the Imperialists – *Don't let it happen to you!*' The poster of the little boy sitting on the kindly-looking older gentleman's knee was ingrained in John's memory, and had been for as long as he could remember. On it, the older man's shadow took the shape of a monster towering over the child, consuming him and the world around them – a manifestation of the Imperialists' dark legacy.

Harding was a sad, old man, and he would die blind to the truth.

It had become starkly apparent during their conversation with Harding, however, that many of the more important cogs in the Yonder Organisation were in fact much older. Not that this was particularly remarkable: there were millions who would happily turn back the clock and undo all of National Socialism's hard work, from those as harmless as Alice's mother to more dangerous individuals such as Joe Harding. As for Ben Chambers, the twenty-something-year-old supplier they had arrested several weeks before, he had been raised by his father, a British soldier who survived the Second Great War, so it made sense that he would have warped the boy. Furthermore, James Summers was old enough to have been born in the 1920s if Harding's idea of his age was anything to go by, which was time enough for him to have been indoctrinated by the Imperialists' propaganda. The claims that both Uncle Billy and The Spaniard had fought at one time or another against the Third Reich and its allies were also unsurprising; they doubtless considered Yonder a form of retaliation for their defeats on the battlefield.

In due course, John and his generation would take the place of these people, and the mistakes of the past would be resigned to history. But what if Peter was wrong when he dismissed them as irrelevant? What if these older individuals were something more threatening than the simple remnants of misguided ideologies? If Yonder had proven anything, it was that they were still capable of causing considerable unrest, especially so amongst the more susceptible members of the working class. Harding was indicative of this, and it was up to John and the Yonder Task Force to put this sentiment down before it got any further out of hand.

At long last, it seemed as though they were beginning to gather the means to do just that.

CHAPTER SIX

Import/Export

John was to spend that afternoon in the East End Docklands, and whilst the rain had stopped, the sky remained overcast as if foreshadowing another downpour. Such heavy rain had done nothing to disrupt the dense, industrial haze that was ever-present along the banks of the Thames, however.

With the Task Force wanting to capitalise on their newest lead, it had been decided that investigating the warehouse with 'Summers' Import and Export' written in big letters on the side was a worthy idea, as although they already knew James Summers was guilty of supplying Joe Harding with Yonder, the implication that this was a centre for the wider distribution of the drug around Great Britain was now a much greater concern. John had been assigned to this task, and his partner on the outing was Detective Inspector Rolf Zeigler, a senior member of the DES who had also been appointed to the Yonder Task Force.

It was suggested that they take John's Morris Minor as it looked the least-threatening vehicle. He thought this a slight against the rundown nature of his car; he would have taken offence were it not so clearly true.

John and Zeigler travelled east along the Thames towards Silvertown, a modernised section of the docklands. It having been all but destroyed during the Blitz, the National Socialist government had taken great care in rebuilding this area on the riverbank to last for several generations, making London more accessible by water now than it had ever been. Today, it was a hub for trade into and out of Great Britain.

After the war, Great Britain had undertaken what some referred to as the "Second Industrial Revolution" when the new government used the vast, open fields to construct huge factories almost overnight, which would provide work for the British people. Soon, foreign labourers had arrived – Dutch, Belgian, French, Scandinavian, and persons of the Greater Germanic Reich – to reap the benefits of this new industrial age and fill the considerable gap left behind by those killed during the fighting. Quickly, the Great British working class became a melting pot of Third Reich nationalities. As a result, the nation thrived, and it had earnt itself the title of the "Industrial Jewel of the Third Reich" by as early as 1947. In a matter of years, National Socialism had systematically ended the economic depression that had ravaged Great Britain throughout the 1930s, as it did in the Fatherland before the war.

Around the nation, the commercial products manufactured – from radios and washing machines to motor cars and tractors – left the likes of London, Plymouth, Aberdeen, and Dublin for mainland Europe, and they acted as the backbone of this booming trade. Beyond this, however, a far more vital industry had been established in Great Britain since the end of the Second Great War: in cities such as Manchester, Bristol, and Birmingham, a landscape of magnificent military factories stretched as far as the eye could see, and they all worked in tandem to assemble weapons and tanks and armoured trucks, which were shipped out from Newcastle and Portsmouth (now the two largest port cities in the world) across the entire Third Reich. It was from these isles that Berlin had equipped its immense and unrivalled armed forces for two and a half decades, secure in the knowledge that their waters were impenetrable.

Unfortunately, it was in these same factory cities that Yonder had established its strongest hold amongst the labourers of both British and foreign parentage. Hence, as it was a threat to the high production levels that had been maintained in Great Britain since the war, it was obvious why this scourge was fast becoming such a particular worry for the government.

Zeigler did not utter a single word during their journey to Silvertown. He was much older than John, fifty-five or fifty-six if John remembered correctly, and the oldest detective in the DES. When he joined the department, John had wondered why Zeigler – a German-born man who had served with the Wehrmacht in the Second Great War before becoming a well-decorated police officer – had not been promoted from DI to a more comfortable position. Having enquired about this with Peter, it appeared the rumour was that Zeigler had refused to become a member of the SS and had therefore been denied progression into the higher ranks of the establishment, within Scotland Yard or beyond. His reasons for this were known only to himself.

The DI's face often reminded John of a granite statue: grey, sharp, and unmoving. His neat hair now matched his skin tone, whilst the thin moustache on his top lip added an extra degree of authority to his appearance. When he walked, Zeigler's lean body seemed to hardly move under his coat, with his arms stiff at his sides and his shoulders perfectly square with his back. He was a daunting presence, and especially so given that he towered over John at what must have been not far off two metres tall.

They found James Summers' warehouse easily enough, and John rolled the Morris Minor to a halt across the road from the entrance.

'Remember, I will do the talking,' Zeigler stated in his gravelly German monotone before he climbed out of the car. This would have made sense anyway, what with Zeigler being senior in rank. However, there was also something about a German accent that people found intimidating, which was a remarkably useful tool when probing for information. 'You take a look around and see what you can find,' he continued as they crossed the road.

John acknowledged the order. His job was to poke around the warehouse whilst Zeigler kept Summers busy. It had been decided by the Task Force that, although arresting Summers for supplying Joe Harding with Yonder would be a much-needed victory today, determining his larger role in its distribution would be more beneficial to the investigation as it might lead to a broader comprehension of the Yonder Organisation's whole inner workings. Plus, such a display of force would only reveal to the Yonder Organisation its unprecedented vulnerability in London, and it would be foolish for the Task Force to surrender this newfound advantage so readily. This visit, therefore, was strictly reconnaissance.

For everyone else present, it was an average working day at the Summers' Import and Export warehouse. In the loading bay at the front, several men in grey overalls were packing a lorry with nondescript crates. John could hear the electronic buzz of unseen machinery inside, and the sound of someone barking instructions, which were not unusual noises for such a workplace. He could feel a bitter cold emanating from within, though, due to there being little insulation from the weather in this cavernous metal building; it must have been a difficult job at this time of year.

The premises cast a distinct impression of the utmost ordinary, but then John recalled how Harding had described Summers as being a man the DES would not think to look twice at.

They would have to be vigilant.

A potbellied man with a clipboard turned away from the lorry in the loading bay and stopped them as they tried to enter the warehouse. 'How may I help you, gentlemen?' he asked, adjusting a pair of square glasses on his round face, which sat below his bald head.

Zeigler produced his police identification, and John followed suit.

'I am Detective Inspector Zeigler. This is my partner, Detective Sergeant Highsmith. We are here to talk with Mr Summers. Is he in?' Zeigler asked in his coarse baritone.

The man with the clipboard, who spoke in a polite English cadence and was unmistakably old enough to have lived through the war, stiffened at the sound of the German accent. He suddenly became much more aware of the way he held himself, and was now standing to a sort of attention before Zeigler's austere, grey eyes. He stuttered, 'Y-yes, sir, he's in.' Then, remembering where he was, the man raised a hand in a shambolic fashion and stammered, 'H-heil Hitler!' There was panic in his voice at having forgotten the presumed formality.

Making nothing of it, both John and Zeigler returned the words with a half-salute.

Composing himself, the man directed them where to go with a stubby index finger, and he watched as the two detectives moved between several stacks of boxes and crates and then started to ascend a rusted metal staircase along the far-left wall of the building.

At the top of these stairs was a corridor that let on to several small offices. Studying the titles on the doors as they went, John and Zeigler passed those of the warehouse foreman and the transportation supervisor before they came to the final room on the row. The white words painted on a frosted glass window read 'Managing Director: J. B. Summers'.

Before leaving for Silvertown, John had telephoned the Ministry of Identification to enquire about James Summers. The following details came back:

Nationality: British.
Date of birth: 8th February 1928.
Marital status: married (wife, Charlotte Summers).
Children: one (male, David Adam Summers).
Profession: managing director, Summers' Import and
 Export.

The 'B.' on the frosted glass stood for Bradley, and there existed no criminal record for the man.

It was all thoroughly reasonable, and all suspiciously normal.

John could hear talking on the other side of the door, but the voices were muffled, incomprehensible. When Zeigler knocked hard on the frosted glass, it stopped abruptly, and a man of James Summers' description appeared at the door. Harding had been correct: Summers was an exceptionally average man by appearance, with no discernible features, barring a pair of plain, black glasses pushed high on his nose and jet-black hair, which was combed back. A five o'clock shadow was already forming on his dimpled chin, whilst his bloodshot eyes and the bags beneath them suggested he was perhaps getting less sleep than he should be, although John was not one to judge on that aspect.

Summers opened his mouth to speak, but Zeigler already had his identification in his hand. 'Mr Summers, I am Detective Inspector Zeigler. This is my partner, Detective Sergeant Highsmith,' he repeated his lines. 'May we have a moment of your time?'

'Yes, of course,' Summers replied after an extended, hesitant pause – one caused, firstly, by hearing Zeigler's accent and, secondly, from the declaration that they were police officers. After opening the door wide, he said to someone else in the office, 'Maria, we'll have to finish this later.'

A striking young woman stepped into view then. She stared briefly at Summers with a set of large eyes, the irises of which were so dark John could scarcely distinguish the brown from the black of the pupils, before disregarding the two detectives as she walked through the door. She wore a pair of knee-high boots, and her slender body was clad in a long, brown leather coat that fastened at the neck, so only her head was visible. Her features were dour and narrow, but petite and well-proportioned. With olive-hued skin and dark hair, this Maria looked to John as if she had something other than British blood in her veins.

John watched her as she walked away, then he followed Zeigler into Summers' office.

The office, like the man, was unremarkable: there was a desk with three chairs opposite it, a typewriter sat on the desk, a series of tall filing cabinets positioned in the far-right corner, and a potted plant placed on a table to the left. It was more normal than DCI Werner's office anyway, given that on the desk there was a series of photographs depicting Summers with two people, who were presumably his wife and son. Through a window to the right was a view of the Thames, which was miserable and uninviting today. The low drone of a foghorn was just about audible. From where he was standing, John could also see the wharf below on which Summers' employees went about their work, transferring goods from a boat onto the dock.

Summers moved behind his desk, and as he sat down, he said, 'Please, take a seat.'

Both John and Zeigler did so across from him.

'What brings you to Silvertown, detectives?' Summers then asked tentatively, clearly unsure how to begin this conversation.

Zeigler spoke again: 'Mr Summers, there has been a series of break-ins in this area over the past several months, which were thought to be unconnected up until recently. We are becoming increasingly concerned, however, that it is the work of a single group operating in or around the docklands, and more specifically in the Silvertown district.' Their identifications did not indicate the police department John and Zeigler represented, and therefore they could keep any mention of drugs or Yonder out of this conversation and lead Summers to believe they were here on entirely different business. This story about break-ins had been chosen back at Scotland Yard as a simple, unassuming means of deception.

'Crikey!' Summers leant back in his chair. He was immediately calmer, as though this was somehow positive news. 'Officers, I've vetted my workers myself. I can assure you they're good men. I've never had any trouble for nearly six years.' There were hints of a rough inflection in his voice, as if Summers were trying to conceal his true nature from the detectives.

'You must understand, Mr Summers,' Zeigler continued (and to John, it sounded like his German accent had become thicker), 'that we are taking this situation very seriously, and though you claim to know these men, you yourself must admit that you cannot be certain of their actions outside of business hours.'

'Yes, of course not.' Summers hastily withdrew his previous confidence.

'Mr Summers, do you have a list of all of your workers?' Zeigler asked.

Summers nodded and made a noise to indicate that he did.

'Then, would you care to share it?' It was a request only out of politeness, as a refusal to do so would be an unambiguous admission of guilt – if not about Yonder, then about *something*.

'Yes, certainly,' Summers replied, although he was visibly unsettled by the order. They were not there about Yonder, it seemed, but any investigation into Summers' Import and Export could be dangerous, or even fatal. Summers would understand that. As a result, however, he would be more than willing to hand over any information they asked for, if only to get the detectives to leave – just as Joe Harding had been. And whilst he would be unlikely to employ a known felon, that being far too risky a prospect for an active criminal, the DES would still be able to work their way through the names on Summers' payroll and rout out any unscrupulous elements.

Doing as instructed, Summers stood and walked over to the row of filing cabinets in the corner, pulled out a drawer, and began flicking through the folders inside.

As he searched, Zeigler said, 'Whilst we look through this, would you mind if the detective sergeant took a walk around the warehouse and spoke to some of your staff?'

Again, it was not a request, and as such, Summers agreed promptly, still trying to hide his continued unease. They would have to be careful not to push him too hard, otherwise they ran the risk of scaring Summers into not only cutting all future ties with the Yonder Organisation but perhaps even into persuading other members that they were in danger as well.

Presently, John stood up, thanked Summers for his cooperation, and exited the office.

He stepped lively along the corridor, descended the staircase, and walked out across the loading bay. Then, slowing down to appear more casual, John approached the plump man with the clipboard and asked, 'So where's this lorry going?' as he came to a halt beside him.

The man was startled by the sound of John's voice, but when he saw that Zeigler was not with him and heard John's English accent, he became noticeably less fretful. 'Cardiff,' he answered at last, after examining the clipboard.

'How many lorries do you send out each day?' John tried to come across as more curious than investigative.

'Four, maybe five. We usually get that many coming in as well, so we work on a steady rotation. And we reload the boats on the wharf with cargo headed for the Continent, so we're kept pretty busy,' the man explained.

'And what are you transporting this afternoon?' John's tone was conversational.

'These' – the man drew his finger across the clipboard – 'are cuts of salted meats. Pork and ham, mostly.' He was completely at ease now. It was odd: although a German accent could persuade somebody to give up everything out of fear, John always found that he fared just as well in coaxing information gently from people by speaking with a soft English lilt.

He pulled an impressed face at the plump man's answer. 'Fancy.'

If what Harding had told them was true, and Summers was involved in the distribution of Yonder around Great Britain, then this would be the perfect place to do it. As an open gateway, it could pass through here with little attention and go in every direction alongside the agricultural produce from Europe.

John stepped in closer to the man. 'Listen,' he said, lowering his voice, 'you must hear a lot around here. Do you know anything about these break-ins?' He would not deviate from the planned narrative. 'That's what we're here about, you see. A few places have been knocked over in the past couple of months, and we're starting to get worried back at Scotland Yard. We think they might all be connected.' John was worried, and he was asking this man for his help.

'Oh,' the man mumbled, and rather skittishly, he answered, 'No, I've heard nothing. I didn't even know anything had happened.'

'The other warehouses are keeping it quiet, trying to protect their reputations, I suppose.'

The man nodded his understanding.

'Have you seen or heard anything suspicious?' John asked.

'Suspicious?' The man clicked his tongue and tapped his double chin with the rubber at the end of his pencil. 'Nothing suspicious, not really.'

'You want to take a look at that bloody dago. Shifty little wanker, if you ask me.' A young man had appeared in the window of the lorry's cabin, his Irish accent thick and fast.

'Dago?' John knew it as a derogatory slur, typically used for a person of Italian or Portuguese origin – or Spanish.

'Yeah, the Spaniard. He comes around here every week or two. He's out the back now with his pretty lady friend,' the Irishman explained.

The "Spaniard"...

'Shut up, Nolan!' the man with the clipboard cut in. He turned to John. 'He's just pissed because the Spaniard gave him an earful a while back for loading with *less care than he perhaps should have used.*' He raised his voice towards the end of the sentence so the Irishman, who had already disappeared back into the cabin, would hear him. 'He told Mr Summers to fire him. That really got Nolan's back up.'

A Spaniard, here... John knew the coincidence was too great, but even so, he could not leave without at least a cursory glance at this man.

'Well, listen: if you see anything, you say something. We don't want this place to be next,' John declared, bringing the conversation to a close and making sure to maintain his guise of the concerned police officer as he did so.

The plump man vowed that he would keep an eye out, and John thanked him for his assistance before he moved back towards the warehouse.

He tried not to seem too eager as he crossed the warehouse, heading towards the wharf. John pretended to inspect some crates waiting to be loaded into a lorry, which were stamped on the outermost wood with a blue ink that read 'Provence, France'. He watched with a staged interest as a man in a bright-yellow helmet zipped past him on a forklift. The workers gave funny looks to this stranger in a navy suit who was fascinated by the mundanity of their labours, but they were all too busy to really care.

*

When John stepped out onto the wharf several minutes later, he stopped to light a cigarette, affording himself a moment to scan the open space for this "dago" without arousing suspicion. And there they were: not ten metres away was the woman with the olive skin, her back to John and her dark hair cascading down the dull leather of her coat. No doubt she was this 'lady friend' the Irishman had referred to. Facing her was a much older, shorter man, his head of greying, curly hair an indication of his advanced age, although physically he was heavyset and powerful-looking. He too wore brown leather, and he smoked a thin cigar. Both of them were irregular beneath London's murky sky.

He does look old enough to have fought in the Spanish Civil War, John thought.

The man had already noticed him, but for now, John feigned ignorance of their presence. *Act casual,* he told himself.

When the woman turned to look at him as well, the man having informed her of John's arrival on the wharf, John guessed they were related – perhaps even father and daughter. They had the same Mediterranean skin, small nose, low cheekbones, and large eyes. His face was wider than hers and his chin more rounded, and he shared little of her innate beauty, but the resemblance was remarkable, nevertheless.

Could he be The *Spaniard?*

The woman turned her back to John again, and he gazed out over the river as if deep in thought and tried to enjoy what remained of his cigarette. Then, performing an exaggerated surprise as though he had just spotted them for the first time, John tossed the butt to one side and began walking towards the pair.

'Excuse me,' he said at a distance of about six or seven metres from them.

They ignored him.

John called again, 'Excuse me, sir, ma'am.' That was impossible to disregard, given that she was the only woman within earshot.

They both turned to face him, but neither of them spoke.

'I'm Detective Sergeant Highsmith.' John flashed his identification as he approached them. 'My partner and I are investigating a series of break-ins in this area over the past couple of months.'

Nothing. Between them, the man and the woman offered only uninviting scowls as a response to John's statement.

'Do you work for Mr Summers?' John asked the direct question in the hope that it would yield at least a one-word answer.

'We are business associates,' replied the woman in a clean southern English accent, which took John by surprise given her distinctly foreign appearance.

He cleared his throat. 'May I have your ID cards? I want to keep a record of whom I've spoken to.' John asked this with a smile, but as with Summers, it was a demand rather than a request as failing to show an ID card would mean their immediate arrest. Those living in Great Britain were required to carry an ID card at all times, whilst anyone visiting carried a visitor's permit. This law was first introduced under the Third Reich to curb illegal immigration, and had since become a cornerstone of national security; it was much easier to catch criminals when the police knew who everybody was. They could be forged, but it was extremely difficult to do so convincingly, and if the ID cards these two produced were fakes, then they were bloody good fakes.

The man was Antonio Ramos Serrano, and he was born in 1910, so he was definitely old enough to fit the description of The Spaniard. His nationality was Spanish, and his ID number was 308913482. John looked up at him from the ID card to compare his face to the photograph. This picture must have been about twenty years old, and the ID card was suffering from considerable wear, yet it was unmistakably him. He had aged badly, though, with his face now resembling the outside of a walnut in texture.

Maria Turner was the woman's name, so these two were perhaps not quite as related as John had first thought. She had been born in 1947, and her nationality was British, which explained the accent. Her ID number was 782039574. Her photograph was much more recent, being a couple of years old at most.

John took out his notebook and jotted down their names and ID numbers. This was all he would need to check up on them later.

'So, Mr Serrano,' John began as he handed the ID cards back, but he stopped when the man uttered something unintelligible and shook his head. 'Is there something wrong, Mr Serrano?'

'Mr Ramos,' he replied with the trace of a foreign accent. Without the help of the ID card, John would not have known it was Spanish, never having met many Spaniards himself. He had also assumed that the latter part of his name was how this man was supposed to be addressed, but apparently that was incorrect.

'Sorry, Mr Ramos,' John apologised. 'How long have you been working with Mr Summers?'

'Since he took over from his father,' Ramos answered through the cigar. His leathery face, almost the same colour as his jacket, was an enigma.

'Doing what, exactly?'

'Importing. I have a business in Spain, and I work here to keep trade steady,' he clarified.

'And what do you trade in?'

'Foodstuffs: fruits, nuts, olive oil,' came the not-so-candid reply.

John nodded. He was not familiar with international trade strategies, so he could contest none of this. 'Whereabouts do you cultivate such delicacies?' He wanted to find out as much as he could about this man before he outstayed his already tentative welcome.

'We do not cultivate them. Our processing plant in Burgos is merely a go-between for the farmers.'

John had never heard of Burgos, but then that was not surprising. 'And what is your role, Miss Turner?' he addressed the woman.

'*Mrs* Turner,' she corrected him, with a thinly veiled contempt.

'Apologies, Mrs Turner.' *She's married. So she could still be related to this Ramos, then,* John noted.

'I am Mr Ramos's accountant,' was her brusque answer to John's previous question. Again, it was as plausible as anything else they had told him.

'Do you make visits to this warehouse often?' John enquired.

'Every couple of weeks we come to discuss business in person,' illuminated Ramos. John offered the man ample time to elaborate further on this, but Ramos provided nothing more than a cloud of cigar smoke and an uncomfortable silence.

The conversation having reached its abrupt conclusion, John thought it best to return to the story Zeigler was spinning back in Summers' office: 'As I said, we've been troubled recently by a series of break-ins in the area. Have either of you seen anything suspicious? Any unfamiliar people loitering near the other warehouses in Silvertown? In a car or a van, perhaps?'

'I do not take notice of such things,' was all Ramos had to say on the matter.

John did look to Mrs Turner expectantly, but she stared back at him and said nothing at all.

After another brief moment of awkward silence, John declared, 'Well, if you see anything out of the ordinary, please do report it. I would not want your goods to fall into the hands of thieves.' He smiled, which neither Ramos nor Turner reciprocated, so he concluded, 'Thank you for your time, Mr Ramos, Mrs Turner. Have a nice day.'

When they bid him no such pleasantries in return, John stepped away.

Feeling sceptical eyes on his back, John approached a man having a cigarette out on the wharf and ran through the same scenario, asking for his ID card and enquiring about anything unusual he might have seen. He paid no attention to the man's rambling response, though, his mind already elsewhere. If this Ramos was *The* Spaniard, and he was in charge of smuggling Yonder into London as Harding had claimed, then an established foreign company that imported goods from Europe would be an ideal front. It could come here with Ramos's produce, hidden away somewhere Customs would never find it, and once it was on this dock, it could go straight into the back of Summers' lorries to be distributed around Great Britain.

It would be a seamless chain, from the smuggler to the distributer to the suppliers, and then on to the dealers.

John stole a glance back at Ramos and Turner, and he saw that the pair were still watching him from a distance. This was all conjecture, he knew, as they could just as easily be exactly who they said they were: a surly Spaniard and his business partner, or his daughter, or whomever. But to have found them here, and for Ramos to fit what little they knew about The Spaniard so flawlessly...

He was getting ahead of himself. John would take this to Zeigler and see what the DI thought of it before he allowed himself any further speculation.

Wanting to cover his tracks regardless, John walked back through the warehouse and repeated the same line of investigation twice more, writing down two further names and ID numbers in his notebook. He then returned to the loading bay to find both the potbellied man and the Irishman still loading the lorry with salted meats, so John took their information as well and apologised for having forgotten to do so earlier. If Summers was to ask around now, he would find that John had done the same with everybody he had spoken to, which would hopefully deter any lingering uncertainty as to the detectives' intentions.

Expecting that Zeigler must be running out of questions for Summers by this point, John returned to the first floor.

*

Summers was in the middle of a sentence when John entered the office, explaining the intricacies of import/export security procedures. He was much more relaxed now than when John left; evidently, Zeigler had convinced him they were here about the local break-ins.

John sat back down and waited for Summers to finish. Then, their attention turned to him. 'Everything looks good to me,' he said, 'and nobody has seen anything suspicious. You run a tight ship, Mr Summers.'

Summers smiled and thanked John for the compliment.

John thought for sure that they were in the clear and Summers had accepted their story without any doubt, so he decided to push for something extra: 'I was wondering, Mr Summers, if we could have the manifest for your imports and exports?'

Summers' expression changed instantly to one of apprehension.

Zeigler shifted in his chair, stifling a nervous twitch.

Before any questions could be asked, John explained his reasoning: 'I think these thefts might be an inside job. Think about it: every shipment is logged in advance, so there are dozens of people across Great Britain who know exactly what goods you have in your warehouse at this very moment, when another shipment will be arriving, and when it'll all be leaving again. They could easily feed this information down to London, and have an accomplice break in when they know there's expensive cargo being stored here overnight. If we cross-check the manifests of the warehouses in Silvertown that have already fallen victim, we might find a correlation between where the goods were destined for when they were stolen. If we could check your manifest, Mr Summers, we might be able to cross off certain destinations as safe and even figure out if some of your own goods are at risk.'

It was a long and, admittedly, shallow lie, but the more John spoke, the more Summers seemed to believe what he was saying. 'Oh, I'm sure that would be no problem at all,' he replied at last with an auspicious smile.

It had worked.

When Summers stood up and walked over to the filing cabinets again, Zeigler shot a look of pure bewilderment at John, and John tried to maintain his demeanour of confidence.

'How far back would you like to go?' Summers asked as he rifled through one of the filing-cabinet drawers.

'Well, the first break-in we think is connected with this case was six months ago, but there may have been earlier ones, so' – John made up a reasonable number – 'say about eight or nine months, if you have them. The further back, the better, to be on the safe side and save us coming back to bother you again.' That was five months before the first reports of Yonder and would therefore work to support their deception.

Summers must have favoured the idea of the detectives not returning because, in the end, he handed John the company's manifest for the past twelve months, which captured information on the cargo, its point of origin in either Great Britain or Europe, and its final destination. At a glance, John saw it included only a line or two of text for each shipment, but that would be more than enough.

It took everything John had to remain composed. Zeigler thanked Summers once again for his cooperation and bid the man farewell, and the two detectives exited the office without any further delay.

*

'What was *that*?' Zeigler asked John when they had reseated themselves in the Morris Minor. He spoke the words with a mixture of relief and confusion, although, in his heavy accent, it sounded more an accusation than anything else.

John put the vehicle into gear and pulled away from the warehouse. 'If Summers is involved in moving Yonder around Great Britain, and this import/export business is his means for doing so, then wherever those lorries terminate is a de facto layover in this web of distribution,' he explained.

Zeigler was silent whilst he considered this. 'We can use the manifest to track where Yonder is going, then use that information to close the net on this "web of distribution", as you call it,' he said eventually, understanding John's reasoning. If it came to pass that Summers' Import and Export was in fact the hub for nationwide distribution, they now knew for certain where he was sending the Yonder that came through his warehouse.

At any rate, John would also be able to check whether there was any legitimacy to Antonio Ramos Serrano's story now they had Summers' international trading information.

He told Zeigler about the conversation he had on the wharf with Summers' suspicious Spanish business partner, who just happened to be old enough to have fought in the Spanish Civil War *and* had the means to smuggle Yonder into Great Britain from overseas.

Zeigler listened whilst John spoke, seemingly intently, but when he finished, the DI said no more than, 'Good work. It sounds promising,' with far less enthusiasm than John had hoped for. When John looked over at him, however, he noticed that Zeigler was smiling, and he could have sworn he saw a streak of admiration break across the man's stony visage.

At a red traffic light, John lit a Reemtsma and took a deep lungful of smoke, savouring yet another step forwards in the Yonder investigation.

In the distance, a flash of lightning lit up the sky, and a crack of thunder roared overhead. Then, it began to rain.

CHAPTER SEVEN

The Ministry of Identification

In a waiting room at the Ministry of Identification, John sat on a low chair with a large coffee-table book open in his lap. The *Atlas of Europe* was twenty years old, though it was still new enough to feature the changes to the landscape of the continent after the Second Great War. John studied the map of Europe: the Greater Germanic Reich was a large area encompassing Central and Eastern Europe, with the lesser states having been brought together under the direct rule of the Fatherland so Berlin could unite the Volksdeutsche – the ethnic Germans – and better control those other, unpredictable peoples. It looked much neater now than it had done in the 1930s.

John turned to the map of Spain and ran his finger down the index of city names. Burgos was near the top, and he traced the coordinates to a box in the north of the country.

There it was: a dot on the map.

So, Ramos's processing plant was in northern Spain. Having skimmed the Summers' Import and Export manifest, John had found 'Santander, Spain' – a port city on the northern

THE MINISTRY OF IDENTIFICATION

coast of the country – to be the place of export for a produce company based out of Burgos named '*Delicias Inspiradas*', which he assumed translated as 'Inspired Delicacies'. It was a prolific company as well, making large shipments several times a week to Summers' warehouse in Silvertown, from where the cargo then went off in different directions all around Great Britain. It afforded a degree of viability to Ramos's story as a food merchant, John had to admit.

His curiosity satisfied momentarily, he closed the atlas.

The Ministry of Identification – known more commonly as the MoI – was all but deserted, as was to be expected at half past six on a Thursday evening. John could see Euston Road from where he was on the fourth floor in the Foreign Nationals Department wing of the building, which was quiet save for the sound of several solitary cars that passed by in the darkness below. The little waiting room he sat in was cosy, with a water cooler and paper cones in one corner, and worn-but-comfortable padded grey chairs placed around a scuffed coffee table. John had found the *Atlas of Europe* on a bookshelf, next to several other oversized tomes: *The Art of Adolf Zeigler*, *Wernher von Braun: Der Raketenmann*, *Berlin: A Tour in Pictures*, and *Adolf Hitler – Der Ewige Führer: The Eternal Leader*. Next to the bookshelf was a magazine rack containing out-of-date and dog-eared editions; this waiting room was clearly not the most visited corner of the building.

John was inspecting these magazines, debating whether or not to retrieve the one with the headline: 'How King Edward VIII United a Broken Great Britain', when Lewis Roberts stepped into the waiting room.

'Got it,' he announced with a smile, waving a blue-coloured file at John. 'Took me ages to find. The system we have for foreigners isn't the best.'

John had known Lewis since they were best friends at school. He had seen less of him over the past two years, since Lewis had both got married and been promoted to the Foreign Nationals Department in the MoI, but there existed no ill will for it, and they still got together for a drink whenever they could to catch up on one another's lives. Besides, it had never done John any harm to have a close friend working at the MoI.

The two men headed into Lewis's office down the hall from the waiting room. 'I don't think there's an awful lot in here to help you, I'm afraid,' Lewis explained as he sat down at his desk and John took the seat across from him.

This office was cosy too, and John had to contain his jealousy when he thought about his own workspace back at Scotland Yard: there was an expensive-looking high-backed leather chair, a spacious wooden desk, and soft lighting, which did not lay waste to his retinas the moment he passed beneath it. A single, side-hung casement window looked down onto Euston Road. A holiday snap of Lewis and his wife Monika in front of the Eiffel Tower was propped up on the desk, the couple grinning merrily into the camera. That was another source of envy for John as he had never seen the world beyond Great Britain. The photograph must have been several years old now, though, because the Lewis sitting before him had rather let himself go. This was a "perk" of his seniority in the MoI no doubt, caused by the late nights, sedentary job, and unhealthy snacking – it happened to a lot of men when they jumped a rank. Even with the extra weight, Lewis was still afflicted by the same square head John had always teased him about.

Lewis had done well for himself, and he was much smarter than he often let on. In five or six years' time, he would likely be the head of this department. They had both come far from pretending to be Focke-Wulf Fw 190s in the playground, their arms outstretched, chasing one another and making machine gun noises. But, like John, Lewis also looked tired: his dirty-blond hair was dishevelled, and there were dark circles under his sagging eyes.

'Whatever it is, I'll take it,' John replied. Anything was better than nothing.

The blue file was now open in Lewis's hands, and he proceeded to read aloud from the frontmost page: 'Antonio Ramos Serrano, ID number: 308913482. Born on 12th of August 1910. Nationality: Spanish.' That was the same information John had found in Ramos's ID card. 'According to his record, he came over to Great Britain in November 1945. All his papers are stamped and signed. Wife: Isabel López Guerrero. One daughter: Maria Ramos López, born 2nd of June 1947.'

So Mrs Maria Turner is *his daughter?* John ruminated.

'No record of any arrests or cautions. He applied for a trade licence in early 1946, attached to some company called "*Delicias Inspiradas*", whatever that means. His last recorded address is a London one, updated in May 1966: 27 Faulks Road in Hackney.' Lewis looked up from the file. 'I'm sorry, John, but anyone who came over so soon after the war can be a bit of a mystery. The system was bare bones back then, and they were letting everyone in to stabilise the population whilst asking few questions. It's still imperfect now. If you hadn't seen him this afternoon, he could just as easily have been dead, and it went undocumented. Wouldn't be the first time that's happened!' Lewis's frustration with the system under which he worked was evident. 'And for anything before 1945, well, you'd have to call Madrid for that. We don't have anything on file from before they get here unless it's criminal.' He tossed the open file onto his desk, disheartened.

John waved a dismissive hand. 'Don't worry, it was always a long shot,' he said with a smile, though there was nothing here to smile about. The information confirmed Ramos's story and also what John had read in the manifest from Summers' Import and Export. Plus, if he arrived in Great Britain after the Second Great War, as the record showed, then this man could not possibly be The Spaniard, if what Joe Harding had told them was to be believed.

'Laura should be along with the file on the woman any second now.' Lewis pulled a packet of cigarettes from his trouser pocket and offered one to John.

John was going to say that they need not bother with Turner's file, because if Ramos was not who John thought he was, then she would be of no concern either. Lewis had been excited by the prospect of helping him with an investigation, however, and was almost grateful for the distraction, so John decided to see this through to the end.

Whilst they waited, the two old friends sat talking about work, having already covered family when John first appeared at the door to Lewis's office. It was nice to be out of the police circle for a spell and to be able to talk to someone who was unfamiliar with Yonder and their war against drugs in the city. Lewis was struggling with his own vocational torments, though: immigration had gone up twelve per cent in the two years since his promotion, and although this meant new labourers and a potential increase in manufacturing for Great Britain, it had also led to a strain on his department's already limited resources. The record peak of monthly applicants was in June, when over 40,000 names came through the MoI's Foreign Nationals Department. They were in desperate need of more staff, and the head of the department was currently battling for an expansion on its budget. Lewis sank deeper into his chair as he spoke, this being a noticeably distressing subject for him.

A knock on the door ended their conversation, and Lewis's colleague Laura came in holding an orange file, which she handed to him. Lewis thanked her, and when she left, he started to read aloud again: 'So, Maria Turner. ID number: 782039574. Nationality: British. Born 2nd of June 1947 in Leicester State Hospital. Name at birth: Maria Ramos López. Mother: Isabel López Guerrero. Father: Antonio Ramos Serrano.' At least this confirmed that John was correct when he assumed Ramos and Turner were related.

'Married to Edward Turner in October 1966. No criminal record. Home address is 42 Fleming Road in Dagenham, last updated in February 1966, and the last registered profession is "accountant, *Delicias Inspiradas*", as updated in September 1966. But other than that, there's nothing noteworthy in here.' Lewis heaved a weary sigh and dropped Turner's open file down on top of Ramos's. He looked disappointed, as though he had anticipated some momentous revelation in one of those files.

'Thanks anyway, Louie. You've cleared a lot up for me,' John said through that same forced smile. He was disappointed too, but at least he could cross Ramos's name from his notebook now.

'I can find the mother and the husband, if you want?' Lewis asked, trying his hardest to be of some further assistance.

'No, no. You go home and get some sleep.' There was no point. It was a dead end.

'Yeah, you too, John,' Lewis conceded.

It was only by chance that, when John stood up to leave, he glanced down at the two open files on the desk. There was Maria Turner scowling back at him, the same photograph as in her ID card, if John recalled correctly. In the grainy portrait, her eyes were as good as pitch-black, and her Mediterranean skin and severe features were imposing against the pale background. And whilst another face gazed up at him from Ramos's file, it was a face John had never seen before, and definitely was not the man he had encountered earlier that day behind James Summers' warehouse.

'That's not Ramos,' John said to Lewis, pointing at the photograph.

'What do you mean?' came Lewis's puzzled reply.

'I met Ramos this afternoon. ID Number: 308913482.' John compared the number in the file to the one in his notebook. It was the same, and he had double-checked it in Silvertown when he wrote it down. 'That's not him.'

'Are you sure?' Lewis was leaning over the file, scrutinising the text.

'Positive.' The faces were completely dissimilar. This one was thin, even gaunt or sickly-looking. His eyes and nose were different as well, and the mouth was too big. John remembered then that Ramos and Turner had looked related, so he placed the two photographs side by side for comparison. 'Do they look like father and daughter to you?' he asked Lewis.

Lewis did not even have to consider it: 'No, not in the slightest.'

'I'm telling you, Louie, I saw her today with an older man who I pegged as her father the moment I saw him.' John picked up the picture from the Ramos file. 'And that's not him.'

'John, this must have been Ramos when he first arrived in Great Britain.' There was an immigration form in the file, accompanied by a handwritten signature and a red stamp, which read 'APPROVED: Ministry of Identification' with the National Socialist eagle at its side.

Lewis continued, 'Everyone who comes into Great Britain legally has one of these documents filled out. That was the rule even in the 1940s, when half the ports were still rubble. Their file is supposed to be updated when the individual is married or has a child or dies, or something, but like I said, it's a flawed system. And even then, no one checks the photograph, and the person in question is very rarely ever called in. We just update the file and put it back. Especially if there's never been any criminal activity. It would take too long.' Lewis ran a hand through his ratty hair and groaned; his frustration was apparent once more.

John was already thinking. This rendered everything he had thought he knew about Ramos obsolete, but most importantly, it brought into question his reason for being in Silvertown. 'I think I will see the wife's file,' he said to Lewis as he considered the photograph of "Ramos" again, 'and Edward Turner's too, if you have it.' If Ramos was now suspect, then why not his wife or his daughter's husband?

If Turner was indeed his daughter.

None of it could be trusted.

Lewis nodded, and then he was gone.

John spent the next twenty minutes pacing back and forth across the office, chain-smoking a series of cigarettes. His head was a mess from trying to put together puzzle pieces that did not fit, and formed a picture that made no sense. How could the photograph in Ramos's file be different to the one in his ID card, but Maria Turner's were the same? How was the produce company *Delicias Inspiradas* real, but the man an imposter? And what did this mean for James Summers and Yonder? Did Summers know he was working with a man who was not who he claimed to be? There was still no proof that they were working together in an illegal capacity and no indication that Ramos was involved with Yonder, John reminded himself, but all of this made that possibility much more probable as far as he was concerned.

With the beginnings of a headache forming behind his eyes, John went to the window and flung it open. He placed both hands on the window frame and took a deep breath of fresh air, and peered out into the rain. Shifting his thoughts, he wondered what Alice would be doing right now. John had called home earlier to let her know he would be back late, but Alice would still be worrying anyway, as she always did.

John watched a couple who walked along Euston Road below, huddled together beneath a single umbrella, and he felt alone all of a sudden.

Presently, Lewis burst back into his office, and John turned away from the window so he could focus.

Out of breath, Lewis placed another blue file on his desk, and as they both sat down, he declared: 'Well, Isabel López Guerrero is dead.' He spun the open file around so John could see it for himself. It read 'DECEASED: 07/12/1949', and the cause of death was stated plainly as 'Road traffic accident'.

John continued down the page from there, but the rest of the information confirmed what they already knew: Isabel López Guerrero had been married to Antonio Ramos Serrano, she had one daughter named Maria Ramos López, and she had arrived in Great Britain in 1945 on the same day as her husband. The only unique factor was her death in what appeared to be unsuspicious circumstances.

'Her last registered profession was as a secretary in that company, the foreign one her husband runs,' Lewis explained. 'And there's a photograph, but' – he looked back at the picture from Ramos's file – 'that could be anyone, now, couldn't it?' Lewis threw up his hands and slumped back into his chair.

John picked up the photograph of Isabel López Guerrero. As with the man in the Ramos file, this woman shared no resemblance with her supposed daughter.

It was whilst John was examining this photograph that Laura entered the office once again. 'Louie, I've got Edward Turner for you,' she said, but there was a hesitation in her voice when she passed the second orange file to him.

Lewis noticed this too, and he eagerly tore open the file to read its contents. His face gave nothing away, but without uttering a single word, he immediately passed the file across the desk to John.

Inside, John found a single sheet of typing paper, and written at the top of it in black ink was 'TURNER, EDWARD. DECEASED. INFORMATION REDACTED. 17/01/1967.' In the centre of the page a stamp read 'APPROVED: London SS Counter-Terrorism Unit', below which was a scribbled signature John could not make out. Unlike the other three files, there was no accompanying photograph.

John read the text on the page several times before emitting a single, surprised, 'Fuck.'

The red eagle on the stamp stared up at him – the steadfast protector of some unknown secret.

He closed the file and placed it on the desk, not sure what to think any more.

'I'm sorry, John,' Lewis said. 'It looks like you might have found something, but I certainly can't help you with it.'

Laura was still standing by his desk, enthralled by whatever was transpiring in this office.

John was rereading the Ramos file. There was something here – there had to be. The photograph, The Spaniard, James Summers, and Yonder: he refused to believe that it was all a coincidence. And especially with the SS Counter-Terrorism

Unit being involved! Was it linked to Ramos? Or to his "daughter"?

'May I take these?' John stood up and gestured at the files scattered about the desk.

'Of course, but make sure you sign them out downstairs, otherwise it'll be my arse!' Lewis claimed, and he laughed aloud as he stood up to meet John.

The attempted levity to lighten the mood fell flat, but John laughed along anyway; at least that would make Lewis feel better.

John and Lewis hugged – they had known each other far too long for a handshake – and John thanked the still-loitering Laura for her help (she was no doubt waiting for him to leave so she could grill Lewis on what this was all about). John then exited the office with a final, 'Thanks, Louie.'

*

It was gone eight o'clock that evening when John arrived home. He had toyed with returning to Scotland Yard, but he knew from experience that if he continued working this late, he would not get to bed until well past midnight. It would be better to start fresh in the morning, after a good night's sleep.

John found Alice lying on the couch in the living room, watching the television. It was a game show on which the contestants answered general-knowledge questions for money, and they were in the middle of a round titled 'Twentieth Century History'.

'What was the name of the space mission that took Ulrich Zimmerman and his team to the moon in 1967?' asked the quizmaster.

'*Sternwanderer Sechs*,' answered a female contestant.

There was a *ding* sound to confirm this was correct, and the quizmaster announced, 'Well done! That's another 100 Reichsmarks.'

'Hello darling,' Alice declared with a smile when John stepped into the living room. 'Good day?'

'Better than most,' John replied. He lifted Alice's head, slipped under her, and sank into the couch. 'How's your mother?' he enquired through a yawn.

'Oh, she's fine. Her arthritis has been acting up again, though. She could hardly stand by the time we sat down for lunch.'

'Who became the president of the United States of America in 1937 after the death of Franklin D. Roosevelt?' the quizmaster questioned.

'Erm, Joseph Kennedy?' a man answered with little confidence.

A loud buzzer indicated that this was incorrect.

'I'm sorry, Harold, but it was John Nance Garner, Franklin Roosevelt's vice president. Joseph P. Kennedy was not elected president of the United States until 1940. That's minus 100 Reichsmarks.'

'Has she been taking her medication?' John played with a lock of Alice's hair.

'Apparently, it makes her sleepy *and* dizzy.'

'So no, then?'

'Nope,' Alice sighed.

'On which day in February 1944 was the war criminal Winston Churchill executed?'

'On the 18th of February.'

Ding.

'Very good. 100 Reichsmarks.'

'Did you buy anything nice?' John asked.

'Just bits and pieces, really. But I did get some more clothes for the baby. Wait there one second, and I'll bring them in.'

Alice stood up carefully and walked out of the living room, holding her stomach.

John tilted his head back and closed his eyes. He was so tired that he could no longer string together a coherent thought.

'What is the name of the black athlete who is infamous for cheating in the 1936 Berlin Olympic Games?'

'Jesse Owens,' John said aloud.

'Jesse Owens,' a man on the television answered.

Ding.

'Correct. That's 100 Reichsmarks.'

John stifled another yawn, and he rubbed at his eyes with his knuckles.

Alice returned with a paper bag and lay back down with her head on John's lap. She then produced a tiny pink outfit with a little yellow duckling on the front, and John's face broke into an uncontrollable grin.

'That's adorable,' he said, taking it from her. It was so soft and so small. Another outfit in the bag was baby blue with a cartoon elephant on it, and the third one was bright yellow with a puppy.

John looked from the outfits to Alice, and an intense anticipation for their future together bubbled inside of him.

'How old was our Führer, Rudolf Hitler, when he became "Führer of the Third Reich" on the 17th of February this year after the untimely passing of his father – our beloved Ewige Führer – Adolf Hitler?'

'Thirty-four?' was the female contestant's unsure answer.

Ding.

'Correct again,' replied the quizmaster. 'That's another 100 Reichsmarks.'

CHAPTER EIGHT

The Yonder Task Force

The next morning, John, Peter, Arnold, and Zeigler were assembled with Detective Sergeants Alfie Walker and Alexander Cooper around a desk in the DES office, and Detective Inspector Tomas Colbeck stood beside them. It was these seven men who made up the Yonder Task Force – with the exception of their colleague Detective Inspector Jeremy Russell, the only member of the DES at present to have been indisposed by this flu that was going around. DI Colbeck was in charge of the Task Force. He stood at a similar height to John, and set into his soft features were two amber eyes. He wore his thick, light-brunet hair in the same undercut style as Peter, and it afforded him the appearance of a younger man. In actuality, he was a seasoned detective and fifteen years John's senior. Alfie and Alex, on the other hand, were both younger than John, but they were good men who were more than qualified for the job. They were often mistaken for brothers, sharing bright-blond hair and similarly pronounced cheekbones; being old friends, they were practically brothers anyway.

It was these seven men (or eight if the flu-ridden DI Russell was included) who had been working tirelessly for the past month and a half against the Yonder Organisation, and these seven men who were on the receiving end of DCI Werner's ire as they chased down dead leads and useless rumours. But that was changing now: suddenly, there were undeniable signs of progress.

The detectives had convened around this desk to update one another and DI Colbeck on how they were faring with their individual assignments. Peter and Arnold began, having spent yesterday afternoon cataloguing the dealers given up by Joe Harding, and whilst none of them had been arrested yet, this process was expected to begin as early as tomorrow morning. Peter was unambiguous in his frustration with the task to which he had been assigned, however, and he made it known that this busy work was beneath him. It was a long and arduous chore, and the results – as they had been so many times before – would likely be limited as very few of the dealers they brought in ever gave them anything substantial. There would be little glory here for Peter, and he knew it.

As for Zeigler, Alfie, and Alex, upon Zeigler's return to Scotland Yard the previous evening, the three of them had concerned themselves with making sense of the shipping manifest from Summers' Import and Export. On working through the document, they isolated eight cities as points of delivery from the warehouse in Silvertown: Manchester, Birmingham, Newcastle, Cardiff, Glasgow, Norwich, Southampton, and across the Irish Sea Bridge to Dublin. By highlighting these destinations on a map, it appeared that Summers delivered cargo to every single corner of Great Britain.

'From there, the picture paints itself: Manchester to Liverpool and Leeds, Cardiff to Swansea and then north through Wales,

Southampton down the coast to Bournemouth and Plymouth, Glasgow into the factory cities further north, and Dublin acts as a gateway to the rest of Ireland,' Alex explained.

Once they had gathered something like concrete evidence to substantiate Summers' involvement in the distribution of Yonder, they would contact the respective DESs in these areas and organise a coordinated strike against the various destinations on the manifest. Until such a time that this could be achieved, DI Colbeck ordered them to sit on the information in order to protect their own investigation.

The Task Force's attention turned to John then, and having heard the others discuss their rather measured progress, he felt much prouder of – or, perhaps, smugger about – his own. He and Zeigler began with their visit to James Summers' warehouse, and John described his run-in with Ramos and Maria Turner on the wharf. He then followed this with his trip to the MoI, his conversation with Lewis, and the subsequent realisation that Ramos was not who he claimed to be.

'With everything Joe Harding told us, I believe this man might very well be The Spaniard,' he stated at last, trying not to sound too matter of fact about it.

There were impressed faces all around when he detailed the steps to this discovery, except for Peter, naturally, whose scowl John had to avoid the entire time he was speaking. He was no doubt envious that John had been out investigating whilst he was stuck in the office, sifting through the dealers. John could smell Peter's cologne even from the other side of the desk, and the sweet scent made him inexplicably anxious.

'Very interesting,' DI Colbeck stated in his assertive tone of voice. Whilst his German accent had softened somewhat over the years, it was still apparent that the man hailed from the Fatherland. 'Do you have anything further to go on?'

'Just two home addresses for now: one for Ramos, and one for Turner,' John explained.

DI Colbeck nodded and said, 'Good work, John,' with a confident smile.

A flutter of triumph whipped around John's stomach at the compliment. DI Colbeck was the man John would have preferred to be behind that desk in the little room on the other side of the DES office. Not only had he completed a tour of duty on the Eastern Front as a young man, he had also risen up through the ranks of the Metropolitan Police on his own merit, starting out as a uniformed street constable the same as most others. Furthermore, he was – simply put – a more capable leader than DCI Werner: he gave the Yonder Task Force their orders, and if they went awry, as they had done so many times over the past month and a half, he took responsibility for it as their superior officer. That was in stark contrast to the DCI, who barked commands and then became agitated if they were not completed to the letter, irrespective of the situation.

'Anything else?' DI Colbeck asked.

There was, and John had been saving it for last. 'Just this,' he said, handing over Edward Turner's MoI file. 'It's for Maria Turner's husband, Ramos's son-in-law,' he added as he watched DI Colbeck read the lines of text.

DI Colbeck made an odd, surprised sound, then he dropped the open file on the desk so that everyone could see its contents for themselves. Alex let out a low whistle, and Arnold exhaled deeply. They all understood the implications when they read the words 'London SS Counter-Terrorism Unit'.

'Okay, Detective Sergeant' – DI Colbeck looked up at John – 'you found the addresses for Ramos and Turner, so I want you to follow up with them. See what you can find, but be careful about it. Detective Inspector' – DI Colbeck gestured towards Zeigler – 'you go with him.'

Zeigler nodded his understanding.

As for the rest of the Task Force, DI Colbeck declared that they were to continue with their current assignments for the time being. At the order, John half-expected Peter to shout and stamp his feet like a sullen child, but, instead, he offered DI Colbeck a cold, hard glare from across the desk before he walked away. DI Colbeck paid him no mind.

Having delegated jobs to everybody else, DI Colbeck picked up Edward Turner's MoI file. He read it again, then announced, 'I will take this and see what I can find.' John was confident he would know exactly whom to speak to.

With that, DI Colbeck dismissed them, and the remainder of the Yonder Task Force dispersed in different directions.

As John walked back to his desk, Zeigler approached him. 'John,' he said in that thick German accent of his, 'I have several telephone calls I want to make about the manifest before we leave. Will you wait?'

Usually, John would have done just that, never having been so bold as to head out on his own, but he felt remarkably sure of himself in that instant, especially after impressing DI Colbeck in the way he had. The truth be told, he believed that this lead on The Spaniard was his alone to pursue, and, like Peter, he did not want to miss out on his personal moment of glory.

So he made his excuses to Zeigler, which culminated in him saying, 'And this will probably be a wild goose chase anyway. You should stay here and try to find something worthwhile, whilst I go knocking on doors.'

Zeigler was uncharacteristically unsettled by the notion of John leaving by himself, and although he tried to say so in a respectful manner, John could not help but feel condescended to by the DI. Besides, it was John who had deftly talked his way around Ramos and Turner yesterday in Silvertown, and who had both got the shipping manifest from James Summers and found Ramos's suspicious MoI file. The insinuation, then, that this task might be too much for him to handle was insulting. He did not need Peter or Zeigler with him all the time, to 'do the talking' and hold his hand.

After a short back and forth between them, John eventually talked Zeigler around to the idea that him going unaccompanied should be no cause for concern. Zeigler still seemed not entirely convinced, though; annoyingly so, actually.

Resisting the urge to say anything further on the subject, John grabbed his grey suit jacket from the chair at his desk and made for the door, all the while thinking to himself, *What's the worst that could happen?*

CHAPTER NINE

Number Twenty-Seven

Before leaving Scotland Yard, John stopped at the Fraud Squad office on the second floor and filled his jacket pocket with a handful of spare photographs from their case files. His alibi, should he come across either Ramos or Turner again, would be to show them these photographs, claim that they depicted suspects for the break-ins around the docklands, and ask if any of them looked familiar. When they inevitably gave him short shrift, John would thank them and leave in the knowledge that the DES cover story remained intact.

This entire ploy turned out to be unnecessary, however, when John knocked on the door of Turner's last registered address at 42 Fleming Road in Dagenham, because it was a dead end. A family lived there now – a husband and wife and their two young children. The friendly couple explained to John that they had started renting the house over two years ago from a Mr Baker, and a telephone call to the number they provided left him able to cross out the address in his notebook: Mr Baker confirmed that a man and a woman named Turner had lived there, but they had moved out of the residence in January 1967. They left no forwarding address, and Mr Baker had not heard from them since. January 1967 matched up with the date of Edward Turner's death, so Maria Turner's absence was not a great surprise. If her husband had been embroiled in some form of terrorist activity, it would make sense that she too was involved in some capacity, and with the SS Counter-Terrorism Unit breathing down her neck, it would have been foolish to have remained at her State-registered address.

Discouraged, half an hour's drive later, John pulled up in the Morris Minor across from 27 Faulks Road, Ramos's last known address in Hackney. This endeavour seemed somewhat pointless now, considering it was doubtful whether Ramos would still be living here either, but with nothing else to chase at the moment, John had decided to investigate regardless.

The street itself was more or less deserted, with only a few cars parked against the kerb and not a single person in sight. It was a Friday morning, so most of the residents would be in work. The houses were semi-detached and pre-war but well-built. There was a passage to the left of number twenty-seven leading through to the rear.

John climbed out of the car, crossed the road, and peeked through the front window of the house. Whilst the front room was still, the furniture arranged inside it gave the impression that it was occupied. Turning to the door, John knocked hard twice, with the resulting echo rattling around the quiet street.

There was no answer.

Undeterred, John walked around to the side of the building and headed down the passageway towards the back of the house. A large metal gate in the path had been left ajar, and the rusted hinges squealed in rebuke when John pushed through it; it was a hostile sound. On the other side, he found himself in a distressed, narrow garden: the grass was in desperate need of a good mowing, weeds had sprouted between the gaps in the concrete flagging, and most of the plants in the single flowerbed along the far wall had fallen lopsided.

Disregarding the garden, John climbed onto the back step and gave the handle on the back door a gentle tug, fully expecting it to be locked. On the contrary, the handle shifted under his touch, and the door opened inwards.

John remained motionless on the back step, uncertain as to what he should do next. There had been nothing to indicate that this was Ramos's house, so he could be trespassing in the home of another perfectly pleasant family.

I knocked on the front door and no one answered, but when I checked the back door, it was unlocked.

John pushed the door open wide and stepped into the kitchen. 'Hello? Is anybody home?' he called, yet nothing stirred within the house.

I shouted, but no one replied. Concerned, I went in to make sure that nobody was in trouble inside.

The reason to enter was sound enough, and if the occupants came home, he would be able to explain himself to them – and to DCI Werner.

His purpose resolved, John closed the back door shut behind him.

Downstairs was exactly how John would expect to find any other house on this street: a kitchen with the regular utensils and appliances, and a living room with an old three-piece suite. Despite this, the home lacked the usual, tangible sensation of another human presence. An eerie stillness was rigid in the air. It had no decoration of any description, beyond the discoloured magnolia wallpaper and worn, grey carpet. A fine layer of dust had settled on – well, everything. John tapped the top of an armchair with his hand and the little grey specks puffed up in a spiral, only to dance back down again and land on the fabric. For all intents and purposes, 27 Faulks Road looked lived in, and yet from where he stood right now, it was apparent to John that nobody had visited in a long while.

He returned to the kitchen, opened the cupboards, and found them void of any food whatsoever.

It was all quite peculiar.

From the dimly lit hallway by the front door, John set off up a flight of carpeted stairs. The old house groaned reluctantly beneath his weight as he made the ascent. At the top, he found three closed doors on a landing. Behind the first one he opened was a large bedroom with a window that looked down onto the street. This bedroom was also sparsely furnished, with an old-fashioned metal bed frame and accompanying mattress, a bedside table, a tall wooden wardrobe, and a chest of drawers. The standout oddity up here was that the bed was not made up, so either it was laundry day or this was a sure sign that nobody was living here. John crossed over to the chest of drawers and pulled each drawer out individually; the empty spaces seemed to confirm that the latter was correct. The wardrobe was bare as well, save for several abandoned wire clothes hangers.

Satisfied for now that this bedroom heralded nothing of importance, John exited it onto the landing. He opened the door to the back of the house to reveal an empty spare room. The final door on the landing was the bathroom, but there was nothing unusual in there either.

John placed his hands in his trouser pockets, walked back across the landing to the bedroom, and stared out of the net-curtained window into the street. If John were a criminal, he would know exactly what was in his MoI file, like his currently registered address, for example. And if he were to become deeply involved in an undertaking such as Yonder, during which time there was a high probability of him being investigated by the police, he would know that staying at said address could be dangerous. Therefore, he would pack up his clothes and any food he had, and then he would head someplace else – somewhere he knew he would be safe no matter what.

Was this what Ramos had done? He could very well be living with Turner now, given that her own current address was not in the MoI's records.

John sighed aloud. This was all high speculation, he knew. Ramos might have moved out of this house years ago, even before Turner left the one on Fleming Road. He would have to find out who owned the property and see if the paper trail led anywhere. Other than that, he was not sure what use it could be to the DES.

Just as John turned to leave, the sound of a car in the street below distracted him, and he watched a dull-blue Auto Union 1000 come to a halt outside number twenty-seven. Two men stepped out, and John heard them talking through the thin window glass.

'D'you 'ave the key?' one of them said with a coarse northern English inflection.

John stiffened. Did he mean the key to number twenty-seven?

'No, I thought you had it,' claimed the second man in what sounded like a French accent.

John could no longer see them on the pavement below, even when he strained against the window.

'I told you to get it off of Mr Ramos! 'Arry'll be waitin' for us at Göring Station any minute now,' the first man declared, annoyed.

Mr Ramos…

So this is *his house.*

'You said no such thing!' argued the Frenchman.

'"*You said no such thing!*"' The Englishman mimicked his companion in a mocking French accent. 'Go round the back. The back door should be unlocked,' he ordered.

'Shit,' John whispered. He hurried across the landing to the back room, and peered out of the window in time to see a large man come lumbering around the corner from the side passage.

The back door rattled, and John tried to convince himself that he had heard a lock click into place when he closed it. If it had, then these two men would have no choice but to leave, and he would be able to escape.

His hopes were promptly dashed when John heard the back door open and the thud of ominous footsteps downstairs in the kitchen.

He was trapped.

He had to hide.

Where?

He hesitated for a second...

The bedroom.

John stole back into the bedroom, trying not to make even the slightest of sounds as he did so. There, he saw two possible hiding places: under the bed or in the wardrobe.

Bed or wardrobe?

Wardrobe or bed?

Wardrobe, he decided. At least then he would be standing up and not flat on his stomach if they found him. John flung open the wooden doors and pushed the metal hangers to one side; he cursed under his breath when they clattered together. Holding them still, he scrambled in. The wardrobe was not tall enough for him to stand fully upright, so John had to hunch his shoulders and stoop awkwardly in order to get into position.

Downstairs, the front door opened.

'The back door was unlocked,' said the Frenchman.

'*Oh, really?*' exclaimed the other man in an overly sarcastic tone. 'Upstairs. Let's find this bloody key Mr Ramos is so desperate for and get out of 'ere.'

Fitted badly, the wardrobe doors left a narrow gap between them when closed. It was enough for John to be able to see out into the bedroom, although only the door, the bedside table, and the rightmost edge of the bed were visible.

John drew his Walther and pulled back the hammer. The snap of the metal was excruciatingly loud, and he swore again in both frustration and panic.

Then, he waited.

The sound of footsteps starting up the carpeted stairs was unmistakable, and John struggled to control his breathing as his anxious heart pounded wildly in his chest.

'Not that room, this one,' the Englishman instructed from the landing.

The bedroom door rattled, and John stopped breathing altogether.

They were coming in.

John watched on in terror as the door opened and the two men entered the bedroom. One of them was taller, and of a sturdy build with broad-shoulders and large forearms, and the other was shorter and unusually thin. The thin man sported a tatty, unkempt beard that was quite unfashionable nowadays, and his devious, little eyes darted about the bedroom from behind his hooked nose and beneath a well-defined and thinning widow's peak. The second man, who had come around to the back of the house, was bald in contrast, and he had a brutish look about him, with deep-set eyes and jug-like ears.

The gun was heavy in John's hand, and he was already sweating underneath his woollen suit. He wanted desperately to wipe his forehead, but he dared not move.

'Check those drawers. Mr Ramos said the key is in one of 'em,' the thin man stated, and he motioned towards the bedside table. He was the Englishman, and the one in charge of this duo.

Obeying the command, the second man – the Frenchman – crouched down by the bedside table and opened the topmost of its three drawers. John scolded himself for his folly when he realised that he had not checked the bedside table, but the prevailing sensation of dread was enough to largely drown this out.

Whilst the Frenchman rummaged through whatever was in the bedside table, John debated whether he should attempt to arrest the two men. He had a weapon and could easily hold it on both of them at the same time, but if they were also armed, it would take only a split second for one of them to draw and shoot him dead.

John thought about Alice, and about their unborn daughter.

It was too great a risk, he knew, taking on both men at once.

He should have waited for Zeigler.

You arrogant idiot!

As the Frenchman moved down to the second drawer, the Englishman became visibly irate. '*Well?*' he snapped, and he flung his arms about.

'I do not see any key,' the Frenchman replied. He opened the bottom drawer and pawed through it, then shrugged.

The thin man groaned and emitted a ferocious expletive: 'Fuck this! You keep lookin'. I'm goin' back to the car.' He stepped out of the bedroom, and John heard him muttering to himself as he descended the staircase, 'Bloody fool's errand, comin' all the way out 'ere for a key. Ramos can't come 'imself – *he has too much to do* – but then 'is bag is *so* precious…'

When the front door slammed shut, the house fell silent, and John endeavoured not to breathe for fear it would be too loud.

Through the sliver of an opening in the wardrobe doors, John watched the broad-shouldered Frenchman – who was now becoming annoyed himself – tip the contents of each of the bedside table's drawers onto the bed. He then proceeded to dig amongst the mess, which looked to John like nothing but odds and ends.

John paid little attention to what was on the bed, though, because with the Frenchman's back now to the wardrobe, his finger twitched on the trigger of the PPK-L. This was his chance: he could take the Frenchman whilst he was alone and hold him at gunpoint as they went down the stairs. Then, he could ambush the Englishman out by their car and force them both to lie down on the tarmac whilst he used the radio in the Morris Minor to call for backup. Controlling them would not be difficult if they were on their stomachs with their hands behind their heads, and John would even be able to ask them about this key they were so interested in.

It all sounded straightforward enough in his head…

As John strategised, the Frenchman dropped something on the floor, and it clattered out of sight under the bed. He grumbled in what John assumed was French and knelt down to find this object again.

'*Now!*' an internal voice told John. '*Step out and shout, "Police! Hands in the air!"*'

His feet stayed stuck to the wood.

The voice ordered John to act, to disregard the consequences and work it out as he went. That confident voice in his head was his daring side. But his cautious side cried back just as urgently, pleading with him to stay hidden and to wait for the men to leave, and to be thankful he would survive this ordeal.

The argument raged back and forth, and the Frenchman remained kneeling, searching under the bed for whatever he had lost.

John took a definitive breath.

I'm going to listen to the daring side, he decided.

He raised the Walther and prepared himself to spring out of the wardrobe.

Three, two, one...

He did not move. An invisible force held him back.

'Come on!' the daring voice insisted. *'Don't be a coward!'*

John shifted his weight, placed his free hand on the wardrobe door, and took another determined breath.

'Come on!'

Three...

Two...

One...

The Frenchman suddenly stood erect and turned to face the wardrobe.

He stared directly at John, and John froze.

Had the man heard him moving inside the wardrobe?

'Quick! Lift your gun and shoot him!' the voice in his head barked.

John did nothing.

As it turned out, the Frenchman had not heard him. Instead, he was now examining the metal key in his hand. The Frenchman read the label attached to it and exhaled in relief.

And then he was gone, and John was again listening to a set of footsteps bounding down the carpeted stairs.

He sank back into the shadows of the wardrobe, and the pistol fell limp at his side.

The opportunity had passed. He had missed his chance.

He heard the front door open and close again, and outside the men began to speak.

'Found it!' the Frenchman announced in a pleased fashion.

'Took you long e-bloody-nough,' was the Englishman's less-than-impressed response. 'Get in. We've got to go meet 'Arry at Göring Station.'

A bickering squabble ensued between the two of them as car doors were slammed shut, but John did not move until the engine had turned over and faded into the distance. Then, he practically tumbled out of the wardrobe. His legs were dead weights, and he struggled to keep himself upright whilst the sound of his heartbeat pulsated around his head.

Wiping down his dripping face with the rough sleeve of his suit jacket, John relaxed the hammer on the PPK-L. He returned the weapon to the holster under his arm – impotent and useless.

'Fucking coward,' he uttered with disgust into the abject stillness of the bedroom.

CHAPTER TEN

Göring Station

'John, this is DI Colbeck. Where are you? Over,' came the DI's voice through the radio.

'I'm going west towards Göring Station, in pursuit of two men who work for Ramos,' John explained into the handset. 'They came to Ramos's house looking for a key, and I overheard them say they were headed to the train station next. Over.'

One car ahead of him, John could see the Auto Union 1000, with the Englishman and the Frenchman visible through the back window. It had taken him only a moment of self-loathing to decide to go after them, and he was lucky enough to have caught up with the car just around the corner.

'Did you say a key? Over,' asked DI Colbeck. But before John could answer his voice came back, 'Wait, where is Detective Inspector Zeigler? Over.'

'Shit,' John muttered to himself before he pressed the button on the handset. Opening up the channel, he said, 'I came without him, sir. He had things to do, and I didn't want to waste his time. Over.'

John sighed. *What a dreadful excuse,* he thought.

Whilst the radio remained silent for a long second, John could almost hear DI Colbeck's disappointment through the hissing of the static. When he did speak again, however, there was no change in his intonation: 'Peter and Arnold are not far from Göring Station. They went to the Ministry of Identification for the files on Harding's dealers. I will radio through to them, and they will be waiting for you when you arrive. Keep us updated. Out.'

The channel went dead.

As he crossed London, making sure to never lose sight of the Auto Union 1000, John could not help but reflect on what happened back at Ramos's house. He tried to convince himself that he would have done it – that if the Frenchman had not turned around, he would have burst from the wardrobe and ordered him to be still. John played out the scenario in his mind over and over again. Each time he did so, it seemed as though it would not have been so difficult.

That voice in his head laughed and called him a liar, and claimed that he never would have committed to such a bold act.

At a red light, John peeked at his tired reflection in the rear-view mirror. He knew Peter would have shot and killed one of the men back at the house and then arrested whomever remained standing. Who to kill? Well, that would have been a coin toss.

Perhaps that was what John should have done.

He rolled away from the lights and let another car come between him and the Auto Union 1000. John had not fired his gun at a real person before, much less killed someone.

Could he have shot a man in the back?

He did not think so.

Did this make him weak-minded?
He preferred not to think about it.
The voice in his head sneered at the remark.

*

Having followed the Auto Union 1000 across London, John eventually found himself on foot on Euston Road, where Reichsmarschall Hermann Wilhelm Göring Station – or Göring Station, as everyone called it – came into view. It was one of several buildings in London that had been redesigned by Albert Speer, the renowned "Architect of the Third Reich", after being damaged during the war, and it was a masterpiece. A set of wide marble steps led from the street to the entrance, and the tall building was enclosed on either side by two enormous square pillars made of white stone, which reached up towards the sky. Between these pillars, the entrance facing the street was nothing but clear glass, except for the huge ornate clock set into its centre. Inside, a long water feature filled with colourful fish ran the length of the train station, its fountains playing an uninterrupted melody of trickling water. Apparently, when the sunlight hit the spray from these fountains just right through the glass ceiling above, it formed a rainbow, although John had never seen this phenomenon himself to verify its authenticity. Large maps and timetables decorated the walls, and grand advertisements for cigarettes and beauty products were placed intermittently in between them. At the far end, archways led commuters out onto the platforms, and to the left of these were the stairs down to the Underground.

The train station was completed in 1946 for the arrival of Reichsmarschall Göring himself. To immortalise him, a bust of the Reichsmarschall sat at the front of the water feature.

Under his mighty face, his neck was adorned with the "Star of the Grand Cross of the Iron Cross", the honour that was bestowed upon the man after the resounding success of his liberation forces during Operation Sea Lion in June 1943. Reichsmarschall Göring's sudden death last year had been the cause for great sadness across the Reich, and it made this monument to his legacy all the more poignant.

With the Englishman and the Frenchman several paces ahead, John spotted Peter and Arnold loitering near the water feature's edge when he stepped into Göring Station. He smiled and waved at them, and the two detectives waved back in an exaggerated act they had been taught to perform in these exact circumstances, in order to throw off any suspicions that they might be officers of the Reich.

At least John's gaiety was a tactical device, anyway. Peter's lips had twisted into that sly, smug smirk as soon as he saw him, the DI unable to contain his delight at the fact that John had needed to radio for his help.

'Prick,' John mumbled through his false smile.

Hiding his displeasure, John stopped in front of Peter and Arnold. He whispered, 'It's the two men at my ten o'clock, passing the corner of the water feature. One has a beard, and the other is bald.' Even amongst the dozens of bodies around them, John could smell Peter's dry cologne hanging heavy in the air, and he had to stop himself from shoving Peter backwards into the water feature to mask the cursed scent.

Peter turned around and saw straight away whom John had described. 'Okay. Follow me,' he said without hesitation.

Arnold fell in at Peter's side, and John followed begrudgingly behind them. As was to be expected, Peter had taken complete control of the situation, just as he had done with Jennifer Campbell and at The Rag-and-Bone. Although

John could hardly complain this time, considering it was his own arrogance that had caused this particular mess.

Peter led the way along the left wall of the water feature, and they slipped between the crowds of bustling commuters; the shops set back into the walls were packed full of early weekend travellers, even at this time of day. Ahead of the detectives, the Englishman and the Frenchman walked beneath an archway into a side room. The sign above the archway read 'Lockers', and John guessed that one of them would be the companion to the key in the Frenchman's possession.

When the three detectives reached the archway, Peter stopped beside it and peered into the room. As he did so, he dictated, 'Arnold and I will go in first. John, you count to ten and follow us in. Then count to ten again and draw your weapon. Understand?' He looked back at John and impatiently awaited acknowledgement of the order.

The plan was not up for debate, it would seem.

John gritted his teeth and nodded.

Peter gestured to Arnold and the two detectives disappeared into the locker room, and John began to count.

One.

Two.

'Mine's number thirty-four,' Peter said out loud inside the locker room.

Four.

Five.

Six.

'My one's over here, I think. One-six-five,' came Arnold's reply.

Nine.

Ten.

John stepped through the archway.

Inside the locker room, a series of small metal lockers stacked in twos lined the walls. Other than that, the room was empty save for the Englishman, the Frenchman, and the three detectives, and four snow-white pillars that stood silent sentinel.

One.

Two.

John crossed the room, searching for his own non-existent locker.

'I can't find my bloody key,' Peter said to Arnold.

'You didn't leave it behind, did you?' Arnold called back.

Five.

John glanced over his shoulder. The Englishman and the Frenchman were standing at an open locker somewhere in the late hundreds, but they were blocking his view of whatever was inside.

Seven.

Eight.

John slipped his hand inside his jacket, and he gripped the Walther in a tight fist.

Nine.

Before he could reach ten, Peter put their plan into action. '*Police! Hands up!*' he growled.

John hastily drew his pistol and turned it on the two men. Arnold had also acted accordingly, with his gun already levelled at the Frenchman.

The men did not raise their hands immediately. Instead, over several seconds, there was a baffled silence as they tried to comprehend what was happening and how they had got to be on the unfortunate side of three handguns.

John stood strong, with his Walther aimed squarely at the Englishman's chest. They would not get away from him this time.

At last, the Englishman recognised that they were in no position to do anything other than what Peter had commanded, and he lifted his arms into the air. The Frenchman followed suit mere moments later.

'Move away from the locker,' Peter ordered.

They did just that, and Peter approached it to take a look inside. 'Detective Sergeant.' He signalled for John to join him whilst Arnold kept his gun on the two men.

There was a single article inside the locker: a small, well-worn, beige leather satchel, which was propped up against the side. Intrigued, John watched Peter pull the bag towards them, and with little ceremony, he tore it open.

The first thing Peter found in the satchel was a pale-blue passport with '*ESPAÑA PASAPORTE*' printed across the front. He opened it. It was issued in 1935, and the man who had called himself Ramos in Silvertown gazed up from the page, except in this document his name was Miguel Carrasco Menéndez. He was much younger here, even more so than in the photograph in his ID card. The rest of the information was illegible to John, it all being in Spanish.

Joe Harding said The Spaniard had fled Spain before the Second Great War began. If that was true, and if Ramos was The Spaniard, then he could have used this passport during his escape to Great Britain – in John's mind, at least, that was the rationale for its being here.

Underneath the passport, Peter next uncovered a thick bundle of used banknotes held together with a length of string. He flicked through it and guessed that it must have been at least 1,000 Reichsmarks, which was a considerable amount of money to keep in a train-station locker by any account. Then, beside these banknotes, there was a pistol. It was slighter even than the Walther PPK-L and had the words 'Looking-Glass' engraved into the side of it. It was not loaded, but the handful of loose rounds rolling around the bottom of the satchel implied that it was for more than ornamental purposes. With nothing else unique about them, Peter put the banknotes and the handgun to one side.

Tucked away at the bottom, the final object in the satchel was an old handkerchief, and lovingly wrapped within the cloth there was a ceremonial medal. John had never seen one like it before. It was a beautifully crafted piece with the golden profile of a face set into a white centre. Eight red points came out from the middle, which was encircled by an emerald-green wreath. A golden crown adorned the decoration at the top – it was definitely not something awarded by the Third Reich.

When Peter removed the medal to take a closer look, a folded piece of paper fell out from inside the handkerchief and onto the floor. John bent to pick it up, and on unfolding it, he discovered that it was not a piece of paper at all, but a photograph. It was a practically antique black-and-white one at that, depicting five men who stared straight into the camera. All of them were dressed in military uniform and brandished war-era rifles. John turned it over, and scrawled on the back in faded blue ink was '*Guadalajara, 7 de marzo 1937*'.

He considered the writing for a moment, then looked back at the image. Could this be proof of Ramos's involvement in the Spanish Civil War? The date suggested that the photograph was taken during that time, whilst '*Guadalajara*' was about as Spanish as any other word John had ever seen. On scanning the faces, he recognised Ramos amongst the men, at a similar age to the photograph in the passport, John thought. Not being particularly familiar with the regalia and uniform of the combatants in the Spanish Civil War, John handed the photograph to Peter in the hope that somebody back at Scotland

Yard would be able to confirm whether these men were in fact Communist soldiers in the conflict. If they were, then it was yet further evidence that Ramos could be The Spaniard – although this was still predicated on the assumption that Joe Harding's story about The Spaniard and his service for the Communists in the Spanish Civil War was based in truth.

So, their revelation had been a passport, banknotes, a pistol, a strange medal, and a photograph from 1937. John studied the contents of the satchel: it presented so many more questions than it did answers.

'What is this?' Also stumped by this series of curiosities, Peter rounded on the Englishman and the Frenchman, who were still standing to one side under the watch of Arnold's pistol. 'Why did Ramos send you after that bag?' he asked them.

The men remained silent.

'*Answer me!*' Peter demanded. He strode up to the Englishman and grabbed him by his shirt collar. John was certain that violence upon the Englishman was to follow then, with a sort of impromptu interrogation taking place in the locker room.

At least it seemed more than likely, until someone called from the archway, 'Jasper, are you in h—'

John, Peter, and Arnold all turned to face the newcomer: a third man had strolled straight into the middle of this confrontation, and a rabbit-in-the-headlights expression beset his face when he saw what was happening. Then – having been allowed a second to come to terms with the situation – quick as a flash, his hand darted under his jacket, and the man produced a weapon of his own.

John was just about able to register the pistol before the first bullet was fired. By the time the second rang out, he was leaping for cover behind the nearest stone pillar. The third and fourth shots came with the sound of screaming outside in the train station, and hurried footsteps in the locker room as the Englishman and the Frenchman scurried for the exit.

John glanced over to the pillar that was parallel to the one he was behind, and was glad to see that Peter and Arnold had both had the same idea as him; several pockmarks in the white stone behind which they were hidden provided evidence of how lucky they had been. Regardless, Peter was already moving, and he called, 'With me!' to John and Arnold when he took off across the room.

Without thinking twice, John stepped out into the open and made after him.

The three detectives exited into the station, which was now in a state of panic. Peter searched for the men in the crowd, but the frightened mass of people blocked his view. John, taking the initiative for a change, pushed forwards and leapt up onto the high edge of the water feature, and surveyed the sea of chaos below. As might have been expected, at the sound of the gunshots a surge of commuters had moved for the front entrance of the station that opened onto Euston Road, and they had become an impenetrable wall of fear. On seeing this, John spun on his heel, and from there he spotted the three men, who were fighting their way towards the platforms at the other end of the building.

'*Peter!*' he yelled. Then, without looking back, John sprang into a sprint along the wall of the water feature.

John easily gained ground on the men, who continued to fight the crowd, and he came to within five metres of them as he ran out of wall. There, the three men split up, with two of them veering left towards the Underground and one – the Englishman – charging for the platforms ahead.

John paused on his elevated position. From this vantage point, he watched the Englishman break out of the crowd into open space, all of the civilians having escaped the area. Identifying an opportunity for redemption, John raised his pistol. He recalled the conversation he had with himself in the Morris Minor after leaving Faulks Road, and his futile attempt to convince the condemning voice in his head that he could have shot one of the men.

John aimed the Walther at the Englishman's back and followed him as he ran. He saw the bright-orange target on Scotland Yard's firing range in his mind, and took a deep breath to steady his hand.

It was time to prove that voice wrong.

John exhaled and squeezed the trigger.

The bullet sailed wide and hit the floor in front of his fleeing target, who ducked his head at the sound of the gunshot but did not slow down.

John aimed again, further to the left, and fired a second round.

It too missed.

Fuck!

He cupped his right hand in his left, rooted his feet on the stone wall, and prepared himself for another attempt as the Englishman got ever further away.

Before he could fire, a third gunshot came from somewhere nearby, and the figure in the distance yelped and crumpled to the ground. John looked down to see Peter standing below him, lowering his smoking pistol.

Bastard.

With not a moment to spare for John to be embarrassed by his dismal shooting – that would wait until later – Peter instructed Arnold to see to the downed Englishman and told

John to follow him again as he set off in the direction of the Underground. This trouble with the Englishman had lasted not even ten seconds, so there was still ample time to catch up with his two accomplices. John was on Peter's heels almost before he finished giving the order.

From the station, the detectives bounced down a flight of steep concrete stairs that led to a long, white-tiled passageway, and John was hit by the sudden chill that was a permanent feature of all underground railway networks. Ahead of them, the two men reached the end of this passageway. Repeating their previous tactic, they split up, with one of them disappearing left around the corner, heading deeper into the Underground, whilst the other man went right, which led back towards the station platforms above.

Together, John and Peter hurtled along the passageway. When they came to the other end, in tandem they both rounded a corner each – John taking the left and Peter the right – but they pointed their weapons at empty spaces: the two men were nowhere to be seen.

John looked to Peter, and Peter nodded – his instruction was clear. Without either of them having spoken, Peter started up another set of stairs, and John continued further into the Underground.

With his pistol raised in front of him, John went along the tunnels at a cautious, jogging pace. Even though the Underground was like a maze, with passageways diverging sporadically in every direction, he found he was able to follow this man with ease: he just had to listen out for the cries of distress, which were made by the terrified commuters the man had left in his wake. These commuters all regarded John with the same fear when he passed them with his gun aloft.

It was then, as he scooted between these panicked men and women, that a disconcerting realisation came to John: he was in a foot chase with an undoubtedly armed man. A swell of anxiety bubbled in his mind, and the cautious voice in his head implored him to stop and think about how dangerous this was:

'Turn back!'

'Now!'

'This man will kill you.'

'What will Alice do if he does?'

John suppressed this agitation and marched onwards.

At this point, he had been in the Underground for no more than a minute. Up ahead, another indistinguishable tunnel stretched out before him, tiled in the same bright-white ceramic as all the others. A group of well-dressed, middle-aged men and women fled past John in the opposite direction, which reassured him that he was still on the man's trail. Here, the passageway led towards Platform 12, where it dropped down onto the train tracks in the distance.

The man is probably on the tracks already, John supposed with dismay. He would never catch him now.

John finished this thought as he stepped out onto Platform 12. He did not think to check whether the man was waiting around the corner for him this time, though, and consequently, his assailant's opening gambit came as a complete surprise: an unanticipated punch to the stomach knocked John off balance, then a second strike batted the PPK-L out of his hand and sent it rattling away across the platform.

Swiftly regaining a sense of composure, John faced his attacker in time to see the muzzle of a gun pointing at his head. He instinctively lashed out towards it. Although the weapon fired, and John heard a ringing in his ears, the bullet missed him, and a similar clatter indicated that he too had disarmed his opponent. John then landed a clenched fist against the man's jaw, which caused him to reel backwards and left them on an equal footing for the ensuing struggle.

It was the third man who had been waiting for him around the corner: the one who opened fire on them in the locker room only minutes before. He was shorter than John, but bulkier of build and a similar age. And whilst he was clean-shaven like his French companion, this man had a thick crop of black hair on his head.

None of this was of any great concern right now as the two men began to exchange a series of blows.

John had not been in a fistfight before. He had engaged in countless scuffles during his years as an officer of the Reich, usually whilst arresting a disagreeable thug, but a *real* fistfight had simply never occurred. It was fortuitous, then, that John discovered there and then on Platform 12 that he had a natural aptitude for the act: he was able to hold his own against the third man, and gave just as good as he got. Nevertheless, what he got was considerable, and after a short bout of this sparring, he was beginning to feel the effects of a third hit to the head.

John's decisive stroke was a lucky jab into his opponent's stomach, just below the sternum. When the third man stooped forwards as a result, John hit him hard in the cheek and sent him tumbling to the ground. On seeing an opportunity present itself, and not having lost sight of his Walther this entire time, John then made a desperate attempt to retrieve the pistol, his one and only lifeline. It was no more than a metre away, but as it turned out, the gun was far enough out of reach that John would not be able to take it from the floor *and* turn it on his assailant before the man could gather himself and give chase. Instead, when John scooped the pistol up and spun around, his arm already extended, the man ploughed into him with his shoulder, and the weapon discharged in John's hand before it was thrown from his grasp once again.

John only realised that he was on the platform's edge when it took him longer than a second to hit the ground. The third man had clearly not noticed their proximity to the edge either, and he sailed through the air along with John.

When John finally found the train tracks below, the impact almost knocked him unconscious. A high-pitched ringing echoed around his head. His vision went dark for a moment and was blurry when it returned. He let out a low, slow groan. His ribs were pressed hard against the metal rails, whilst the total weight of his assailant atop him left him breathless. Everything hurt.

The third man lay across him, rendered motionless by the fall. Summoning what little energy he could, John rolled the man onto his back and his lungs filled with oxygen again.

With great difficulty, and with a cough and a splutter, John stumbled to his knees and, without thinking, climbed on top of the third man. Evidently not being quite as unconscious as John had first thought, the man opened his eyes, and when he saw John looming over him, they were lit by dread. John seized a handful of his black hair, and the man clawed at John's face in a desperate attempt to fend him off; it was a feeble effort, however. John batted the limp hand away, and it fell back down onto the stones between the train tracks.

Having rendered him defenceless, John hoisted the man's head several centimetres from the ground, and then slammed it against the stones with all his strength.

Then he did it again.

And again.

And again.

The fifth time, the sheer exertion of the act became too much for John, and when the man's head thudded into the stones once more, John toppled over him and landed back down across the rails.

John lay there for what felt like a lifetime, his mouth filling with the taste of iron. Eventually, he gathered the resolve to move and began the long process of standing. His head throbbed, and every movement was an overwhelming struggle.

Once upright, John looked down at the man on the ground, but he was no longer a threat. The stones between the rails were wet with his blood, and his hollow eyes gazed back at John. He was dead.

Leaving the body where it was, John found his Walther amongst the train tracks. The once-shiny metal of the brand-new pistol was now all scuffed from being tossed about the platform, and there was a chip right in the tip of the muzzle.

Bloody fantastic.

John returned the weapon to the holster under his arm, not that being armed had done him any good all day. Then, he hobbled to the short ladder at the end of the platform and hoisted himself up it. There, he took a seat on a platform bench. He breathed shallowly through his sore ribs with the foreboding suspicion that something was broken, and stared at the floor.

In that instant, the fact that he was not dead was John's only prominent thought. Everything else – Yonder, Ramos, the leather satchel, and even the corpse on the train tracks below – fell to the back of his mind, and he focused on the sensation of being alive.

In pain, but alive.

Grunting as he did so, John stood up and started the journey back towards the surface.

*

Upon emerging into the dim daylight of the train station, John found Peter with not a scratch on him next to the broad-shouldered Frenchman, who was in handcuffs and surrounded by Arnold and a half-dozen uniformed police officers. The Englishman was gone, having been rushed away already in the back of an ambulance.

When Peter saw John's condition, he came straight to his side with an air of genuine worry. John was actually taken aback, not being accustomed to such compassion from the DI; that was until Peter asked irately what had happened to their final suspect, and it became apparent that this concern was reserved for the third man and not his injured colleague. John pointed Peter and the ever-present Arnold towards Platform 12, and they disappeared without so much as an 'Are you okay?'

A paramedic on the scene took John to one side and gave him the once over, checking his vision and patching up a cut above his eyebrow. He also examined John's ribs, an agonising process that confirmed nothing was broken, just badly bruised. He then gave John two painkillers and suggested that he would benefit from a proper assessment in a hospital. John dismissed the idea, and cradled his sore head in his hands.

Several minutes later, Peter and Arnold returned with dire expressions on both their faces.

'We were too late,' Peter told John.

John stared back at him, too tired for the pretence of confusion.

'The half past one train arrived at Platform 12 before we could get down there,' he explained.

It took John far longer than he would have liked to admit to figure out exactly what that meant.

CHAPTER ELEVEN

Concussion

'And now a shoot-out! In Göring Station! *Are you fucking insane?*'

This was the shrieking culmination of DCI Werner's tirade against John, Peter, and Arnold, and the accompanying DI Colbeck. 'One man dead and another in the hospital, and a bunch of bullet holes somebody is going to have to pay to fix!' As he stood behind his desk, DCI Werner's face was bright red, his eyes looked fit to burst out of his skull, and his hands were clenched into tight, enraged fists on the wood. 'Commissioner Krüger has already been on the telephone. He wants a full report from the three of you before you do anything else.'

John felt that the DCI was overlooking the significance of their actions at Göring Station, as he so often did. They had recovered the leather satchel from the locker room after the chase, with its contents intact, and the DES now had the Englishman and the Frenchman in custody. And these were not any old dealers either, but two men who must have been very close to Ramos. True, the link between Antonio Ramos

Serrano / Miguel Carrasco Menéndez and Yonder remained tentative, but it was so patently apparent he was involved in something nefarious that his connection to James Summers' warehouse was all the proof John needed for now to continue the investigation into the man. Besides, if the black-and-white photograph from the satchel did turn out to be from the Spanish Civil War, then the prospect of him being The Spaniard would be undeniable.

John would have gladly explained all of this to DCI Werner, but he knew his rank did not permit him to speak right now.

'You give me nothing but excuses for weeks, and then when you *finally* start to accomplish something, you embarrass me like this!' chided the DCI. The shrill German accent gave a gravitas to his accusations that made John uncomfortable. Plus, when he said they had embarrassed *him* specifically – and neither the Metropolitan Police nor the DES – it offered an unfavourable indication of the man's priorities.

DCI Werner waved a hand at John, Peter, and Arnold. 'You three get out. Write up your reports and have them on my desk within the hour. Detective Inspector' – he pointed at DI Colbeck – 'you stay where you are.' The way the younger man spoke to DI Colbeck irritated John; he had obviously never been taught to respect his elders – the jumped-up little bastard.

Having been dismissed, John, Peter, and Arnold raised their right arms in salute and stood to attention. When DCI Werner sat down and refused to acknowledge them any further, however, they exited his office in a silent single file.

*

Sometime later, John was sitting at his desk. He was working tiredly at the Imperial Model 50, as he tried to concentrate through the most intense headache he had ever experienced. Each click and clack of the typewriter's keys was excruciating, and the usually subtle hum of the office was so acute that it scrambled his mind to the point he could barely think straight.

In an attempt to clear his head, John turned away from the typewriter, lit a Reemtsma, and took a long lungful of smoke. This was followed by a fit of uncontrollable and painful coughing, and he ended up doubled over at the desk.

He put a hand to his sore ribs and grimaced.

After returning gingerly to an upright position, John placed the cigarette between his lips and leant back on the uncomfortable desk chair. He regarded Peter on the other side of the office, typing away as if he had not a care in the world; he would likely be finished in half the time John was. And Arnold was yet to even begin his report, amusing himself instead by talking merrily to another DES detective.

They seemed so unconcerned by everything that had happened.

In considerable agony, John continued with his own report. After briefly recounting his visit to 27 Faulks Road – he saw no need to describe in much detail how he had hidden from the Englishman and the Frenchman – he moved on to the events at Göring Station: 'Detective Inspector Baer and I examined the contents of the locker whilst Detective Sergeant List watched the two suspects. That was when the third individual appeared and opened fire. We chased the three men through the train station, and when they were clear of the crowd, Detective Inspector Baer and I opened fire in an attempt to subdue one of them.' John had never considered himself much of a wordsmith, and he struggled to get the ink onto the page.

John almost hit "I" on the typewriter then, before he remembered that it was not he who had shot the Englishman.

He had missed.

Twice.

Idiot.

It was the bloody PPK-L! John had known this would happen; the first time he had cause to fire his weapon outside of the firing range, and he missed. *I would have hit the Englishman at double that distance with my old PPK,* he stubbornly exaggerated to himself.

Grumbling under his breath in embarrassed petulance, John resumed tapping at the keys: 'Detective Inspector Baer hit the suspect. We left Detective Sergeant List on the scene to detain him, and Detective Inspector Baer and I went after the remaining two suspects. I followed one of them into the Underground and Detective Inspector Baer chased the other man onto the station platforms.'

John stopped abruptly mid-paragraph. He had not thought about the Underground since leaving Göring Station, and he had refused to address what occurred on Platform 12. But as the words on the page approached what would transpire down there, amongst the white-tiled walls and between the metal train tracks, it all came rushing to the forefront of his mind, and the reality of his actions became unavoidable.

He had killed someone.

In the line of duty, and in self-defence, but still: he had taken a life for the first time, and he did not know how to feel about it.

Was this something to be proud of? Peter often bragged about the men he had killed as an officer of the Reich, tales in which he was the brave hero fighting against the enemies of the State. But sitting at his desk, thinking about how he had smashed the third man's head against those stones over and over again, John did not feel heroic, or brave, or proud.

In all honesty, he mostly felt guilty. He had killed a man – a man who was perhaps someone's husband or even someone's father, people who would now be wondering where he was. And he was young too, or at least no older than John, so his having been manipulated as a boy was self-evident; be it by his parents, older "friends", or Ramos himself, John would never know. Those his age who were conditioned by the enemies of National Socialism could never truly be held accountable for their distorted beliefs, John had always thought. He had been lucky to find himself under the guidance of the State in his youth, but for those who were left vulnerable to the depraved philosophies of Imperialists or Communists, their eventual corruption was inevitable. John never did share this opinion with any of his colleagues – it would be considered weak of him to feel such empathy – but it was individuals such as the third man who had been lost to the enemy long before they were ever given a chance to prove themselves valuable members of the Third Reich.

And now this man was dead, and the blood was on John's hands.

As those words came to him, John looked down at his hands, and his stomach turned: they were red and sticky and covered in what looked like blood.

That's impossible. There had been none of the third man's blood *literally* on his hands. He would have noticed otherwise, and he was certain he had washed them in the hours since leaving Göring Station. John closed his eyes tight, and told himself he was exhausted and it was just his imagination. He took several deep breaths and tried to settle his now racing heart.

His whole body shivered. He was cold, as if he were down in the Underground again, skulking along those endless, twisting tunnels.

He opened his eyes, feeling calmer after a moment's respite.

This calm did not last long when he glanced down again, only to find that his hands were still red and the blood was even darker and thicker than before.

Fuck.

Am I going mad?

In an effort to escape this disturbing vision, John placed his hands out of sight on the desk and fixed his gaze on the maroon carpet below. There was something down there, though, something in amongst the shadows at his feet. It was round. Or roundish, anyway.

John squinted and tried to make out what it was.

Suddenly, a set of eyes glowed in the darkness, and a head appeared in the void underneath his desk. The face of the third man materialised upon it, and he glared up at John with a piercing ire. 'You murdered me,' he accused, but his lips did not move.

Now outright unnerved, John leapt up from his chair. He cast his eyes across the office. The pressure in his head was so tremendous that his vision became blurred, the shapes around him distorted and warped, and the office drone intensified into a wall of insufferable, interminable noise.

He had to get out of that room.

Recalling the only corner of Scotland Yard in which he had ever achieved more than a second to himself, John staggered out into the hallway and headed in the direction of the fifth-floor WC.

The fluorescent lights in the corridor did nothing to help his current distress. Beneath their torturous glare, John's headache worsened considerably, and bright specks appeared before his eyes as he stumbled forwards.

He saw those white, ceramic passageways in his mind, and the path leading out onto Platform 12.

John tumbled through the door of the WC and was just about able to keep himself steady against the wall. From there, he lurched across the room to the washbasin and ran the hot tap. The porcelain turned a dark red, and John scrubbed furiously at his hands under the water, trying to wash the imaginary blood from between his fingers.

His head was a cavalcade of extraordinary pain. Each time a particularly brutal throb arched across his skull, John would feel the impact of the third man's fist against it.

He looked into the mirror over the sink: through dizzy tunnel vision he saw a pale, sickly face gazing back.

And then John remembered that moment when the third man had tackled him as he stood on the edge of Platform 12, and the terrible panic that consumed him as he was lifted over the side. In his dizziness, he experienced again a sensation of falling, falling, falling backwards, and his whole body tensed in anticipation of the back-breaking impact against the train tracks.

It never came, and John was left to plummet into an endless abyss, descending evermore into the cold, dark madness of his mind.

Back in reality, John burst into one of the WC's stalls, dropped to his knees, and vomited violently into the toilet.

Afterwards, he slumped against the wall and closed his eyes.

*

'John?' A voice sounded close by.

'*John!*'

John opened his eyes to see a worried DI Colbeck standing at the threshold of the stall.

'Are you okay?' DI Colbeck asked, and he placed a gentle hand on John's shoulder.

John nodded. His head was clear now, as if somebody had pulled the plug and all of the filth had drained out of it. He looked at his hands, and although they were still a shade of red, it was pink from the minor scalding as a result of the hot water, and not imagined blood.

With DI Colbeck's help, John climbed to his feet, hit the flush on the toilet, and watched the evidence of what had occurred here disappear. He then went back to the washbasin, rested against it, and took several slow, calculated breaths.

'It is all right, John,' DI Colbeck reassured him in a sympathetic tone. 'You did good work today. You have done the Reich proud.'

John's response to this statement was an audible scoff. It was involuntary, but even so, he understood where the reaction came from: the waking nightmare he had just endured, reliving what took place in the Underground, was still fresh in his mind, whilst that guilt he felt over killing the third man had not vanished down the toilet with his vomit. To make matters worse, this trip to the WC had only exacerbated the aching in his ribs. Right now, John felt sorry for himself, and being told he had done the Reich a service with his exploits was not what he wanted to hear. Usually, he would not have been so careless as to display such an emotion openly – and especially in front of a superior officer – but in his rattled and tired state, the sentiment had slipped out.

John regretted it instantly.

DI Colbeck noticed this sneer, of course. He crossed the room and stopped opposite John, his kind face now serious. 'It may seem unlikely at the moment, but one day you will think back on what happened this afternoon and you will remember what it was that you did for your Reich.' His tone was near scolding, and John could have sworn the DI's accent thickened as his passion intensified. 'We must all make sacrifices for the well-being of the State. I have been shot three times in defence of it myself – once on the Eastern Front and twice since I joined the Metropolitan Police – and I wear each scar with honour. And I have killed people – men and women, individuals who conspired to harm the Reich. It is often an awful decision to make, yet it is nevertheless a necessary one.' DI Colbeck pointed at him. 'The sacrifice you made today is what is expected of you, John. You missed those men at Ramos's house, but now you have righted that mistake. You fought for the values of National Socialism, and you almost died defending them.' He grabbed John's arm and leant in closer: 'You should be proud of that pain you feel, because it is evidence of what *you* have done – in the name of the Reich!'

John was speechless. He had not expected DI Colbeck's change in demeanour, but he knew the DI was correct. He should not have been feeling sorry for himself: he should have been feeling honoured. Some men travelled halfway across the world to the Eastern Front to serve the Reich, and many of them would never achieve what he had done on Platform 12 that afternoon. As for the sympathy he had experienced for the third man – that bordered on irresponsible. Although the man may very well have fallen victim to bad influences in his youth, his choices were still his own, and he chose to oppose the Reich. Therefore, John should feel nothing even akin to guilt for having killed him. In its place, that guilt gave way to a profound sensation of triumph.

'Thank you, sir,' was all he could think to say.

DI Colbeck smiled. His expression reverted to one of benevolence, and his amber eyes softened.

John was all of a sudden reassured about his entire existence.

'It is your day off tomorrow, is it not?' DI Colbeck asked, changing the subject.

'It is, sir.'

'Good. Spend some time with your family and come back whole on Sunday. We need you here in good shape.' DI Colbeck patted him firmly on the shoulder, and a slight grin broke out on John's weary face. 'When you have finished your report, give it to me, and I shall pass it to Werner,' he said with what sounded like distaste at the name. 'Then you go home and get a proper night's sleep.'

'I will, sir. Thank you,' was once again all John could muster.

DI Colbeck nodded, and exited the WC without another word.

John remained there long enough to rinse from his mouth the sour taste of vomit, before he returned to the DES office. DI Colbeck was already there, but he did not acknowledge John when he entered the room, their conversation never having happened as far as anybody else was concerned.

After sitting himself at his desk, John realised he had been gone for only ten minutes, although the experience felt much longer. Wasting not another second, he got back to the task at hand and was soon scrawling his signature at the bottom of the completed report.

'Goodnight, sir,' John stated in a professional monotone when he handed it to DI Colbeck.

'Goodnight, Detective Sergeant,' DI Colbeck replied at a similar pitch, maintaining their shared pretence.

With short farewells to Alfie and Alex – Zeigler was not present, and Peter and Arnold had departed with the intention of heading down to The Basement for a "visit" with the

Frenchman – John left the DES office, surprisingly satisfied with how this day had concluded.

*

Alice called out to him with delight when she heard John step through the front door before six o'clock in the evening for a change, although this soon became concern once she saw his bruised face. He had decided he would tell Alice everything, from his hiding in the wardrobe at 27 Faulks Road to the fistfight on Platform 12, and not only because he refused to lie to her about his injuries, but also because it would help to keep him sane. He needed to talk it through with someone who had nothing but compassion for him – someone who would share his pain.

Alice did just that: she sat there and held him tight as he spoke, not questioning his actions and not doubting his performance, but just listening.

When John came to the climax of his day, however, he realised he was hesitant to tell Alice about what happened on the train tracks below Platform 12. What if she thought different of him now? What if she did not want her child to be around a killer? John had come to terms with it himself after what DI Colbeck said, but what if Alice did not see it the same way?

He need not have worried. Whilst Alice was shocked by the death of the third man (she burst into tears at the thought of her husband fighting for his life, and it took her a moment to compose herself again), she was quick to reassure him that what he had done was justified. 'If he was who you say he was, then he deserved nothing less,' was her final, candid take on the matter.

John also described to her the incident in the fifth-floor WC. 'You probably have a concussion,' was Alice's diagnosis. He was lying on the couch with a cold flannel across his forehead, and she had been pressing down on each of his ribs individually until she was satisfied for herself that nothing was broken.

John and Alice ate dinner together, then they retired to the couch to watch the television. By eight o'clock, John was finding it difficult to keep his eyes open, and when Alice noticed, she took him by the hand and led him to bed.

As he lay there, wrapped in his wife's tender embrace, John found that the prevailing sentiment in his mind was one of neither guilt nor honour, nor triumph, but relief: relief that he was not dead, and that he would still be able to watch his daughter grow up beside Alice.

John fell asleep in her arms, and he did not stir until his alarm sounded at half past six the next morning.

CHAPTER TWELVE

Saturday

It was a welcome change to be heading out of the city, leaving the noise behind for fresh air and open roads, especially given recent events. Mark, Alice's brother, lived in Hertford, a quaint little town an hour's drive from Acton, which was far enough away from Scotland Yard that John hoped to put the Yonder investigation to one side, even for a short while.

Alice had been hesitant as to whether he should be driving at all after his fall, never mind for nigh on an hour, but John convinced her that he felt fine so long as nobody touched the lump that now protruded from the back of his head. Anyway, he would be back in work tomorrow, so he would just have to persevere. Alice was more uncertain still about that, but John tried to dismiss her concerns: he had to return to work, as another day away might mean slowing the progress the Yonder Task Force was making, and he did not want to be responsible for the consequences should that happen.

In the Morris Minor, their baby's name was the hot topic, and whilst John and Alice traded suggestions – Janice, Barbara,

Harriet, Lauren – none sat right with the two of them. John suggested Eva, but Alice thought it a bit on the nose. After a brief reflection, John agreed.

Alice soon drifted off to sleep (this late stage of pregnancy was draining what little energy she had left), so John turned on the radio to drown out his lingering inner thoughts. Dieter and Judy were in the middle of a conversation with a caller, something about a neighbour's dog that frequently escaped into their back garden. John only half-listened to the chatter. With one hand on the steering wheel, he cruised absent-mindedly down Autobahn 17 at 100 kilometres per hour, with London having long receded into the rear-view mirror.

The discussion ended with some advice about confronting the neighbour. 'It's ten o'clock,' announced Judy in her pristine English accent, 'and time for a round-up of the news for you this morning.'

John turned up the volume, and Judy spoke again. 'Our top story: a date has been set for the seventh Greenland Conference, at which the Führer is scheduled to meet with President John F. Kennedy and Emperor Akihito for the first time since he became the "Führer of the Third Reich" earlier this year. The Führer is reported to have said that he is excited to meet his fellow world leaders, and that he is determined to preserve the strong relationship established by the Ewige Führer and their respective countries in an effort to maintain world harmony. The conference is set to take place in Nuuk on the 18th of March next year. It is expected that the key points of discussion will be trade relations and a continued commitment to atomic non-proliferation amongst the three powers.'

'I am sure you know, Judy,' Dieter added in his heavy German inflection, 'that it was the fathers of President Kennedy and Emperor Akihito – President Joseph P. Kennedy and

Emperor Hirohito – who met with the Ewige Führer for the first-ever Greenland Conference in 1945. I think I speak for all of us when I say that it will be *wunderbar* to see the children of The Big Three continue the current trend of peace and prosperity, particularly in light of the passing of our beloved Ewige Führer.'

Judy confirmed that he did in fact speak for all of them.

The news continued from there for several stories, and then it came to what John was listening out for, buried in the middle of the segment. 'A brief pursuit in Göring Station yesterday afternoon involving the Metropolitan Police meant the transport hub was closed to the public until early this morning. The Ministry of Transport has apologised for any inconvenience this caused commuters, and it says all services are now fully operational again. The incident ended with the arrest of the suspects in question, and no one was injured. We applaud the Metropolitan Police for their dedication to keeping us, the citizens of the Third Reich, safe from harm.'

And that was it: the whole ordeal was explained away in less than thirty seconds. Sure, rumours would circulate from those who were present about what "really" happened, but one would debunk another, with two stories never the same – for the majority, this account on the radio would be considered factual. The 'incident' and to what it pertained to was not the sort of thing the government permitted for open discussion in the media.

The news segment came to an end, and Dieter finished by saying, 'We will leave you for now with the latest hit record from Miss Sandra Goodrich.'

The music started to play, and John relaxed into his seat, encouraged by the fact that at least the radio personalities were pleased with their exploits in Göring Station.

Shortly afterwards, John was driving through Hertford. Being one of the few areas in this part of England to survive the war without a scratch, there were still old-English stone buildings dotted about the town. This architecture always fascinated John, as a reminder of the nation's humble past before the imperialistic nature of more recent generations had corrupted it. The newly built houses out here were impressive as well, though John admitted only to himself that he thought this largely out of jealousy: Mark's home was far grander than his and Alice's, with two extra bedrooms and a considerable garden out the back for their children to play in – it was a castle compared to Pullman Road.

When John pulled into the driveway, Jane – Mark's wife – appeared on the front step. She was several years older than both John and Alice, but it showed only in the faintest of wrinkles at the corners of her eyes and mouth; Jane had never had a grey hair in all the time John had known her, and her skin had a suspiciously youthful glow to it.

The youngest child of the family, Isabelle, was waiting eagerly at her mother's side, and as soon as the Morris Minor came to a halt, she darted out towards Alice's opening door.

'Hello Izzy,' Alice said as she embraced the girl. She spoke in the delicate tone of voice she had used with children when they were on her ward at the hospital – it was a caring, reassuring tenor.

'Hi Uncle John!' Isabelle exclaimed when she saw him walking around the front of the car.

'Hey Izzy!' he replied with perhaps too much enthusiasm. John was not as good with children as was Alice. He always felt awkward around them – in particular, the younger ones –

and was never sure what to say or how to act. He just hoped it would come naturally to him when his own child was born.

John and Alice followed Isabelle back to her mother, and they both greeted Jane with a kiss on the cheek and a hug. Then, the four of them entered the house. The décor inside was astutely modern, due to Jane having a keen eye for detail: the walls in the hallway were a pale and clean blue, and a dark wooden banister ran up along beige-carpeted stairs to the first floor. Next to the front door, a glass vase stood with a bouquet of colourful flowers on a seemingly constant rotation; at least, the flowers were always there whenever John and Alice visited. Ahead down the hallway was the kitchen, with its bright-white surfaces and shining metallic appliances.

Jane led the way into the living room through a door on the left, where Mark and their middle child, Alfred, were sitting on the couch. It was a long and spacious room decorated in a dark floral pattern, and a tall bay window at the far end looked out on the front garden. In the corner, the largest television set John had ever seen outside an electronics shop was lit up with the bright colours of Saturday morning cartoons. Currently, a popular show about a Third Reich battalion that fought to foil evil Communist schemes played across the screen.

As they entered the living room, Mark welcomed John and Alice, with a big hug for Alice and a sturdy handshake for John. At thirty-nine, he was considerably older than his younger sister – or half-sister, as Alice actually was, with Mark having been born to their mother's first husband. Unlike his wife, Mark was showing his years, with greying hair at his temples and the sagging features of a man on the cusp of middle age. John and Alice said hello to Alfred as well, but the boy was not listening, engrossed instead by the flashing images on the television. The four adults shared a laugh about this, then John followed Mark into the kitchen whilst Alice went out onto the patio with Jane; the weather was mild this morning, and they intended to make the most of it.

Mark flicked the switch on their electric kettle, and it burst into life. 'So, how's work?' he asked, and he pottered about, fetching mugs and milk. It was idle chit-chat, and the exact sort of thing that would be discussed over the course of the day: work, the weather, current affairs, the children, and a film or television programme of some description, perhaps. John could hear Alice and Jane outside talking about the final weeks of Alice's pregnancy – an easy topic of conversation to relieve any initial awkward silences.

'It's fine,' John replied to the question in a trite manner. 'Stressful. Late hours.'

Mark pointed with a teaspoon to the cut above John's eyebrow. 'Perk of the job?' he enquired sarcastically.

'You could say that.' John forced a laugh. 'A suspect got a little rough, and I took the brunt of it,' he explained with caution. The line was much clearer with Mark and Jane than it was with Alice: they were to know no details about his work, no matter how trivial. 'How are things at the bank?' he asked, shifting the focus away from his own profession.

'So-so,' Mark answered as he readied a pot for the tea. It was his toils for the Reichsbank that had earnt him this house in the countryside, and John would often come away questioning his career choices after paying Mark and Jane a visit. 'We have a couple of people off sick with this flu that's going around, and we're a bit stretched for staff until they come back,' Mark elaborated.

John acknowledged that this must be difficult. For the Task Force, losing DI Russell to the flu had made the Yonder investigation significantly more demanding.

'Listen, I need to talk to you about something.' Mark's voice fell to a whisper, and it became uncomfortably evident that he had no intention of discussing the ins and outs of the financial sector. 'This drug, Yonder – apparently, some kid in the city killed his friends whilst he was on it.' Mark tipped the boiled water into the teapot. 'Someone at work heard about it, and he said the boy was only three or four years older than Mark Jr.' He set the kettle down and turned to face John. 'What's going on? Do you know anything? Should we be worried?' he concluded with an unexpected onslaught of questions.

John's blood ran cold. Had the news of these deaths really circulated so quickly? It always shocked him whenever someone outside the DES mentioned Yonder, but given the drug's rampant popularity across Great Britain, it was only to be expected that it would have become a cause of major unease for regular citizens like Mark and Jane. And now, with the deaths of Jennifer Campbell's teenage friends, it was also natural for them to be worried for the safety of their own children. Mark and Jane did not know that John worked in the DES, though, just that he was a detective sergeant for the Metropolitan Police, and therefore they had no idea it was in part his fault this situation had become so dire.

In any case, John feigned ignorance on the whole subject. 'I'm not told much about that sort of thing, to be honest,' he lied.

Mark started to pour the brown liquid into the mismatched mugs. 'Well, you'd better tell whoever does handle it to get their act together, because it's a fucking nightmare.' He added milk to the tea. 'Is that okay for you?' He gestured towards a mug.

'Perfect,' John replied, downright sick to his stomach.

No more was said about the looming drug problem when the two men joined Alice and Jane on the patio. Instead, the four of them made jokes and laughed and told stories about this and that, basking in the pleasant winter sunshine.

John sat uneasy in the garden chair the entire time, his back and ribs sore against the hardwood; however, he affected a cheery disposition. Mark's faultless assessment that the Yonder situation was a 'fucking nightmare' tormented him, and he struggled to concentrate on what was being said. He was distracted by thoughts of Jennifer Campbell and her friends, and of the other misguided individuals who might be falling victim to this drug whilst he sat sipping tea. An image of that pink bedroom flashed before his eyes, and in his still-throbbing head, John could almost hear the sound of the teenage girl sobbing downstairs. He cursed Mark for reminding him of that house, even though he knew full well that his questions stemmed from a concern for his family. Perhaps if the parents of those teenagers had also been so concerned, their children would still be alive.

Several cups of tea later, John was taken by the need to relieve himself. He happily took his leave – the conversation had progressed to Alice and Mark's mother, a topic for which John had no particular fondness – and headed upstairs to the bathroom. It was then, during this moment of solitude, that he realised there had been neither sight nor sound today of Mark Jr, the eldest child of the family. So, with little desire to return to the patio just yet, upon exiting the bathroom, John decided he would invade on the boy's privacy and see how he was faring.

John crossed the landing and stopped in front of a door, and he rapped softly on it.

A young voice called, 'Come in.'

On the other side of the door was a bedroom John would have cherished as a boy. Several self-assembly plastic Second

Great War aircraft, painted with a steady but unpractised hand, were suspended from the ceiling with string, and a series of tiny metal soldiers in various Third Reich military uniforms stood to attention atop a tall chest of drawers, keeping watch over the room. Next to the bed, a bookcase was stacked with adolescent fiction, all with names like *Our Fatherland*, *A Man of the Volk*, and *Son of the Reich* on their spines – a genre of literature that had become increasingly popular over the past decade. A dog-eared copy of *Mein Kampf* lay on top of the bookcase; it was the English version that had been adapted specifically for teenagers so they might follow the intellectual material more easily. Hanging on the front of a wardrobe was a Hitler Youth uniform, comprised of the traditional tan shirt with a black neckerchief and shorts, together with a black leather belt and what was no doubt its owner's most prized possession: a Hitler Youth knife.

Fourteen-year-old Mark Jr, in a short-sleeved shirt and shorts, sat cross-legged on the bed, his head resting in his hands, reading a book.

'Hey, Mark,' John said to make his presence known.

Mark Jr looked up, smiling, and replied, 'Hi, Uncle John.'

John had always got along with his eldest nephew, and even more so now that he was old enough to hold an actual conversation.

'What're you reading?' John asked.

Mark Jr lifted the book for him to see the front cover: *Beware the Man with the Red Star*.

John knew it well. It was an older title from the late 1940s, about a Kriminalpolizei detective in mid-1930s Berlin who was hunting down a Communist spy. 'That was one of my favourites when I was your age,' he declared.

'I like it, but it's a little bit old now.'

'Well, just like me, then,' John claimed with a chuckle.

Mark Jr laughed as well, the ice now broken.

'How's school going?' That was John's go-to topic of conversation with any child, even one as old as Mark Jr.

'It's okay, but I'm struggling with maths,' Mark Jr admitted reluctantly. John noticed a mathematics textbook on the floor next to the bed, likely discarded there in frustration.

'Don't worry, I was never any good at maths either,' John confessed, and the two of them shared another smile. Mark Jr was an intelligent boy, but doing badly at school in any subject would be more than enough to dissuade him of such, especially at his age. John would gladly reassure him that it was not the end of the world.

Not wanting to dwell on the matter, John pointed at the uniform on the wardrobe. 'Do you have Hitler Youth tomorrow?'

'I do!' Mark Jr perked up at the notion.

'Any idea what you'll be doing?'

'They said last week that we'd be going for a march in the woods and learning how to start a campfire, if it isn't raining.' He frowned at the possibility.

'The forecast is for clear skies, so you might just be in luck!' John stated, and the boy's face lit up with delight.

John recalled his own hikes through the woods with the Hitler Youth, usually with Lewis at his side, singing marching anthems such as 'The Rotten Bones Are Trembling' – they were amongst his happiest memories from his childhood.

'So how have *you* been, Mark?' John asked, prolonging his time away from the patio.

'Okay, I guess…' Mark Jr left a long pause after his answer, as though he wanted to say something else, but he could not quite make up his mind whether he should.

'You guess?' John probed, troubled by this reticence, but Mark Jr just nodded. In an attempt to coax this "something" out of him, John sat down on the edge of the bed next to the boy and nudged him. 'Come on. What's bothering you?'

Evidently deciding that John could be trusted, Mark Jr told him: 'I can hear Mum and Dad talking in their room sometimes. Last night, they were talking about a boy who killed some of his friends. Dad sounded really worried.' He scratched at his arm. 'I would have asked who the boy was and what happened, but Dad doesn't want us asking about that sort of thing. He says it's not something children should worry about.' The boy, or more a young adult now, was disheartened by the prospect of still being treated like a child.

John swore – to himself, of course – understanding right away to which 'boy' Mark Jr alluded. It seemed that he would not be able to avoid the spectre of Yonder at all today.

John felt compelled to respond to this intimate revelation, but exactly how he should do so was not that straightforward. The simplest option would be to lie to Mark Jr and claim he had heard nothing about this boy's death. Or he could agree with his father, say that Mark Jr need not worry about such matters at his age, and leave it there. But then John remembered Jennifer Campbell's tearful account of how her friends had attempted to pressure her into trying Yonder, and how they thought taking it would be 'fun'; whilst he did not think for one second that Mark Jr was so gullible as to fall for such nonsense, peer pressure could be a dangerous obstacle for a teenager, and he felt duty-bound to make certain his nephew understood the severity of the situation.

'The boy took drugs, Mark,' John revealed at last.

Mark Jr's eyes widened in surprise.

'He and his friends – the ones he hurt. They thought it would be fun, but the boy reacted badly, and, well...' John did not need to finish that sentence. Instead, he continued to the crux of this talk: 'That's not the type of boy the Reich needs, Mark. To be a valued member of society, you must be better than boys like that: boys who think they're above the laws set down by the State. Because they cannot defy the State, and like all criminals – traitors, thieves, murderers, *and* drug users – sooner or later they all end up the same way: dead.'

To ensure that his point had been made, John added: 'Promise me, Mark, that if you ever hear anybody at school talking this way about *anything*, not just drugs, you'll report them immediately.'

Mark Jr nodded and promised he would do just that. Then he stared down at his bed, lost in thought.

There was no need to mention the broader crisis surrounding Yonder and what it stood for, John decided, as Mark Jr's father was correct in that aspect: someone so young did not need to worry about it.

That was John's burden to shoulder.

Then, out of nowhere, Mark Jr asked, 'Did your dad not talk to you about this stuff either?'

Somehow, John swore to himself louder this time, and he rebuked the inquisitive nature of the boy.

As before, a lie would be the least complicated way out of this quagmire, he knew. But when Mark Jr looked up, and John saw a burning desire for the truth in his brilliant, blue eyes, he found that he could think of little reason to hide it from him. 'My father died in the war when I was young. Younger than Izzy,' he explained.

Mark Jr sat bolt upright, suddenly interested. The war would be a thing of intrigue for him at his age: a defining moment in history when Great Britain had been salvaged from the ashes of its past by National Socialism. 'Did he fight against the Imperialists?' he asked, captivated.

John sighed. 'No, Mark, he fought on the wrong side. And so did my mother. She died in the war as well, and I grew up in a boarding school.' It was the same story for most of the boys in the boarding school, as it was for many children across Great Britain at that time. He had no recollection whatsoever of his parents, but then he preferred it that way if he were being honest with himself. To think about them fighting against National Socialism, the vanguard of liberation that not only saved Europe from ruin but also raised him as its own in their absence, had always caused John a deep resentment.

'Oh,' was Mark Jr's blunt response to this admission. He was visibly disappointed by the answer.

John was silent, consumed for an instant by this old bitterness. Then, realising that Mark Jr was still looking at him, he said, 'But *your* father is a good man, Mark, and you should be proud of him.' John placed a hand on Mark Jr's shoulder, and whilst he thought it might have been too much, the boy seemed comforted by the gesture.

With that, their conversation came to an end, and John left Mark Jr to his book.

He returned to the patio, and when he was met with the inevitable question of what had taken him so long, John smiled and said, 'Oh, I was just talking to Mark about school and Hitler Youth, and whatnot.'

*

Eventually, the visit itself also ended, and with long goodbyes and promises to do it all again soon, John and Alice began the drive home.

In the car, John told Alice about his conversation with Mark Jr, more out of guilt than anything else. It was not his place to give the boy such advice as he had, that being Mark's job, and even more so when it was something Mark Jr knew his father considered too mature for him. Always a source of great comfort, Alice placed her hand on his arm and reassured him that he was correct to have put the boy's worries to rest. She knew her brother would never do so, and if John had not done it, who else would have?

John did not mention the subsequent discussion he and Mark Jr had about his own parents; he had lamented long enough on that sore subject for one day. Besides, Alice was never truly able to appreciate this sentiment of unchecked resentment. Whilst her father fought in the war against the Reich as well, he survived, and like so many others, he was able to pay back his debt to society afterwards. He had worked in one of London's many factories up until his death seven years ago, and was therefore one of the millions who were instrumental in transforming Great Britain into the Industrial Jewel of the Third Reich. Alice was at least able to admire the choices her father made after the fighting, then.

John's parents had found no such redemption.

They had just died, deluded and misled.

CHAPTER THIRTEEN

The Ninth Floor

John entered a sombre DES office the next morning. As the only other member of the Yonder Task Force present, it was left to Alex to inform him that, the previous afternoon, DI Jeremy Russell – the only detective in the DES to have been taken ill with the flu as yet – had succumbed to his symptoms. Such a sudden death would have been a shock under any circumstances, but for DI Russell – a perfectly healthy man in his forties – to have been killed by so commonplace an ailment was quite unbelievable. John was disappointed in himself, then, when he was stricken by an immediate relief that it was not he who had caught this apparently deadly virus. He knew it was a natural instinct to be thankful that he was well, but even so, it was an uncomfortable sensation in light of the situation.

In the succeeding awkward silence at Alex's desk – he had nothing of value to say in response to this news – John lit a cigarette, and after the appropriate moment, he clumsily manoeuvred the conversation towards the Yonder investigation and what he had missed yesterday.

Regarding the contents of the leather satchel from the locker at Göring Station, Alex revealed that John's assumption had been confirmed: the photograph of the men dressed in military uniform indeed depicted Communist soldiers in the Spanish Civil War – it had been identified as such by an expert on the matter. Not only that, but the medal found alongside the photograph was the Order of the Spanish Republic, an honour awarded to only a select few for their ill-advised efforts on the Communist side during the Spanish Civil War, a fact that gave credence to Ramos's status as an enemy of the Spanish state.

John blew smoke from his cigarette up towards the ceiling. Given that they now knew for certain Ramos had fought in the Spanish Civil War for the Communists, and bearing this in mind alongside his ability to smuggle Yonder into London from abroad through *Delicias Inspiradas* via Summers' Import and Export, Joe Harding's rumoured account of The Spaniard fit him to the letter. Alex added that he had put in a request to Customs for the records on Ramos's produce company – including receipts, the British cities into which he imported, employees, and permits – but he conceded with a shrug that the man on the telephone told him this enquiry could take anything up to several days to process.

Whilst this was all promising progress, John moderated his expectations. That Ramos was a criminal was no longer in question, and at some point in the near future a call would be put out nationwide for his arrest for possession of a falsified ID card if nothing else. Still, whether he had anything to do with the Yonder Organisation remained up for debate.

In a hushed tone, Alex then told John about Peter's latest activities. Yesterday, Peter and Arnold were sent by DI Colbeck to visit the Englishman, whose name they now knew was

Jasper Jones, in London State Hospital. Jones was in a critical condition after being shot by Peter in Göring Station, however, with the bullet having punctured his right lung, and whilst Peter and Arnold waited all morning, there were complications in surgery, and in the end, they left without talking to him. So, for now, Jones was useless to them.

That left the Frenchman as their only interrogable suspect, who turned out not to be a Frenchman at all, but a Belgian named Sebastien Dubois. According to Alex, following their return from the hospital, Peter and Arnold spent all of yesterday afternoon in The Basement with the man, but Peter was frustrated when he surfaced in the evening, and Arnold had informed Alex that Dubois remained utterly unbreakable. Peter had already left for The Basement again that morning, just before John arrived, impatient to continue his work.

John tried not to imagine what was happening down there, but he hoped it would yield something more significant than bruises and blood.

Presently, DI Colbeck stepped out of DCI Werner's office, with a sullen expression etched upon his face. John had never seen him so downbeat before. After the Yonder Task Force's public display in Göring Station, DCI Werner had no doubt taken to belittling his DI with much greater ferocity than usual – from the safety of his big desk in his little office, of course. That would likely be a daily vilification now, and John could not help but feel responsible.

'Detective Sergeant Highsmith.' Looking up, DI Colbeck had noticed him, and he crossed the room towards John.

John stiffened. Some men would channel abuse from a superior down the chain to their subordinates, and he was not confident he would be able to withstand a berating from DI Colbeck in front of his fellow detectives. But DI Colbeck was not "some men", and instead, he asked, 'How are you feeling?' with genuine concern when he stopped next to Alex's desk. That impression of dismay had already disappeared; the DI's moment of despair was swallowed up by his unwavering professionalism.

'I'm fine, sir. Ready to get back to it,' John replied, alluding as much to his physical state as to his state of mind. He vividly recalled their conversation in the fifth-floor WC on Friday and was embarrassed in hindsight for his childish reaction to what had occurred in the Underground beneath Göring Station.

DI Colbeck nodded and said no more about it.

Actually, he changed the subject entirely: 'I have a friend in Counter-Terrorism who said he would have time to talk to us this morning. I want you to come up to his office with me, John, to help me explain what the situation is with regard to Edward Turner.'

With everything that had happened since his visit to Lewis's office, John had forgotten all about Maria Turner's deceased husband and his MoI file, which had been redacted by the London SS Counter-Terrorism Unit. Their investigation into Edward Turner was active as recently as January 1967, so it was not a stretch of the imagination to presume they might still have information at hand that would shed some light on his widow or his ex-father-in-law — such were John's raised expectations.

'I'd be glad to help, sir,' was John's response to the offer. He had never worked so closely with DI Colbeck, both before or during the Yonder Investigation, and so was keen to seize the opportunity.

'Good. We shall go now, then,' DI Colbeck declared.

Before he knew it, John was being led out of the DES office in the direction of the lifts.

*

Whilst organised terrorism was now a thing of the past, in the late 1940s and early 1950s this had not been the case. As a matter of fact, it had been the single greatest threat to the nation in its heyday, and at one point in 1954, when reports of explosions and acts of subversion became a weekly occurrence, many thought that full-scale civil war might have erupted at any moment. Although smaller groups did advocate their own twisted agendas during this time, the most prevalent terrorist organisation, the King's Loyalists, had a manifesto that included reinstating the "Usurper King" – who had escaped Great Britain with his family in 1943 and gone into hiding – to the British throne and establishing a government allied with the Soviet Union, all as a means to reignite the Second Great War. These objectives were attainable via a singular goal: destabilising Great Britain from within through violence and fear. This included the distribution of dangerous anti-Reich propaganda, the frequent sabotaging of military factories, and even the assassinations of several high-profile politicians and public figures. Then, just when Great Britain appeared destined for ruin, The Purges happened: a meticulously planned, large-scale assault against these terrorist groups. An unqualified success, it wiped the King's Loyalists from existence, and the tension lifted from the streets overnight as opposition to National Socialism dissolved. There were still SS Counter-Terrorism Units active nationwide today in spite of this, because no matter what the State did for the people, there remained those who conspired against it; yet there had been no mention of these subversive elements in the media for fifteen years, and as far as John was concerned, they were no longer a tangible threat.

What Edward Turner had done, then, to win the attention of the London SS Counter-Terrorism Unit, he could only speculate.

The lift came to a halt on the ninth floor, and John realised he had been holding his breath in anticipation for the entire duration of the ride; but this was not so odd, he recognised, given where they were going. Unlike the DES, SS Counter-Terrorism Units consisted entirely of SS agents, what with national security being above the pay grade of Metropolitan Police detectives. Like many police officers, for as long as he could remember, John had aspired to be a member of the SS: an elite agent who was responsible for keeping the Third Reich safe from its most dangerous enemies. To be up here, then, heading into their offices on invitation, was as exhilarating as it was nerve-wracking.

Having traversed the winding corridors of the ninth floor, DI Colbeck stopped in front of a door labelled 'London SS Counter-Terrorism Unit', and he knocked with purpose on the wood. He then waited there in silence, whilst John fought the urge to shuffle anxiously at his side.

Seconds later, a man appeared at the threshold. He was dressed in a grey suit only a shade darker than the one John was wearing, yet he seemed to stand taller in the wool, and John could tell that he was an SS agent even without his black uniform.

'May I help you?' the man asked with a hard stare, suspicious of these unfamiliar faces. He was unmistakably German and no more than a couple of years older than John.

'We are here to see Standartenführer Thompson. I am Detective Inspector Colbeck, and this is Detective Sergeant Highsmith,' DI Colbeck answered, with an authority John did not think he would have been able to summon at that exact moment.

John was shocked to hear the British name: Standartenführer *Thompson* would be something of a rarity amongst the ranks of the SS at such a high standing. Within the Wehrmacht, the equivalent rank was that of Oberst – a colonel. At one time, these positions had been reserved for men from the Fatherland, and that their government had come to trust the British with such responsibilities was a sign of a new era.

'Okay,' the SS agent said with indifference, and he opened the door wide for John and DI Colbeck.

The workspace on the other side was not dissimilar to the DES office, and it surprised John that he was dissatisfied as a result; in his head, he had built up the SS offices as some fantastical place. Perhaps the imposing rooms with the high-backed leather chairs and grand mahogany desks, the likes of which were depicted in films about the SS, were reserved for the SS Main Office over in Dean's Yard, the much larger building that acted as the central hub for the SS in Great Britain. Regardless, it was still far nicer up here, with bigger desks, newer models of typewriter, and a bright, natural light that illuminated the room through the tall windows that lined one wall – almost blindingly so after being downstairs. Counter-Terrorism men sat at the desks, going about their work, and they looked up only briefly to scrutinise the two detectives who had just entered their world on the ninth floor.

John and DI Colbeck were led across the office by this SS agent towards a door that had 'SS-Standartenführer J. Thompson' written on the nameplate. The man then turned away without having uttered another word and left DI Colbeck to knock on the door, this time with a whimsical tap.

'*Come in,*' bellowed a voice from the other side, and DI Colbeck did so.

This workspace too was markedly ordinary. As was to be expected, it was furnished with the usual articles: a desk, a chair, a typewriter, a bookshelf; what was notable, however, was that the room was in perfect harmony with itself. The desk was the correct size for the office, and whilst the typewriter upon it was worn with use, it was evident that its owner had cared for the machine, since the discoloured keys were cleaned and polished. Evenly spaced on the bookshelf were framed photographs of official-looking individuals and certificates of commendation – John observed that one of them was signed by both Commissioner Krüger and Prime Minister Bormann. A large window to the left overlooked Victoria Street, and the optimum amount of daylight poured across the room.

'Good morning, James.' DI Colbeck announced their presence in a joyful lilt. His rigid demeanour relaxed when the door closed behind them, and his whole posture became somehow more natural. He offered a half-salute. 'Heil Hitler.'

Standartenführer James Thompson closed the file he was reading and placed it to one side on his desk, and with a broad grin, he stood to meet his friend. He appeared to be a similar age to DI Colbeck, although his receding hairline added several years. A pair of simple half-rim reading glasses sat below a wide and wrinkled forehead, and a shaved jawline came to a sharp point at his chin. He afforded the exact appearance of an SS-Standartenführer, John thought, with his heavy brow and deep-set eyes – he was the complete antithesis of DCI Werner. The black cap on his desk had a silver Totenkopf fixed prominently upon it, and the holster at his hip contained a Lugar P08, John knew.

The Standartenführer removed his reading glasses and raised his hand to the side of his head. 'Tomas, I was wondering when you'd show up. Heil Hitler.' He was a slender man, even in his SS uniform; nevertheless, his voice had a distinctive weight to it.

'This is Detective Sergeant John Highsmith,' introduced DI Colbeck.

John greeted Standartenführer Thompson with a high salute.

'John is the detective who came by Edward Turner's MoI file,' DI Colbeck promptly added, finding a subtle way to get straight to the point of this visit.

'Yes, of course, Edward Turner,' Standartenführer Thompson acknowledged as he sat back down behind his desk. He offered John and DI Colbeck the two chairs opposite. 'Tell me, John, what do you already know?'

'Very little,' John admitted, taking a seat. 'We know more about his widow, Maria Turner, but it's all basic information. Her father is the one we're interested in right now, but we're coming up short on him as well.'

Standartenführer Thompson nodded. Then, without needing to be prompted any further, he leant forwards, resting his elbows on his desk, and began to speak: 'We followed Turner's activities for only a short while. Edward Turner, that is. I was surprised when Tomas mentioned the name.' He chuckled. 'You're lucky it was one of my operations, otherwise you would have been stonewalled by one of my colleagues.' Interdepartmental politics so often got in the way of police work, and John knew that the Standartenführer's friendship with DI Colbeck was the sole reason for his current candour.

Standartenführer Thompson continued, 'Turner was part of a cell that surfaced around mid-1966, one of these groups of youngsters who have been trying to establish themselves as the next generation of terrorists since the beginning of the decade. Although, it was theorised by some in this office that this particular cell was working under the instruction of a faction of older terrorists, presumably members of the King's Loyalists who went underground after The Purges. They were nothing but talk for several months, and we were hoping to use them in an operation to rout out this suspected larger group, but towards the end of the year, they started acting up: they set fire to metalworks, robbed numerous cargo trains transporting materials to military factories, and even succeeded in setting off an explosive device in a government building.'

John recalled an explosion in a government building not far from Scotland Yard several years ago. He had always thought it was a gas leak; it had never once occurred to him that it might have been an act of terrorism. He supposed this was proof of the fine work Standartenführer Thompson and his agents were doing in keeping these subversives at bay, and of the government's continued dedication to protecting its citizens from things they did not need to worry about.

'Eventually, they began discussing plans to assassinate high-profile individuals, and we were ordered to step in and dismantle the cell before anything greater could come of it. At that stage, we had identified eight of its members, including Turner, but, unfortunately, none of them ever made it back to us for questioning.' Standartenführer Thompson slumped back in his chair and exhaled, seemingly still frustrated that this particular operation had ended in bloodshed.

'Do you think Maria Turner was involved?' DI Colbeck asked. John had wanted to put forth the same question, but he could not quite bring himself to address the Standartenführer without first being instructed to do so.

'She was already Turner's girlfriend when we first took notice of him, and they married not long before we made our move, but she was never linked to any of her husband's activities before or after the wedding – if she ever even knew what he was up to. We did plan to keep an eye on her to see if she picked up where he left off, but she vanished like that' – Standartenführer Thompson snapped his fingers – 'when Turner was eliminated. I hadn't heard the name since until I got your message.'

That 'vanished' would be when Maria Turner left the house on Fleming Road, John supposed.

'So you never got as far as her parents, then?' DI Colbeck queried, although it was more of a statement than a question.

'Someone will have looked into them, but as I said, she wasn't our priority.' That sounded like a considerable oversight to John, but it was not his place to comment.

Besides, it was already apparent that Standartenführer Thompson had nothing to offer the Yonder Task Force: he barely knew who Maria Turner was, never mind her father.

John sighed to himself, disappointed.

'Who is her father, anyway? Why is he so important?' Standartenführer Thompson then asked, curious suddenly.

DI Colbeck said nothing, but he gestured for John to answer the question.

John was happy to oblige. 'According to an individual we interrogated, a key figure in our investigation is a Spaniard who fought on the Communist side of the Spanish Civil War. He was actually somewhat notorious, so much so that he became an enemy of the Spanish state, and to escape his crimes, he fled to Great Britain sometime before the Second Great War began. At least, that's how the story goes. That brings us to Antonio Ramos Serrano, Maria Turner's father. I met him on Thursday at a place of high interest, and I took his ID card and wrote down his name and ID number. Everything was in order, and it was definitely him in the photograph in the ID card. I then took the ID number to a friend of mine at the

Ministry of Identification, who pulled his file. Now, the ID number and the name were a match, *but* the photograph in the MoI file is of an entirely different person to the Antonio Ramos Serrano I met. However, I also met his daughter, and the photograph in her file is the same woman, just as it was in her ID card.'

Standartenführer Thompson had sat up as John spoke, becoming more attentive. 'So the man you met as Antonio Ramos Serrano is *not* the man in his MoI file? And he's Spanish, you say?'

John motioned that this was correct, but he remained silent.

The Standartenführer made an odd noise when he confirmed the detail, as if this scenario sounded familiar to him. 'Do you know anything else about this Ramos character?' he enquired.

John answered again. 'Well, we now know for certain that he fought for the Communists in the Spanish Civil War, which does lend credence to this idea that he's our man. Beyond that, though, all we have is a Spanish passport dated 1935 and a falsified MoI file that states he arrived here in 1945 alongside his wife. She died in 1949.'

Standartenführer Thompson was quiet then for a long moment, and he stared intently at the desk with his fingers interlaced on the wood, deep in thought. In the protracted silence, John felt his pulse quicken. This account of what the Yonder Task Force knew about Ramos had clearly stirred something in the Standartenführer's mind, and all at once there appeared the prospect of them not leaving his office empty-handed.

At last, Standartenführer Thompson said, 'When I joined the SS Counter-Terrorism Unit in 1949, part of my job concerned tracking down foreign nationals who were involved in terrorist activities here in Great Britain. A considerable faction of the King's Loyalists in particular was made up of such people – foreigners, a number of whom were Spanish, remnants of the Communists who scattered into Western Europe after *Generalissimo* Franco came to power and ended the Spanish Civil War.'

It was John who was sitting up in his chair now, enthralled by the possibilities of where this story might be heading.

'By the time The Purges brought the King's Loyalists' reign of terror to an end in 1954, I'd personally worked on seven cases that resemble your own – an ID card matching the person who held it and an MoI file with the same information but a different photograph, and all of them were Spanish. What we discovered was that the King's Loyalists were paying Spanish nationals to enter Great Britain legally, reassigning their identities to terrorists actively working against the Reich here, then smuggling these Spaniards back home to Spain without them ever passing through any border controls. The ID card would be altered to fit the terrorist – which was much easier than trying to counterfeit one from nothing – and the original document in the Ministry of Identification would slip to the back of a cabinet. If anyone ever checked on one of these individuals, they would call it in and never see the file for themselves. Instead, they would find that the ID number and the name matched the MoI's paperwork and that the person in question was clear of any known criminal activity. In the meantime, these terrorists with the doctored ID cards were able to travel freely around Great Britain so long as they were careful – passing through checkpoints, buying train tickets, and entering government buildings as they pleased.' Standartenführer Thompson crossed his arms. 'The cases were rare, and we never did uncover how the Spanish nationals were smuggled back to Spain.'

John had to steady his hands. Following his visit to James Summers' warehouse, he believed he could hazard an educated guess.

'What are you saying?' DI Colbeck probed. 'That Ramos was one of these terrorists given a new identity by the King's Loyalists?'

'It would make sense,' Standartenführer Thompson claimed. 'If he was an active member of the King's Loyalists, then he would have needed a reliable identity – and even more so if he was labelled an enemy of the Spanish state. We have a list somewhere of the Communists the Spanish government is still trying to hunt down for the crimes they committed during the Civil War, so he would have been picked up and sent home the minute he surfaced. The seven I dealt with were all on that same list. The Spanish Civil War was won largely with the help of the Third Reich, so it made sense to them that if they fought us here then they fought the same enemy. This Ramos no doubt came to Great Britain in 1938 or '39 and found sanctuary with the Imperialists. How these individuals survived the Second Great War and the Occupation, however, is a complete mystery.'

'What about his wife?' John spoke up, desperate to fill in the gaps.

'The same story, I'd imagine. She may have known this Antonio Ramos Serrano beforehand, or they might have met for the first time in 1945 when they were assigned these new lives. But, in either case: a married couple arrive in Great Britain legally, your man and this woman take their identities and pose as husband and wife, and the original couple is smuggled back to Spain. They must have been two of the first to go through this process, though, if it happened as early as 1945. All of the cases I dealt with were dated after 1948, when the King's Loyalists came out of the woodwork after the Occupation Forces left.'

The pieces surrounding Ramos had fallen into place as Standartenführer Thompson described this illicit practice. Was it possible the Yonder Task Force was on the trail of an old terrorist this entire time without knowing it? John never would have dared venture out to 27 Faulks Road alone if they had…

Just as Standartenführer Thompson came to the end of this explanation, his composure changed from that of impassive to apprehensive, though he tried to hide it from John and DI Colbeck. 'Do you have any idea what this man's name was before he became Antonio Ramos Serrano?' he asked, feigning apathy towards any potential answer.

'It was Miguel Carrasco Menéndez,' John answered, 'according to his passp—'

He was not allowed to finish his sentence: when Standartenführer Thompson heard Ramos's believed real name, he jumped to his feet and hurried from the office without excusing himself, leaving John and DI Colbeck to sit there in his wake, quite perplexed.

'Well…' DI Colbeck raised his eyebrows in amazement.

A thought had occurred to John in the seconds since Standartenführer Thompson's unexpected departure, and he shared it with DI Colbeck: 'What if Yonder is organised terrorism?' It had never even crossed his mind before now, but all this talk had him thinking.

'What do you mean?' DI Colbeck's demeanour was now serious as well.

'We know that Yonder is supposed to be a "medication" for the fools who take it – a so-called "cure" for their so-terrible existence – or indicative of some kind of a working-class "silent protest", but what if it's more than that?' John turned around to ensure they would not be overheard, but the door was closed. 'Men who fought for the Imperialists in the war were the driving force behind terrorist groups such as the King's Loyalists, and they've been a recurring theme in our investigation. Joe Harding, Uncle Billy, and even that supplier Ben Chambers' father. And what's the betting that James Summers' father fought as well? He ran the warehouse in Silvertown at one time, which would have been the perfect place to smuggle out of Great Britain these Spanish nationals the Standartenführer was telling us about. And then there's Ramos, a Communist soldier in the Spanish Civil War and almost certainly a King's Loyalist.' John paused, allowing himself a second to catch his breath and DI Colbeck a moment to wrap his head around this bombardment of information, before he stated, 'What if it's these same men, these terrorists, continuing the work they began after the war under the guise of the Yonder Organisation? Standartenführer Thompson said that Edward Turner's cell was perhaps working with surviving members of the King's Loyalists as late as 1967, so they must still exist in some capacity today.'

DI Colbeck shifted uncomfortably in his chair at the notion. 'To what end?' he asked, as much to himself as to John.

John strained for something, a reasoning, but he could conceive of nothing meaningful. 'I have no idea. For profit, to finance something bigger?' he guessed.

'But if they have the money to fund Yonder, could they not just use that money to fund... *it*?' DI Colbeck was right: a drug ring would only bring unwanted attention to a larger cause. Anyway, Yonder was not an expensive drug to buy, being a fifth of the price of opium, so there would be little profit in it.

It made no sense.

Maybe it was not organised terrorism.

But then why would Ramos, a Communist soldier and probable terrorist, be involved? There had to be a reason beyond Yonder's status as a "medication" or a "silent protest";

such motives were surely too trivial a motivation for a man like Ramos.

DI Colbeck had just opened his mouth to add something else to this debate when Standartenführer Thompson burst back into his office. Not noticing that they were in the middle of a conversation, or perhaps not caring, he started talking at once: 'I may have some good news for you. About an hour ago, an informant of ours who hasn't been active since The Purges made contact again. Back then, he was enlisted by the King's Loyalists to help compromised terrorists escape to the Continent – information he dutifully passed on to us. With his assistance, SS Counter-Terrorism Units across the Third Reich were able to bring some of National Socialism's most dangerous enemies to justice.'

The Standartenführer had recounted this story of past glories with enormous pride. *How strange,* John thought, *that for him, those years of terror had been exhilarating, whilst for everybody else, they were immeasurably distressing.*

'Anyway,' continued Standartenführer Thompson, returning to the present conversation, 'our man said that an old member of the King's Loyalists surfaced this morning. Apparently, something has gone dreadfully amiss, and he needs a way out of Great Britain for himself and another – a woman.'

John's heart skipped a beat.

'The informant claims this man is Spanish…'

John leant forwards, and next to him, DI Colbeck slid to the edge of his seat.

'…and that his name is' – Standartenführer Thompson raised his hands at the revelation – '*Miguel.*'

John took a sharp intake of breath.

Could it really be Ramos?

If so, this 'woman' would without a doubt be Maria Turner.

The DES had run the bastards into a corner, and now Ramos was trying to secure a way for them to escape.

'He's set to meet our informant later this morning, at his antiques shop in Shepherd's Bush,' Standartenführer Thompson declared. 'Several of my agents will be standing by, ready to pick this Miguel up and bring him in.'

DI Colbeck was quick to interject: 'James, the DES must speak to this man.' There was a hint of uncharacteristic trepidation in the DI's voice, and John understood why: this was an SS Counter-Terrorism operation, after all, and therefore "Miguel" was an SS Counter-Terrorism suspect – and the SS had a reputation for refusing to share such "resources" with the lowly Metropolitan Police.

By now, Standartenführer Thompson was standing behind his desk. As he spoke again, he leant forwards, placing his palms flat on the wood and towering over the still seated John and DI Colbeck: 'Once we have him, Tomas, you and your boys can ask him all the questions you want.'

A wide smile stretched across DI Colbeck's face, and John could not help but do the same. Standartenführer Thompson was a more amiable person than some of his colleagues, it would seem.

Whilst DI Colbeck and the Standartenführer set about discussing this operation, John sat back in his chair. His smile had already disappeared. A tight knot had settled in the pit of his stomach, and he could not decide whether it was due to unbridled excitement or wild unease. In the end, he put a hand to his tender ribs and determined that it was both.

CHAPTER FOURTEEN

Smith and Sons' Antiquities and Crafts

It was fortunate that there was a café directly over the road from Smith and Sons' Antiquities and Crafts, with a table set up next to a large window that faced onto Uxbridge Road. It was a quaint little place, trimmed in a rustic, dark wood and decorated with hanging baskets. There was even a bookshelf for its patrons to peruse whilst they sipped tea and ate a slightly-too-expensive piece of cake. It was empty right now but for an elderly couple, and although it would fill up in the next half hour as lunchtime approached, this had been perfect for John, Zeigler, and Arnold, as they were able to take up their position at the table by the window without any hassle.

That was where John now sat, in the corner with his back to the wall, and Zeigler and Arnold were sitting opposite him. With some persuasion, DI Colbeck had talked Standartenführer Thompson into allowing the detectives to watch the apprehension of "Miguel" from a distance, and John had ferried the three of them to Shepherd's Bush in the Morris

Minor. Smith and Sons' Antiquities and Crafts was the shop belonging to the SS Counter-Terrorism Unit's informant, who was indeed named Smith, and it was here that their suspect was supposed to be meeting him any minute now. Three Counter-Terrorism agents were already stationed inside, poised for their opportunity to strike.

It was silent at the table, due to the three detectives having exhausted all of their small talk in the first five minutes after taking their seats. John occupied himself by fiddling with an empty teacup – one of those thick, white ones every café used – and he looked out of the window along Uxbridge Road, waiting impatiently for Ramos to appear amongst the weekend shoppers. Zeigler too was fixated on the street outside, his grey eyes searching for anything suspicious. Arnold, on the other hand, gawped blankly at the back wall, lost somewhere in his own thoughts.

John forced himself to leave the teacup alone, conscious that his fidgeting might be irritating the other two detectives (or at least irritating Zeigler), and he slipped his nervous hands into his trouser pockets. He knew there was still no certainty that this "Miguel" would be Ramos, yet John had already decided it *must* be him, his expectations now completely untempered. He refused to consider what the DES would do should this turn out not to be the case. They had nothing else to go on with regard to The Spaniard, and the prospect of this operation being worthless to them was too depressing to contemplate.

It was several further restless minutes before Zeigler broke the prolonged silence at the table by mumbling, 'John,' under his breath.

John looked at him, and Zeigler gave a subtle nod towards the window. When John followed the direction of his gaze down Uxbridge Road, he immediately saw to what Zeigler was signalling: in the distance, two figures were walking up the street on the other side – a man and a woman.

Even from this far away, John could see their olive skin glowing beneath the bright winter sunshine. The man was shorter, and older. The woman was buttoned up against the cold in a familiar brown leather coat and her face was partially obscured by long, dark hair. They were both unmistakable to John: it was Ramos and Turner, and they marched in tandem towards Smith and Sons' Antiquities and Crafts.

'That's them,' John announced, suppressing a quiver of excitement. That it was not just Ramos but Turner as well was so much more than they could ever have hoped for.

Arnold was paying attention now, and he peered out of the window at the pair. 'Are you sure?' he asked.

'Positive,' John stated, making certain that his impatience at the question was not evident in his tone. He would not have forgotten them so easily.

Oblivious to the three detectives watching them from the café, Ramos and Turner approached the door to the antiques shop and stepped through it without so much as a moment's indecision.

And then nothing happened. People milled about Uxbridge Road, going about their day, and cars passed in both directions, but the antiques shop was still.

John stared out of the window, waiting for some sign that the operation had been a success and that the Counter-Terrorism agents had apprehended Ramos and Turner. This was their big chance to break the Yonder Organisation wide open, and they could not afford to waste it. No sign came, however, and as the seconds ticked by, John felt the tension intensify around the table; Arnold tapped out an anxious tempo on the wood with a fingernail, whilst Zeigler moved not a single muscle.

Just as John was beginning to question whether or not the pair had in fact been Ramos and Turner, a series of gunshots shattered the serenity of the Sunday morning. The passers-by in the street screamed and ducked for cover wherever they could, and porcelain smashed on the café floor after a waitress dropped her tray in fright, but the door to Smith and Sons' Antiquities and Crafts remained closed.

There was a split second of confusion amongst the three detectives before the reality of what was happening sank in. Then they were scrambling to their feet, and all at once fighting their way between tables and chairs towards the café's door. John had been in the furthest corner, and as a result, it took him several extra seconds to navigate this maze of furniture, and so by the time he stumbled out onto the pavement, he saw Arnold and Zeigler were already racing across the road.

In his haste to catch up, John did not think to look before he tried to follow them onto the tarmac, and an approaching car screeched to a halt mere centimetres from hitting him. His heart in his mouth, John stepped back off the road – the driver had not waited to let him by – and he was able only to watch from a distance as the two detectives made it to the other side and to the entrance of the antiques shop.

Arnold entered it ahead of Zeigler, their weapons drawn, and the roar of another volley of gunfire sounded inside the building.

Cursing his delay, John burst through the door an instant later, but the tinkling of the bell was the only sound that met him. His Walther raised, he crept forwards, and the outcome of this brief shoot-out unfolded around the room: Arnold was splayed backwards into a splintered shelf of little glass figurines, his eyes wide in motionless horror and two holes in his chest.

He was dead.

Zeigler stood across from Arnold, hidden behind a shelf of decorative plates. He had also been hit in the exchange, his left shoulder now stained with blood, but the gunshot wound was not fatal.

John scanned the shop floor. The man he assumed was Smith cowered behind the counter, his grey head visible above the faded wood. Two of the three present SS agents had already succumbed to the same fate as Arnold: one of them was practically riddled with bullet holes, and the other bore a single dark-red wound at the side of his head. The final Counter-Terrorism man was alive, but he had been shot in the stomach and was slumped against a display cabinet in the corner of the room, his consciousness waning.

Ramos and Turner were nowhere to be seen.

Reading his mind, Zeigler snarled, 'They ran off into the back of the shop,' through gritted teeth.

John idled in the middle of the room, unsure as to what he was supposed to do next. He and the injured Zeigler would make for a less-than-formidable team against the armed and dangerous Ramos and Turner. But backup would not arrive for some time, and they could not allow the pair an opportunity to escape.

But then the two of them advancing further into the shop, into what might be a bottleneck of shelves and gunfire, sounded like sheer fucking insanity to John.

He regarded Arnold's body. John had never been particularly fond of the man, yet he was John's colleague nonetheless and had not deserved to die. They had to get Ramos and Turner, to avenge this murder of a fellow detective; right now, everything else – including the Yonder investigation – was of secondary importance.

'We have to go after them,' John declared at last, with as much confidence as he could muster.

In response, Zeigler tightened his grip around his Walther and grunted his approval of the idea.

Before they set off, John ordered the still-hiding Smith to call Counter-Terrorism and report what had happened, and to then help the wounded SS agent in any way he could. Smith said nothing either, but he snatched the telephone cradle from the counter and began to dial a number, having understood the instruction.

With his finger resting across the trigger guard of his pistol, John motioned for Zeigler to follow him – he could hardly expect his superior to go first, given his condition – and he edged his way deeper into the building.

The back room of the shop was a large, dimly lit space. The same as the front room, it was cluttered with trinkets and knick-knacks of every shape and size: a shelf lined with old silver teaspoons was atop another shelf of dinnerware and teacups, next to which stood a tall glass display cabinet full of rings, brooches, and bracelets. Paintings were stacked five deep against the wall, forming a collection of abandoned artwork that would never again see the light of day. A suit of armour in the corner startled John, who very nearly shot at the inanimate figure.

Content that nobody lay in wait amongst these rows of jumble and treasure, the two detectives arrived at a staircase that led up to the first floor, the only way out of the back room. A sign attached to a discarded chain read 'STOP! STAFF ONLY' – the words were just about legible beneath a wet, red smear.

Zeigler whispered, 'I think I hit Ramos.'

At least they were on a somewhat level footing, then.

John took point again, and Zeigler followed close behind him as they ascended the staircase.

At the top, a long landing presented itself, along with three doors and another flight of stairs at the far end. John tried the first door, but it was locked, as were the second and the third. The knob for the third door was crimson, however, being slick with someone's – presumably Ramos's – blood.

Before a discussion could be had about their next move, there was a distinct squeaking noise heard coming from the floor above them. Distracted from the bloodied doorknob, John and Zeigler took off at a quickened pace up the second staircase, heading towards the building's third and final storey. Through the spindles under the banister, John could see that this floor was of a similar layout to the previous one, with two doors opposite the stairs and no doubt a third at the end of the narrow landing. Which one Ramos and Turner might be hiding behind was anybody's guess.

John rounded the corner and continued onto the landing, and he felt a bullet zip past his head almost before he heard the gun fire. He was already diving for cover when the second shot came, and the first door on the landing gave way beneath him as John hurtled into it with his whole body and went crashing to the ground.

John gathered himself as best he could. His bruised ribs throbbed, and his head was rattled from the impact with the floor, but the second bullet had missed him. He sat up, and through his dizzy vision he saw Zeigler was still on the stairs, with his back to the wall and his pistol levelled towards where the gunfire had originated.

John dragged himself to his feet and stood against the doorframe. There, he took a deep breath, and without thinking too hard about it this time, he counted: *Three, two, one.*

On one, he stole a glance around the corner, and a third bullet exploded part of the doorframe next to his head.

John thought his heart would give out as he brushed splinters of wood from the sleeve of his jacket. But, he had seen their attacker: Ramos was sitting alone at the other end of the landing, propped up against the third door, with his gun aimed at the detectives and nowhere to run.

They had the bastard.

Or at least they almost had him, because a challenge now presented itself: how would either he or Zeigler make it those several metres without being killed?

A fourth and fifth bullet sailed along the landing, and Zeigler took a fast step backwards.

How many rounds did Ramos have left?

It did not matter, John realised: one would be more than enough.

In the end, Ramos did not leave the detectives to formulate their own plan. Down the landing, there was a shuffling, and then, loud enough for John and Zeigler to hear him, he said, '*Adiós, mi niñita.*'

John had no clue as to what the words meant, but he expected that they would be followed by a sixth and final gunshot; he would have saved the last bullet for himself, too. Ramos was a terrorist, a fact that was now undeniable, and he would know what awaited him should he be arrested. Suicide would be simpler – and less painful.

John looked across at Zeigler, and he returned a frustrated scowl. Zeigler knew full well himself what was about to happen.

It was over. There was nothing they could do.

John bowed his head, defeated, and waited for the inevitable crack of another gunshot.

Click. The dull noise echoed around the landing.

'No…' Ramos muttered in the distance.

Click, click, click. That same sound again.

'No!'

John raised his head from his chest, utterly baffled.

Across the landing, the truth of the matter had already dawned on Zeigler, who stepped with absolute composure from his cover on the staircase. When he was not promptly gunned down, John peeked out around the doorframe. The situation finally made itself apparent to him when he saw Ramos turn his weapon on the approaching DI to no effect, shout something incomprehensible, then lapse into unconsciousness as Zeigler drove a knee into his head. The misfired pistol clattered to the floor, and Ramos slumped to one side – he left behind an indent in the door where the force of Zeigler's blow had cracked the wood.

John exhaled unsteadily. But, he kept his gun to hand: whilst Ramos no longer posed a threat, Turner was without a doubt also armed, and she had to be up here as well.

Or so John thought.

He had assumed Ramos was defending the door at the end of the landing, and that his daughter would be waiting for them on the other side of it, ready to make a last stand of her own. John and Zeigler never did find out what was in that room, though, because just as John placed a hand to the door, two gunshots rang out downstairs, and so the detectives tore their way back towards the shop floor. They were moving so fast, John scarcely had chance to notice that the door on the first floor with the bloodied knob was now wide open.

Upon returning to the front room of the shop, they found Smith crumpled on the floor next to the gut-shot SS agent, each of them with a bullet hole in the head. It took John only a second to piece together the series of events: Ramos had given himself as bait whilst Turner hid in the room with the bloodied doorknob, and when John and Zeigler continued up to the second floor, she slipped out behind them. For good measure, on her way out of the building, she had executed Smith – the man who betrayed her and her father – and the Counter-Terrorism agent.

She would be long gone by now.

They had lost her.

Arnold's vacant stare judged John from where he lay, condemning his stupidity. John sighed, knelt beside the body, and closed those accusing eyes.

He examined the room and the massacre before him.

So many dead – and all in the name of Yonder.

John just hoped Ramos would be worth such a high price.

CHAPTER FIFTEEN

Shackles

Backup in the form of a dozen uniformed police officers and Counter-Terrorism agents soon arrived, along with DI Colbeck and Standartenführer Thompson, but too late to be of any use.

Presently, John stood with DI Colbeck and the Standartenführer inside Smith and Son's Antiquities and Crafts, and the three of them watched from a corner whilst paramedics went about lifting the deceased onto trolleys. He could feel a fury radiating from DI Colbeck as he looked upon Arnold, who had been one of his longest-serving colleagues in the DES. His reaction was only intensified when Zeigler revealed it was not the detained Ramos who shot him, but the escaped Maria Turner. DI Colbeck neither said nor did anything to make his feelings known, of course – that would have been far too unprofessional for a man of his standing.

Arnold's body was covered by a white sheet, and John, DI Colbeck, and Standartenführer Thompson – Zeigler had already been whisked away by the paramedics – stepped out of the antiques shop. There, they stopped next to Ramos, who was lying face down on the pavement, handcuffed, and still very much unconscious.

Standartenführer Thompson was the first to speak. 'I imagine you must have some pressing questions for this man?' he growled, his total contempt evident.

'We do,' DI Colbeck confirmed. Whilst his own voice was composed, the anger behind his eyes suggested he would have preferred to kick Ramos to death where he lay.

'Then we should go,' declared Standartenführer Thompson. 'We'll take the Spaniard.' He waved, and two imposing Counter-Terrorism agents began to move towards them.

These two men had arrived with the Standartenführer in a luxury-model black Mercedes-Benz, and John guessed they had not been chosen to work so closely with him for their pleasant conversation. They were as good as identical, with cheekbones that could cut glass and austere, expressionless faces beneath the peaks of their caps. When they hoisted Ramos up from the ground, John observed that they had hands like garden shovels, and between them, Ramos seemed to weigh nothing. They were dressed in perfectly cut SS uniforms, yet there was something not right about how they wore the black fabric, as though their huge, muscular bodies did not befit such formal attire.

Standartenführer Thompson ordered, 'Tomas, you and your detective sergeant follow us.'

'Back to Scotland Yard?' John asked.

'Not this time. Counter-Terrorism has someplace else prepared for men like Ramos,' was Standartenführer Thompson's cryptic response. He then turned on his heel, crossed Uxbridge Road, and disappeared into the front passenger side of the Mercedes.

The two Counter-Terrorism agents hurled Ramos onto the back seat, then they climbed into the car themselves.

DI Colbeck suggested they take John's car, the Morris Minor being parked just down the road, and John agreed. They lingered on Uxbridge Road, however, for Arnold to be brought out of Smith and Son's Antiquities and Crafts and towards the back of an ambulance. It was frightening to think that he had been alive when John watched him enter the shop, but that by the time he himself went through the door, Arnold was already dead. He could not help but wonder what might have happened had he gone in first, and if it would not have been him on that trolley instead. He shuddered, and felt an urge to hug Alice.

Arnold's body was loaded into the ambulance, and John and DI Colbeck took their leave.

*

John followed the Mercedes west until London's city streets and brick buildings gave way to country lanes and a landscape of fields and trees. What they were doing all the way out here, venturing ever further into the middle of nowhere, he had not the slightest of ideas. He wanted to ask DI Colbeck, but decided that doing so would only prove his apprehension about whatever was waiting for them when they stopped, which he was consciously trying to suppress. Besides, DI Colbeck was likely no less clueless.

It was with trepidation, then, that John turned off a country lane and onto one of said fields. At the other end of a neglected cobbled road, what came into view must have been their destination, given that it was the only structure in sight: a derelict barn. This building was a remnant of an agricultural past, a practice that had died out when a programme of large-scale food cultivation commenced on the Continent under

National Socialism, with the aim of providing all the sustenance the Third Reich might ever need. As a result, there had been no reason for Great Britain to continue working the land, and the people who had once inhabited the countryside went to find employment in the newly built factories. The fields returned to nature and became overgrown and wild, and such places as barns and farms were left abandoned.

That was by all except the SS, it would seem.

The Mercedes came to a halt in front of the barn. As John rolled up behind it, a now-hooded Ramos was bundled out onto the stone path. Then the Counter-Terrorism agents were on him again, and lifting the man to his feet, they dragged him towards the building. Standartenführer Thompson appeared from the car, and he beckoned for John and DI Colbeck to follow them before he headed that way himself.

Unperturbed by any of this, DI Colbeck did as instructed.

John was allowed but a second to wallow in his silent unease before he hurried after him.

Inside the barn, rusted field tools lay scattered about a rotting floor, and the wooden pillars and beams were cracked and broken. Sections of the roof had fallen in, and the clear, blue sky on this pleasant December afternoon was visible through it. The whole structure looked set to collapse, and John would have readily assumed that nobody had visited this place in several decades had he stumbled upon it by chance – but he was not here by chance. When John entered the barn and saw an open trapdoor in the centre of the floor and a flight of concrete stairs leading down from it, his stomach turned in an ominous, wrenching sensation.

DI Colbeck did not hesitate to descend beneath the earth, and John followed him once more without delay.

He shivered as the daylight disappeared above his head.

At the bottom of the stairs, there was a heavy metal door left ajar for them. John had wondered during the drive to the barn what place could possibly be more imposing an environment for an interrogation than The Basement, with its bare lightbulbs and cold metal tables. His scepticism was dashed the moment he passed through that door.

On the other side, John was met with a large chamber. The floor was concrete, and there were no windows in the grey-brick walls, so any notion of the time of day was lost completely. The only source of light was a single spotlight erected near the back, which cast long shadows across the chamber. Beyond the light, the sound of a small generator could be heard; its soft drone echoed around the room and it polluted the chamber with dense petrol fumes. As his eyes adjusted, John noticed a series of metal shackles hanging from the low ceiling. Against one wall, there was a table, and whilst he could not make out from where he stood what had been laid upon it, he imagined it would include much-employed instruments of pain and torment.

The chamber had the appearance of a medieval dungeon, and had no doubt been painstakingly designed to this specific motif to put fear into the hearts of those unlucky enough to find themselves down here.

Ramos was one such individual. Illuminated by the spotlight, he was suspended, naked, in the centre of the chamber by one of these sets of shackles, his arms stretching unnaturally above his head. His feet, swaying several centimetres above the floor, were also chained so he could not move his legs. He was still hooded but now conscious, which was made apparent by his grunts and yelps of pain. Standartenführer Thompson's men had wasted no time in getting to work, and having removed their black tunics and rolled up their sleeves, one of them was taking long swings at Ramos's back with a thick length of wood, whilst the other stood in front of him and used closed fists to pound his ribs and stomach. Ramos rocked backwards and forwards with each blow, unable to defend himself as the chains rattled together.

This scene inside the chamber unfolded before John, along with the prospect of what was to follow, and he met it with an unparalleled angst.

He had to remind himself that the man hanging from the shackles possessed information the Yonder Task Force needed and that he would never surrender it of his own accord. However long this process lasted, then, was a decision only Ramos could make: if he gave them what they wanted, there would be no cause for it to continue. Therefore, everything that transpired in this chamber due to his refusal to cooperate was of his own choosing – and nobody else's.

As for John, although he did not yet know what the plan was, he understood that he would be expected to play his part in it. And he would do so, without question, such was his duty as an officer of the Reich.

Ramos cried out as the length of wood struck his back for the umpteenth time, and John repeated this vow to himself again.

And again.

And again…

For now, the beating upon Ramos ceased.

Standartenführer Thompson turned to DI Colbeck. 'Do you have your questions?' he asked.

DI Colbeck nodded.

'Then let's see where we stand.'

The two of them moved forwards. John had already taken his place at the back of the chamber, behind the spotlight, where he willingly hid himself away amongst the shadows.

Standartenführer Thompson instructed his Counter-Terrorism agents to remove Ramos's hood. They did so, and the man blinked furiously as it was torn from his head, the blinding dazzle of the spotlight an assault on his retinas. John saw that one of his eyes was stained red, with roots of blood striking inwards towards the pupil, but then that might have been from Zeigler's knee. The bullet hole in his thigh was Zeigler's doing as well, from when he returned fire on Ramos and Turner back at Smith and Son's Antiquities and Crafts.

Ramos tilted his head down, away from the light.

Then, the interrogation began.

Standartenführer Thompson stepped between Ramos and the spotlight. 'I'm Standartenführer Thompson. This' – he gestured at DI Colbeck, who was standing at his side – 'is Detective Inspector Colbeck. His colleague, Detective Sergeant Highsmith, is just beyond the light, but you likely cannot see him. They're the men who have been hunting you and your little band of subversives, Ramos.' He stopped abruptly, then said, 'That is your name, isn't it? Antonio Ramos Serrano. Or do you prefer Miguel Carrasco Menéndez? The King's Loyalist or the Communist: which one shall we go with this afternoon?' The Standartenführer delivered the statement with a chuckle. He was making Ramos aware that they had already figured out who he was, and so there would be little point denying his past crimes.

John was surprised, then, when Ramos raised his head to reveal a smirk playing across his face. John's previously arrived at assumption was realised at last: a straightforward beating would not be sufficient to break this man.

Standartenführer Thompson was obviously not expecting such a display of defiance either, as upon seeing Ramos's smile, his own face dropped. With no more than a glance, he signalled to one of the Counter-Terrorism agents, who instinctively marched over and hit Ramos twice in the side of the head with a hulking fist.

Ramos's head dropped onto his chest and he groaned in pain.

'You did not answer my question. Do you go by these names?' the Standartenführer asked, this time without the chuckle.

Ramos spat blood onto the floor and offered a single-word answer in his thick accent: 'Yes.'

Standartenführer Thompson continued his questioning. 'So, we know you worked alongside the King's Loyalists as Antonio Ramos Serrano, and we know you fought for the Communists during the Spanish Civil War as Miguel Carrasco Menéndez. Would you care to fill in the gaps for us?'

Ramos sneered at the question. Then, he came out with it: 'I fought the Fascists in Spain for the Second Republic, then I fought the Nazis in North Africa for the British. Then, with that battle lost as well, I fought them in this country when they shipped us back – part of the guerrilla war we were forced into after the Nazis invaded. But even when the swastika flew over Buckingham Palace and the people surrendered themselves to the enemy, I refused to stop. I joined the King's Loyalists, and I continued the fight.' He looked up and stared Standartenführer Thompson steadfastly in the eye. 'For almost two decades, I fought your kind. I killed them in scores. Then The Purges happened, and there was no one left to fight alongside.' Ramos sighed. 'No matter what we did, no matter how hard we tried, it was never enough.' He hung his head, no longer smiling, but instead dejected by this apparent failure.

'Why did you fight us?' Standartenführer Thompson asked, seemingly to satisfy his own curiosity more than anything else.

'Because fascism is a parasite, and the Nazis are the host – a plague upon this world of apocalyptic proportions,' Ramos hissed.

John could not fault his command of the English language. He could, however, fault Ramos's philosophies: how someone could have been conditioned by Communism – or the Imperialists – to think so lowly of National Socialism was beyond comprehension. After having been consumed by such an outright rejection of the world since the end of the Second Great War, perhaps the inevitable fate of this man would be an act of kindness – one which would free him from that poisoned mind.

Standartenführer Thompson was equally unimpressed, and for his comments, Ramos paid a heavy toll at the hands of the Counter-Terrorism agent.

When he was satisfied that this slander had been answered for, the Standartenführer said, 'Detective Inspector Colbeck has some questions for you now, Ramos. I hope for your own sake you are as forthcoming with him as you were with me.' He moved aside and allowed DI Colbeck to take centre stage. Standartenführer Thompson had everything he wanted with this confirmation that they had detained an old terrorist; for the time being, anything else regarding Yonder was not his problem.

DI Colbeck did not start with his questions straight away. He instead lit a cigarette and took a long, slow lungful of smoke. John felt an urge to light his own, but he did not want to disturb the DI's theatre. He was different down here, in this chamber: no longer the kind-faced man who comforted John in the fifth-floor WC back at Scotland Yard – he now bore an emotionless demeanour and a severe, uncompromising gaze. John understood that DI Colbeck must adopt this persona of a ruthless interrogator, given what they were here to do, but even so, it was disturbing to witness how proficient he was at assuming the character.

DI Colbeck blew a cloud of smoke towards the low ceiling and, finally, addressed Ramos: 'Are you currently involved with a drug known as Yonder?'

Ramos's head was still on his chest after the Counter-Terrorism agent's latest efforts, and he made no attempt to answer DI Colbeck's question. He would have known that his own future had been determined when the pistol misfired in the antiques shop, so now it would be a simple matter of keeping everything he knew about the Yonder Organisation to himself.

'Are you responsible for smuggling Yonder into Great Britain?'

Again, Ramos said nothing.

'Are you known by the alias "The Spaniard"?'

Silence.

'Do you work with a man called James Summers?'

Nothing. Not even a murmur.

With this unresponsiveness becoming immediately tiresome, DI Colbeck changed his approach. 'There is an easy way for this to end, Ramos: you tell me what I want to know, and we will make a deal. That deal will include protecting your daughter, should she cooperate—'

'María will die before she yields, you fucking Nazi!' Ramos snarled at DI Colbeck, suddenly provoked by the mention of his daughter, and he bared his teeth like a caged animal. It was the same tactic Peter had used against Joe Harding, but it would not work on this man – such was obvious.

DI Colbeck did not acknowledge the outburst. Instead, he took another drag on his cigarette and lifted it up to watch the embers at the tip smoulder in his shadow. Then, before Ramos knew what was happening, DI Colbeck grabbed him by the nape of the neck, pulled him forwards in his shackles, and jammed the lit end of the cigarette into his left eye. Ramos made a wild, agonised sound, screaming so loud that John thought it impossible no one would hear him, even out here in the middle of nowhere. He twisted madly against his constraints, trying his hardest to escape DI Colbeck's grasp as the cigarette was driven deeper into his skull, all to no avail.

John watched aghast from behind the spotlight, but he was nevertheless unable to look away.

When DI Colbeck stepped back and tossed the crumpled cigarette to one side, there was a ferocity on his face that disturbed John – no, that *frightened* him to his very core. It was visible for no longer than an instant before his expression settled back to impassive, yet John could still somehow see it there, hidden between the wrinkles in his skin. Maybe it had always been there. Maybe this "ruthless interrogator" was not a persona after all, but it was the "kindly mentor" that was the man's front – the façade he wore in public to conceal this brute lurking beneath the surface.

John lowered his eyes to the concrete floor, away from the still-flailing Ramos, and he hid his trembling hands in his trouser pockets. He was yet to resign himself to the fact that this interrogation was going to be far more intense than his last one; far more intense than any interrogation he had ever been a part of, actually. Ramos was not Joe Harding, and nor was he Frank Boyd – both men who were easily influenced using simple manipulation techniques and a small amount of physical violence. John just had to focus on the reason they were here, the reason they were doing this: if they could break Ramos now, then they would be able to unpick the whole

Yonder Organisation and perhaps even bring the investigation to a swift conclusion. He had to remember that, no matter what came next.

John glanced up and saw blood trickling from the corner of Ramos's eye, and he repeated this resolve to himself again.

And again.

And again...

When Ramos's cries had subsided into a spluttering whimper, DI Colbeck continued with the same line of questioning:

'Are you currently involved with a drug known as Yonder?'

Nothing.

'Are you responsible for smuggling Yonder into Great Britain?'

Nothing.

'Are you known by the alias "The Spaniard"?'

Nothing.

'Do you work with a man called James Summers?'

Nothing. Ramos dangled in his shackles, quiet now but for the gentle clinking of the metal. His ruined eye twitched erratically, and his other eye was closed.

Unmoved by DI Colbeck's bout of aggression, Standartenführer Thompson chimed in: 'We have so much planned for you, Ramos, but you won't have to suffer through it if you give the detective inspector what he wants.' Then, in a tone that brimmed with malevolence, he added, 'I promise you, we *will* get it in the end.'

At the threat, Ramos lifted his head and, with a piercing resilience in his functional, bloodshot eye, he said, 'Do your worst, you Nazi bastard.'

Standartenführer Thompson returned Ramos's gaze, and he replied with a single, foreboding word: 'Okay.'

With that, the interrogation *truly* began, and John was called out of the shadows at the back of the chamber to participate.

He has information we need, John reminded himself as he joined DI Colbeck and Standartenführer Thompson in the spotlight, *and he will never surrender it of his own accord.*

He repeated this over and over whilst the Counter-Terrorism agents took Ramos down from his shackles.

I will do whatever I am ordered to do, without question, he insisted when DI Colbeck handed him a set of rusted pliers.

And, true to his word, John did just that.

Small bones were broken.

Fingernails and teeth were removed.

Lungs were starved of oxygen.

Red-hot pokers were applied to soft flesh.

Sections of skin were flayed and discarded.

Yet, having endured each of these miseries, Ramos did not break.

He thrashed and fought against them and made this process a struggle at every turn.

But he refused to talk.

He screamed and cried and wailed in unyielding agony, making sounds John did not think possible from a human being.

Still, he remained resolute.

The smell of his blood filled the chamber when it spilt across the concrete floor.

And he gave them nothing. Not a single scrap of information.

Ramos got what he asked for, though, without a shadow of a doubt, because Standartenführer Thompson most definitely did his 'worst'.

CHAPTER SIXTEEN

Clear Liquid

Time had lost all meaning to John, being confined to these four walls in an endless trance of artificial light and shadows. He had not looked at his watch in – well, he did not know how long. The world outside was like some half-remembered dream from another lifetime. This chamber beneath the barn was all that existed now, as if it were drifting on a plane beyond reality.

At this point, there was silence in the chamber save for the relentless rumble of the generator. One of the Counter-Terrorism agents sat back in a chair, the soiled penknife in his hand dangling between his legs. His eyes were glazed over with a vacant gaze of discernible boredom. The other SS man was propped up against a wall with his arms folded and that same expression of apathy he had worn the entire time they were down here fixed across his face. Standartenführer Thompson, on the other hand, was deeply frustrated. He had been chain-smoking a series of cigarettes, the stubs of which now littered the concrete floor like VE Day confetti. As for DI Colbeck, he had disappeared into the shadows behind the spotlight some time ago and made not a sound since.

John was sitting low on a chair with his shoulders hunched and a cigarette burning away between his fingers. He did not smoke it, but stared down at the red stain on his knuckles and shirt cuff – blood that was not his own. His other hand was placed against his ribs, the lingering pain there having been aggravated by the afternoon's undertakings. His sodden shirt was pasted across his back and stomach, and he could taste the bitter sweat that clung to the stagnant air, the chamber having taken on the properties of a furnace the instant this interrogation began.

Ramos was secured in his shackles again, unconscious. He hung there like a pig on a butcher's hook, his body mutilated almost beyond recognition. DI Colbeck's opening gambit with the lit cigarette was child's play in comparison to what had followed.

After flicking the stub of his latest cigarette to the ground, Standartenführer Thompson crossed the chamber to the Counter-Terrorism agent who was standing against the wall. 'Radio for the doctor,' he ordered.

Although John had known he was going to speak, the sound still made him flinch after such an extended period of silence.

The Counter-Terrorism agent nodded and headed for the door. When he pushed it open, a swell of frigid wind swept through the chamber, and John stayed a desire to chase after it. He had become accustomed to the thick stench of sweat, petrol fumes, and stale cigarette smoke down here, and to the unnatural heat of the chamber; he was forced to swallow the bile that rose in his throat when this brief respite of fresh air gave way to that miasma once more as the door slammed shut.

The Counter-Terrorism agent soon returned, and the chamber settled back into a taut, uncomfortable quiet.

*

Sometime later (it might have been five minutes or it might have been an hour – John could no longer tell), there was a knock at the door. The Counter-Terrorism agent answered it, and the click-clack patter of high-heeled footsteps entered the chamber.

The wearer of these shoes was an older woman, with a neatly cut bob combed into place, which was white but for the faintest hint of blonde. A pair of frameless, rectangular glasses sat on the bridge of her nose, and behind them were two indifferent grey eyes. Her face was set into a scowl, yet this seemed more her natural disposition than a reaction to the circumstances in which she found herself. This was amplified by her hollow cheeks and unusually high cheekbones, which gave her angular features an otherworldly quality. Her beige raincoat swayed just below her knees, underneath which a stark white blouse and a pair of straight black trousers sat on her thin frame. She carried a black leather doctor's bag in her left hand, and her right hand was slipped casually into the pocket of her coat.

She was an anomaly in the chamber.

'Thank you for coming, Doctor Beauchene.' Standartenführer Thompson addressed the woman in fluent German and with a degree of respect in his voice that John was yet to hear from him.

'You know my services are always available to the Schutzstaffel, Standartenführer,' Doctor Beauchene replied, also in German but with an accent, and it took John a moment to decide it was French. 'I take it this is the subject?'

'It is.'

'Hmm.' She was unfazed by both the menacing nature of the chamber and the disfigured state of Ramos.

Without any further discussion, Doctor Beauchene walked to the table at the side of the room and dashed the various bloody tools upon it to one side. In their place, she set down her bag. She removed her raincoat and proceeded to roll the sleeves of her blouse up her forearms. With a snap, the bag was then unlocked and the top of it opened wide.

'I must inform you, Standartenführer, that whilst my methods have improved significantly since last we met, they are still far from infallible: we have had success with less than fifty per cent of subjects using this current formula. However' – she considered the suspended Ramos – 'it would appear that you are out of other options, yes?'

'We are,' Standartenführer Thompson confirmed.

'Some men have a strong physical resolve,' Doctor Beauchene began as she removed a syringe and a vial of clear liquid from her bag, 'and they simply will not be broken by brute force. But these same men' – she unscrewed the lid from the vial and dipped the syringe into it – 'cannot protect their minds from science, Standartenführer. Soon' – she drew the fluid into the syringe – 'we will have no need for instruments of violence to gain access to the thoughts of our enemies.' She held the syringe up to the light and flicked the tip of its needle with her middle finger.

'I await the day,' Standartenführer Thompson remarked.

Doctor Beauchene paid him no attention. She was already approaching Ramos, an ominous twinkle of anticipation having settled in her eyes. She stopped, though, when she saw he was unconscious. 'Please, Standartenführer, wake the subject,' she requested.

Standartenführer Thompson ordered the Counter-Terrorism men to do so, and one of them struck Ramos hard across the face with the back of his hand.

Ramos burst back into life, and he searched the chamber with that frantic, bloodshot eye of his, uncertain for a second as to where he was. He soon remembered, and worry crossed his maimed face when he noticed this new figure standing before him, the syringe primed in her hand. When Doctor Beauchene smiled a small, eager smile and resumed her advance on him, Ramos started to squirm fretfully in his constraints again, and he mumbled anxious, incomprehensible words under his breath as the shackles rattled together. He clearly recognised that this woman represented a changing of tactics with regard to his interrogation, and it visibly terrified him.

Doctor Beauchene was not deterred. After stopping in front of Ramos, she pierced the skin of one of his legs with the syringe's needle and pushed down on the plunger until its clear contents had emptied into him. She then stood back and waited.

Ramos continued to struggle for a moment, much feebler now than when they began. He stopped eventually, though, and his head dropped onto his chest. He was not unconscious, which was evident by his eye still being open, but he had become suspiciously tranquil.

John watched this process unfold from where he was sitting, not sure what to think. All this talk of success percentages and subjects was strange to him. And what was in that vial that had put Ramos at such ease? Was it morphine? Or some opiate? The name "Beauchene" was unfamiliar to him, but then the Third Reich was famed for its brilliant doctors who had propelled the field of medical science forwards with their innovative ideas.

But this?

This was sinister.

Doctor Beauchene motioned for Standartenführer Thompson to join her in front of Ramos. 'Start with some simple questions, and I shall determine whether the dosage is correct. But make haste: whilst it varies from subject to subject, the effects of my formula can take a fast toll,' she explained, in a callous and clinical tone of voice.

Standartenführer Thompson nodded his understanding. Speaking English again, he turned to Ramos and asked, 'Can you hear me, Ramos?'

Ramos replied, '*Sí*,' but he did not lift his head to look at the Standartenführer.

'In English, if you don't mind,' Standartenführer Thompson instructed.

'Okay,' Ramos said in a soft, rather sleepy register.

'I have some questions for you, Ramos. Will you answer them?'

'Okay,' came the same, slow response.

Happy for now with the 'dosage', Doctor Beauchene indicated that Standartenführer Thompson should proceed.

Meanwhile, John remained sitting to one side in muted apprehension, none the wiser as to what was happening.

'Is your real name Miguel Carrasco Menéndez?' questioned the Standartenführer.

'Yes.'

'Did you fight for the Communists in the Spanish Civil War?'

'Yes.'

'Did you come to Great Britain before the Second Great War began?'

'Yes.'

'Did you change your name to Antonio Ramos Serrano?'

'Yes.'

'Did you commit crimes against the Third Reich on behalf of the King's Loyalists?'

'Yes.'

Although Ramos had admitted to this much already, the blithe nature by which the words left him surprised John more than the confession.

'What did you do for the King's Loyalists?'

'*Contrabando. Bombas. Sabotaje. Asesinatos.*'

'In English.'

'Assassinations.' Countless good and respected individuals had been murdered during those dark days, and John could only imagine how many had been by Ramos's own hand.

'Are you currently involved with a drug known as Yonder?'

John leant forwards in his chair.

There was a change in Ramos's demeanour when Standartenführer Thompson asked him this: his body tensed and his hands clenched into tight fists above his head, as though he were trying to resist answering the question. At last, he did say, 'Yes,' once again, but it took him much longer to speak the word this time, and when he did so, it was through gritted teeth.

John stood up at the answer, roused by a flicker of hope; this was the first time Ramos had acknowledged Yonder's existence all afternoon. Whatever that clear liquid was – and it categorically was not morphine – it had taken effect.

With that, Standartenführer Thompson stepped away. 'I think it's time for you and the detective sergeant to take over,' he declared.

When John turned around and saw that DI Colbeck had emerged from the shadows behind the spotlight, his gaze fell to the floor. The mere sight of the DI caused his hands to start trembling, so John folded his arms and dismissed the lingering doubts in his mind that had been set aside the moment this interrogation began.

Wasting no time, DI Colbeck moved towards Ramos and asked the same question he had put to the man at least a dozen times today: 'Are you responsible for smuggling Yonder into Great Britain?'

Ramos struggled against the answer again, and his body shuddered in the shackles. 'Yes.'

'Do you smuggle Yonder via the company *Delicias Inspiradas*?'

He let out a long, guttural groan and growled, 'Yes.'

'Are you known by the alias "The Spaniard"?'

His breathing became laboured. 'Yes.'

If nothing else, at least John now knew for certain he had been correct when he theorised that Ramos was The Spaniard.

'Do you work with a man called James Summers?'

Ramos did not answer DI Colbeck's question this time, or if he did, it was lost amongst a series of grunts and snorts whilst his body began to convulse erratically. Before anything further could come of the matter, however, Doctor Beauchene was injecting him with another dose of her clear liquid, having anticipated a change in his composure. This raucous behaviour lasted for only several seconds before Ramos's head fell back onto his chest and he was silent once more.

As he settled, Doctor Beauchene went to retrieve a little notebook from her leather bag. She then set about scribbling something into it, unable to hide her fascination with how Ramos was reacting to her 'formula'. She addressed DI Colbeck and Standartenführer Thompson without averting her eyes from the page: 'You may have to hurry, gentlemen. I do not know how much more he will be able to handle.' She gave no hint as to what she alluded when she used the term 'handle', but John assumed the worst.

'Do you work with a man called James Summers?' DI Colbeck repeated the question now that Ramos had returned to his docile state.

'Yes,' he answered.

John exhaled. They were back on track.

When Ramos had spoken this time, though, there was a detached, mechanical quality to his voice, as if he were no longer trying to resist the question. Either that, or with a second dose of the clear liquid coursing through his body, he was no longer *able* to resist.

'Does he distribute Yonder around Great Britain?'

'Yes.' The word was harsh and unemotional.

'How does he distribute Yonder?'

'*Camiones.*'

'In English,' commanded Standartenführer Thompson from the side of the chamber.

'Lorries.'

'And they leave with the Yonder from James Summers' warehouse in Silvertown?' continued DI Colbeck.

'Yes.'

This put to rest any speculation in that regard, then: the Yonder Organisation used the lorries from Summers' warehouse to move Yonder across the nation under a legal licence. With this information, the Task Force would not only be able to raid Summers' Import and Export with impunity, but they would also be able to spread the word to other DESs around Great Britain and set into motion a chain reaction that would cripple the drug's distribution network.

DI Colbeck posed his next question: 'Where is Yonder being manufactured?' It was not in Great Britain if Ramos was smuggling Yonder over from Spain, so it was either on the Continent itself or somewhere even further afield.

'Venezuela,' Ramos replied without hesitation, much to John's surprise. It was such an odd place for Yonder to have originated, but then this did have a certain logic to it: Venezuela was half a world away, and far beyond the reach of the Third Reich, so the Yonder Organisation would be able to manufacture the drug there without fear of being discovered. The revelation was nevertheless worrying, though, as not only would transporting Yonder across the Atlantic and into Spain necessitate considerable effort and substantial financial backing, but it would also require a vast web of conspirators spanning two continents to accomplish such an enterprise. John had never considered that they might be operating on so grand a scale.

'Where in Venezuela?' queried DI Colbeck.

'Venezuela,' repeated Ramos.

'Yes, but *where* in Venezuela *precisely?*' DI Colbeck asked with deliberate emphasis, like he would if he were speaking to a small child.

There was a pause, as though Ramos was thinking about his answer. Then: 'Venezuela.'

Irritated, DI Colbeck gave up.

Standartenführer Thompson took over. 'Are there any others in your organisation who used to be King's Loyalists?' His question concerned his own agenda far more than it did the Yonder Task Force's.

'Yes,' Ramos answered.

'Who?' Standartenführer Thompson added quickly, his interest piqued.

Ramos said, 'Yes,' into his chest again, and nothing more.

Standartenführer Thompson grumbled and did not bother asking a second time. It would appear that the clear liquid had rendered Ramos incapable of giving anything beyond basic, ambiguous answers. John glanced over at Doctor Beauchene, who was writing in her notebook, infuriatingly captivated by the fact that she had reduced their most valuable asset in the Yonder investigation to little more than a monosyllabic vegetable.

It was with limited confidence, then, that John put forth a question of his own to Ramos. Edging closer to him, John asked, 'What does Yonder mean? What is its purpose?' He refused to believe that it was a "medication" or a "cure", or the figurehead for a fashionable "silent protest", given what Ramos had endured to protect the Yonder Organisation. Why would he offer so much of himself for something so inconsequential?

'Freedom,' was Ramos's terse response.

'Freedom from what?' John probed. 'National Socialism? The Reich?' Was it really so straightforward?

'Freedom from... from... life...'

'Freedom from *life*?'

'Ye... ye... yes...' Ramos's words became slurred.

John leant towards him, straining to understand the answer.

As he did so, Ramos let out a tremendous ear-piercing wail that took John completely by surprise, and he could not help but recoil in shock. DI Colbeck and Standartenführer Thompson withdrew as well, alarmed by this unexpected eruption of tormented agony. When John looked around, he saw concern on the faces of both Counter-Terrorism agents for the first time that afternoon.

The only person in the chamber who remained composed was Doctor Beauchene. She was already approaching Ramos, with the syringe filled with yet another dose of clear liquid in one hand and the now half-empty vial in the other. As she drew nearer, however, Ramos started to flail back and forth, and just when she reached him, he lurched outwards, hitting her and launching the vial out of her hand and across the chamber. But the syringe was still safely in her grasp, and Doctor Beauchene drove it into Ramos's leg and pressed down on the plunger. The same as before, he soon calmed into that state of unusual stillness, with his head on his chest and those howls of anguish subsiding.

The vial of clear liquid clattered across the floor and rolled to a halt at John's feet. He bent to pick it up and read the label fixed to the glass: 'Formula B150663. #17'. It meant nothing to him, and when Doctor Beauchene extended a hand, John placed the vial in her palm, and she turned away without thanking him.

Instead, she declared to the room, 'Very few subjects have ever made it to a fourth dose, gentlemen.' Her words implied an imminent end to the interrogation, underscored by a trace of anticipation for whatever might happen next.

They did not return to this idea of Yonder being 'freedom from life'; Ramos's description fit the drug's narrative well enough, what with all that nonsense about "freeing" people from the National Socialist world they considered so dreadful. Besides, they would likely get little else out of him on the subject anyway.

But what should their next question be? What could they ask that would provide them with reliable and coherent information whilst Ramos lingered in this absent-minded stupor?

The chamber fell silent.

DI Colbeck opened his mouth to speak, but he changed his mind.

Standartenführer Thompson's shoes scraped restlessly against the concrete floor, but he offered nothing.

And all the while, the seconds ticked by, and Ramos edged ever closer towards whatever inauspicious fate Doctor Beauchene's words had condemned him.

And then a question came to John that they should have put to Ramos the instant Doctor Beauchene injected him with her clear liquid: 'Who is the leader of your organisation?' he asked.

'Uncle Billy,' Ramos stated in that same mechanical monotone.

John's eyes widened in disbelief: Uncle Billy actually existed!

DI Colbeck challenged Ramos: 'Who is Uncle Billy?'

'Uncle Billy,' Ramos repeated the name.

'What is his *real* name?'

For the first time since being subjected to the clear liquid, Ramos lifted his head. He stared unblinkingly past John and DI Colbeck, his eye fixed on the blinding spotlight behind them. 'William,' he muttered.

John's heart hammered in his chest.

'William *what?*' DI Colbeck demanded.

Ramos's body stiffened, and the name was stifled in his throat before he could fully speak it aloud: 'William A... William A...'

They were so close.

'*William what?*' DI Colbeck yelled the question this time.

'Will... William...' Ramos stuttered. Then, through a clenched jaw, he barked, 'Uncle Billy.'

DI Colbeck ran a frustrated hand through his hair.

A thin layer of foam had formed at Ramos's mouth, and he growled, 'Uncle Billy,' again with a spray of spittle.

'Fuck,' John breathed.

'*Uncle Billy!*' Ramos shouted the name suddenly, as if he were calling out to this man. His eye started to quiver in its socket, and the foam at his mouth turned red. He began to convulse again – violently this time, with his whole body writhing in the shackles. Then he screamed wildly and roared, 'Billy! Billy! Billy!' Blood dribbled down his chin from his remaining teeth biting into his own flesh, and the screams became almost a crazed laughter: '*Billy! Billy! Billy!*'

John stumbled backwards, horrified by the deformed and frenzied figure before him.

What had they done to this man?

To his body?

To his *mind*?

A gunshot rattled around the chamber, and Ramos's head dropped back onto his chest, the bullet hole at his chin having ended his misery.

Doctor Beauchene stood behind the smoking revolver, a tiny thing she had produced from nowhere. 'Psychosis is a common symptom of prolonged exposure,' she explained, and she dropped the gun into her leather bag. She spoke without regret, like she had just disposed of a laboratory rat.

John realised his mouth was agape, and so he made a conscious effort to close it.

'I will take the subject,' Doctor Beauchene announced. She was writing in her notebook and offered no explanation for why she might want the body. That aura of intrigue had dissipated with the gunshot, her grey eyes revealing nothing but indifference once more. 'When you have concluded your investigation, please let my office know if the information he provided was of any use. It will be most beneficial to my studies to know whether or not the subject was lying.'

Standartenführer Thompson thanked Doctor Beauchene for her assistance. When she offered no further pleasantries in response, the men gathered themselves in a shambolic fashion and filtered from the chamber without another word.

Up in the barn, it was much later than John had expected it to be, with the field already shrouded by darkness. He squinted at his watch in the moonlight, and it read just shy of twenty past six – it had been midday when they descended into the chamber.

John shivered. A bitter breeze was chilling him to the bone as it ruffled his sweat-dampened shirt. He would have preferred to not linger out here; with the reminder that a world above that chamber existed, the reality of what they had been doing all afternoon began to push its way to the forefront of his mind, and what little energy he could rally became focused on repressing those thoughts for as long as possible.

Evidently, the others did not share this desire.

'So, Tomas, did you get what you needed?' Standartenführer Thompson enquired as they exited the barn onto the stone path.

'For now,' was DI Colbeck's tentative reply. He stopped next to the Standartenführer. 'Thank you for your help, James.'

'Listen, if there are old King's Loyalists involved, I want to be there when you take them down.' Standartenführer Thompson offered his services with a smile.

DI Colbeck declared that he would be delighted to have him along when they moved against the Yonder Organisation. John could not help but think that this was no more than a cynical ploy by the Standartenführer, though, to encroach on the DES's impending glory.

Either that or it was a sincere gesture of support…

It had been a long day, and exhaustion was setting in. John just wanted to go home.

DI Colbeck read his mind. 'John, you take your car and head home. James, may I ride back to Scotland Yard with you?'

Standartenführer Thompson confirmed that he could, and John felt relief fill his body.

John walked to the Morris Minor – past what must have been Doctor Beauchene's Porsche 911, its steel grey a fitting colour for the woman. He climbed in and watched the others approach the Mercedes. Before DI Colbeck got in onto the back seat, he looked to John to bid him goodnight; that reassuring face John knew so well smiled at him, and his gentle, amber eyes met John's through the windscreen.

Even in the darkness, John could see that "ruthless interrogator", the vicious man who had assaulted Ramos with a lit cigarette, and who had instructed John to do far worse in the hours since. It was only a glimpse, but it was there nonetheless, creeping around the edges of his façade now that they had returned to the surface.

John's hands were shaking uncontrollably beneath the steering wheel. He placed them flat on his knees and forced himself to smile back.

He waited for the Mercedes to leave first. Then, after a final glance at the barn – which seemed so innocent out here in the middle of nowhere – John set off across the field, and he began the journey home along the dark country roads.

CHAPTER SEVENTEEN

Sleepless

John lay wide awake that night. The bedroom had been consumed by a pin-drop quiet after Alice fell asleep, and the sound of Ramos in the throes of death rang around his skull. Worse still, whenever he closed his eyes, John would see Ramos's mutilated figure there, dangling from those shackles in an endless, distorted oblivion.

*

During the drive home, John had turned the radio up loud to drown out the voices in his head. He had paid no attention to the words spoken by the presenters, though, nor had he hummed along to the music they played. He had focused on the road ahead, not thinking about what had happened that afternoon or what would happen tomorrow, but stopping and starting, finding the familiar landmarks and following them towards Pullman Road.

When he had walked through the front door, Alice had welcomed him with a kiss and a hug, but she had recognised straight away that something was amiss by his demeanour.

Not questioning him directly, she had asked, 'How was your day? Did you catch bad guys?'

Alice had delivered the attempt at cheerful brevity with a sweet smile, but John had not responded in kind. 'It was fine,' he had said, like a taciturn child returning home from school. 'I'm going for a shower.' Even with the windows wound down, all the way home the car had been beset by the stink of the chamber: that foetid mixture of petrol fumes, sweat, and stale cigarette smoke. It was as if it had seeped right into his skin, and John had been desperate to wash it away.

'Oh, okay,' Alice had mumbled as he had climbed the stairs by the door, dejected by this rebuff. John had become adept at hiding a bad day from her, burying any negativity beneath a veneer of happiness and love; today, it was different, and he had not been able to summon the emotional fortitude required to maintain the pretence.

He had dropped his clothes on the bedroom floor and stepped into the bathroom. In the shower, he had scrubbed himself with soap until he was raw, yet somehow that stench had lingered up his nose. And he had still been able to feel Ramos's dried blood between his fingers and under his nails, long after it was gone. Eventually, he had turned the water so hot that it very nearly scalded him.

He had soon lost track of time.

When John had emerged from the bathroom, he had found Alice sitting on the edge of their bed. She had his shirt in her hands, and he had seen that the blood was not only on the cuffs: dark streaks of it ran up the forearms, and spots of it were flecked across the chest. He had not noticed before.

'John?' Alice had looked up at him.

He had shaken his head.

'John, what happened?' she had asked. Usually, she would not pry, knowing as she did that he would never share certain details with her. Then again, he had never before come home covered in someone else's blood, so Alice's persistence was understandable.

'Arnold's dead,' John had replied, hot tears filling his eyes.

'Oh John, I'm so sorry,' Alice had whispered. She had motioned to the shirt. 'Is this... his?' She meant the blood.

'No,' John had choked out as he shuffled in the doorway.

Alice had said no more. She had dropped the shirt back to the floor, and standing up, she had crossed the room to him and put her arms around his waist.

John had placed his head on her shoulder and begun to cry.

They had stayed there in an embrace for a short while. Before long, Alice had led John to the bed and lain down next to him, and she had stroked his hair until she thought he had fallen asleep. She had then slipped into her usual position beside him and drifted off herself.

*

That was where John lay now, not asleep, but staring up at the bedroom's art deco ceiling whilst the thoughts he had suppressed that afternoon danced across his mind to the tune of Ramos howling in agony.

When the interrogation had first begun, John's resolve that whatever they did was justified because Ramos possessed information the Yonder Task Force needed was excuse enough. But the sufferings they had then inflicted upon the man – it had been barbaric! They as good as tore him limb from limb, each act upon his body worse than the one that preceded it. John had neither done nor seen anything like it before. Plus, it all came to naught when Ramos proved to be unbreakable, and any semblance of justification he was working to melted away.

Yet John did everything that was asked of him, without question, just as he had vowed he would do – and just as he had always done.

When the noises Ramos made became harrowing to the point that it was almost unbearable to be in the chamber any longer, John had retreated to a blank space in his mind. He moved unconsciously, refusing to let in the incessant soundtrack of screaming, and refusing to look into Ramos's tormented eyes. His hands acted of their own accord when they followed orders to do unspeakable things, and John watched the interrogation unfold before him as though it were playing out on a television screen. It had been easy enough to achieve this detachment in the chamber, out of sight of the world above. But now, with nothing except for Alice's soft snoring to keep him company, John remembered every second of that afternoon and every action he had performed, and he was wracked with guilt. And it was not that niggle of guilt that settled in his stomach when they had interrogated Joe Harding; nor was it the grinding, uncomfortable guilt he experienced after killing the third man in Göring Station. No, this was a heavy, tiresome guilt that weighed upon John's chest, as if someone had dumped a boulder on him where he lay and he was being crushed beneath its terrible mass.

What they had done to Ramos reminded him of the stories he had been told as a boy about the Imperialists and the atrocities they committed during the liberation of Great Britain at the end of the Second Great War: German soldiers captured by the Imperialists were routinely tortured and executed, and then left on display for the advancing troops to find. According to John's childhood history teacher, in some of the most extreme instances, heads were put on spikes in a seemingly medieval ritual as a warning to those who dared challenge the Imperialists' rule. These brutalities became synonymous with the utter immorality of the Imperialists, and only worked to incite a greater dedication in the German soldiers to freeing Great Britain from them. Even before the war, though, for centuries the Imperialists had imprisoned and murdered millions of innocent people all around the world in the name of the "British Empire", so such inhumanity was no surprise.

John had always wondered how he could have descended from such a savage race, but after today, and after the hurt he had wrought upon Ramos – he saw more of his ancestors in himself than ever before.

He was no better than them.

As for what this implied with regard to Standartenführer Thompson and his Counter-Terrorism agents – and DI Colbeck – John was unsure. This was not the first time any of them had interrogated a suspect in such a manner, so much was apparent.

Maybe none of them were any better than the Imperialists.

Maybe nothing had changed…

As John lay there questioning everything he believed in, a phrase popped into his head. It was something he remembered from school that had been said to the children when they were reprimanded for their misbehaviour: *Jedem das seine*.

He mouthed the words to himself. The insinuation in the maxim was: Everyone gets what they deserve.

Ramos had been no run-of-the-mill criminal like Joe Harding or the third man. Before his pivotal role as a drug smuggler for the Yonder Organisation, he was an agent of violence as a soldier for both the Communists and the Imperialists, and then as a terrorist for the King's Loyalists. He had readily admitted to these crimes before the interrogation proper was even underway, as though his direct involvement in the murder of what was probably hundreds – if not *thousands* – meant nothing to him. If those who had died as a result of Yonder were added to this tally, the number of deaths Ramos was accountable for became unimaginable.

The man was, in a single word: evil.

That was the difference, then, between John's actions that afternoon and the transgressions the Imperialists had perpetrated during their global reign of terror, against both the innocent citizens of the British Empire and the brave German soldiers who fought to liberate Great Britain from their clutches: Ramos *deserved* everything that had happened to him. He had brought it upon himself by the choices he had made, past and present. If the pain this man had caused over the last three decades were to be calculated, where would it stand in comparison to what he had endured today? He had done so many terrible things – was this not retribution in kind for his crimes?

Did it even come close to true justice?

Jedem das seine.

John needed to change his outlook. He was an officer of the Reich, a tool of the State, and he was not supposed to burden himself with such trivial things as guilt when the security of the nation – nay, the Third Reich! – was at stake.

He knew that.

And he was not an Imperialist, fighting to preserve power and influence over innocent peoples, or to uphold some corrupted belief system.

He was a National Socialist, and a proud one at that.

He recalled the words to 'Horst-Wessel-Lied', the anthem of the Third Reich: *'Zum Kampfe steh'n wir alle schon bereit!'* – 'We are all ready for the fight!' That did not only refer to the war with the Imperialists or to the battle that continued against the Communists on the Eastern Front; it was the fight for National Socialism wherever evil tried to destroy it.

Ramos and Yonder were a part of that evil, and therefore they had to be eliminated – by any means necessary.

John turned over in the bed and exhaled through the ache in his ribs. He would do whatever he could to protect the Third Reich and National Socialism – the greater good in this world. That was his duty, and was how he paid back the debt he owed to the State for having raised him in the absence of his parents.

'You should be proud of that pain you feel, because it is evidence of what you *have done – in the name of the Reich!'* DI Colbeck's talk with him in the fifth-floor WC was particularly relevant once again: everything he had done today, he did in the name of the Reich.

John closed his eyes and, repeating this to himself, he pushed any remaining self-doubt far to the back of his mind.

He did finally fall into an uneasy sleep, which was plagued by dark images and troubled dreams: John wrestled with the sight of Ramos writhing in his shackles; of Doctor Beauchene and the chilling fascination she wore when she injected her clear liquid into the man; and of DI Colbeck, whose face became contorted and unrecognisable, almost monstrous.

But when he awoke in the morning, that nagging, lingering guilt had subsided; his moment of uncertainty had passed, only to be replaced instead by a weariness and a muggy headache.

CHAPTER EIGHTEEN

A Loose End

It was a little after nine o'clock in the morning when John found himself sitting beside Peter in the DI's BMW once more. They were on their way to London State Hospital to visit Jasper Jones, the man Peter had shot in Göring Station. Although he was still in a bad way, Jones was awake and coherent according to a phone call earlier that morning, and as a result, he was ready to be questioned by the DES.

The same could not be said for Sebastien Dubois, the broad-shouldered Belgian they had arrested alongside Jones in Göring Station, who had been taken away that morning beneath a white sheet. Peter had beaten the man to near death the previous afternoon whilst interrogating him; John guessed that Peter must have heard about what happened to Arnold at Smith and Sons' Antiquities and Crafts, and that the resulting fury had fuelled his visit to The Basement. Alex told John that he had been down there for most of the afternoon and had surfaced only when DI Colbeck returned to Scotland

Yard and ordered it. It was already much too late for Dubois, though, and he died in the night from his injuries.

John could see dark bruising on Peter's knuckles when he turned the steering wheel, but that was the only lasting impact Dubois' death had afforded him: killing a man had disconcerted him not one bit. With candid disregard, he dismissed the incident as a mishap, and it was not mentioned again. After what John had done to Ramos in the pursuit of answers, he supposed he was in no position to judge.

Visiting Jasper Jones was more or less a way to kill time at this juncture, as although DI Colbeck had put in a request to DCI Werner for approval of a raid on James Summers' warehouse in Silvertown, it would take time for the green light to come back from the powers that be before they could begin preparations. Granted, Jones was a loose end who would be questioned sooner or later, but he was still insignificant when compared to the devastating blow they were ready to deliver against the Yonder Organisation. It was more important than the assignment Alfie and Alex had been given, at any rate: they were to investigate the connection between Yonder and Venezuela about which Ramos had spoken, but even DI Colbeck stopped just shy of admitting that this would be a waste of everybody's time.

Nevertheless, John would have gladly traded places with either Alex or Alfie. He was less than pleased to have been partnered with Peter again, especially given that they were on their way to what might be yet another interrogation. He just hoped Peter would be forced to exercise a modicum of restraint since they were questioning Jones in a public space, but the familiar, malevolent grin that stretched across his face when DI Colbeck assigned them the task was downright unsettling. That heavy cologne of his swirled around John's head, intensifying the clawing headache that had dogged him all morning; in the end, he had to wind the window down in order to escape the overwhelming aroma.

Having endured the awkward silence of the car ride – John had refused to engage Peter and pretended instead to read through his notebook, and Peter seemed content to let him do so – they pulled into a parking bay at the back of the hospital.

Peter instructed, 'Follow me. I know the way to Jones's room.'

John acknowledged the order with nothing more than a nod and climbed out of the BMW.

London State Hospital was identical to every other hospital John had ever visited, with clinical, white walls and that distinct smell of disinfectant. Doctors, nurses, patients, and visitors scurried about the place, paying little or no attention to the detectives as they crossed the foyer to reach the lifts and travelled up to the third floor. From there, it was a short walk along the corridor to Jasper Jones's room.

The uniformed constable stationed at the door did not ask for any identification when they approached him, but he greeted Peter knowingly as, 'Sir,' with an outstretched arm in salute.

Peter responded by raising his hand to the side of his head, and John consciously did the same – the formalities of rank still made him uncomfortable, he noticed.

Dismissing the sensation, John followed Peter into Jones's room, and the constable closed the door behind them.

The room was indistinguishable from any other patient's room in the building: there was a bed; a lamp; a window; a side table; a worn-out, padded green chair for visitors; a machine making a ceaseless *beep, beep, beep* sound; and, of course, a patient. The one thing out of place here, however, was that the patient was handcuffed to the metal bed rail by his left wrist.

Jasper Jones was lying there, asleep, with an oxygen mask over his nose and mouth and a square of padded dressing covering the area beneath his right nipple.

John remembered Jones's bearded face from when he was hiding in the wardrobe at 27 Faulks Road. Back then, Jones had been a formidable threat and a cause for great anxiety; now, lying in that bed under a soft blanket, he was no more than a small and pathetic man.

There had been no discussion about what would happen next, and no back and forth on the strategy the detectives were to employ to extract any information out of Jones. Yet, as was custom by now, Peter was already at work – he unplugged the heart monitor, and the *beep, beep, beep* stopped – having once again taken complete, unilateral control of the task at hand. Not surprised in the least and unwilling to break the habit of a lifetime, John kept his comments to himself and stood to one side in silent obedience.

Peter followed the clear tube on the oxygen mask down to the side of Jones's bed, and in a calm, calculated movement, he twisted the plastic so that it contorted in his hands and cut off the flow of air. There was a split second when John questioned this action, but then he recalled his revelation of the night before: they were here to find out what this man knew, and that could not be achieved with kindness or a gentle touch. And besides, Jones was another enemy of the Reich who was complicit in all of the deaths caused due to Yonder, so he deserved little else.

Jedem das seine. John repeated the phrase to himself with a certain resolve.

As the oxygen in his mask became thinner, Jones stirred in the bed. He opened his eyes, unsure at first as to why he was unable to breathe, and this confusion then became abject fear when he saw the two suited men standing over him.

Peter leant down towards him and whispered in his ear, 'Make a noise, and your inability to breathe will become permanent.'

It was rather a dramatic threat, John thought, but Jones understood its message well enough, and he was quiet when Peter removed the oxygen mask.

'Do you remember me, Jasper?' Peter asked.

Jones shook his head.

'I'm the man who shot you,' Peter clarified through a ruthless smile. 'Your two friends are dead. I did Dubois myself, and my colleague here did the other one.'

Jones examined John out of the corner of his eye, and John responded with a composed, steady stare.

Or at least he tried to. In his mind, John was back on the train tracks below Platform 12, and he was slamming the third man's head into the stones over and over and over again…

He was lost in the memory for a moment.

It felt like a lifetime ago.

Peter's voice returned him to the present. 'I would not regret making the set, Jasper. *You* need to give me a reason not to.'

Jones's eyes filled with anger at the remark, but that fear remained on his face, as though he believed Peter might actually kill him in his hospital bed.

'So, do you have anything for me?' Peter asked.

Jones said nothing.

Peter waited for several seconds before he accepted that Jones was going to concede nothing voluntarily. When this became evident, he produced a set of handcuffs from his jacket pocket and without a word proceeded to shackle Jones's free wrist to the bed rail. Jones tried to resist him, but with not even enough energy to lift his arm it was a useless effort, and he was rendered defenceless against the metal.

Before he continued, Peter removed his suit jacket and took great care in placing it over the padded green chair, straightening its shoulders until they were in the right shape. He rolled up his sleeves, and from a trouser pocket, he produced a penknife. Peter then stepped towards Jones, and after taking a long look at him, he dashed the blanket from the bed and onto the floor to reveal the semi-naked man, who was dressed only in thin hospital trousers.

Jones was breathing unsteadily by now, and beads of nervous sweat had formed at his thinning hairline. He did not struggle in the handcuffs, but stayed perfectly still save for the heaving of his chest. Even his eyes were motionless, with both of them fixated on Peter.

'I was told about your injuries,' Peter said, and he began to peel the padded dressing from Jones's torso, 'and I must admit, I did not intend to put you in the hospital. This place is far too nice for the likes of you.'

Jones winced and glanced down at the exposed wound. It was messy and raw, with black sutures holding the skin together.

'To be honest, I would sooner have put you in the ground,' Peter confessed, as he removed the last of the dressing and tossed it away. He lifted the blade out from the penknife's wooden handle. 'Your boss, Ramos – he's dead as well. We already know he smuggled Yonder into Great Britain, and we know James Summers' warehouse in Silvertown is the centre for its distribution nationwide. So, in actual fact, there's not an awful lot left for you to tell us.'

Jones's composure changed then, as it became clear they knew far more than he had expected.

'But there is always something else, Jasper,' Peter claimed. He ran the tip of the penknife across Jones's bare stomach.

'Something you can give us to stop me from doing what you know I'm about to do.'

John could hazard a guess as to what Peter was 'about to do'.

'First, where is Maria Turner hiding? Second, who is Uncle Billy?' Peter asked, and Jones shuddered beneath the steel point of the penknife. These were the two questions DI Colbeck had instructed them to put to the man, and although they had asked about Uncle Billy because they wanted to dismantle the Yonder Organisation, the question about Turner's whereabouts owed more to the Task Force's desire to seek revenge for Arnold's murder.

'I don't know.' Jones garbled the words in his coarse northern accent, and his narrow eyes flickered between Peter and the penknife.

'Last chance,' Peter warned as he drew the blade towards Jones's wound.

'Please, don't!' Jones whimpered, and he started straining against the handcuffs.

'Hold him down, Detective Sergeant,' Peter commanded.

When John hesitated, Peter turned to him and said, 'C'mon, John, grab his shoulders.'

John swallowed hard and approached the bed.

What I do, I do because it is my duty. I do it to protect the Reich.

'Zum Kampfe steh'n wir alle schon bereit!'

John set his hands firmly on Jones's shoulders and held the squirming man in place.

'We are all ready for the fight!'

Before he could shout out, Peter placed a hand over Jones's mouth so he was able to make only a muffled cry for help. He then slipped the blade between the sutures that were interwoven across the wound and severed them, one by one, with erratic, ragged movements. Each time he did so, a muted yelp came from Jones, and John had to wrestle against him to keep him still.

John wanted to be appalled by how abruptly this situation had escalated into violent interrogation, but such a reaction would be quite preposterous after yesterday. If nothing else, these sounds of stifled misery were almost pleasant compared to the noises Ramos had made.

Although Peter had proven a vivid point already about what Jones could expect should he refuse to cooperate, he did not allow Jones a second chance to answer his questions when the final suture was broken. Instead, he tilted the penknife into the now open wound and commenced digging around in the dark-red flesh. Blood spilt out over the sides and cascaded down onto Jones's stomach and into the bedsheets, and the man writhed in inaudible agony. All the while, the clatter of the handcuffs against the metal bed rails consumed the room.

Using all his weight to keep Jones pinned down, John leant forwards, and he was struck unawares by the sweet and sickly scent of Peter's cologne. It was somehow stronger than before, though: a ripe, festering stink that swamped his nostrils and clung to the back of his throat. He was so close to Peter that he could see the perspiration seeping from his clean-shaven skin, and it was all John could do not to gag or retch.

After ten gruelling seconds of this torment, Peter removed the blade from inside Jones, who collapsed into the bed. He was trembling beneath John's hands, and tears rolled down the sides of his face onto the pillow.

'When I move my hand, I want nothing but answers,' Peter demanded.

Jones nodded hastily.

Peter took a step back, and John released his shoulders.

Jones shuffled up the bed until he was propped upright. 'Fuck it. If you know all that, then it's over anyway, whether Ramos is dead or not. And I owe 'em nothin',' he professed, and he gritted his teeth against the throbbing pain in his chest.

Ramos and Dubois would have been disgusted by such a profound surrender, John thought.

'Turner's got a flat in Stevenson Place, on the south side of the river. Ramos was staying with 'er, but I'm tellin' you she won't 'ave gone back there, not if you got 'er old man. And I don't know where she'll 'ave run off to instead.'

John believed he was telling the truth. He took his notebook from his jacket pocket and wrote 'Stevenson Place' on a clean page.

Jones continued, 'I saw 'im a couple of times, Uncle Billy. Older bloke, like seventy or somethin'. English. White 'air, combed back, and glasses. Kind of lanky. Thin. But 'e 'ad a... a presence about 'im, you know. Always carried this walkin' cane with a silver dog's 'ead on the handle – or some kind of animal, anyway. And I never got a proper name before you ask, 'e was just Uncle Billy. 'Im and Ramos were old friends from back in the days of the King's Loyalists.'

John was surprised. He had hoped that Jones might have heard Ramos talking about Uncle Billy and maybe gathered a handful of vague details in the process, but had not expected that he would have ever seen the man in person. Nevertheless, an older English gentleman with a walking cane and glasses was hardly a breakthrough for the Yonder Task Force, as that could describe countless men in London alone. It was further confirmation that Uncle Billy existed, but nothing more.

Jones also filled the detectives in on James Summers' backstory – or to be more precise, his father's. Jones had met

Summers many times, and on one such occasion, he had divulged proudly to Jones that his father aided the King's Loyalists before The Purges, smuggling into and out of Great Britain for them via Summers' Import and Export. And not just weapons and contraband, either, but people as well: it was Summers' father who had smuggled Standartenführer Thompson's Spanish nationals back to Spain for the King's Loyalists, which in turn provided terrorists such as Ramos with the freedom to roam without restraint on altered ID cards. The produce company – *Delicias Inspiradas* – and trade licence the original Antonio Ramos Serrano had signed his name to back in 1946 was the foundation for this, and although Ramos's name remained on the documentation to this day, it was always an asset belonging to the King's Loyalists that they had used to facilitate this smuggling operation. These ex-King's Loyalists in the Yonder Organisation had returned to the warehouse in Silvertown when the concept of Yonder arose to recruit the son in place of the father, knowing full well that he was already indoctrinated in their foolish ideologies.

At this point, Jones claimed to know nothing else, insisting that he was little more than a dogsbody to Ramos, so Peter flicked his cigarette butt out of the window and turned back towards the bed. He had stepped to the side and lit that cigarette the instant Jones started speaking, his disappointment in the man for yielding so soon palpable in his expression; it was as though Peter had wanted a reason to continue the interrogation, and Jones's willingness to cooperate robbed him of the pleasure.

He addressed John: 'Go and find a telephone and get in touch with Colbeck, and tell him that we're headed for Turner's flat.'

Thinking nothing of the order, John exited the room.

Doing as instructed, he found a public telephone at the other end of the corridor, and several minutes later, John was on the line with DI Colbeck. He was similarly astonished to hear that Jones had talked with such abandon, even though he too recognised that the description of Uncle Billy was not an awful lot to work with. John also told him about James Summers' father, but DI Colbeck was less shocked by the link between the warehouse and the King's Loyalists. In the final moments of the conversation, DI Colbeck agreed that heading to Turner's flat was the best use of their time for now, and he wished John luck before ringing off.

John walked back along the corridor with a skip in his step. He thought himself quite foolish for having dismissed Jones as no more than a loose end in the investigation, and relief absorbed any lingering notion of guilt he might have felt for their rough treatment of the man.

He smiled, content with the morning's proceedings.

That fleeting spark of relative happiness was swiftly snuffed out when John entered Jones's room to find him motionless in the bed, gazing with empty eyes up at the ceiling.

Peter was gone, but he soon reappeared behind John, with a worried look on his face. 'After you left, he started choking,' he explained through shallow breaths as the constable and a nurse in a dark-blue uniform burst into the room behind him.

The nurse rushed to the side of the bed and checked Jones for signs of life, but she shook her head.

He was already dead.

'*Fuck!*' Peter shouted, but there was a suspicious, artificial tone to the outburst. He demanded that the nurse do something, and when she said there was nothing to be done, he barked a series of expletives at her until she was forced from the room in search of a doctor.

John watched on from the corner, not showing any indication as to what he was thinking: *Has Peter really just murdered Jones in cold blood?* He had given them everything they had asked for and more, so perhaps Peter had decided there was now no reason for him to live. He had beaten Dubois so severely that he died, but at least that was during the process of interrogating him – or so Peter claimed…

John stared down at the body in the bed, then he dared to glance at Peter. He did appear concerned, but it seemed to John as if it were affected – as if the whole thing were a performance.

A doctor arrived before long with the same nurse in tow, but he asked no further questions of the detectives once Peter explained what allegedly "happened". And although the doctor exchanged a troubled look with the nurse when he noticed Jones's open wound and the bloodied bedsheets, neither of them were bold enough to mention it as John and Peter took their leave.

*

Once back in the BMW, Peter again expressed his disappointment at Jones having died, a sentiment that was followed by him declaring, 'But I suppose he had already told us everything he could, so fuck him.' And that was the final word on the matter: he did not ask for John's opinion, nor did he seek validation of his own. Instead, Peter put the car into gear, and he set off in the direction of Stevenson Place.

Jedem das seine, John thought to himself, with a grim cynicism.

CHAPTER NINETEEN

1965

In the aftermath of the Second Great War, there was an urgent housing crisis in Great Britain, as not only had many homes been reduced to rubble during the fighting, but also the unprecedented migration of people from both the countryside and the Continent to its cities in search of work in the factories had forced them into cramped and squalid living conditions. Acting accordingly to resolve the issue, the National Socialist government had commissioned the building of thousands of residential tower blocks all around the nation, and within a matter of weeks, the workers were moving into their new State-provided housing. South London had been a focal point of this housing regeneration, and today dozens of these high-rise buildings soared like enormous obelisks along the skyline on this side of the Thames, each twenty storeys high with hundreds of tenants residing within it. The buildings were not elegant and the flats were not modern, yet they were homes nonetheless, and it was deeds such as this that had demonstrated the truly generous nature of the Third Reich.

Maria Turner's flat was on the sixteenth floor of one such tower block named Stevenson Place, which was several kilometres west of where John and Peter had visited The Rag-and-Bone. The flat was an unwelcoming dwelling, John had to admit, although that was the fault of the occupant and not the architect. The small living room was sparsely decorated, with there being no photographs or ornaments to speak of, and the faded wallpaper was more late-1940s than late-1960s. A threadbare three-seater couch was pushed against one wall, and on the opposite wall there was a narrow kitchenette stocked with only the most basic of utensils. Between them, a sliding sash window looked out across South London; up here on the sixteenth floor, the wind caused it to rattle indignantly in its loose fittings. Despite its scant furnishings, the living room was spotless and tidy, as though Turner had been anticipating their company.

John and Peter had entered the flat with their pistols drawn, having easily acquired the key from the aged caretaker downstairs. It was a pointless exercise, however, as Jasper Jones had been correct in that Turner would not be home. Peter therefore instructed John to search the bedroom for anything of interest whilst he stayed in the living-room-cum-kitchen, the only rooms in the flat besides the bathroom.

The idea of leaving Peter alone again was unnerving. On the drive over from London State Hospital, John had tried to rationalise what had happened to Jones, yet he kept on arriving at the same disturbing conclusion: Peter must have murdered the man. There was no other explanation. Regardless, there would never be an inquiry into his death, and even if there were, John would say nothing to contradict Peter's version of events – that sort of thing was not done.

To distract himself from these distressing realities, John focused on the bedroom. Also neatly organised, it was furnished with a bed, a wardrobe, a dresser, and a bedside table. He opened the top drawer of the dresser, which was full of women's underclothes. He turned around to find the wardrobe also packed with clothes: dresses, blouses, skirts, trousers – nothing unusual. Just then, Peter shouted from the living room that there was a newspaper dating back to 5th December, which implied that neither Turner nor Ramos had been here since Friday, the day they had apprehended Jones and Sebastien Dubois in Göring Station.

If that were the case, John thought, *and Turner and Ramos did abandon the flat on Friday under the – correct – assumption that one of the men would give them up in a desperate attempt to save themselves, then perhaps something of value to the DES had been left behind.*

Wasting no time, John tipped the contents of the dresser drawers onto the bed, emptied the wardrobe, and scoured the bedside table for anything remarkable, but there was nothing.

Where would I hide something so it could not be found so easily should someone pay an unexpected visit? he asked himself.

On his hands and knees, John inspected the bases of both the bedside table and the dresser, but there was just bare wood. And he removed the drawers one by one, checking for anything taped to the undersides of them, but again he came up empty. He even slid the wardrobe away from the wall, only to reveal a blank space behind it.

With the room turned upside down, John sat on the bed, disheartened and in a lather of sweat. This endeavour was always one of long odds, he knew, but even so, he had allowed himself to hope that there might be something at least vaguely pertinent to the Yonder investigation tucked away amongst Turner's personal effects.

All but ready to admit defeat, John gripped the edge of the mattress and pulled himself upright. As he did so, the dull sound of something scraping against the metal frame underneath was just about audible, and he realised with contempt for his incompetence that there remained one obvious place he was yet to check.

After standing up fully, John lifted the mattress away from the wire bedframe. And although two of the things he found in this hiding space were somewhat expected by now – a bundle of Reichsmarks and a loaded handgun, this one with the faded engraving 'Pistole MAB Kaliber 7.65' on the side – the third thing was different: the third thing was a book. Bound in a soft brown leather, its age could be inferred from the worn corners. There was no indication as to what this book was from the cover, and neither an author nor a title was given on the spine.

Curious, John perched himself on the bedframe and opened it to the first page. It became apparent at once that this was not any old book: it was Maria Turner's diary.

Handwritten, it read:

19 January 1965

I thought keeping a diary would be a good idea now I'm leaving home. I've been told this will be an important and exciting time for me, but moving away will be so strange that I feel like I need someone, or something, to talk to. Papa was NOT happy when I first told him, but I can't stay here in Portsmouth my whole life just because he'd like me to. Mr Ashworth always said I could have a job at the British Reich Museum and I cannot turn down the opportunity to work in London!

> I leave tomorrow. It will be hard, but I have to think of it as an adventure.
>
> As for this diary, I'll have to find a place to hide it just in case I write something I shouldn't. As papa always told me, if there's one thing the Nazis are good at it's hanging people who write books.

John had to read that final sentence several times before he believed what was written. Such open sedition stated as a flippant afterthought was staggering. He thought back to Turner's MoI file; she must have been about eighteen in 1965, so she was still only a teenager. Had it been normal for her to refer to people as "Nazis" this candidly? It was learnt from Ramos, no doubt, the man impressing his tainted ideologies upon his daughter.

John scanned the next entries in the diary, but there was nothing else particularly egregious in Turner's words, just her musings on her move to London, her cosy flat on the north side of the river, and her days at the British Reich Museum – where she had indeed gained employment as a trainee archivist. In fact, there was no malice at all in the girl, and no indication whatsoever of the woman she would one day become.

Then, a name appeared:

> 10 February 1965
>
> I made friends with one of the tour guides at the museum today, a girl called Nancy who came over during her lunch break and introduced herself. We sat and talked about this and that, and when I mentioned that I had only been in London for a couple of weeks

and didn't know anyone yet she invited me out with her and her girlfriends. They go to the local pub to spend their wages on a Thursday evening, and she said I should join them one week. Her fiancé and his friends go as well, and apparently there is a lovely boy named Edward who is there sometimes who I just have to meet! I said I'd think about it, but Nancy wouldn't take no for an answer so I agreed.

I think I will go. It will do me good to make some new friends and have some fun. I can't be BORING all my life!

This boy, Edward: was it Edward *Turner*, Maria Turner's future husband and the eventual target of the London SS Counter-Terrorism Unit?

John flicked through the pages and the lines upon lines of writing. So much must have happened between then and now to set this pleasant teenager down a dark path towards Yonder. Would there be answers in the diary? If not regarding Yonder, then at least ones that would help John to understand Turner herself?

It was an intriguing prospect.

'What did you find?' Peter had appeared at the bedroom's doorway, evidently having found nothing himself.

'A pistol and some Reichsmarks, and what looks like Turner's diary,' John explained. He had forgotten that Peter was with him in the flat, and his presence caused John immediate discomfort.

'Her diary?' Peter asked, mildly curious.

'Uh-huh,' John confirmed. 'Could be something, but' – he shrugged with deliberate disinterest – 'it's probably nothing.'

He held the diary out to Peter. 'Do you want it? Or should I hand it in to DI Colbeck?' he gambled, believing he already knew the answer to this question.

As expected, Peter scoffed. 'I'm not wasting my time on some girl's diary,' was his dismissive response.

John nodded, hiding his delight. He would give the diary to DI Colbeck, then, and offer to continue reading it himself. There was something about it that fascinated him.

'Detectives? *Hullo?*' someone called from the living room.

Peter stepped out of the bedroom to investigate, and John followed him with the diary, the pistol, and the bundle of banknotes.

They met the building caretaker at the door to the flat, where the short, timid, old man stood waiting for them, his entire bearing the picture of angst. 'Sorry to bother you, but s-someone keeps calling f'you on the radio in your car. I thought you m-might want to know,' he stuttered in an accent not dissimilar to how Joe Harding had spoken, although there was no arrogant bite to this man's words. He held his flat cap in his hands and fiddled with its rim as he addressed the space between John and Peter, unable to look either of them in the eye.

John heard a familiar intake of breath come from Peter. He had witnessed the DI reduce grown men to tears in the past, taking off on a rampage of shouting and threats for no particular reason; quite frankly, John thought he enjoyed such mindless hostility. But John was tired of these unnecessary beratings and of Peter's merciless disposition. So, just before he could embark on his impending tirade, John interjected with a smile: 'Thank you for telling us. It must be important.'

The caretaker was noticeably taken aback by this friendly rejoinder, no doubt due to the forceful manner by which Peter had secured the key to Turner's flat from him earlier. Knowing not to question John's kind words, however, he happily declared that it was no trouble at all and took his leave.

Peter rounded on John then, as if to say something, with that vicious breath still inside him and his eyes ablaze with ire. He did not speak, though, but instead let the air out slowly between his clenched teeth, and he walked away without so much as a 'Let's go.'

Sporting a cautious, triumphant grin, John followed Peter out into the hallway, and he closed the door to Turner's flat behind them.

CHAPTER TWENTY

Return to Silvertown

As it transpired, it was DI Colbeck on the radio, and John and Peter did not return to Maria Turner's flat after their conversation with him. During their visit to Stevenson Place, the request to DCI Werner for permission to conduct a raid on James Summers' warehouse that afternoon had been approved with enthusiasm – for the DCI too, the idea of closing the Yonder investigation was tantalising – and John and Peter were being called back to Scotland Yard to participate.

Having answered this summons, John soon found himself up in the DES office, sitting at DI Colbeck's desk beside Peter. There was a lull in proceedings whilst the pieces for this operation were moved into place, which was time enough for the detectives to be debriefed by DI Colbeck on their morning.

As was to be expected, he was shocked to hear about Jasper Jones's death, but when Peter advised that it was likely due to the rough nature of their interrogation, DI Colbeck made no further comments; they had got what they needed from Jones, and neither he nor anybody else at Scotland Yard would be troubled by his subsequent fate.

Next, the conversation turned to Maria Turner's flat, beginning with a short exchange on Peter's behalf during which he conceded he had found nothing of interest. So – and making certain to not act smug about his own measured success – John detailed the handgun and the bundle of Reichsmarks, including where he found them, and then he produced the diary. 'As far as I can tell, it's Turner's diary. I read the first couple of entries, and it seems to me like it could be rather'– John searched for the right word before settling on his choice – 'revealing.'

'Revealing, you say?' asked DI Colbeck, interested.

Unable to think of a more adequate description for the contents of the diary, John passed it over the desk to DI Colbeck and waited for him to read the first entry.

When he had finished, DI Colbeck closed the diary and studied the featureless cover. 'Good work, detectives,' he acknowledged. Then he paused and contemplated the brown leather before he said, 'But I am afraid we do not have time for this right now. Today will be demanding enough as it is.' DI Colbeck opened the top drawer of his desk and, placing the diary in it, asked, 'When this business in Silvertown is concluded, would you continue reading it for me, John? I am eager to know what secrets lie in wait inside.'

DI Colbeck spoke the words with a smile, and whilst John returned this warm gesture, it was insincere. Although he had come to terms – as best he could – with his own actions in that chamber beneath the barn, when John now looked at DI Colbeck, he could not help but see the "ruthless interrogator" who had blinded Ramos with a lit cigarette. The compassion had drained from his face, and that gentle light behind his eyes was extinguished. John gave no hint as to any of this in his expression, of course, and he stayed a quiver in his voice when he replied that he would gladly read the diary.

The debrief completed, DI Colbeck asked John and Peter to follow him out of the DES office and towards the lifts. They were heading up to the eighth floor, where the briefing for that afternoon's operation would soon take place.

*

That had been at half past twelve, and it was just turned three o'clock when John arrived at Silvertown. He was in the back of an unmarked, dark-blue BMW New Class 2000 with Peter, and DI Colbeck was sitting behind the wheel. Next to him in the front passenger seat was Standartenführer Thompson, DI Colbeck having kept his word in allowing him along on the raid. The car itself was parked around the corner from Summers' Import and Export, out of sight of any suspicious onlookers.

Idling in front of them was a similarly nondescript silver Triumph 2000, although that vehicle was packed with neither DES detectives nor Counter-Terrorism men: they were Waffen-SS agents, renowned marksmen who were recognised the world over as fierce combatants. These particular agents formed part of an assault unit that worked with the Metropolitan Police when their usual duties found them in need of something closer to a military operation, as they did today. Half a dozen further Waffen-SS agents were currently surrounding the warehouse from the wharf at the back; they would enter the building from the rear and secure the loading bay.

It was a straightforward plan, by all accounts.

Presently, all parties involved were waiting for a quarter past three, the time it had been decided that the raid would commence. Even given their military-trained support, John still felt sick anticipating what might happen at the warehouse; a tight knot of anxiety had swelled in his stomach during the drive across London. Unsurprisingly, the other three men were not at all fazed by the impending action: DI Colbeck had conveyed nothing but an impatience to be done with the Yonder investigation; Standartenführer Thompson agreed that he must be weary of it by now; and Peter was busy pouting like a bad-tempered child because DI Colbeck had ordered him to sit in the back with John, which, to Peter, was a blatant indication of his implied inferiority in the car.

John did his best to ignore them and lit a Reemtsma with an unsteady hand.

As he did so, a large, rust-orange-coloured lorry came around the corner, and it rocked the BMW when it went hurtling past. It was followed at pace by a tall, mint-green van, and John watched them both disappear into the distance through the wing mirror. *They're lucky,* he thought, *to be heading in the opposite direction of the raid.*

There had been absolute silence in the BMW since DI Colbeck had parked it against the kerb. The only discernible sound had been that of the foghorns echoing from the Thames – a standard melody for a Monday afternoon on the dockside. It was DI Colbeck who eventually broke this serenity, when he glanced down at his watch and stated, 'Two minutes.'

Preparing himself, John drew his Walther and pulled back on the slide, the brass of the chambered round winking at him in today's bright sunlight, and he checked his jacket pocket for the spare magazine. This process completed, he stared down at his own watch, and time seemed to slow as his heartbeat quickened. He took a deep breath and held it, and the second hand wound its way ever closer towards the number twelve.

Three…
Two…
One…

The Triumph 2000 shot away, and DI Colbeck took off after it. In succession, the two cars rounded the corner at the top of the road, then they bore down on Summers' Import and Export at high speed.

When the Triumph 2000 skidded to a halt in front of the warehouse, four Waffen-SS agents emerged from it. Dressed in a black, military-style uniform and wielding MP100 automatic submachine guns, they darted towards the loading bay in tight formation as though they were storming an enemy stronghold.

Before DI Colbeck could bring the BMW to a complete stop, Peter was already out onto the tarmac, determined to be ahead of either of the men in the front two seats in this raiding party. And although DI Colbeck was visibly riled by his apparent enthusiasm, Standartenführer Thompson sported more a look of quiet admiration, the exact significance of which John was not certain. Whatever the case, nothing was said about it; instead, the three of them scrambled from the car and followed Peter towards the warehouse.

One of the Waffen-SS agents announced their presence in a guttural, German-accented bark: 'Officers of the Reich! Everybody down on the ground!'

The warehouse staff did not react straight away, confusion having taken effect. When the order was repeated by another roar from the wharf, however, they all fell to their stomachs as the reality of what was happening became all too clear.

As armed bodies swept through the loading bay, John saw the plump man he had questioned during his previous visit to the warehouse, the one who had carried a clipboard and was terrified of Zeigler. He peeked up from his place on the ground and appeared to recognise John as well, and whilst John felt sympathy for him for being caught in the wrong place at the wrong time, the bottom of a Waffen-SS agent's boot forced the man's bald head back into the concrete, and he knew not to raise it again.

With this assertive approach, the loading bay was secured in scarcely a minute.

Their initial objective accomplished, DI Colbeck turned to John. 'Lead the way to Summers' office, Detective Sergeant.' He motioned for Peter and Standartenführer Thompson to accompany them, and John guided the group up the rusted metal staircase at the side of the building.

All afternoon, John had been inwardly dubious as to whether or not they would find James Summers in his office. He would have known about Ramos's arrest by now from Turner, and if John were in his position, he would have escaped London with his family the moment he got the news. This concern was unfounded when they came to the door with the white words on the frosted glass window that read 'Managing Director: J. B. Summers', because when DI Colbeck pushed it open the man was revealed: he was standing there behind his desk, shaking like a leaf with his hands in the air. John did notice that the office was bare compared to when he was last here, though, with all of Summers' personal effects now missing – he may not yet have fled the city, but he was certainly in the process of doing just that.

Peter gave none of them a chance to address Summers before he strode across the office, moved behind the desk, and whipped the man in the head with the butt of his pistol.

Such aggression was unnecessary, John thought, when Summers let out a yelp and collapsed to the ground, but then he had come to expect nothing less from Peter. He glanced over at DI Colbeck and Standartenführer Thompson, and saw that both men were watching on with zero regard for Summers' well-being; the Standartenführer actually looked impressed by Peter yet again, as if this violence was something to marvel at.

Peter dragged Summers up from the floor and dumped him into the chair behind the desk. A deep wound had formed at his temple, and the right side of his face was covered in blood. Peter did not wait to hit him a second time and cracked the lenses in his glasses when he struck Summers full in the face.

'Tell me where the Yonder is!' Peter demanded as Summers reeled in pain.

'I don't know what you're talking about,' Summers sobbed through blood and broken teeth.

'Tell me!' Peter repeated. 'Harding and Ramos gave you up!'

Summers' eyes widened in horror at the mention of his two associates. 'I don't—' he tried to lie, but Peter belted him across the head again.

John holstered his weapon at this point. Summers was no danger to them any more, if ever he had been.

Proceeding with this – as far as John was aware – unplanned interrogation, Peter grabbed Summers by his shirt collar and pushed him down onto the desk. He then placed the muzzle of his pistol against the nape of the man's neck and snapped back the hammer. In a far more calculated tone, he declared, 'Tell me, or I'll personally go to your house and kill your wife and son.'

John took a step back, now more wary of Peter than of anything else. He was rabid and uncontrollable. John regarded DI Colbeck, but he made no move to rein Peter in, his face set to the same cold grimace he had worn when confronted by Ramos dangling from those shackles. Standartenführer

Thompson, on the other hand, continued to observe this demonstration with a brazen fascination.

'It's not here!' Summers admitted with a shriek. That technique of threatening a suspect's family so often worked wonders for Peter.

'What do you mean?' DI Colbeck chimed in.

'What was left of the latest shipment, about 200,000 pills – it's gone! They went out this afternoon,' Summers whimpered.

John let out a defeated sigh.

Peter muttered, 'Bastard!' under his breath before he flung Summers back into the chair and, for good measure, hit him again in the face with his pistol.

'When did they go?' asked DI Colbeck, as calm as anything.

'About ten minutes ago,' Summers cried, barely able to speak any more.

The sight of that lorry-and-van convoy passing by the BMW played across John's mind, and he said as much to DI Colbeck.

On the other side of the room, Summers nodded and exclaimed, 'Yes, that was them! Their route is on my desk. Please, just stop hitting me!' The man cowered in the chair, his face a pulpy mess.

Peter ignored his plea.

DI Colbeck stepped forwards and snatched the most prominent stack of papers from Summers' desk. He skimmed through them and, having found what he was looking for, moved towards the door. 'Detectives, secure Mr Summers and bring him downstairs,' he instructed John and Peter, and then he left the office with Standartenführer Thompson.

John watched them go before he turned back to the desk. Peter was still standing over Summers, seemingly undecided as to whether he should resume this beating.

After a long moment, during which Peter neither said nor did anything, John decided to speak: 'Let's get him up and take him—'

Peter lifted his pistol and shot Summers point-blank in the head. The force of the bullet caused him to collapse backwards into the chair, the whole thing almost tipping over.

'*Fuck, Peter!*' John rounded on him as he lowered the Walther to his side. 'Why did you…? *He could have told us more!*' he shouted.

'Well, he's not going to now, is he,' was Peter's callous reply.

'*Are you fucking insane?*' John grabbed him by the lapels of his suit jacket and shoved Peter into the wall behind the desk. He had no recollection of deciding to do this; it was as if sheer anger had taken control of him.

'Careful, Detective Sergeant,' Peter warned without the slightest rise in the timbre of his voice, and John felt something stick into his ribs, 'accidents happen all the time. Summers just had one, and it would be unfortunate if you were to fall victim yourself. Who would look after Alice? And your child?' That sly smirk John knew so well crept across his face.

John's blood ran cold. He felt like he finally recognised Peter for who he truly was, as the last remnants of his façade were left scattered about the drab office carpet. He was a killer, a vicious thug bent on nothing more than pain and cruelty. Dubois, Jones, and now Summers – and who knew how many countless others over the course of his career, all of whom were dead because of this man's thirst for violence.

As this realisation struck him, John took a sharp, startled breath, and his throat filled with the dry, sickening scent of Peter's cologne. He choked on it: that raw and putrid odour that oozed from every pore on the man's body like some maddening, inescapable poison. It swam around his head and seeped into his mind. It was so powerful that it caused John's vision to blur, and he felt his consciousness waning under its unbearable influence.

John let go of Peter and backed away.

Peter holstered his pistol, straightened his jacket, and strode out of the office without once looking back at either John or the man he had just executed. Only that foul fragrance remained in his wake.

John stared down at Summers, and that phrase from his childhood came to him once more: *Jedem das seine*. Summers had deserved little else than a bullet for his role in the Yonder Organisation; still, those words were somehow hollow now, with the knowledge of what Peter had done without consideration for anything beyond his own bloodlust.

He must tell someone about what had happened here, John knew. Peter could not be allowed to get away with such an audacious act of self-indulgence – it was not right.

Determined to out him, John exited the office.

On his way down the metal staircase and into the loading bay, John noticed that Peter was already mid-conversation with DI Colbeck. As he approached them, DI Colbeck addressed him: 'Are you all right, John?' When John offered only confused silence in response, he added, 'Detective Inspector Baer said that Summers tried to attack you.'

Shifting his gaze, John saw Peter glaring at him over DI Colbeck's shoulder with an intensity that was spine-chilling. Peter's remark to Summers that he would have gone to his house and murdered his wife and son had he refused to talk sounded more like a promise than an empty threat now, and after what Peter said about Alice and John's unborn daughter – what would he do if John challenged his story? There would be few repercussions for Summers' death, if any at all, and

John would make an enemy of a man he knew to be capable of terrible things.

'I'm okay,' he replied at last, verifying Peter's version of events. That determination he had harboured but an instant before had vanished, and as fear took its place, John felt all of a sudden worthless.

Satisfied that he understood what had transpired upstairs, DI Colbeck focused back on the task at hand: the plan for how they would seize the lorry that was transporting the Yonder pills.

It was decided that four Waffen-SS agents would head out in the Triumph 2000, going after the lorry-and-van convoy by following the route on the document from Summers' desk. It had been no more than fifteen minutes since it left, and in the mid-afternoon traffic, a lorry that size would be easily caught up to with the aid of a police siren.

With that settled, Standartenführer Thompson proclaimed, 'Tomas, you should go as well. This is your investigation, after all, so you should be there to make the arrests. Take the detective sergeant with you.' Then, to reassure them that this end of the operation would be furthered in their absence, Standartenführer Thompson placed a hand on Peter's shoulder and said, 'Detective Inspector Baer and I will clean up this mess.'

John was immediately uneasy. He recalled the unsettling expression of intrigue the Standartenführer had worn whilst Peter beat Summers bloody, and he believed nothing good could come of the two of them being left alone together.

Apparently sharing none of these misgivings, DI Colbeck agreed with Standartenführer Thompson, and he wasted no time in gesturing for John to follow him out onto the road.

John did so, and as he climbed into the front passenger side of the BMW, he tried to dismiss the uncomfortable awareness that he was being watched by Peter from the warehouse. The bite of Peter's cologne lingered up his nose, and he was glad when DI Colbeck turned the key in the ignition and the air was instead filled with the harsh smell of exhaust fumes.

The Triumph 2000 came to life beside them, and it raced off in the direction the lorry-and-van convoy had gone. To the accompaniment of the squeal of tyres against tarmac, John was thrown back into his seat when DI Colbeck made after it once again.

CHAPTER TWENTY-ONE

Tarmac

Even though his heart was currently residing somewhere between his throat and his mouth, John was obliged to admit that DI Colbeck had a way about him behind the wheel of the BMW. With a portable police siren wailing away on its roof, the DI tore north across London, passing other cars with only centimetres to spare, ignoring red traffic lights, and careering around corners almost on two wheels. He followed the Triumph 2000 with ease, as though he had done this a thousand times before.

It was not long before the rust-orange lorry appeared up ahead, with the mint-green van trailing immediately behind it.

The Triumph 2000 drew swiftly closer to the rear of the van, and John pondered with uncertainty what the Waffen-SS agents intended to do next, with this part of the plan having been but alluded to back at the warehouse. Would they signal the convoy to stop and surround it? They wielded considerable firepower in the form of their MP100s, but then it was impossible to know who was in either the lorry or the van, whether they were also armed, or whether they outnumbered the Waffen-SS's ranks. Regardless, if the lorry was transporting Yonder, they would be unlikely to surrender it so readily.

Somehow responding to this exact thought, the narrow doors at the back of the van were flung open ahead of the Triumph 2000. A man appeared in the breach, and whilst one of his hands was firm against the side panelling for balance, he held aloft a pistol in the other. His arm outstretched, the man aimed the weapon at the Triumph 2000 and fired what was no doubt its entire magazine into the windscreen.

The Waffen-SS driver swerved wildly as the hail of gunfire rained down upon them, and they crashed head-on into a parked car at the side of the road.

DI Colbeck made no attempt to pull over and help the Waffen-SS agents, and John understood why: if the contents of that lorry were precious enough to kill for, they needed to secure it at all costs. So, rather than stopping, the DI floored the BMW's accelerator and began to close the gap between them and the van, despite the gunman in the back who was frantically – but unsuccessfully – trying to reload his pistol.

'John, I will get beside the van, and you shoot,' DI Colbeck commanded without taking his eyes off the road.

John played the scenario out in his head: if they could immobilise the van, then the lorry would be much easier to seize further down the road, even if it was now just the two of them. This whole situation was becoming ever more precarious with each passing second, though, with DI Colbeck now doing over eighty kilometres per hour in a fifty zone, the lorry and the van having sped up in an effort to escape their pursuers. They were on a long stretch of two-lane dual carriageway in a built-up residential area, and the lorry hurtled down the outside lane with the van several metres behind it.

Putting his plan into action, DI Colbeck veered the BMW into the inside lane and accelerated further still. In that instant, it became abruptly apparent exactly what he was expecting John to do: he could hardly shoot past DI Colbeck and through the driver-side window; therefore, the only way for him to hit the van would be to fire *over* the car from *outside*. With this insight, John sank into the fabric of his seat. That ever-present cautious voice in his head demanded that he did not even consider such a reckless act – yet he unholstered his Walther all the same. With DI Colbeck in audience, that voice was not quite as convincing as before; as it turned out, John feared looking like a coward in front of his superior far more than he feared for his own well-being. So, and in what might have been a comical fashion under less perilous circumstances, John struggled to wind down the passenger-side window, with the cheap plastic handle slipping in his damp, trembling hand, and he mustered what little courage he could manage in preparation for this reluctant feat of heroics.

When DI Colbeck pulled alongside the van, he shouted, 'Now!'

Silencing those better impulses, John hoisted himself out of the window until his whole torso was exposed. At such a high speed, the wind whipped under his suit jacket and tried to drag him from the car, and he had to anchor himself against the window frame whilst his heart stopped short of bursting from his chest. There, balanced precariously, he leant across the roof of the BMW and emptied the Walther into the side of the van.

Perched on the door of this speeding vehicle, John then waited for some indication that DI Colbeck's plan had worked.

Nothing happened, and the van continued on its path without faltering. John was not sure how, but each of those eight rounds had failed to do anything beyond ruining the paintwork.

He slid back onto the seat and stared down at the PPK-L in disbelief. The urge to toss the cursed thing out of the window was belayed only by the knowledge that he still had the spare magazine in his jacket pocket.

DI Colbeck spoke again, his irritation at John's ineptitude evident in his voice: 'The driver, John! Aim for the *driver*!' The emphasis on the word 'driver' was unmistakable, and John wanted to throw himself from the car in place of the pistol for having been so foolish as to waste his first magazine on the van's side panelling.

Disregarding the notion, John reloaded the Walther and readied himself to climb out of the window once more, all the time imploring that one single bullet would find its intended target.

What happened next was nothing more than bad luck.

The detectives charged down the inside lane with DI Colbeck holding the BMW level alongside the van. As he did so, however, a car emerged from a side street ahead of them and pulled out onto their side of the road. Its driver saw them too late to stop, and DI Colbeck was going far too fast to do anything other than swerve; he did just that, only to come up against the side of the van with a thud and bounce back out into the middle of the lane. By then, the other car was half-exposed, and the BMW ploughed into this vehicle with tremendous force.

John was slammed into the dashboard amongst a thunderous din of glass shattering and metal scraping against metal, and everything went dark.

*

John awoke upside down.

He was disorientated, unsure where he was.

Then he remembered the crash.

He was against the roof of the BMW.

It must have rolled over...

He could taste blood in his mouth.

Everything was sore.

He could not move.

Someone groaned beside him.

Out of the corner of his eye, John saw DI Colbeck. He was alive, and conscious, and against the roof of the car as well.

John turned his head – *Fuck that hurts!* – and peered out of his smashed side window. With the way the BMW had landed, even through his at present blurred vision he could see the wreckage of the car they had hit back up the road; its bonnet and front fender were a gnarl of twisted metal.

I hope the driver is okay.

DI Colbeck began to move, and John turned to face him. He grumbled expletives in German and contorted himself against the roof of the car until he had managed to reposition himself onto his knees. With enormous effort, he crawled out of his own side window, wincing as he went over the broken glass. When he was clear, he struggled to his feet and disappeared but for his legs behind the car door.

He was all right.

John was glad.

DI Colbeck took several laboured steps forwards, such that he became altogether visible to John, but he came to an abrupt halt in the middle of the road.

He was looking at something, his eyes fixated upon it.

John strained to see what it was, but the frame of the car

was blocking his view, and he could only move his head so far before it hurt too much.

What was DI Colbeck staring at with such intensity?

All of a sudden, he had his pistol in his hand.

He aimed the weapon, and a gunshot cracked outside.

John flinched at the unexpected sound, and DI Colbeck tumbled to his knees.

It was not his gun that had fired.

From the other side of DI Colbeck, a figure stepped into view.

They were difficult to make out, and John blinked furiously to try to correct his still-distorted vision.

The world came back into focus, and this figure took shape along with it.

It's a woman, John realised.

It's Maria Turner!

She stopped next to DI Colbeck and gazed down at him. She was clad in that same long, brown leather coat that fastened at the neck and walked in knee-high boots similar to the ones she had worn on the wharf behind Summers' warehouse. Her hair swirled around her olive-hued face in a flurry of dark, silken strands that danced on the wind.

DI Colbeck glared back at her, and John saw determination in his eyes. But when he tried to lift his Walther again, Turner guessed his intent and kicked the weapon out of his feeble grasp with a fast movement. She then raised her hand to reveal a pistol of her own and proceeded to level it at his head.

The scene unravelled before John, with DI Colbeck on his knees, defenceless, and Turner standing over him, her face beset by total indifference. He wanted desperately to leap out from the car and tackle Turner to the ground, but he could not move: his body felt so heavy, it was as though someone had turned up the gravity inside the BMW.

He could at least fire at Turner instead and send her into retreat if nothing else. John tightened his grip around the Walth—

His hand was empty.

He tried to search the BMW from where he lay, but that bastard PPK-L was nowhere to be seen.

It had abandoned him.

He was unarmed.

He was immobile.

He had to do *something*!

In the end, it took every bit of energy John had in him just to lift a limp arm several centimetres and whisper, 'No,' before Turner pulled the trigger, and DI Colbeck collapsed in a heap on the tarmac.

John let out a gasp of dismay, but it made scarcely a sound.

Somehow hearing him anyway, Turner focused on the BMW, and she stared at John through the smashed side window.

His whole body stiffened in pure, unfettered terror.

It was his turn now, he knew.

He was going to die.

From somewhere far away, the faint echo of police sirens came within earshot, and as unexpectedly as she had appeared, Maria Turner was gone. Closer by, an engine revved violently, and alongside the rumble of tyres across tarmac, it disappeared into the distance.

John held his breath and waited for something to happen.

The sirens became gradually louder, but that was all.

He exhaled.

It was over.

He was safe.

He looked out into the road. DI Colbeck lay with his back to the BMW, and John urged him to move, to get up.

The wind ruffled his suit jacket, but he remained still.

Turning away, John closed his eyes.

He was so tired; a long and arduous week of gunfights, fistfights, and interrogations was catching up with him at last.

It was time to rest, if only for a moment.

He would see Alice in the morning.

That would be nice.

But for now, he would sleep.

Sleep.

Sleep…

CHAPTER TWENTY-TWO

Boyhood Fantasies

It was stifling in Herr Weismann's classroom at this time of year. The windows only opened a few centimetres, and the sun beat down through them onto the back of John's neck. In the spring, this was liberating after the chills of winter, but now, in the height of June, it was thoroughly uncomfortable.

Lewis Roberts was sitting at the next desk along to John, his square head resting on one hand and his eyelids drooping as he drifted in and out of a light sleep. Herr Weismann soon noticed, as he always did, but instead of calling Lewis's name, the middle-aged, bearded teacher threw the piece of chalk in his hand across the classroom with considerable force. The chalk – Herr Weismann being a practised marksman with the soft white projectile – hit the desk and missed Lewis by a whisker when it ricocheted off the wood.

Lewis bolted upright, and when he saw Herr Weismann scowling at him, he stood to receive his punishment.

'Roberts' – Herr Weismann never addressed them by their forenames – 'which building was the main objective during the Battle of Canterbury?' The words, uttered in a growling German baritone, boomed around the small brick room.

Lewis stood there in silence; he had not been listening, that much was obvious. He shuffled anxiously and refused to meet Herr Weismann's eyes.

'Highsmith' – Herr Weismann turned his attention to John, and he too stood up – 'can you help Roberts?'

Without having to think, John answered, 'The cathedral, sir.' He *had* been listening.

'Thank you, Highsmith,' Herr Weismann stated, his voice void of any emotion. His gaze shifted back towards Lewis. 'Roberts, since you think paying attention in my classroom is unnecessary, you shall write 500 words on the Battle of Canterbury for tomorrow instead.'

Lewis stared down at his desk and said nothing. The chubby little boy was very awkward around his teachers.

'Sit,' was the final word on the matter.

Herr Weismann straightened his tweed waistcoat across his rounded stomach and returned to his lesson on the Battle of Canterbury.

Despite the intense heat in the classroom, John listened with rapt captivation. He was eleven years old, and this was the first time he had been taught the real particulars of the war – it was thrilling! Their studies were now in mid-1943, the boys having covered most of the Second Great War with Herr Weismann this year.

On the blackboard at the front of the classroom were written the events that preceded the Battle of Canterbury:

May 1943: The Battle of the English Channel.

4th June 1943: The aerial bombardment of Sussex and Kent begins.

14th June 1943: Operation Sea Lion succeeds.

15th June 1943: The Blitzkrieg across Sussex and Kent begins.

21st June 1943: The Battle of Canterbury begins.

John loved this room. It was decorated with old German posters depicting strong men and women in their service of the Reich, and there was a big map of Europe on the wall that plotted the path to victory across the continent. The map was out of date, being from before the war when Central and Eastern Europe were broken up into smaller nations; it was much neater now as the Greater Germanic Reich.

Herr Weismann spoke to the class: 'Finally, after three days of fierce fighting, the German troops broke the line of defence around the *cathedral*' – he shot Lewis a disdainful glance, and Lewis squirmed in his chair – 'and stormed the building. There, they found the Archbishop of Canterbury kneeling at the altar, praying to his God for salvation. He was captured and subsequently executed for his slander of the Third Reich. With this main stronghold fallen, we swept through the city with little further resistance, and the Battle of Canterbury was declared a pivotal victory in the liberation of Great Britain.'

As if timed to perfection, when Herr Weismann finished his sentence, the bell rang out for the end of lessons.

'Next time, we shall discuss the long march towards London. Stand,' he instructed, and the boys did so. Then, in a singular movement Herr Weismann both stood to attention and extended his right arm. In that gruff voice of his, he declared, 'Heil Hitler.'

'Heil Hitler!' The class repeated the words back to their teacher, each of them with an arm raised high in salute.

Herr Weismann lowered his arm. 'You may leave.'

As the children scrambled around the desks in the direction of the door, Herr Weismann bellowed, '*Do not forget, Roberts, I expect your 500 words on my desk first thing in the morning!*'

Lewis skulked out of the classroom, and John followed behind him. Herr Weismann was already wiping his notes from the blackboard, not giving the two boys a second thought.

'How did you even know that?' Lewis asked in disbelief.

They were descending the wide stone steps into the schoolyard at the front of The Rudolf Hess School for Boys. It was the end of the school day, and boys of all ages were emerging into the dazzling afternoon sunshine, glad to have escaped those stuffy classrooms once more.

'Herr Weismann said it,' John replied.

Lewis groaned, and John chuckled at his friend's misfortune.

'Oh, shut up!' Lewis muttered, and he gave John a boisterous shove on the arm. Then, his voice bristling with excitement, he asked, 'Do you want to come back to my house?' That was often their routine after school: to go to Lewis's house and play in his bedroom.

But John could not this afternoon. 'I can't. I have classes,' he grumbled. Whilst Old Ford Boarding School was not a "school" as such, with the administration electing to send their boarders to The Rudolf Hess School for Boys instead, they still held extra classes for the boys of John's age on a Tuesday and a Thursday, and today was a Tuesday.

'Just come for a bit, then,' Lewis pleaded.

John studied the big clock on the side of the school building. It was half past three now, and classes did not start until six o'clock, and with no homework to do tonight, he realised he had time to play.

'Okay, but only for a bit!' John cheerfully conceded, and Lewis's face lit up with a smile.

On their way to Lewis's house, they took the path through Victoria Park, where the boys found two long sticks and played at sword fighting. Overexaggerated shouts of effort were offered as they clashed on the grass, and John acted out his death when Lewis ran him through (under the arm) with his (pretend) straight sabre. His opponent vanquished, Lewis proclaimed himself supreme ruler of "Frankazaria", their own fantasy world, or at least he tried to before John leapt up and speared him to the ground. John then named himself ruler in Lewis's place.

Lewis complained, 'You can't do that! You're dead!'

John's response was to stand over his friend and exclaim, 'You cannot kill Baron von Highsmith!' with his wooden broadsword aloft in triumph.

The two of them continued to Lewis's home, a narrow terraced house in a quiet, clean part of London.

When they arrived, Lewis opened the front door and announced that they were home, and his mother – or Mrs Roberts, as John always addressed her – appeared from the kitchen to welcome them. She gave Lewis a hug and a kiss, and then she did the same with John, who was a son to her as much as Lewis was; as a matter of fact, she and her husband would have adopted him long ago given half the chance, but British-born individuals were not legally permitted to do so. Not that John was aware of any of this, and he nevertheless treasured spending time here, where he was treated as one of the family. And although he relished in the Roberts' company, their house, and their rich food, it was the privacy of Lewis's bedroom that John appreciated the most. There, he was allowed to play and to fantasise without fear of reprimand, unlike at Old Ford – "fun" was not a condoned practice in such a dull place.

Wasting not a single second of what precious little time they had today, the boys dashed straight up the stairs to Lewis's bedroom. After discarding their schoolbags, they took their positions around the "Fort of Frankazaria", which was the cardboard castle Lewis's father – Mr Roberts – had helped them to build several months ago. Lewis retrieved a shoebox filled with small metal figures from under his bed. Their play was a mismatch of centuries, with knights on horseback going up against Wehrmacht soldiers, these two factions engaged in an endless struggle for dominion over the Fort.

Baron von Highsmith's knights fought valiantly against Generalfeldmarschall Roberts' troops that afternoon, deflecting bullets with their swords, much to Lewis's amazement. But the Wehrmacht soldiers eventually drove them out of the castle, and John retreated with his men to the mountain peaks atop Lewis's dresser, where they would gather their strength whilst he devised a counteroffensive.

In no time at all, it was five o'clock, and Mr Roberts was returning home from work. He greeted the children in the same affectionate manner Mrs Roberts had, and then he sat down on the bedroom floor and asked who was currently in control of Frankazaria. After a brief recounting of the afternoon's events, he even provided John with tips for how Baron von Highsmith might retake the Fort. John took Mr Roberts at his word: he was a detective for the Metropolitan Police, and although John was clueless as to what this entailed in terms of actual work, the mere fact that he was an officer of the Reich had resulted in his relentless admiration of Lewis's father.

Before Baron von Highsmith could put this advice into effect, Mrs Roberts was at the bedroom door. After reminding the boys what time it was, she asked John if he did not have to be back at Old Ford for classes that evening – the question was rhetorical, with Mrs Roberts knowing his schedule just as well as he did. So, being forced to return to the glum normality of the real world, Baron von Highsmith abandoned his men for the day with the promise that he would return soon to reclaim the Fort that was his "birthright". He did not understand what this phrase meant, having heard it in a film or read it in some book, but it sounded heroic, so he said it anyway. Lewis seemed to agree, and he retorted that Generalfeldmarschall Roberts would defend Frankazaria with his life as John exited the room.

John trod a shaded path back through Victoria Park on his way to Old Ford. In the absence of his and Lewis's raucous play fighting, the walk was peaceful. With his hands hanging limp in his shorts' pockets, he took to watching the little birds as they flitted between the jovial green trees and swooped low across the freshly cut grass. A grey squirrel darted across the path, scurried up a tree, and vanished out of sight. The soft quacking of ducks bathing in the Yacht Pond drifted on the air. A gentle breeze ruffled his shirt, and John drew a long, deep breath; he had not a care in the world to burden him on this pleasant summer's evening.

The park path came to an end, and as John crossed the Parnell Road Bridge over the canal, Old Ford Boarding School loomed into view. The towering building's brown-and-red-brick exterior was more akin to an institution than a home. Two forbidding, old-fashioned Palladian windows were set into the front façade, like ancient eyes that scrutinised the boys and judged their worth as they entered it. The door was three metres high and made out of an ominous, heavy oak, and at eleven years old, John still struggled to push it open. The entire structure was foreboding; but even at his tender age, John understood how supremely lucky he was to have been taken in and raised under the watchful eye of its staff.

He entered Old Ford at half past five and traversed the cavernous, dim corridors and tall stone staircases on the way up to his dormitory at the top of the building on the fifth floor. There, John tossed his schoolbag into the locker next to his bed and retrieved his copy of *Beware the Man with the Red Star*, which had been a present from Lewis's parents for his previous birthday. He lay down and opened the book. At this point in the story, the hero – a Kriminalpolizei detective named Adalard Finneman – was investigating the death of his partner at the hands of a Communist spy. Finneman did not know about the Communist spy yet, though, and John only knew the identity of the murderer because this was the third time he had read the novel, his copy now dog-eared and tatty. After finding a comfortable position on the bed, he began to follow the text once again and lost himself on the troubled streets of mid-1930s Berlin.

Boys filtered in and out of the dormitory, but none of them paid John any mind. He was a quiet child, and whilst not unpopular, he was never the centre of attention either, happily keeping to himself.

At ten minutes to six, the bell for evening classes sounded. John turned down the corner of his book, and amongst a crowd of boys his age, he crossed Old Ford to reach the classrooms on the other side of the building and found his seat in Room 2B.

As in Herr Weismann's history classroom, the walls in Room 2B were adorned with various posters, the difference being that these ones were printed far more recently and in English. 'Your grandparents were tricked by the Imperialists – *Don't let it happen to you!*' one read. 'Fulfil your role in society and help National Socialism become even stronger!' This poster showed four men at work: one was in a factory, another appeared to be a teacher, the third one was a policeman, and the final one was a soldier. They all smiled; all healthy, young men. 'If you see treachery, report it. The Third Reich will thank you!' In this one, a young boy about John's age spoke to a kneeling police officer, and he pointed towards two evil-looking men with big noses and curly hair, who were clearly conducting some nefarious business in the shadows of an alleyway.

There was a great deal of chatter in the classroom as the boys took their seats, but the distinct clicking of high-heeled footsteps on the tiled corridor outside brought these conversations to an immediate end.

The door opened, and Frau Haage stepped across the threshold.

John was always startled by the tall, thin figure in the black uniform. Her features were long and sharp, and her pitch-black hair was pulled back into such a tight bun that it seemed to cause her pale skin to stretch unnaturally across her narrow face. A pin on her lapel bore the two SS Bolts, in bronze on a black background, and the highly polished metal glowed when it passed beneath the golden evening sunlight, which cascaded across the room through an open window.

With a rigid gait, Frau Haage walked to her place behind the desk at the front of the classroom, and the boys stood in unison to meet her.

Her thin lips parted. 'Heil Hitler!' she called in a piercing German accent, her skeletal hand high in the air.

'Heil Hitler!' echoed a chorus of young voices.

Frau Haage sat down, and the boys waited for her to say, 'Be seated,' before they did the same.

She then began today's lesson: 'You are the children of Great Britain. As such, it is your duty to lead this nation into the future through loyalty and dedication. Those who refuse to accept their role in society will be condemned by the Führer and by us, the people, as traitors to National Socialism.'

Frau Haage stood up. 'I am a citizen of the Third Reich, and I obey the word of the Führer,' she said in German.

The boys recited the statement, also in German: 'I am a citizen of the Third Reich, and I obey the word of the Führer.'

Frau Haage sat down, and she continued in English. She talked of the Imperialists and their corruption, and of how the Führer had worked tirelessly to purge the world of their tyranny. Beyond this, he had reformed the Jewish, Slavic, and Romani populations into honourable races; guided the African sub-species into the service of the Reich; ended the religious indoctrination of the Church; cured the homosexuals; relieved the suffering of the terminally and mentally ill; and unified Europe, a continent broken by centuries of belligerence. All those who still opposed him – the Communists and their ilk – would one day throw down their arms in recognition of his passion for world harmony and surrender themselves unto the mercy of National Socialism.

John hung on Frau Haage's every word. He was fascinated by her account of how the world would be in 1,000 years' time: an Aryan utopia without war or hunger or suffering. And when she told them that they would all readily give their lives in service of this ambition, John agreed that he would, without question.

The clock wound its way around to half past six, and Frau Haage's lesson was at its end. Before she took her leave, she stood, and the boys did the same. When she declared, 'Heil Hitler!' they all called out the words with an arm raised towards the ceiling in a united pledge of their devotion. Frau Haage then instructed them to sit back down, and she strode out of the classroom without another word.

The following lessons – mathematics with Herr Bilz and German language with Herr König, with a half-hour break in between for dinner – came and went, and the boys were dismissed at nine o'clock.

By ten o'clock, John was in bed with the lights out.

He lay awake for a long time that night, thinking. Lewis and Frankazaria preoccupied him at first, and he planned for how Baron von Highsmith might retake the Fort. When that subject became tiresome, John went over the mathematics he had just been taught by Herr Bilz. He quickly gave up on this, his distaste for numbers in no way lessened by the quagmire that was algebra, and his focus settled instead on Frau Haage. In spite of her unnerving appearance, she said things that John liked to hear, reassuring them of the safety of the Third Reich and reiterating how they were all one people under National Socialism. And the way she described the Führer, as a caring and paternal man who loved each and every child of the Reich, made John feel as though he had a purpose in serving National Socialism – in order to make the Führer proud if nothing else.

John rolled over. He had been told by numerous adults as of late that he should have an idea of what he wanted to do when he was older, of exactly how he would serve the Third Reich, and the question now weighed on his mind. There were so many options to choose between that to pick just one was difficult.

Seeking guidance, he had asked Lewis what he would do once they left school, but Lewis shrugged his shoulders and offered a terse, 'Dunno,' as an answer, so John decided to not mention it again.

As he pondered this question for the dozenth time, the poster on the wall in Room 2B of the four men at work popped into his head, one in a factory, one in a classroom, one a policeman, and the other a soldier. The prospect of working in a factory or being a teacher did not intrigue John because they were, or at least he believed them to be, boring jobs. But the other two – the policeman and the soldier – would give rise to a future of excitement and adventure as far as he was concerned.

John thought about Mr Roberts, an officer of the Reich and a man whom he idolised; he thought about Adalard Finneman from *Beware the Man with the Red Star*, who battled against Communist spies to keep the Third Reich safe; and he thought about the two bombs that had been set off in Central London earlier that month, and the men who were now tasked with pursuing the villains responsible.

He could do that – he could be a police officer.

The idea of joining the Wehrmacht was less alluring, if only for the fact that Lewis would never follow him halfway across the world to wherever a military career might take him. John refused to leave his best friend behind, no matter how hopeless he sometimes was.

John soon drifted off to sleep with this newfound resolve to serve projecting itself across his dreams: fantasies in which he arrested bad guys and chased down Communists as a true hero of the Third Reich. It was this same eager determination that would guide him through the Hitler Youth as a boy, into the Police Technical Training Academy straight out of school, and eventually into the ranks of the Metropolitan Police.

Then, one day, his ambitions as an eleven-year-old would bring John to the Drug Enforcement Squad and to the centre of the Yonder investigation. Like destiny, they would lead him to The Rag-and-Bone, to James Summers' warehouse, to 27 Faulks Road and Göring Station, to Smith and Sons' Antiquities and Crafts, and to that chamber beneath the barn in the middle of nowhere.

They would lead him to the BMW with DI Colbeck. To a high-speed car chase. To mangled steel and shattered glass, and the ruinous effect of a single gunshot.

CHAPTER TWENTY-THREE

Job Done

It felt like an eternity passed before John woke up.

He had dreamt about his childhood: those afternoons up in Lewis's bedroom, the history classes he loved so much, and days out with the Hitler Youth when they would go hiking amongst the trees. And he dreamt about Alice – her smile, her laugh, her radiant green eyes; he could feel her smooth skin beneath his fingertips, and all the while the soft tenor of her voice played like a melody around him. He was aware he was asleep, yet he did not fight to wake up, being content to drift between these happy memories.

Gradually, however, far more disturbing images began to weave themselves in amidst these pleasant dreams. Soon, John's mind was overrun by them, and he was unable to wake up no matter how hard he tried. He was beset by memories of the Yonder investigation: the never-ending nights, the frustration, fleeting glances of cracked skulls and slashed wrists. Distress and agitation reigned. Then fear seized control as monsters took to roaming freely about his head, faceless shadows that forced John to hide in narrow corners of a dark world. When these fiends caught up with him – and they always did – the Walther would not fire at them, his finger stiff against the trigger. And there were long periods of falling, falling, falling backwards into perpetuity, never finding the floor but endlessly anticipating the impact. Bodies dangled from shackles, their flesh deformed and mutilated, but still they laughed: shrill, terrible, crazed laughs.

And then it all stopped.

John looked up and found himself on his knees in the middle of a road. It stretched on forever into the distance, but there were no cars, and the only sound that remained in the entire world was that of a low wind tugging at his suit jacket.

He exhaled, thankful for a moment's reprieve from those haunting visions.

The distinct rasp of shoes scraping on tarmac drew his attention, and John turned to see a figure standing at his side. He took in that shining, olive skin wrapped in leather and two cruel, inky-black eyes set into a spiteful visage.

It was none other than Maria Turner.

She was staring down at him, her severe, merciless features framed by her dark hair, and John realised he was terrified.

Turner raised her arm and aimed a pistol at his head.

John gazed into the barrel. He knew he was going to die, but his body refused to act; it refused to bat the gun away or to even leap up and run. He just knelt there, waiting for the inevitable to happen.

Turner snapped back the hammer.

'For my father,' she snarled, and then she fired.

John opened his eyes. The sound of the gunshot thundered in his ears, but he was awake – of that he was certain.

He was less sure about where he was, though, and he struggled against his own hazy concentration to gather his bearings. He was in a bed with the covers pulled high on his chest. A *beep, beep, beep* repeated itself on a continuous loop nearby, but he could not turn his head to locate the source; the weight on his shoulders was too great.

Sometime later – everything was a muddle – someone was speaking to him: 'John?'

He looked around and saw a woman in a dark-blue uniform.

'John, can you hear me?' she asked.

John tried to answer, but the words stuck in his throat as if it were packed with dust. He nodded instead, but it was a feeble, slight movement.

The woman in the blue uniform left his side, and the room was still once more.

Little by little, the events prior to his long sleep returned to John. He retraced the Yonder investigation and the week when everything came together with Joe Harding and James Summers, Ramos and Turner, Sebastien Dubois and Jasper Jones, and Standartenführer Thompson. When he tried to piece together that last afternoon, however, it became much more difficult. He remembered arriving back at Scotland Yard with Peter from Turner's flat, and that the briefing for the raid on Summers' warehouse took place shortly afterwards, but beyond this, everything was a blur until he was in the BMW with DI Colbeck, closing in on the lorry and the van. And even then, all John was able to recall from the chase was the sight of the car pulling out in front of them and the devastating impact of metal on metal.

He moved his legs under the covers, and the nerve endings erupted in a searing agony. The crash had happened, of that there was no doubt, but the rest of it was lost to him.

Presently, a tall man in a white coat entered the room, accompanied by the same woman in the blue uniform.

'Good morning, Mr Highsmith. I'm glad to see that you're back with us,' he said, and he stopped next to the bed.

John tried again to speak, but he produced only a hoarse croak.

'It's okay, John,' the nurse – he was beginning to come to his senses – encouraged, 'drink this.' She placed the rim of a glass against his lips and poured a steady trickle of water into his mouth. His shrivelled tongue expanded beneath it, and it cleared the lump in his throat when he swallowed it down.

John took a slow breath. 'Where am I?' he asked, finding a gruff version of his voice.

'London State Hospital,' replied the doctor, and he lifted a pair of glasses to his eyes. He studied the medical chart he had taken from the end of John's bed. 'You've been here for three days.'

Although the doctor said the words in a dismissive manner, the news could not have come as more of a surprise to John. It would be at least Friday by now, he figured. He had been laid up in this bed all week, then, whilst the Yonder investigation had gone through its most important phase without him as the London DES effectively curtailed the distribution of the drug around Great Britain. There were suddenly so many questions rattling around in his head: Did anybody ever catch up with the lorry he and DI Colbeck went after? Was DI Colbeck all right after the crash? Had Maria Turner been apprehended? Had they figured out who Uncle Billy was? Had they found anything else at James Summers' warehouse? What new leads were the Task Force following now? – the sensation was maddening.

Yet all of these burning questions fell away in an instant as if they were of no importance at all when a far more crucial matter presented itself, and John asked, 'Where's Alice?'

'She's already on her way,' the nurse answered with a comforting smile. 'She's been here every day since you arrived, so I don't think she'll dally now she knows you're awake.'

John thanked the nurse. Just knowing that Alice was okay was enough to quell any further questions for the time being, countless and boundless though they were.

The nurse was correct, and before long, Alice was at the door to John's room, her cheeks wet with tears. She rushed to his side and threw her arms around him, and only agreed to let go when John reminded her that he was in considerable pain. Restraining herself as best she could, Alice took one of his hands in both of hers and held it tight. There was utter relief on her face and unconditional love in her bright eyes. She sat down on the edge of the bed, and John kissed the back of her hand. He was guilt-ridden for having put her through such an ordeal, but he did not mention it; Alice would insist it was not his fault anyway.

Alice told John that Lewis had visited him whilst he was asleep, and Mark and the children as well (though not Jane, who had been taken ill with this flu that still plagued the nation). Plus there were several men from Scotland Yard – two younger ones and an older gentleman with his arm in a sling – but she did not get their names. The younger ones were Alex and Alfie, John assumed, knowing full well that Peter would never have made the journey, and he was unable to think of anybody other than DI Colbeck who might have been this older man. John then asked how the baby was doing. Apparently, she had been giving Alice a right kicking of a night for the past couple of days, and Alice had come to the conclusion that she could sense John was not in the bed next to them. John grinned broadly at the statement, and although he did not quite believe it himself, it was nevertheless a charming thought.

After an appropriate amount of time, the doctor – or Doctor Wood, as he now introduced himself – returned, and he set about explaining John's condition to them: 'Considering the collision you were in, Mr Highsmith, you came away exceptionally lightly. If not for sheer luck, you would be dead.'

Alice wiped away fresh tears, and whilst John squeezed at her hand in reassurance, he was struggling to grasp this notion that nothing but luck had saved his life: not his police training, nor his desire to live long enough to meet his daughter, but plain, blind luck – pure and simple.

Continuing, Doctor Wood asked, 'Do you remember what happened?'

John said he recalled the morning of the crash well enough, but that the afternoon surrounding it was patchy at best. The doctor nodded, wrote something in his notes, and claimed that a certain amount of disorientation was only to be expected after such a traumatic experience.

He then went on to describe the full extent of John's injuries, which was a remarkably short conversation: 'You were banged up rather badly in the crash, Mr Highsmith, so there's a lot of bruising to your arms, legs, head, and back. Although, some of this does appear to predate the incident.' Doctor Wood observed John with a raised eyebrow, clearly curious about these older injuries – the remnants of his fall onto the train tracks below Platform 12, no doubt. But when John offered him no explanation – he was not in a position to know the exact circumstances of any of his bruises, past or present – the doctor pried no further. 'Anyway, nothing has been broken, and there will be no lasting damage as far as we can tell. As I said, this was a case of extraordinary luck.'

That word again: 'luck'.

A shiver ran through John's body: he should have been killed.

He was not kept much longer. Doctor Wood conducted a series of tests, which was an arduous process that included John staring into bright lights and having his tender skin poked and prodded with a blunt metal instrument. But, when he was finished, the doctor determined that there was no reason he should remain in the hospital another night. John did not need to be told twice, so with the warning that he might experience some dizziness over the coming days, and the strict instruction that he must seek medical attention without delay if his condition worsened, Doctor Wood discharged John from his care.

*

Shortly afterwards, John and Alice arrived home in a taxi. Within the hour, however, he was showered, shaved, and dressed, and heading for Scotland Yard in the Morris Minor, which had been returned to Pullman Road on Tuesday by a uniformed constable. Alice protested vehemently against this decision whilst John pulled on his trousers with a delicate touch and fastened a waistcoat around his battered torso, as she contended that he had surely earnt at least one more day to rest, but John could not be persuaded. Those questions he had stifled that morning about the Yonder investigation were already forcing their way back to the forefront of his thoughts, and he could not bear to wait until tomorrow for answers.

In the end, Alice yielded to his determination, and with a kiss, she begged him to be careful as he left the house.

*

None of his fellow detectives stopped to greet him when John hobbled into the DES office at half past two that afternoon; in all likelihood, most of them had not even noticed his absence. Ignoring them regardless, John made a beeline towards DI Colbeck's desk. When he saw the DI was not at his station, he turned on his heel and quickly found the two men he knew would have the answers he so desperately sought: Alex and Alfie. They were sitting at Alfie's desk, neither of them having spotted John yet.

When they did see him, they both stood to meet John with a mixture of shock and relief.

'It's bloody good to see you up and about,' Alex proclaimed in a delighted tone. 'We thought you were still in the hospital.'

John shook his head and had to hide the twinge of pain that shot around the base of his skull at the vigorous movement. 'I was discharged this morning,' he clarified. Then, with not another second to spare on idle chit-chat, he asked, 'Where's DI Colbeck? I need to talk to him.'

Alex's face dropped, and Alfie breathed a sorrowful sigh beside him. 'I'm sorry, John, but he's dead. Someone shot him,' Alfie explained in a sombre cadence.

The statement hit John in the chest like a runaway freight train. Bright, white lights flashed before his eyes, and he tumbled into the chair next to Alfie's desk. The dream that had woken him from his long sleep that morning – that vision of Turner looming over him with a gun pointed at his head – was not a dream at all, in a sense: it was what John had watched unfold through the smashed side window of the BMW when Turner shot DI Colbeck, but with John in DI Colbeck's place. It all came flooding back to him, as vivid as if it had happened only moments ago.

His pulse became erratic, and John had to take several deep breaths so he did not vomit on the maroon carpet.

It occurred to him then that neither Alex nor Alfie, nor anybody else in the DES for that matter, would know who had killed DI Colbeck, so he told them: 'It was Turner.'

Alfie stepped forwards. '*Maria* Turner?' he asked.

'She was there, after the crash. Must've been in the van or the lorry,' John elaborated. 'Has she been arrested yet?' Turner had to pay for what she had done.

'No, John,' answered Alex. 'Nobody else has seen her since the antiques shop, when she killed Arnold.'

John clenched his jaw to stop himself from screaming aloud. Maria Turner had murdered two of their detectives, plus at least one of Standartenführer Thompson's Counter-Terrorism agents at Smith and Sons' Antiquities and Crafts, alongside Smith himself, and she had got away scot-free.

He placed a hand on Alfie's desk and dug his fingernails into the wood.

Maria Turner.

Maria fucking *Turner.*

The name burrowed into his mind like a parasite, and a surge of furious hatred rose inside of him. He would kill the bitch if ever he saw her again.

Having contained this swell of emotion, John enquired as to what else he had missed since the raid on James Summers' warehouse.

'We've been working our way through the list of known dealers, but beyond that, not an awful lot has happened around here,' Alfie admitted. 'We did find the lorry you and DI Colbeck were chasing. It was left abandoned in an Autobahn lay-by, but any Yonder was long gone.' Alfie shrugged his shoulders.

John was overcome by an excruciating sense of quite how pointless it was to have gone after the lorry. That, and it became apparent that DI Colbeck had died for nothing. John half-wished he were still unconscious in a hospital bed, unaware of any of this.

With a more upbeat lilt, Alex took over. He told John that the DESs from the eight cities in Summers' shipping manifest had spent the last three days raiding dozens of warehouses and businesses up and down the nation, and each of them had reported the presence of Yonder at a number of their targets. Along with the confirmation from Customs that the only warehouse *Delicias Inspiradas* had ever imported its goods through in Great Britain was Summers' Import and Export, it was believed that the Yonder Organisation's distribution network was now completely dismantled. 'The going theory is that over the next couple of weeks their reserve of the drug will run dry. It might be that they try to establish themselves again in the future with another smuggler, but as far as DCI Werner's concerned, the investigation is as good as over,' Alex concluded.

'What about Turner, then? And Uncle Billy?' John asked with an edge of frustration in his voice. There were so many loose ends, surely the investigation could not be resolved this readily? And he still questioned the true intent behind Yonder. It being a "silent protest", a "medication", or even 'freedom from life' as Ramos had described it – they were all such insignificant motives when compared to the behemoth the Yonder Organisation had become.

Alex spoke again: 'We have no way of finding either of them, John. Anyway, DCI Werner says it was our job to stop Yonder, and so if the supply on the street does run dry, then that's it: job done. He's told us to keep the investigation open for the time being so we can process any dealers as they come in, but the Task Force itself is set to be disbanded at the beginning of next week if there are no significant developments.'

So it *was* over? Just like that? John was less than surprised. DCI Werner would not care about finding Turner or Uncle Billy once Yonder was finished in London, so long as it was recognised that he had excelled in his duty as the head of the city's Drug Enforcement Squad. John wanted to storm into his little office and scream and shout and demand that they did not rest until the bastards were in handcuffs, but he knew it would be nothing more than an embarrassing waste of energy.

'What does Peter think about all this?' he asked instead, although he at once regretted his curiosity. As it turned out, Detective Inspector Baer had more important things to concern himself with than Turner or Uncle Billy, given that he was soon to be an SS-Sturmmann, the equivalent of a Gefreiter – a junior lance-corporal – in the Wehrmacht.

At least, this was according to Alex: 'He's been up on the ninth floor with Standartenführer Thompson all week. We've seen nothing of him.'

It was then that John at last remembered what had transpired at Silvertown on the afternoon of the crash: Peter had executed Summers, but not before he had beaten the man bloody at his desk whilst the Standartenführer watched on in chilling awe. Peter's promotion into the ranks of the SS was not all too unexpected, then. John actually feared for those who would soon find themselves in the crosshairs of SS-Sturmmann Baer, because there would be no stopping his sadistic tendencies once he wielded even a modicum of genuine power.

Jedem das seine. He would have laughed aloud at the expression, were the circumstances not so discouraging.

There was something else John had forgotten from that afternoon, though, something that also took place in Summers' office. The memory was just out of reach, loitering on the periphery of his mind.

It was something distressing, even fear-inducing.

What was it?

'Careful, Detective Sergeant...'

John felt a stab of pain between his ribs.

'...accidents happen all the time.'

He stood up and excused himself from Alfie's desk.

'Summers just had one...'

As if materialising in the air itself, the dull, sickening scent of Peter's cologne descended around him.

'...and it would be unfortunate if you were to fall victim yourself.'

He knew it was not real, yet he could not escape the suffocating veil that consumed and smothered his senses.

'Who would look after Alice?'

And that smell – that putrid, raw stink; it was not even cologne any more, but rotting, festering flesh.

'And your child?'

It smelt like death.

John hastily lit a cigarette, and as he breathed in that first familiar lungful of smoke, the smell faded away, together with this memory of Peter. If nothing else, his promotion to the ninth floor meant John might never need see the man again.

In an effort to clear his head, John took a slow walk over to DI Colbeck's desk. He traced a line across the faded wood with his finger. A fine layer of dust had settled there, as though the DI had been gone for not days but weeks.

John stared down at his empty chair, and he recollected what DI Colbeck had said to him in the fifth-floor WC after the events at Göring Station, advice that had guided him through a tortured moment: *'You fought for the values of National Socialism, and you almost died defending them. You should be proud of that pain you feel, because it is evidence of what* you *have done – in the name of the Reich!'* An ache ran up John's leg and arced across his lower back, and he had to steady himself on DI Colbeck's desk. Those words were true now more than ever, even if going after the lorry had proven to be a fruitless endeavour, yet John could only wonder whether DI Colbeck would have said them had he known his own life was so soon to end, and that the woman who ended it would not be hunted down like a dog by his colleagues and superiors.

He sighed and bowed his head.

John was distracted from this cynicism when he saw that the top drawer of DI Colbeck's desk was not flush with the wooden frame. With absent-minded curiosity, he pulled on the handle. Several scraps of notepaper, a series of half-sharpened pencils, a handful of paperclips, and an opened packet of Reemtsma cigarettes were amongst the odds and ends discarded inside. John paid little attention to this assortment of DI Colbeck's personal effects, however, because his eye was drawn to something else in particular. There, placed in the centre of the drawer, was Maria Turner's diary.

It took John a long second to register what it was, but when he did his heart leapt in his chest. He had forgotten all about the diary after finding it in Turner's flat at Stevenson Place. And so must have Peter, the only other person in the DES who knew of the leather-bound volume's existence besides John himself and DI Colbeck.

John recalled the first entries and the pleasant demeanour of the girl who wrote them. The idea that the diary might chronicle how Turner had transformed from this girl into the woman who killed no fewer than three people at Smith and Sons' Antiquities and Crafts had intrigued him when he found it under her mattress; that was before he bore witness to her murdering DI Colbeck, and before he knew her crimes would go unpunished. Now, even the thought of Maria Turner was enough to send a vicious anger coursing through his entire body, which was unfortunate given how she had become an unrelenting fixation in John's mind. To read something she had written, then, was no longer simply intriguing: it was a momentous, earth-shattering prospect.

And beyond this insight into Turner's seditious, twisted mind, the outside chance that somewhere in those pages the origins of Yonder might be revealed to him, along with the true reason for its existence – well, that was too great an opportunity to pass up.

CHAPTER TWENTY-FOUR

Handwritten

Before John was able to continue where he left off with Maria Turner's diary, DCI Werner emerged from his office. When the DCI noticed him sitting at his desk, he offered John no more than the briefest of pleasantries, and then proceeded to demand that he write up his full account of the raid on James Summers' warehouse.

So, rather than focusing on the task at hand, John spent the next half hour clacking away at his typewriter, reliving that awful afternoon in excruciating detail. He was even inclined to include that Peter shot Summers because the man tried to attack him, despite the fact that but a glance at the body would have told a different story. And he reported that it was Turner who shot DI Colbeck, of course. The words appeared before him on the page, and John's heart sank: it was as if committing his death to paper had made it somehow – *permanent*.

A dull headache was scratching at his temples by the end of this exercise, and in a manner most unlike John, he did not bother to read the document over before he signed it and handed it in to DCI Werner.

John then returned to his desk, and after lighting a fresh cigarette, he immediately turned his full attention to Turner's diary.

There was nothing of significance for several entries after 10th February 1965, the date he read to back at Stevenson Place. Well, nothing of significance to John, anyway. There were remarks about her work at the British Reich Museum as a trainee archivist for Mr Ashworth, a running commentary on her budding friendship with her co-worker Nancy, and complaints aplenty about her new landlord – but nothing that alluded to Turner's impending descent into criminality.

Then:

5 March 1965

I finally went out with Nancy and her friends last night. We went to a little pub called The Dutton Arms where they meet up for drinks on a Thursday. Nancy introduced me to her friends, a lovely bunch who seemed to take to me quite quickly, and then she introduced me to Edward Turner.

Edward. Such a nice man! I sat and talked to him for most of the evening. He was very interested in my Spanish heritage and said he has some friends from Spain himself. He even tried to speak some Spanish with me, and I think I impressed him when he realised I'm fluent. He's a little bit older than me, but he still spoke to me like I'm an adult, unlike most men do.

> It was nice to be out having a drink and some fun. There weren't many girls in the pub other than Nancy's friends, but they didn't care when the old men gave them funny looks so I tried my best not to care either. I suppose after a while you just get used to it.

The entry continued from there for another half a page: first, with Turner's plans to see Nancy for lunch that weekend, and then ending on some ideas she had for decorating her flat, but there was no further mention of Edward Turner.

To see that man – that terrorist – described as the perfect gentleman was unsettling. Would it be Edward who eventually guided Turner towards the life of a subversive? Because her father had not done so at this point, or at least not to the extent that she was shooting officers of the Reich in the street.

The diary progressed through March 1965 with little consequence, and Turner continued to display not even the slightest hint of animosity towards anybody beyond her landlord (who, in fairness to her, did sound like a rather disagreeable man). Even Ramos was humanised by her words, often being portrayed as a gentle and sage figure whom she missed terribly.

The certainty of how it would all end was painful to think about.

As the daylight through the narrow windows gave way to dusk, John read on. The further he read, however, the more the words on the pages began to blur, and he found himself reading the same sentences over and over again as he tried to concentrate on what was written. Soon, his head was dipping onto his chest, and he was jolted from the verge of sleep by the thud of the diary hitting the carpeted floor when it slipped out of his hands.

He repositioned himself in the hard desk chair and rubbed at his tired eyes with his knuckles. The diary would have to keep until tomorrow, he conceded, when he would be able to afford it the appropriate attention.

For the time being, John scooped it up from the floor and dropped it into the top drawer of his desk. He then exited the DES office without so much as a farewell to any of his colleagues.

*

Alice was thrilled to see him when he returned home. Although John had to stifle a yelp as she flung her arms around his bruised body, he was more than happy to grin and bear the pain; to be wrapped in her warm embrace again after the onslaught of dreadful news he had endured that afternoon was wonderful.

It was not long before John was in bed, his total exhaustion having got the better of him. As he slept, though, those same nightmares that had tormented him in the hospital returned: his memories of the Yonder investigation manifested themselves as a cavalcade of bloodied bodies and monstrous figures that danced across his mind. James Summers joined them now, with a gruesome bullet hole in his head. He asked John why he had allowed Peter to kill him, and why he had told nobody the truth about what happened; John never could answer him. And, as was only to be expected, there was a new, recurring dream in which John found himself upside down against the roof of the crashed BMW. He would look out of the smashed side window into the road and see DI Colbeck there, on his knees before Turner's pistol, and he was forced to watch as over and over again she gunned the DI down, in a never-ending cycle of him collapsing into the tarmac, motionless – dead.

When he awoke in the morning, he was stricken by a crushing lethargy that even a black coffee with breakfast was unable to appease. Regardless, the knowledge of what was waiting for him at Scotland Yard was enough to spur John on, and he was soon heading back into the city in the Morris Minor, with the blistering air through the open window helping to rouse him from this groggy stupor.

*

Only a handful of detectives were present in the DES office when John arrived that morning, which included neither Alex nor Alfie, nor Peter. Without anyone to distract him, John readied himself to settle in with Turner and her teenage chronicle.

And he would have done just that had some inconsiderate bastard not placed his Walther PPK-L in the centre of his desk for him to find. John knew it was his by the tell-tale chip in the muzzle from when he had dropped it during his fight with the third man on Platform 12. The weapon's polished metal had been left scuffed after that incident in the Underground, but now there were scratches and dents all along the length of it, together with a small crack in the side of the plastic grip, which were no doubt the result of its unknown trajectory during the car crash.

He gazed down at the handgun and brooded over how he might have saved DI Colbeck's life had it not abandoned him. An alternate version of events played out in his head, a fantasy in which he raised the pistol and shot Turner dead before she could murder him – it would have been glorious!

Whether or not – John straight away rebuked himself – he would have been able to summon the wherewithal to actually hit his target with the PPK-L at that critical moment was another matter altogether.

He sighed and returned the Walther to its place in the holster under his arm.

Trying to suppress these daydreams of triumph, John slumped into his desk chair and retrieved the diary from the top drawer.

It was mid-April 1965 when the handwritten notes yielded anything else of interest:

16 April 1965

I was out again with Nancy and her friends last night. I feel like I've become an integral part of their group over the past couple of weeks, and I have to admit I love it! It's so nice to feel welcome with them, to be able to sit and talk and laugh. On Wednesday I was invited out with them to the cinema which was exciting, even if the film was no good. We saw The Desert Fox, the new picture about Rommel in North Africa during the war. It made me uncomfortable, the way the Nazis were shown as these fearless warriors whilst the British were devious little men who hid in the sand. Papa always told MUCH different stories about Africa. But the other girls lapped it up and I did my part afterwards by saying how terrific it was.

Last night Edward Turner was in The Dutton Arms again though, and he came straight over to me and apologised for not having been back for so long. I sat with him all evening, sharing stories like we were old friends. But when he overheard the girls talking about The Desert

Fox, he leant in close so that nobody else could hear us and asked me if I thought it had been any good. I don't know why, but for some reason I felt like I could be honest with him. It might have been the way he asked, with a hint of contempt in his voice for the others. Or it might have been the beer. It doesn't matter either way, though, because when I whispered to him that I thought it was ridiculous his eyes shined with delight.

At the end of the night he promised me that he would be back again soon. Not anyone else – ME!

I already can't wait!

There it was: the mere suggestion of a subversive inclination, and Edward would have spotted an opportunity to corrupt another young mind. Would it be long now until he shared his true identity with the already-infatuated Maria? Or would he be more careful and keep the girl at a distance before inviting her into his secret life of villainy?

And as for the remark about Ramos, John recalled the man citing his service for the British in North Africa as part of his long battle against 'fascism' during his interrogation. The conflict there had been a brief one, thanks to Generalfeldmarschall Rommel and his tanks; still, it was possible that Ramos both shipped out with and then retreated alongside the British troops who fought on that short-lived front.

John also disagreed with Turner about *The Desert Fox*, a modern classic of British cinema and a tribute to one of the greatest – if not *the* greatest – generals in all of human history. If truth be told, they could use a man of Generalfeldmarschall Rommel's calibre right now on the Eastern Front to help eradicate what remained of the Soviet scourge, but the master strategist had retired to Switzerland after the Second Great War and withdrawn completely from public life. He had earnt that right, of course, given what he had accomplished for the Third Reich. Nevertheless, it was a shame that such a talent was lying idle when there were victories yet to be won.

Edward reappeared regularly in The Dutton Arms in the weeks following 16th April, but Maria did not write about any other untoward conversations between the two of them; she was more interested in his deep laugh and piercing, grey eyes – much to John's frustration. This frustration was only intensified by the fact that it was taking him much longer than he might have expected to read the diary, as although there was no definite structure he could determine for it, Maria often made several new entries a week, some of which were at least two or three pages of mindless prattle.

Mindless, that was, until June 1965, when something noteworthy finally occurred:

12 June 1965

I think Edward is involved in something.

I saw him today in the market when I was doing my shopping. He was just standing there looking at a box of potatoes as far as I could tell, so I thought I'd go over and say hello. It would have been a chance for us to talk without anybody else there to eavesdrop or interrupt. But when he saw me, he stared right at me with those eyes of his and shook his head. I hadn't noticed before, but one of his eyes was black and there were little scratches on his face.

I stopped dead, not sure what to do.

Then I saw them, two police officers coming towards us through the market stalls in their ugly green uniforms. Edward was trying his hardest not to look at them, pretending instead to weigh a cabbage in his hands, and when they walked straight past him he almost collapsed with relief.

I turned to watch the police officers walk away, and when I looked back Edward had disappeared. I went looking for him again, hoping he might have been waiting for me out of the way somewhere, but he was gone.

What has he done to be so afraid of the police? And how did he come by those marks on his face?

I desperately want to know.

But how do you ask someone you barely know something like that? When we talked about that film a couple of weeks ago, it was as if he was suggesting he's like me. I've thought about it so much since then.

But what if he isn't? What if he's like everybody else?

The entry ended there, and John closed the diary. If he was going to keep at this, he would need a strong cup of coffee.

John limped out of the office and headed towards the fifth-floor break room. On the way, he mulled over that last entry. He too was curious as to how Edward had acquired those injuries, but then the answer seemed obvious to him:

it must have been the consequence of some act of terrorism gone awry. Standartenführer Thompson said that Edward's group did not surface until mid-1966, though, so perhaps this was a precursor to his more notorious activities. What else could have made him so wary of two passing officers of the Reich?

John filled the break room's electric kettle with fresh water and absent-mindedly tipped too much instant coffee into the bottom of a discoloured porcelain mug. He was distracted by the entry's final question: 'What if he's like everybody else?' By 'everybody else', Maria obviously meant people like John: regular people who understood that National Socialism was not a blight upon the world, and who did not go around blowing up buildings and murdering the innocent in the name of some misguided ideology. She was yet to express such hostile tendencies in her writing, but the more John read, the easier it appeared it was going to be for Edward to drag Maria down into his pit of sedition. It was a pity, really, because if she had met a nicer, normal man, then this might have been averted, and the subversive ideas that were planted in her mind by her father would have faded into obscurity.

The kettle came to the boil and John poured the water into the mug. After a cautious first sip, he set off again across the fifth floor. Back in the DES office, he placed the mug on his little desk, settled in his uncomfortable chair, and immediately picked up the diary once more.

Nothing was said of this brief encounter when Maria next saw Edward in The Dutton Arms two weeks later, his wounds already healed, but she had the impression that they were somehow closer after that day, as though they now shared an unspoken secret. What exactly this secret pertained to, Maria remained uncertain.

And so the diary rambled on. Although there were no further chance meetings or unusual injuries to speak of, Maria continued to see Edward almost every week at The Dutton Arms, and what ensued was a blossoming of their friendship to the point that she now admitted – to only herself and her diary – she might be in love with the man. Beyond this, John did his utmost to skim through the less relevant moments of her everyday life: her work, her friends, her hopes and dreams; films she watched and music she listened to; things she bought and things she planned to buy; and the unexpected ups and downs of a girl on the very cusp of womanhood – it quickly became tedious.

Then, just when John was beginning to question whether the diary would ever offer anything better than adolescent musings and lovesick nonsense, the inevitable happened:

5 September 1965

There was a knock on my door yesterday morning at about half past ten, and imagine my surprise when I found Ed standing on the other side! He asked me if I was busy, smiling that same cheeky grin I've grown so fond of as he said it. I wasn't, and even if I were, I wouldn't have been for much longer.

We headed out of the city in Ed's car, away from the buildings and into what little countryside is left around London.

The first sense I got of what he wanted to ask me was when we talked about his parents. Ed told me his mother and father were killed during the Occupation when he was still very young, something he had never shared with me before when we were out with the others. I think he remembers them, but I didn't push him for any details. I can't imagine they're happy memories.

It was his use of the word "Nazi" that gave him away though. Papa used to say it all the time, but it's not a word the average person would throw around half-heartedly. Ed said his parents were "killed by some Nazi". He said it in passing, but thinking back now it was obviously a test. And when I replied that I was so sorry for his loss, and didn't raise my arm and shout about National Socialism being the greatest thing to ever happen to Great Britain, I passed this first round.

We left the car parked off the road and Ed continued to test me here and there as we walked through the woods. Did I hear the Führer's speech last week? No, I must have missed it. Have I ever been to see the monument to the German soldiers in Piccadilly Circus? I've seen it, but I've never stopped to read what's written on it. Have I ever visited Berlin? I haven't, and I don't intend to either. It looks like just another boring city to me.

I could see Ed thinking carefully about each of my answers, as if he were sizing me up.

He eventually asked me about my school days and I left him little reason to doubt my true feelings. I said I was always disagreeing or arguing with my eugenics teacher, so much so that in the end papa had to teach me how to lie my way through my classes so I didn't get into serious trouble.

Ed stopped walking when I said that. He had this look in his eyes, one I'd never seen there before, and for a second I was terrified I had misjudged the whole situation.

But then he asked me if papa fought in the Spanish Civil War, and I said he did.

'Which side?' The Republicans, with honour.

'Does he hate the Nazis?' He does.

'Do you?' I despise them. I would kill them all given half the chance, one by one, until the very idea of them was wiped from the earth.

And all of a sudden Ed was kissing me, and then we were making love on the soft ground.

John looked up from the diary.

He had been wrong. This whole time he had assumed that Edward – or Ed, as she now referred to him – would be the influence in Maria's life that sent her tumbling into the abyss, and that he would somehow manipulate her into becoming the murderous subversive she was today. Beyond the odd questionable comment against National Socialism, she had been such an affable, easy-going young girl up to this point, so it was the most logical conclusion. In reality, she was this way inclined all along, without Edward's influence. Ramos would have been moulding her in his image her entire life and teaching her to hate the world she was born into. That part of Maria must have festered and gnawed away beneath the surface, hidden from even her own diary, awaiting the perfect moment to reveal itself.

This was that moment: this sordid act in the middle of the woods, incited by a complete and ignorant abhorrence of the Third Reich.

The whole affair made John sick to his stomach.

After that day, Maria's entries in the diary soon became fewer and further between. With Edward to talk to, she no doubt felt less of an urge to commit her every thought to paper. And when she did return to it, the entire rhetoric of her writing was changed from cheerily inconsequential to unabashedly insubordinate. Maria now condemned aspects of society she had once enjoyed: music and cinema were dangerous propaganda tools, technological and fashion trends were a way to distract the working classes from reality, and her friends were sheep who blindly followed a tyrannical shepherd. And, as her relationship with Edward grew ever more intense, she documented numerous disturbing conversations between the two of them: they claimed that government censorship of the press was a means to control the people, derided the puppet reign of "the False King" Edward VIII, apparently shed actual tears over the warmonger Churchill's execution after the war, and denounced the Reich's employment of the African sub-species as "modern-day slavery".

It was so clear to John that they spoke in simple Imperialist propaganda terms; that Maria could not see this for herself was an indictment of just how deep her father's conditioning ran. And these were incredibly dangerous opinions to be writing down, he thought, but then the girl was young and bold, and she did not care. That someone of this ilk had worked at the British Reich Museum, amongst a collection of the most precious artefacts from the history of the Third Reich, was an outrage.

In December 1965, Edward plunged Maria further into certain darkness:

> 22 December 1965
>
> Ed finally took me to meet some of his friends last night.
>
> We went to a pub, an ordinary-looking place I'd never even noticed before. Ed ordered us some drinks, and then he whispered something to the bartender and led me into a room at the back. I was so ~~nervous~~
>
> No, nervous is the wrong word.
>
> I was EXCITED!
>
> In the back room a group of men and women was gathered, both young and old and of various nationalities. I was introduced to them, and when I sat down to listen to them speak it became clear that they are like us.
>
> They talk about a better world. A free world. And they do so openly, without fear of being overheard and dragged out into the street and beaten to death.
>
> When papa told me these things when I was little, I had always thought we were the only ones who knew

the truth. But Ed has shown me that we are not alone in this terrible world.

It was the most spectacular night of my life.

John grunted at the page of writing. The existence in London of such a place – a little room where subversives would pass around their insidious beliefs – did not surprise him. However, whilst the prospect that he could have walked past the pub in question a thousand times was annoying enough, that he had potentially drank in there before, perhaps even when Maria's new friends were only metres away, was actively infuriating.

In any case, Maria was a part of this group now, and was therefore a step closer to being branded a full-blown enemy of the State.

A step closer to Yonder.

A step closer to murdering DI Colbeck and Arnold List.

By early February 1966, Maria and Edward were living together in the house on Fleming Road. In the meantime, Edward had been teaching her how to drive, how to fight, and how to use a firearm – something she was a "natural" at according to Edward – thus fashioning the girl into the formidable foe the Yonder Task Force was up against today. Although there was never anything in her words that implied direct extremist action against the Reich, Maria did make several comments about one day "helping" Edward and his friends in their "work"; John assumed this was a reference to the crimes that would soon bring them to the attention of the London SS Counter-Terrorism Unit.

This group of theirs in the back room of the pub was mentioned on occasion, but – and this was likely a conscious decision on Maria's part – no location was ever disclosed. One such instance that stood out was in May, when Maria wrote about one of their friends arriving with a stack of newspapers that had been smuggled into Great Britain from the United States. She read them all, cover to cover, then eulogised at length on the Americans and their "democracy". More often, she recounted the stories the older members of the group told her, which usually centred on either the war itself or how marvellous life was before it. In his head, John imagined Maria would sit cross-legged on the floor like a child, listening to these tales of fighting "the bastard Nazis for king and country". She revered these men and women, who were heroes to her now just as her father was.

Ramos himself became a much larger presence in Maria's life when he moved to London in late May to be closer to his daughter, and so another key individual was now in place for the foundation of the Yonder Organisation. John had already made his peace with the fact that Yonder would not be touched upon in the diary, though; it had been a long shot to begin with, and as the right side became thinner in his hand, he knew the odds were dwindling with every passing page.

He then turned to the entry dated 9th July 1966:

9 July 1966

Ed came home last night giddy as a schoolgirl, and when he eventually sat down to tell me what had happened, I understood why.

He met a man, a Swiss chemist who has been living in the United States since the war. He relocated there after the British surrendered in 1944 and it became evident the Nazis had no intention of respecting Switzerland's neutrality in the conflict. He's in London this week for an international conference with his peers in the science community. Ed said he was very friendly and wears his disgust for the Nazis on his sleeve in a way that's unlike anybody else he has ever met.

During the war this chemist began developing a new drug, a psychedelic he calls "LSD". He has continued to study it in America ever since for use in his research into psychoanalysis and psychotherapy, with apparently fascinating results. According to the chemist, in its current form the drug allows a subject to psychologically "suspend the boundaries" between this reality and an unfathomable, beautiful altered reality of infinite possibilities that is hidden from our everyday consciousness. He even went so far as to describe this process to Ed as a "spiritual, euphoric experience", all whilst claiming that his LSD has none of the addictive or destructive tendencies of something like heroin.

Speaking to this man gave Ed an idea for a revolutionary way to strike back at the Nazis.

We have never stopped believing that although the people of Great Britain salute and bow their heads, they still want to be free of their oppressors. But in a world in which there is not a SINGLE aspect of their lives the Nazis do not dictate with an iron fist, it's easy to understand how the people might have FORGOTTEN what it is to be free in order to survive day by day. In fact, there remains only one place in Great Britain today that the Nazis cannot control by force, and that is the MIND, but even then it's impossible for the people to imagine their own liberation for more than several blissful seconds before another heap of propaganda is shovelled down their throats, and these notions of freedom are smothered all over again.

But what if there were a way for the people to exist outside of the shadow of this propaganda? What if there were a way for them to experience something BEYOND this world, this reality, in that one place we know the Nazis cannot control – THEIR MINDS?

Given what his new chemist friend told him about LSD, Ed thinks this drug could do just that. He thinks it could be a way for the people to finally be free – if not in body, then in spirit.

He wants to use this drug, wants to make it mean something, something that the people will own as a symbol of their oppression.

The people would never take a "drug" willingly, however. They smoke and drink to pass the time, but they do not do drugs recreationally for the most part – to them, heroin is a dirty, addictive thing, and cocaine is a high-society indulgence. This LSD would have to be less of a "drug", then, and more like a MEDICATION, so to speak – a CURE to the confines of Nazism. If it is recognised as such, as a cheap and clean way to live beyond the prison that is 1960s Great Britain, then the people will come to view it as a means of liberation. They will take it over and over again to FREE themselves from this world. The Nazis will not be able to stop them, and the bastards will no longer control how the people live every second of their lives.

It would be a SILENT PROTEST, done in the comfort of peoples' own homes, and it would make a louder statement than any rifle ever could.

But if the people were shown the light, having experienced just this GLIMPSE of freedom, could this drug ever lead them to something beyond silent protest and spiritual enlightenment? To actual protest, perhaps, or one day even to open revolution? Ever the realist, Ed would not say either way when I asked him, but he still could not help grinning like a wonderstruck child at the thought.

Ed has it all worked out. This chemist would ship his LSD across the Atlantic (he claims he would be able to produce an endless supply of the stuff given appropriate backing) to Spain where the ports are less heavily monitored, then papa could smuggle it into Great Britain through Delicias Inspiradas and his old contacts in London.

Papa would be on board. He thinks a lot of Ed and his optimistic idealism. Plus he always said he only ever kept overseeing the processing plant in Burgos all these years for this exact reason, so that should the time ever come for it to be needed for its intended purpose again it would still be operational. I could even leave my job at the museum to go and work for him.

The chemist will need some persuading, though – he wasn't thrilled at the suggestion of his drug being used in such an unscientific manner. But Ed has a way with words, and I don't doubt that he will be able to convince the man otherwise.

We have done so little for so long that the mere prospect of achieving something tangible is exhilarating!

John tossed the diary across his desk.

Everything the Task Force had learnt about Yonder was true: it was a 'medication', a 'cure', and a means for the Yonder Organisation to infiltrate peoples' minds and set them 'free'. And whilst Maria and Edward hoped that this 'silent protest' might one day impel the people towards their ultimate desire for direct action against the State, this was all it ever was: a hope. The entire Yonder investigation – the violence, the deaths, the stress; all the things John had done and seen and suffered through – had been to overcome this idiotic flight of fancy.

He returned begrudgingly to the diary and worked his way towards the final entries.

As remarked upon in the entry of 9th July, Maria left Mr Ashworth's employ at the British Reich Museum at the beginning of September and went to work for Ramos at *Delicias Inspiradas*. Then, at the end of that same month, Edward proposed to Maria, and they were promptly married in a small ceremony three weeks later on 18th October. Ramos and several of their backroom-friends were in attendance, and

John could only wonder how many wanted criminals had been gathered beneath the same roof that afternoon.

More importantly, Maria was now Maria *Turner*. The way she wrote about her wedding day, she was so happy, so content, and so blissfully unaware of how everything would soon come crumbling down around her.

And then the diary ended. There were several entries in the weeks following the wedding regarding Maria's new life with Edward, but they included nothing else about this Swiss chemist or their plans concerning his psychedelic drug. In her final entry on 12th January 1967, Maria revealed that she was preparing to go on her first "job" with Edward and his friends, but it was no more than a vague, passing comment; whether this "job" ever took place, given that Edward was killed not a week later on 17th January by Standartenführer Thompson and his Counter-Terrorism agents, John would never know.

Whatever the case, Maria must have given up on the diary after her husband's death. There were pages left blank at the back of it, and whilst thumbing idly through them, John pondered what she might have written had Edward not died or—

One of the pages was *not* blank!

John had almost missed the flash of black ink amongst the white paper, but turning back through the pages carefully, he soon found it again: scribbled across the centre of a page there were two short paragraphs in what was unmistakably Turner's handwriting. There was no accompanying date and no rhyme or reason at all as to why this entry was here. What made it further unique was that parts of the page were discoloured and some of the words were blotted, as though drops of water had fallen on the paper:

Ed. My dear, sweet Ed. Would you forgive us for what we have set into motion? You were always so passionate, so idealistic – I do not think you would have given your support to such a sickening proposal. You wanted to save the people, to free them, but that time has long passed. I have realised that since I lost you.

I am sorry, my love. We have no choice. They grow stronger every day, and we are the only ones who can stop them. It was my idea in the end. I hope you would forgive me, because I am not certain I will ever be able to forgive myself.

John studied the other pages at the back of the diary, but they were all blank. This undated entry was the last thing Turner wrote.

CHAPTER TWENTY-FIVE

A Not-So-Familiar Face

The following morning, John wrote up his report on the contents of Turner's diary, but no matter how he worded it, it always read like a long-winded confirmation of everything they already knew about Yonder and a complete waste of police time. Despite this, John left the report on DCI Werner's desk – who was not in, of course – although he doubted whether the DCI would trouble himself to even open it after his announcement to Alex and Alfie on the imminent reassignment of what remained of the Yonder Task Force.

It was the final entry in the diary that caused John a second restless night in a row. It was a confession by Maria to an already deceased Edward, such was apparent, yet it offered no explanation as to what this 'sickening proposal' alluded to or why she was so wracked with guilt. It was unlikely to be anything to do with Yonder, what with that whole enterprise being Edward's idea in the first place, and John knew so little else about her beyond what she had written in the diary that he could not hazard a guess as to what Maria might have done that Edward would have found so reprehensible. The entry had a sinister quality to it, though, and its ambiguity was enough to drive John to the very edge of madness as he lay awake, tossing and turning until the early hours of the morning.

Given the foul humour he had subsequently woken up in, which was only exacerbated by having spent an hour typing up the report on the diary for the absent DCI Werner, John was in no mood for it when an irksome rumour on the subject of said man circulated the DES office. It went that his superiors were so impressed by his handling of the Yonder investigation that the DCI was set to receive a promotion; this was a promotion into the SS, no less, at the distinguished rank of SS-Oberführer – a rank above SS-Standartenführer, and so the equivalent of a senior colonel in the Wehrmacht. He would soon be heading for the SS Main Office, and a comfortable desk job the likes of which were reserved for men with useless university degrees and reliably German accents.

John had to bite his tongue. DCI Werner had contributed nothing beyond vitriol and incompetence to the London DES since he had become the head of the department, and his impact on the Yonder investigation was no different. Such a grand promotion was, therefore, both unmerited and unreasonable. Moreover, John was now convinced that the man would never read the report on Turner's diary, and he felt personally cheated for having wasted his morning on it.

Desperate for a moment's relief from the oppressive welter of the DES office, John left the other detectives to their gossip and made his way across the fifth floor in the direction of the ever-familiar WC.

Having used the facilities therein, John gazed into the mirror over the washbasin: a clean-shaven, twenty-nine-year-old face stared back, with dark circles under the dull, grey eyes, which were somehow even darker now the Yonder investigation – the source of all his previous stresses – was supposedly over and done with. A series of small cuts and scratches were dashed across his face, whilst what had been a prominent bruise on his forehead was fading from a sore purple to a sickly yellow. Dressed in his pale-grey suit and navy-blue tie, these were the only visible injuries he had sustained during the car crash – under the wool, his skin was a tapestry of discolouration.

He looked like a shell of a man beneath the WC's unflattering overhead lighting, and he felt worse than he looked.

As he examined his weary reflection, John considered for the umpteenth time DI Colbeck's speech to him in this very room about them doing what they did 'in the name of the Reich'. It was difficult to grasp how a man so devoted to National Socialism could give his life for it, yet John remained the only person in the entire Third Reich who cared about apprehending his killer. If he himself had also been murdered that day, he would have died believing his fellow detectives would stop at nothing to bring Turner to justice. Still here he stood, alone, whilst the rest of them idled over departmental politics. It was all incredibly disheartening.

John was taking a slow and reluctant walk back towards the DES office when he came upon a not-so-familiar face. In fact, he failed to notice him waiting by the lifts until the man called, 'Detective Sergeant,' in his gravelly German tone of voice, and even then it took John a full couple of seconds to identify who had spoken.

Zeigler loomed tall in the corridor. However, he was now quite unrecognisable with a bestubbled chin below the thin moustache and his left arm bound up in a sling. Even his demeanour was altered, being somewhat less abrasive than usual.

'Detective Inspector!' John greeted him with a high salute.

'Good morning, John.' Zeigler smiled and returned the gesture with a half-salute.

They exchanged pleasantries, then Zeigler was quick to thank John for having taken the lead during their encounter with Ramos and Turner at Smith and Sons' Antiquities and Crafts. With an eye to his sling, he dwelt momentarily on what might have happened had John not been there. John graciously contended that he need not be thanked as he knew full well Zeigler would have done the same for him; nevertheless, this gratitude from his superior – a man John had always regarded as a daunting yet impressive figure – meant a lot.

Zeigler was not set to be John's superior for much longer, though, as it turned out that he had just visited DCI Werner's office to hand in – or rather, place on the still-absent DCI's desk – his resignation. When John asked why with a measure of disbelief, Zeigler answered, 'I am too old for being shot at, my boy. Between the Wehrmacht and the Metropolitan Police, I have made a fine career out of it' – he chuckled – 'but it is now time for me to go somewhere warm and while away my days in relative harmony, I think.'

John laughed with him. He would be sorry to see Zeigler leave, but the man had most definitely earnt himself some peace and quiet after dedicating more or less his entire life to the service of the Reich.

Before John could enquire any further as to what he planned to do next, Zeigler spoke again: 'I heard about what happened to you and Colbeck, and what that Turner woman did.' A brief pause followed the statement, and then he asked, 'How have you been?'

There was an uncharacteristic concern in his voice that John was not expecting, and it caught him off guard. So much so that, without hesitation, he revealed to Zeigler his exact state of mind: 'Not too good, to be honest.' He realised his hands were beginning to shake with anger, and John hid them in his trouser pockets. 'DCI Werner is going to disband the Yonder Task Force, and not a single person cares otherwise.' He leant in closer to Zeigler, and whispered so that nobody else in the corridor would be able to hear him, 'DI Colbeck died chasing Yonder, but as long as Peter and the detective chief inspector have their promotions, then what does it matter if his killer is still out there, along with Uncle Billy and no doubt dozens more of those bastards? It's not right, sir' – even though Zeigler had decided to step down as his superior, John could not call the older gentleman anything other than "sir" – 'that DI Colbeck gave everything just for *them*' – he pointed a furious, trembling finger towards the DES office – 'to forget about him, and for that sacrifice to mean nothing!' John could feel his heart racing, and so he took a long, calculated breath in an effort to calm himself down.

He instantly regretted this outburst. He was frustrated and tired, and he had spoken out of turn using words he reserved for Alice or his own internal dialogue. He fully expected Zeigler to denounce him on the spot for what he had said – or worse.

Zeigler did no such thing. Instead, when the lift doors opened on an empty carriage, he stepped inside and gestured for John to join him. John did so, and for a fleeting, fearful moment he believed Zeigler might take him straight up to Commissioner Krüger's office to report his comments, until he pressed the button for the foyer.

Then, as the lift started its descent, Zeigler spoke: 'I was there in the summer of 1941 when the invasion of the Soviet Union began. We had been stationed on the border for weeks, awaiting the order, and I remember there being this terrific stir of excitement when word finally got to us that we were to be on the frontline for Army Group Centre's strike through the heartland of the Soviet Union. We were all so desperate to see combat again after having our appetites whetted in Poland and France. Not that the Reds ever put up much of a fight. Their defences crumbled so readily that it even became a game amongst the men to bet on how many kilometres we would have taken by the end of each week. We showed them no mercy and followed commands to throw ourselves at the enemy without a second thought.'

Zeigler stopped abruptly and heaved a heavy sigh. John had studied the Eastern Front at length in school and recalled vividly how his teachers had described to them in magnificent detail the brave exploits of the German soldiers as they fought their way across the Soviet Union. Yet there was something other than pride in Zeigler's voice when he told of his involvement in this campaign, something that sounded to John oddly like remorse.

The lift arrived at the foyer without interruption, and John walked out beside Zeigler onto the stone floor. He did not think to ask where they were going or to question why Zeigler was recounting this story to him – John was too intrigued by what he might say next.

'In the October, there came what was set to be our most difficult undertaking: seizing control of Moscow, the capital of the Soviet Union. But to our surprise, the city fell within a matter of days, and the tens of thousands of soldiers and civilians who were not killed in the fighting surrendered. Any commander with sense would have thought such an effortless victory suspicious, were it not for the fact that we had marched through so many well-fortified positions on our drive towards Moscow. As it stood, it was only natural that this great city too would submit itself before us, so we did not distrust our success. Why would we have? We were fighting for the Third Reich, the most powerful force this world has ever seen, and we were unstoppable.'

Having now crossed the foyer, the two men exited Scotland Yard into a biting December chill. There, they stopped on the forecourt beneath the Union Jack, its inherently bright colours dull and solemn on this grey and windless Sunday morning.

Zeigler lit a cigarette and offered one to John before he continued. 'We had been there for no more than a week when the Soviets launched their surprise counter-attack. You see, they had allowed us to capture Moscow so easily in the hope that we would be blinded by a false sense of our own prowess, and, in their arrogance, our commanders were deceived by this ruse. Given what little resistance Army Group Centre met during its initial offensive, they had already redeployed many of our tanks and a significant number of our infantry to Army Group South to aid with the stalled war effort on the Volga. Consequently, when the Reds descended upon us all at once, they forced Army Group Centre to retreat over 100 kilometres before a new defensive line could be established. They encircled Moscow in the process, and those of us who were unfortunate enough to find ourselves trapped in the city withdrew to its centre to mount a defence of our own. By the time the first Soviet wave was repelled, the dead from both sides were piled high in the streets.'

Zeigler flicked the ash from the tip of his cigarette. 'Considering how celebrated we were for reaching Moscow, one would not have been judged naïve, John, to trust that the Reich would come to our assistance without delay. Our spirits were practically merry whilst we waited to be liberated. We ate and drank what little was left behind by the Reds and thought nothing of our gluttony.' He placed the cigarette between his lips and exhaled a steady stream of smoke. 'It was early November before we got the news that there was to be no relief. The focus on the Eastern Front had shifted southwards towards the Caucasus for the winter, and it was now our responsibility alone to hold Moscow, a so-called "vital" stronghold, until such a time that forces could be spared to restore control in the area.'

Zeigler met John's eye. 'Imagine it: being abandoned by your commanding officers in enemy territory, then those same men order you to defend that ground at all costs.'

John said nothing, and Zeigler shook his head at the apparent absurdity of the situation.

'That is exactly what we did, though: 200,000 of us held the centre of Moscow under the threat of non-stop shelling and despite the frequent raiding parties the Soviets threw at our defences. Very few Reds ever made it further than the outermost perimeter, but with the way they kept on coming at us in those first weeks, it was as if their generals were more concerned with exhausting our fast-dwindling ammunitions supplies than they were about preserving their own numbers.'

Zeigler bowed his head, and his voice dropped an octave: 'They stopped attacking once the weather became cruel at the end of December. It had obviously occurred to them that this struggle was a waste of able-bodied soldiers when they could lay siege to us instead, and having rounds for our rifles was suddenly the least of our worries. Food soon became scarce, and we lined up for a mouthful of soup watered down with snow. Men killed one another over rats and stray dogs, and I envied them when they were executed with a full stomach. Others fell delirious from their hunger, and they wandered out into the cold and never came back. We would find them days later, John' – he looked up, and stared at John with heavy, sorrowful eyes – 'frozen stiff and blue.' There was a visible tremor in his hand, and he gasped, 'They sparkled in the sunlight.'

Zeigler lowered his gaze and scratched at his chin with his thumb. 'Eventually, we turned on the few Soviet prisoners who remained, men, women, and…' He trailed off mid-sentence, then mumbled, 'The things we did there to hold that ground, to survive…'

John's cigarette burnt away in his hand, unsmoked. None of this had ever been mentioned during his history classes, when his teachers had lauded the famed "Siege of Moscow" as an act of stoic defiance by the German soldiers in the face of a devious Soviet ploy to advance back towards Eastern Europe. Even now, after being confronted with this first-hand account of what happened there, John still found it difficult to accept such a harrowing version of events as the truth; perhaps Zeigler's memories of the siege had been warped by time and old age into something far worse than reality, he supposed.

Zeigler cleared his throat, and when he spoke again, his tone was composed: 'The Soviets never were afforded their opportunity to finish us off. With the onset of spring, the Reich's forces on the Eastern Front pivoted northwards and broke through their lines, and at the end of March, the first German soldiers since October entered Moscow. Those of us still alive, which was fewer than 20,000 by then, were named heroes for having defended the city. They even gave us medals to prove it.'

His face fell into a grave scowl, and with a streak of venom in his voice, Zeigler said, 'I tossed that medal into the nearest river. I was *not* their hero. None of us were. They abandoned us, John. They left us to wither and die in that cursed city whilst *our* tanks and *our* infantry were sent elsewhere! We became no better than beasts and did things no person should ever have to do to survive. They rewarded us with leave, mostly because our uniforms no longer fitted our starved bodies, but once we had been sufficiently fed, they returned us to the Eastern Front in plenty of time to face another brutal winter.'

His eyes lit up with wrath in place of sorrow. 'The Reich does not care about any of us, John. It did not care about the fates of its loyal soldiers in Moscow all those years ago, and it does not care about what happened to Colbeck on Monday. We are all expendable. It would cast you aside in a heartbeat if that best suited its interests.' He spat the words across the forecourt, then stuck his cigarette in his mouth to stop himself from saying anything further.

John stood there in stunned silence. He had not anticipated such a plain-spoken statement from this man – a man he admired, no less – about the callous nature of the Reich. Zeigler delivered it with such authority as well, as if he truly believed they were all so easily 'expendable' at a moment's notice.

And John found that he could not help but agree with him: to the Reich, they were indeed all expendable.

But then he had always known that his life was forfeit to the preservation of National Socialism, so this was by no means a revelation. And that was not because the Reich cared so *little* about him that it would eagerly send him to his death; quite the opposite, it was because it cared so *much* for him that John would gladly give his life to protect it. Nobody had ever forced this concept upon him: he had realised it himself as a child, as soon as he was old enough to appreciate the lengths the Reich went to when it chose to raise him as its own.

Zeigler must have misunderstood him earlier, when he ranted about the Yonder investigation. John was frustrated that the Task Force was being disbanded when there remained so many loose ends and whilst DCI Werner absconded with his undeserved promotion, but he would never malign the entire Third Reich and everything it stood for based on this single decision, no matter how contemptible he believed it to be. Even DI Colbeck's death, when held in comparison with the infallibility of National Socialism, was a trivial matter at best – John knew that.

As for the Siege of Moscow, and in spite of how horrendous the whole ordeal sounded, John could not have been any more at odds with Zeigler's verdict. When he found his voice again, he made this known: 'But what you accomplished in Moscow was a turning point on the Eastern Front, wasn't it? You prevented the Soviets from gaining a foothold there, which hindered their advance and bought the Reich enough time to invade the Caucasus and claim the oil reserves it needed to sustain the war effort. By defending the city the way you did, you saved what might well have been millions of German soldiers from being killed during a prolonged struggle for control in Eastern Europe.' That *was* mentioned by his history teachers.

The perfect words materialised in John's mind, and he delivered them to Zeigler with absolute clarity: 'Everything you suffered through, and everything you did to survive: it was all in the name of the Reich.'

It was so obvious to him.

Zeigler did not reply straight away, and through the smoke from his cigarette, John thought he saw a look of disappointment settle in the older man's eyes. When he blinked, however, that look disappeared, and it was replaced by the stony regard Zeigler was renowned for.

Zeigler then smiled and declared, 'You are right, John: all in the name of the Reich.'

John smiled back. Zeigler would not have intended for his comments to sound as dishonourable as they came across, he surmised.

Their conversation came to an unforeseen conclusion a moment later when light raindrops began to patter down on the concrete around them. Signalling that it was time for him to take his leave, Zeigler stubbed his cigarette out on a nearby bin and threw the butt inside.

He said, 'It was good to see you, John. I am glad you are well,' and extended his hand towards John, expecting him to shake it. But given how Zeigler was still at present a detective inspector in the Metropolitan Police, John thought it far more apt to send him on his way in the appropriate fashion, so ignoring the outstretched hand, he stood to attention and raised his arm into a high salute.

Zeigler did not return a salute this time, half or otherwise. Instead, he considered John with those impenetrable, grey eyes of his, and his hand dropped to his side. Then, having said nothing else he turned away, and he started out across the forecourt towards Victoria Street.

John lowered his arm and watched in utter bewilderment as Zeigler vanished out of sight around the corner of Scotland Yard.

A volley of thunder rolled across the sky overhead and the rain became immediately heavier, and with his hands in his trouser pockets, John sloped back inside to escape the impending downpour.

CHAPTER TWENTY-SIX

Bulldog

Upon returning to the DES office, John slumped into his desk chair and lit another cigarette. The conversation with Zeigler had left a bitter aftertaste in his mouth, and it was with relief that he turned his attention back to Maria Turner's diary.

As he skimmed through the pages once again, John realised there were only ever two locations mentioned by name on a regular basis: The Dutton Arms, where Turner drank with her friends (before these friends fell out of favour with her), and the British Reich Museum, where she worked with Nancy for a Mr Ashworth. Surely somebody at one of these establishments would still recognise her? And if they did, perhaps they could point John towards where she might be hiding now.

It was still early, so John decided he would head to the British Reich Museum first during its opening hours. Taking the photograph from Turner's MoI file with him, he left the DES office unaccompanied. He would have asked either Alex or Alfie to join him, but both the detective sergeants retained an infuriating indifference as to the half-finished nature of the

Yonder investigation, and John did not need to be reminded this was likely a fool's errand.

*

As always, the British Reich Museum was a sight to behold. Although the old, weather-worn building had been badly damaged by bombing raids during the Second Great War, it was impossible to tell since the government had painstakingly rebuilt it afterwards to its previous specifications, even using Portland stone that matched the surviving sections to create a seamless visage. Today, it was adorned with the colours of the Fatherland and Great Britain, with respective banners of red, white, and black and blue, red, and white hanging the length of its stone columns. Atop the museum's pediment, a bust of the National Socialist eagle stood perched upon a polished silver swastika, its wings splayed wide in glory, from where it kept a steadfast watch over the treasures housed within.

The interior of the building had seen modifications since the war, and the most considerable change came in the Great Court, which was the main atrium of the museum. At one time, this area had been stacked deep with an extensive library of Imperialist propaganda, books upon books of lies and falsehoods on display for all the world to see. Of course, when the Reich Ministry of Public Enlightenment and Propaganda had arrived in Great Britain during the Occupation, one of its many assignments was to confiscate and destroy any literature that sought to harm the Third Reich and its people, and the books once catalogued here were no exception. Anything deemed appropriate was eventually returned to the museum and remained available to this day in the Reading Room, the large, rounded structure at the centre of the Great Court, and the iron shelves that had held those deceitful materials were stripped down to create a brighter, less cluttered gateway into what was one of the most incredible historical and cultural collections in Europe.

That was where John stood now, waiting for a museum guide to appear. As he idled to one side, out of the way of the Sunday-morning patrons who shuffled about the Great Court, he cast an eye to the three huge portraits that were hanging on the wall of the Reading Room opposite the entrance, and John allowed himself a moment to admire them. The one on the left depicted Prime Minister Martin Bormann, his sober face and stern gaze indicative of his steady tenure in office. The one to the right was of the Führer, the charismatic smile of the young man forever an uplifting sight to see. Since the loss of his father at the beginning of the year, Rudolf Hitler had proven himself just as capable a leader as the late Ewige Führer, something which was no small feat to accomplish – a wondrous future for the Reich was assured with him as their Führer. Between them sat what had become the most iconic image of Adolf Hitler himself: the portrait that was commissioned to commemorate his posthumous ascension to the title of "der Ewige Führer" – "the Eternal Leader" in English – after his death. In the portrait, he appeared with the National Socialist flag draped over his right shoulder, a gesture that was symbolic for how he had carried the weight of the Third Reich during its most turbulent years; it was a poignant yet beautiful tribute to his legacy. Truth be told, there was little resemblance between the father and the son when they appeared on the television together or side by side in a photograph: the Führer had brilliant-blond hair and effervescent, blue eyes, and his cheekbones and jaw were far more pronounced than those of his father. In these portraits on the wall of the Reading Room, however, their likeness was striking, and the Führer was undoubtedly the son of the Ewige Führer.

Shifting his focus, John spotted a young guide – who was no older than seventeen or eighteen – taking up position on the other side of the Great Court, where he waited to be engaged by a visitor.

'Excuse me,' John called to the guide as he crossed the atrium towards him.

'Yes, sir. How may I help you?' he answered, with the forced enthusiasm of someone who works with the general public.

John produced his police identification and said, 'I'm Detective Sergeant Highsmith.' The guide went stiff and stood to a sort of attention when he realised he was being addressed by an officer of the Reich. 'Do you recognise this woman? She used to work here, at the museum.' John had the photograph of Turner in his hand, and he passed it to the guide.

He examined it closely before he shook his head; he had only been working at the museum for eight months, which was far too recent for him to have ever encountered Turner. But he would be more than happy to run the photograph up to his manager – the museum director, Mr Ashworth – should John so desire.

Recognising the name from Turner's diary, John agreed that this was a fine idea, and the guide scooted from his post without another word. John chuckled to himself as he watched him go – the younger ones were always so eager to please.

Whilst John awaited the guide's return, he studied the exhibition posters around the Great Court. The mainstays were present, such as the Bronze and Iron Ages and Roman and Viking Britain (all large collections that evoked life in

Great Britain from long before the Imperialists corrupted it), and a prominent poster advertised the "German Historical Collection": an exhibition on the history of the Fatherland for the thousands of years leading up to the rise of National Socialism. Plus, there was a section dedicated to National Socialism itself, which was an extensive chronicle of the five most important decades in human history. One of the newer, less conventional exhibits was entitled "The Tyranny of the Jew", which addressed a long-proposed idea that had been met with concern by some due to the potential exposure of young children to these nefarious ideologies. John was yet to see the exhibit – he had not visited the British Reich Museum since a school trip when he was fourteen, during which he wandered with awe amongst the artefacts whilst Lewis huffed and puffed, bored out of his mind – but he thought it an inspired decision. It was better to document this type of thing, he believed, and to showcase it in public for the young and old alike to witness for themselves so that such a people were never again allowed to contaminate Europe with their influence.

The guide reappeared before long and announced that Mr Ashworth would like to speak with John on the matter of Maria Turner. Stricken by an immediate curiosity as to what this man might have to say, John accepted the invitation, and he followed the guide away from the public area of the museum through a set of doors with a sign that read 'Staff Only'.

The guide escorted John along a series of corridors. They passed numerous museum employees on the way, most of whom smiled politely at both the guide and this stranger in their midst, and John could not help but wonder about the girl Turner had been at the beginning of the diary when she first started working here. Was she ever one of those people who would smile of her own free will at a passing police officer? Or had she always felt the inclination to murder them on the spot? Given how her disposition flipped so drastically in her writing from one persona to the other after that day in the woods with Edward, John believed the latter was the truth.

Having left the bustle of the museum far behind them, when they reached the third floor, the guide stopped in front of a door with the nameplate 'Mr William Ashworth – Museum Director' screwed to it, and he knocked twice.

A voice from the other side called, 'Enter.'

The door opened into a modest office. Deep bookcases were set against the walls on the left and the right, their shelves lined with various tomes bound in old leather, and placed intermittently amongst them were what could – without closer inspection – only be described as trinkets; most likely, they were items of significant historical value that had been hidden away in this room for the personal enjoyment of the museum director. The carpet was an off-white colour, although considering the surrounding décor, John might have guessed that it was once as vivid as fresh snow but years of heavy use had rendered it dull and worn. The focal point of this office was a wide and magnificent dark wooden desk on the far side, which backed on to a narrow window that, in turn, had an impressive view down into the courtyard at the front of the museum.

Mr Ashworth stood behind the desk with his back to the door, silhouetted by the dim daylight and quietly observing the rain-soaked world outside. From the door, all John could see was a head of combed-back, thick, white hair on a tall, slim frame, garbed in a finely cut suit of charcoal grey and patterned in a subtle check.

The guide led John into the room and declared his presence: 'Detective Sergeant Highsmith for you, Mr Ashworth.'

'Thank you, David,' Ashworth replied in a smooth, perfectly refined English accent.

He turned around to face John, and John took Ashworth in. He was much older than John, but still the man looked well for his age, with his excellent posture and a strong, clean-shaven jawline. The only real indicator of any frailty was the walking cane in his right hand, though John thought this was perhaps as much for show as for anything else since he had also worn a burgundy-coloured knitted bowtie to work, along with a pocket square of a similar shade. A red-and-white Nationalsozialistische Deutsche Arbeiterpartei – the NSDAP; the National Socialist German Workers' Party – membership badge sat high on his left lapel, the swastika in the centre prominent against the grey of his suit. Ashworth considered John from across the office with kind, blue eyes through a pair of round glasses with a simple, black frame, and he offered him a warm grin when he said, 'Good morning, Detective Sergeant. David, you may leave us now.'

The guide stepped away, and the door closed behind John with a squeak as he exited the office.

'So, Detective Sergeant Highsmith, was it?'

John nodded that Ashworth was correct.

'You have some questions with regard to Miss Ramos?' Ashworth had the photograph from Turner's MoI file in his hand.

It took John a second to recall that "Ramos" was Turner's maiden name. 'It's Mrs Turner, actually. She married in 1966. But yes, she is wanted for questioning in relation to her husband, Edward Turner,' he lied. There would be no mention of drug enforcement or counter-terrorism in this conversation. 'I was hoping someone at the museum might know something of her current whereabouts. Or that you would be able to put me in contact with a guide she was friends with when she worked here, a woman called Nancy.'

Ashworth contemplated the photograph. 'Miss— sorry, *Mrs* Turner did train downstairs as an archivist. However, it has been several years now since she left us, Detective Sergeant, so I do not know how much use we will be to your investigation.' His tone was apologetic, but John had expected little else; anticipating any major revelation from this visit would have been absurd. 'As for this guide, the name Nancy does not sound familiar, but then we see so many employees come and go, I could not possibly remember them all.' Ashworth looked up at John. 'I can call down and have a clerk bring up our employment records, if you think they will be of any interest?'

It was better than nothing. 'That would be much appreciated. Thank you, Mr Ashworth.' With any luck, it would not be difficult to find Nancy in the employment records. Maybe she had heard from Turner more recently.

Ashworth smiled broadly, and he picked up the handset from the telephone cradle on his desk.

As he began speaking to someone on the other end of the line, John examined the walking cane in Ashworth's right hand. The shaft was a plain, dark wood, not dissimilar in colour to the desk, and it was topped with a silver handle. The handle was ornate, though, and John busied himself whilst he waited by trying to figure out its design.

From where he stood, it resembled an animal's head.

A wolf, perhaps?

Or a dog?

Ashworth moved his hand when he shifted his weight and revealed that it was in fact the head of a dog. A bulldog, to be precise.

A strange thing to have on a walking cane, a bulldog's head.

John had heard of that somewhere before – that someone wore some manner of silver dog's head on a walking cane. He was certain of it.

It was during the Yonder investigation...

That was it! Jasper Jones said it in London State Hospital, when he gave up everything he knew about Uncle Billy to John and Peter.

Hmm...
The nameplate on the door read 'Mr William Ashworth'.
William Ashworth.
Billy *Ashworth?*
Surely not...

John thought back to the description Jones provided of Uncle Billy: older gentleman, combed-back white hair, glasses, tall, thin, English. And then there was the name Ramos had fought to keep from them in that chamber beneath the barn when he was questioned about Uncle Billy's identity: 'William A...'

...
...
...
Shit.
Is it really him?
No, it can't be...

'Detective Sergeant?' Ashworth was talking to him again.

John returned his focus to the man.

'Somebody will be along shortly with the employment records,' Ashworth explained through that same, incessant smile. 'Might I interest you in a drink in the meantime?' He motioned to a series of expensive-looking decanted liquors by his desk.

'No, thank you,' answered John. He was sure to maintain his composure. The seed of suspicion had been sown in his mind, but he still did not believe it possible that this gentleman – that this pleasant and evidently well-respected National Socialist – was Uncle Billy, the supposed mastermind behind the Yonder Organisation. 'How long did Mrs Turner work at the museum for, then?' he enquired to keep the conversation flowing at a natural pace.

Ashworth was fixing himself a drink. 'Oh, about eighteen months, I would imagine,' he said in his musical lilt, and golden liquid splashed into a crystal tumbler.

'She must have made quite the impression for you to remember her even now,' John probed with care. There was only a fine line between informal chit-chat and interrogation.

'Well, the girl was a breath of fresh air for this tired place – a free spirit brimming with exciting ideas. We were sad to lose her.' Ashworth's grin did not falter even when he spoke of this regret, and John started to convince himself that something was amiss; that jovial temperament of his seemed false all of a sudden, as if an ancient façade was beginning to crumble around him.

'How did she come to work for you?'

'The usual process: we advertised the post, and Mrs Turner was the strongest applicant – a young go-getter whom we were hoping to mould into a valued member of our team here at the museum.'

Taking a sip from his drink, Ashworth remained assuredly blithe, unaware that this latest answer had set John's mind racing. He had reread the opening entry in Turner's diary before he left Scotland Yard that morning – the one in which Ashworth was first mentioned – and he recalled a particular sentence word for word: *'Mr Ashworth always said I could have a job at the British Reich Museum and I cannot turn down the opportunity to work in London!'*

Turner never applied for the job: Ashworth offered it to her.

Therefore, he must have known her before she came to London.

The only way he could have known her back then was through her father.

Her father, the close acquaintance of Uncle Billy.

John was a bloody idiot. It had been there all along, on the first page of Turner's diary.

It was him: William Ashworth *was* Uncle Billy.

Ashworth was regarding him quizzically by now, likely because John had not said anything for several seconds; he had chosen instead to stare the man dead in the eye as this realisation settled across his mind. When he did speak at last, John was unable to hide the note of triumph in his voice: 'That's funny, because I read Mrs Turner's old diary – that's how I found my way here, you see – and in it, she wrote that you had offered her the job, Mr Ashworth. As a matter of fact, it was the reason she moved to London in 1965.'

Ashworth's entire demeanour transformed in that instant: his smile dropped into a scowl, his eyes narrowed behind his glasses, and his right hand tightened around the silver bulldog's head. 'What are you insinuating, Detective Sergeant?' he asked, but even his intonation was changed, having fallen from that cheerful cadence into a harsh, dry monotone.

'You knew her father, Antonio Ramos Serrano, didn't you,' John accused in his toughest detective voice.

Ashworth said nothing.

Holding his nerve, John straightened his shoulders and stated, 'You're Uncle Billy.'

With hardly a moment's hesitation, Ashworth let out a low, slow chuckle, and the hairs on the back of John's neck stood on end. 'Only my closest friends call me that,' Ashworth then replied.

CHAPTER TWENTY-SEVEN

Yonder

John did not react straight away. Ashworth had admitted so readily to being Uncle Billy that there was a considerable delay before he was able to grasp the significance of what had been said. When the Reichspfennig did drop, however, John hastily drew his Walther and pointed it at the man's chest.

Ashworth did not so much as flinch at the sight of the gun, and he took another drink of liquor from the tumbler in his left hand.

'You're under arrest, Ashworth,' John declared. 'You're going to pay for the crimes you've committed against the Reich, and for the harm you've caused it with—'

'Spare me your drivel, Detective Sergeant,' Ashworth cut John off mid-sentence in a weary, disdainful tone. 'You are oblivious to the truth – yet another man striving aimlessly to secure the continued enslavement of this nation.'

John laughed out loud. He had not intended to do so, and it took him by surprise as much as it did Ashworth. Then, almost of its own accord an angry tirade exploded from his mouth and across the office: 'You're all so obsessed by this idea that the British people aren't free, when it's *you* – you and Ramos and Turner – who have been imprisoned this whole time, held captive by the Imperialists and their legacy of propaganda. If you'd have looked up just once in the last three decades, you would have seen everything the Reich has done for us and everything it has accomplished in spite of your disruptions. You lost the war, the Kings' Loyalists are scarcely a footnote in history, and now this whole Yonder fiasco is over and done with. The people will soon forget you ever existed, and they'll finally be able to see for themselves just how free they are under National Socialism when they no longer have you and your kind warping their minds with nonsense.'

Ashworth's face fell. 'It never fails to pain me how easy it was for them to indoctrinate your generation.' There was what sounded like genuine sadness in his voice. 'But you are incorrect, my boy. The people of Great Britain are *not* free. They have been conditioned to salute and to repeat the mantras of the Nazis, and to keep their heads down and do as they are instructed by their masters – a behaviour that is predicated on the promise of violence and death should they dare to disobey. That is not freedom, Detective Sergeant; that is servitude.' Unlike John, Ashworth made his point with a certain grace and fluidity, as though this was a rehearsed speech he had delivered a thousand times before.

'And what? You thought drugging people out of their minds was the answer to this?' John snarled the condemnation at Ashworth. He was tired of this pretence that Yonder was somehow a "cure" for life in Great Britain – it was pathetic.

Ashworth made an affirmative gesture. 'That was the plan at first: to try to free the people from the prison of Nazism through Yonder. We truly believed we could win back their hearts and their souls by providing them with a means to live beyond their oppressors. Then, once they were no longer burdened by these psychological chains and had experienced for themselves how true freedom might feel, we would lead them into open revolution against the State.' It was more or less word for word what Turner had written in her diary.

Ashworth walked around from behind his desk, unperturbed by the presence of the handgun still aimed at him, and he leant against the wood, facing John. As he did so, he continued, 'And whilst open revolution against the Nazis is all well and good, the real triumph of this would have been the mass exodus of workers – British-born and foreigners alike – from the military factories. You see, it is no secret that our home is the cog that turns the Nazi war machine. Bormann cannot open his mouth without saying so. The "Industrial Jewel of the Third Reich": a landscape of smoke and metal. Every bullet fired, every rifle that fires it, and every truck that carries the man who carries the rifle: they all come from Great Britain, assembled by the men and women who are forced into service under the Nazis, and distributed across the Reich by way of the military ports in Newcastle and Portsmouth. Those monstrous factories are their greatest achievement – a real industrial powerhouse that has been put to use to subjugate a third of the planet.'

He wet his lips with a sip of liquor. 'But it is also their greatest weakness: if this British manufacturing base were to fall into disarray, it would cause the immediate collapse of the Third Reich's military production line, and the whole Nazi war machine would promptly grind to a halt – from the soldiers entrenched in snow and rain over on the Eastern Front to the coastal defences down at the Cape of Good Hope. Before The Purges, the King's Loyalists tried to fight this Goliath in the old-fashioned way, but every time we succeeded in putting a factory out of commission, they would build two more to take the strain. It was a noble effort, yet a failure nevertheless.' An unnerving, determined expression crept across Ashworth's face then, and his voice bristled with purpose: 'If we were instead able to *destabilise* this manufacturing base, though, by *starving* the factories of their workers? Well, that would be a different matter entirely, and for the first time in thirty years, the Third Reich would be left vulnerable. Without a steady flow of equipment to reinforce the Eastern Front, the Soviet Army would at long last have the advantage it needs to break the Nazi line and march into Europe. The liberation of the continent could then commence, and it would all have been achieved because of Yonder.'

John spoke up: 'The factory workers will never support your cause! They're loyal to the Reich, even if they sometimes don't see eye to eye with it. And no amount of Yonder will ever change that.' The King's Loyalists had tried to rally the people – and, in particular, those of the working class – against the Reich in the early 1950s using a similar rhetoric of liberating Great Britain from the clutches of the "evil Nazis", and they were categorically rejected by all save a stubborn few. The factory workers would make the exact same decision again today, even with the effects of Yonder clouding their judgement – of that, John had no doubt.

Ashworth placed his walking cane between his legs and traced the grooves in the silver bulldog's head with his thumb, and through a barely contained resentment, he muttered, 'Oh, do not worry, Detective Sergeant, we gave up on that notion when you widowed Maria.'

John emitted a wary grunt at the statement, but he said nothing.

'Edward was the idealistic one amongst us, you see; the one who told us that our more traditional means of rebellion – sabotage and assassinations and the like – would not work because the people will never back a cult of such direct action against the State for fear of the repercussions should it fail. That was why he conceived of Yonder. He said that before any revolution could ever take place, we first had to remind the people what life might exist for them beyond Nazi rule, and that the only way to accomplish this was to open their minds to the possibility. Then, and only then, would they be inclined to join our cause, even if it were only to throw down their tools and walk out of the factories. The older ones such as me were not so easily convinced by any of this. We still remembered how the people refused our call to arms back when the King's Loyalists were at the height of their influence, and we have never forgiven them for it. But to hear Edward and Maria discuss this concept of a "silent protest", these two youngsters who wanted to change the world through enlightenment rather than violence – well, damn them if they did not begin to make us believe again.'

Ashworth bowed his head, and he talked into the off-white carpet: 'Then, before anything could come of this grand proposal, you people murdered the boy. It was our fault, really – me and the other older ones. We were too slow in coming to terms with Edward's ideas, and we pushed our own heavy-handed agenda of rebellion too far, and it got him killed. When he died, that idealism of his all of a sudden seemed so naïve, so childish, and the prospect of using Yonder to liberate the people from the shackles of Nazism was abandoned.'

That made no sense: if the plan for Yonder was 'abandoned', then why had the drug vexed DESs nationwide since it first arrived back in August? And, personally, why had it haunted

John's every waking moment – and most of his dreams – since he was assigned to the Task Force almost two months ago?

Before he could seek clarification on the matter, Ashworth spoke again: 'Maria was never the same after his death. Overnight, she transformed from the girl who had hung on Edward's every word into a woman consumed by the need to wreak revenge against those who killed him. She became hell-bent on the destruction of the Nazi race – by any means necessary. It was then that she devised an idea of her own; an idea to neither fight the Nazis directly as we had always done, nor to convince the people to rise up against them as Edward had advocated. Instead, in her grief, Maria realised a way to tear out the very heart of the British manufacturing base, the resource that, since the 1940s, has been the lifeblood of the Nazi war machine: the British population itself.'

The final entry in the diary: the 'sickening proposal' and Turner's guilt-ridden confession…

'W-what have you done?' John asked, the stammer in his voice betraying that he was terrified what the answer might be.

Ashworth raised his head, and his gaze met John's. 'Did you know that ingesting just one-tenth of a teaspoon of arsenic can kill even the healthiest of adults?'

John caught his breath, and his eyes widened in horror.

'It is not an exact science, mind you. Death can take anything from several hours to several days, whilst some may even survive such a lethal dose with the proper medical attention. But then it has neither taste nor smell and is quite undetectable under examination, unless one knows what they are looking for.'

'You wouldn't…' John contended, but it was little more than a panic-stricken gasp.

'We would,' Ashworth replied without missing a beat. 'Millions of those little blue pills are currently in situ all around Great Britain, comprising a mixture of the regular Yonder formula and just a dash of arsenic. Our people are standing by as we speak, ready to distribute them amongst their dealers. They are not aware that these particular batches of Yonder are laced with arsenic, of course. That information has been kept secret to all but a *very* select few. They will hit the streets any day now; then, within the week, hundreds of thousands of people will have died, and all each death will take is a single pill.'

'Freedom from life.' The vague answer Ramos provided when John asked him about the purpose of Yonder echoed around his head. He had never considered that the man might have meant it quite so literally. 'The government will figure out what you have done as soon as people start getting sick. It will find a way to treat them, and it will fill the factories with those who are not foolish enough to take your drug.' He barked these words with contempt – it was a ridiculous plan.

'Would it be safe to assume that you are unfamiliar with the symptoms of arsenic poisoning, Detective Sergeant?' Ashworth asked, with taunting condescension. 'Well, it is remarkable just how similar they can be to those one might attribute to the common flu virus.'

John's whole body stiffened.

The spike in cases of the flu since October...

'We have been slowly distributing the arsenic-laced pills since mid-October, in amongst the clean Yonder that people had already grown so fond of. The first cities we experimented with back at the beginning of October were Manchester, Leeds, and Sheffield, and the doses of arsenic in that first batch were so minute so that whoever took the pills did not instantly keel over and die – we doubted whether it would work as intended. When concerns about a flu outbreak in the area started to circulate, however, we knew it was having the desired effect. Following that success, we gradually rolled out further lightly poisoned batches across the nation, including in London. We then began hearing the stories that people were succumbing to their symptoms, and the number continued to rise day by day.'

The Walther trembled in John's hand.

DI Jeremy Russell was killed by the "flu" only last week…

'A spate of sudden deaths would have roused suspicions and warranted further investigation, but a flu virus that is touring Great Britain at this time of year is no more than a seasonal illness. Alongside this narrative of a flu outbreak, the people have thought nothing of their symptoms when they fall sick. Many of them have likely used Yonder once or twice before and experienced only pure ecstasy, so it has never so much as crossed their minds that it might be the source of their misfortunes. And Yonder no longer poses a threat as far as the government is concerned, since the Drug Enforcement Squads so efficiently shut down our operation; hence, there is no reason why we would ever factor into their comprehension of what is happening for even the briefest of moments.' Ashworth smiled. 'Your dogged determination has done us a sizeable favour, Detective Sergeant.'

John felt an unhinged rage swelling inside of him.

'Those batches of arsenic-laced Yonder already in situ are far deadlier than anything previously distributed, though. Once they are released into the wild, this "seasonal illness" will see a rampant evolution over a matter of days, and it will soon come to be known as the most destructive pandemic since the Spanish Flu. If we are careful with our supply, it will last us well into the new year. Before long, the entire nation will fall under a strict quarantine whilst the government tries in vain to contain an illness that does not exist. The people will not be allowed to leave their homes, never mind go to work. In the factory cities, where so many took to Yonder that we have struggled to meet the demand, the death toll will be more akin to that of the Black Death. Then, when we begin to propagate the rumour that this illness was caused by the Nazis themselves, as a radical new programme of population control, perhaps, or the result of some scientific experiment gone awry, the people will be quick to proclaim how gullible they were to ever trust them with their lives.'

Ashworth leant forwards on his walking cane. 'In the midst of this chaos, the factories will fall silent. And when they do so, the Soviet Union will seize the opportunity offered by this unexpected vulnerability, and it will strike out over the Eastern Front.'

'You'd kill millions of people, and destroy countless lives, just to allow the Soviet horde to rape and murder its way across Europe?' John asked with furious disbelief. This was absolute madness.

'The Soviets are not barbarians,' Ashworth replied, ignoring John's question. 'That, my boy, is another myth spun by your teachers; another falsehood written into history by the victors. Had the Nazis been defeated, you would have instead been taught of the heroic sacrifices the Red Army endured in the face of abject villainy. Had they been defeated, Churchill and Comrade Stalin would have walked hand in hand across this continent, and Europe would now be enjoying an unprecedented era of alliance with its two greatest powers as the arbitrators at the negotiation table.'

To Ashworth, this dreamt-up, alternate reality of Imperialist–Communist domination was somehow superior to life under National Socialism – how a man could be so blind was beyond John. 'The Soviets are peasants with sticks,' he sneered, 'and they'll be crushed by the might of the Third Reich.'

'That the Soviet Union still exists is convincing evidence to the contrary, would you not agree?' Ashworth was amused by John's statement. 'Our newspapers tout countless victories over the enemy on the Eastern Front, when, in reality, the two armies have not met in open battle for more than a decade. The Soviets reside in such a vast and impenetrable natural fortress of mountain valleys and forests, no amount of Nazi engineering has ever been able to surmount it. But this endless deadlock – this "Great Stalemate", as they call it – has granted them time to amass weapons and vehicles and to prepare themselves for an advance towards Europe. They did try to achieve this in the years after the war, but the sheer density of the Nazi line threw them back into the mountains. But when that line falters, and with the continued support of the Americans, their next offensive will be unstoppable.'

'The *Americans*?' John exclaimed. Of all the things Ashworth had just said, this mention of them was perhaps the most alarming.

'Yes, Detective Sergeant, the Americans. President Kennedy started providing military equipment to the Soviets in secret when he came to power in 1961 so they would be ready to move against the Nazis whenever the time should arise. And they have thousands of agents stationed in Europe, Africa, and Nazi-occupied Asia who, once this occasion presents itself, will be tasked with causing civil unrest on a colossal scale, which will split the Nazis' forces and prevent them from mounting a true defence on the Eastern Front.' Ashworth sipped at his drink and made John wait in agitated suspense, before he said, 'It was no surprise, then, when the American government was told what Edward was planning with Yonder and the potential it had to destabilise the Nazi war machine, that it went to exceptional lengths to be intimately involved with all the arrangements. We did worry that they might back out after Edward was killed and we put forward Maria's proposal instead, but if anything, they became more interested.' Ashworth shrugged his shoulders. 'Where else would we have got so enormous an amount of arsenic?'

John clenched his jaw so hard he almost cracked his back teeth. *The* fucking *Americans.* The relationship between the Third Reich and the United States had always been an amicable one ever since President Joseph P. Kennedy met with the Ewige Führer for the first time in Greenland in 1945. To this day, both still benefitted from prolific trade routes across the Atlantic, whilst the atomic accords signed at that conference had reduced any threat of a nuclear war to zero. Joseph Kennedy's son – the presiding John F. Kennedy – had neither done nor said anything to undermine this during his eight years in office, and he had even committed himself to renewing these treaties with the Führer at another Greenland Conference in the coming March. To think that this younger Kennedy would have gone so far as to not only arm the Soviet Union against the Reich, but also to actively conspire to murder millions of its citizens as a means to bring about its end…

John dared not imagine the ramifications should this information reach Berlin.

'After Edward's death, it was still another two years before we saw the first Yonder pill. The Americans were constructing a manufacturing plant somewhere out in Venezuela, of all places, that would be able to produce the drug on an industrial scale, so we waited. And whilst we waited, we planned for how we would effectively distribute the Yonder. The Americans had taken full control of the operation in South America by this time: our original Yonder supplier opposed the plan to mix it with arsenic, so, unfortunately, he had to be removed. Then, with the Americans' assurances that they would ship every single Yonder pill across the Atlantic into Spain, the manufacturing plant went into full production in January. The Americans even provided Antonio with modified boats so he was able to move the pills up to Great Britain undetected. They were these marvellous vessels that have hidden compartments in the hulls, which the Nazis would not find in a thousand years. Antonio smuggled the first batches of Yonder into London in April, and we worked at growing a stockpile of it so we would not run short when distribution began. Although, as I said, we did still struggle to keep up with the demand once word spread of its euphoric properties.'

Ashworth swirled the last of the liquor around in the tumbler. 'I do not want you fearing for the future when this is all over, Detective Sergeant, as we have no intention of abandoning Great Britain to anarchy. Once our plan for the arsenic-laced Yonder is set into motion and the Red Army has defeated the Nazis in the east, the true royal family will return and claim the throne from the False King. They shall unite the people against their oppressors, re-establish order, and pick up the pieces of this broken kingdom. Then, when the Soviets have routed out the weakened Nazi command altogether, the other governments-in-exile will descend upon the continent to assume control of their own nations.' He paused, then added, 'Under our close supervision.'

Ashworth raised his glass into the air. 'We will rebuild Europe better than it was before, so that monsters such as Adolf Hitler are never again allowed to bring it to ruin. And then we will liberate Africa and occupied Asia, and wipe what remains of the Nazi blight from existence.' He tipped the drink into his mouth and placed the tumbler down on the desk. 'By the way, we have a queen now, and she is a magnificent woman.'

'Fuck you, Ashworth!' was John's impetuous retort. It infuriated him that the man spoke as though the Reich was already defeated and this dystopia of his was just around the corner. 'The Eastern Front will stand strong, the Soviets will be brought to heel, and you'll hang as a terrori—'

Wait. Why had Ashworth told him all of this, revealing their plan in detail to an officer of the Reich whilst standing there at gunpoint? Surely he knew that John would immediately report it to his superiors?

As this uncertainty struck him, the door behind John squeaked. Startled, he twisted on his heel (although the gun stayed aimed at Ashworth), expecting to see a bewildered clerk standing in the doorway.

It was not a clerk.

When John looked over his shoulder, it was none other than Maria Turner who stared back at him from the doorway. The woman had appeared once again as if from nowhere, wearing that long, brown leather coat and those knee-high boots. When Ashworth had been on the telephone earlier, he was not talking to a clerk about the museum's employment records, John realised; he had called Turner, and this whole conversation had been a distraction whilst he awaited her arrival.

It took John but a second to recognise her for whom she was: the Mediterranean skin; the dark hair; the narrow face; the large, brown eyes; the petite, dour features; the low cheekbones; the distinct likeness to her father – and, without thinking twice, he turned the Walther on the woman and fired it at her head. The crack of the gunshot filled Ashworth's office, and Turner reeled backwards into the corridor.

John could not quite believe it: the PPK-L had finally fired true for him, and it had found its target with deadly accuracy!

That's for DI Colbeck, he growled to himself with triumph.

This delight soon faded when John felt a dull ache materialise in his stomach. He looked down and saw that there was now a stain of deep, dark red in the white of his shirt.

No...

John's knees buckled, and he tumbled forwards onto them. He had not spotted the gun in Turner's hand, much less heard it go off.

He took a deep breath and waited for a fierce pain to surge through his body. But it did not come, and in its place, an unusual tingling sensation settled in his abdomen, which was accompanied by an acute numbness.

It was not at all what John might have expected from a gunshot. And this was not at all how he had envisioned his visit to the British Reich Museum would unfold.

He had to get to the telephone on the desk and call Scotland Yard. With Turner taken care of, it would not be difficult to keep Ashworth in check until backup arrived.

John could still emerge from this victorious.

And alive.

Ashworth was speaking: 'Jesus Christ, Maria! Are you okay?' He had crossed the office behind John and was kneeling down in the corridor beside Turner's body.

Of course she's not okay, John scoffed. *I shot her in the head, and the bitch is dead.*

At least, he had assumed as much...

It became apparent he had assumed wrongly: with Ashworth for support, Turner staggered to her feet, and she stumbled unsteadily into the office.

The PPK-L had failed him yet again, the worthless lump of metal!

Turner did not survive the shooting unscathed, however: the left side of her face and neck were already wet and red, and a chunk of that ear was missing. Blood from the wound trickled along her jaw, and heavy crimson drops fell from the tip of her chin onto the carpet. Her face was contorted by pain, but when she focused her gaze on John, he saw a red-hot, murderous fury burning in her eyes.

She lunged towards him, and John raised the Walther with the intention of emptying the entire magazine at her this time. He was far too slow, though, and Turner was able to grab his wrist before he could complete the motion, and the gun fired wide into one of the bookcases against the wall. With her other hand in a tight fist, she then hit John square in the face.

He would have been knocked straight to the floor had Turner not kept hold of his wrist, such was the force of the blow. The back of his mouth filled with blood and a sharp pain ran up his nose. The Walther slipped out of his hand, and it clattered into the carpet. When Turner released him from her grip, John could do no more than slump backwards onto his heels; that he remained vertical was an achievement in itself.

'Our decision to decimate the working-class population of Great Britain was not an easy one to make, Detective Sergeant.' Ashworth stopped beside Turner and glared down at John. 'Many of us were firmly opposed to it at first, me included. It was an unthinkable idea, and an inconceivable act of aggression. But that was before the Americans enlightened us as to the Führer's plans for world domination. Their spies in Berlin have been warning them of his thinly veiled belligerence over this past decade, as his father's health declined and the boy amassed increasing power and influence within the ranks of the

Nazis' upper echelons. Adolf Hitler was content with Europe and Africa and half of Asia, so he signed the peace treaty with Joe Kennedy and Hirohito and set about securing his legacy. Now it is his son's turn, and he wants to determine his own legacy. Rudolf Hitler wants to build on his father's empire, until all seven continents are engulfed beneath the shadow of the swastika. God only knows what weapon he intends to use to accomplish this, but the Americans are not particularly keen to find out. In the end, we decided that neither are we.'

Ashworth sighed. 'There is no honour in mass murder, but we tried an uprising, and it failed. It failed because the people refused to join our cause. So many of our fellow countrymen chose instead to kneel before their new emperor and forgo their freedom in favour of an easy life, and now it is those same people who help the Nazis to sustain their rule. If only they had supported us back then, perhaps all of this could have been avoided.' He bent towards John, leaning on his walking cane, and John stared into his cold, steely eyes. 'Today, they take Yonder whilst believing it to be an act of silent protest when, regrettably, their opportunity to protest has long since passed. In reality, it is an act of war.'

Hovering centimetres away from John's face, Ashworth was all but whispering now. 'What we do, we do to cleanse humanity of the Nazi plague. And if some must suffer in order for us to realise this goal, then they shall do so in the name of the greater good.'

Before he withdrew, Ashworth pulled the NSDAP membership badge from his lapel and tossed it to the floor between them. When John glanced at the bright and bold colours amongst the off-white, a devastating sense of defeat consumed him. Everything he had endured during the Yonder investigation, and everything the DES had done in an attempt to dismantle the Yonder Organisation – it was all for naught. Despite their best efforts, millions of people would soon die. And not in Great Britain alone as a result of these poisoned Yonder pills, but throughout Europe once the Soviets flooded across the Eastern Front and laid waste to the continent.

He urged his body to move, to stand up and dash Ashworth and Turner to one side so he could escape from this office and make it known to the world what was about to happen. But it did not. John felt fainter with each thump of his heart as blood continued to spill out from the hole in his stomach. His arms dangled limp and heavy at his sides, and the room around him was becoming increasingly distorted and blurred. It took all of his remaining strength just to stay conscious.

Ashworth stepped away, and he spoke to Turner: 'Let him bleed to death, Maria. I never did like this carpet anyway.' He then moved towards the door, and with a whimsical note in his voice, he declared, 'One less Nazi to worry about.'

At the instruction, Turner crouched down in front of John. She considered him with those eyes of hers – so dark a brown that they were almost black – and John's entire being was overwhelmed by an unbridled dread.

He felt as though he knew her so well after reading her diary, this woman who had been born to terrorists, who had fallen in love with one, and who, in due course, had become one herself. When John first met her at James Summers' warehouse, he had disregarded Turner as being of little consequence to the Yonder investigation, his attention drawn instead to Ramos; how naïve he had been. Her father had conditioned her as a child, and Edward trained her to be the menace she was today, yet she was a far more serious threat to the Reich than either of them ever were. Turner alone had devised this plan to poison the workers with Yonder, an idea so audacious that neither Edward, nor Ramos, nor Ashworth – the man who, mere minutes ago, John had thought was the mastermind behind the whole enterprise – were able to think it up. It was such a straightforward concept as well, but one that only a truly evil mind might ever have conceived.

And now she was here, a phantom from his nightmares manifested before him. John saw up close for the first time the damage his attempt on her life had caused: her left ear was a mess of blood and skin in amongst her wet and matted hair.

Still pulling to the right...

Turner leant forwards, and she put her hand on the nape of John's neck to steady him. Her touch was soft, gentle even, and he shuddered beneath it.

She placed something against his chest, and John peered down to watch her snap back the hammer on his Walther. He had not seen Turner take it from the floor beside him.

She drew him closer. He could feel her laboured breathing on his cheek and smell the sweetly scented chemicals in the leather of her coat. John could not so much as raise a hand to push her away.

Turner's lips parted, and she said, 'For my father.'

Then, she fired.

John felt the gunshot this time as the hot lead ripped through his chest. He exhaled raggedly and choked on the blood that rose into his throat.

When Turner removed her hand from around his neck and stood up, John expected she would be wearing an expression of smug victory. For she had done just that: she had won. But when she stepped back, she showed no such emotion. In fact, Turner showed no emotion at all. Her face was impassive, and it was then that John understood quite how little his death would mean to the woman, just as murdering both DI Colbeck and Arnold List had meant nothing – neither joy nor sorrow, guilt nor glory – to her either.

They were one thing to her, and one thing only: they were the enemy – a vile scourge that was to be eradicated no matter the cost.

To her, they were nothing more than "Nazis".

Turner did not even spare a moment to admire her work before she walked away, and she exited Ashworth's office without once looking back.

John stayed upright as the door closed behind her, held there by disbelief, before collapsing into the carpet with a muffled thud.

It was all over.

His final thoughts were not of Ashworth or Turner, or this plot to bring about the downfall of the Third Reich. That was all already forgotten, cast into the abyss of his fading consciousness.

No, his final thoughts were of Alice, the woman he would not grow old with. And of his daughter, the child he would never meet.

A thousand summer days played out before him. In them, John and Alice walked together through a secluded meadow with their child, whilst they basked in the warm embrace of a golden sun. Birds sang merry melodies in the trees. Somewhere nearby, the deliberate babble of a small stream was just audible. A low breeze swept across the grass, so that it gave the impression that a sea of shimmering, emerald surf was rolling against the hills around them. They were days that would never exist beyond the confines of his mind, yet in that instant, these were so real he could almost reach out and touch them. His daughter, who was by now a beautiful young girl, ran ahead, and her astonishing-green eyes danced in the brilliant sunshine when she stopped to wave at her father.

Standing beside him, Alice squeezed his hand, and he turned to face her.

She smiled, and John smiled back.

He would have been so happy.

The world grew distant, and John closed his eyes.

This book is printed on paper from sustainable sources managed under the Forest Stewardship Council (FSC) scheme.

It has been printed in the UK to reduce transportation miles and their impact upon the environment.

For every new title that Troubador publishes, we plant a tree to offset CO_2, partnering with the More Trees scheme.

MORE TREES
LET'S PLANT A BILLION TREES

For more about how Troubador offsets its environmental impact, see www.troubador.co.uk/sustainability-and-community

For my parents – everything I am,
and everything I can ever hope to be,
is all because of you.